CRIMSON PARK

The Park Trilogy - Book 2

by

C. J. Booth

Also by C.J. Booth

OLIVE PARK
ANGEL PARK
GIRL NUMBER FOUR
HONEY SUCKLE ROSE

This is a work of fiction. Names, characters, places, and incidents are either the product of the author's imagination or are used in a fictitious manner. Any resemblance to actual persons, living or dead, events or locations, is entirely coincidental.

ISBN 978-0-9838329-2-8

For Elizabeth.

Without you, where would I be?

"Is there any point to which you would wish to draw my attention?'
'To the curious incident of the dog in the night-time.'
'The dog did nothing in the night-time.'
'That was the curious incident,' remarked Sherlock Holmes."
— **Arthur Conan Doyle, Silver Blaze**

"Half-truths are worth more than outright lies."
— **George R.R. Martin, A Storm of Swords**

PROLOGUE

Michael Cooper watched the paramedic pull the blanket up to his sister's chin and thanked a god he didn't believe in because the EMT didn't cover her face.

"Sit down kid," motioned the paramedic.

Michael ignored him, reached out, and gripped his sister's hand. She was breathing, her mouth slack, drool decorated one of her cheeks. Michael couldn't believe she was still with them.

"She was drugged," mumbled Michael.

"What?" The paramedic turned away from Michael and pulled up one of the girl's eyelids.

"It was a good thing," Michael stated.

"The hell you talking about?"

Before Michael could answer, the ambulance's driver slammed the rear doors, closing them in.

"What do you mean drugged?"

Michael shielded his eyes from the blast of the overhead light.

The paramedic grabbed Michael's face, turned it to his own. "Kid! Focus. Drugged with what?"

Michael released his sister's hand, pushed away from the paramedic. Through the back windows, he could see the strobing of red and blue lights, frantic silhouettes shouting, running. A curious face stopped at one of the windows. A profile. Slowly it turned to stare into the back of the ambulance.

"Kid? What was the drug?"

Michael shuddered. "Dunno. Just good she didn't know… what was going on." When he looked again, the face had disappeared.

"What?"

"You all right?"

Michael sucked for air which wouldn't come. "She's a... tough... little kid," he breathed. But, he didn't sound sure, even to himself.

The paramedic leaned in. "Okay. Look, were there drugs in the house? She get into something in the medicine chest?"

Michael didn't answer.

"C'mon kid, help me out here. Help her out."

Michael tried to center. "No house, no medicine chest," he stated simply. He watched his own arm rise up and gesture to the activity happening all around the ambulance. "Don't you know what happened?"

"Listen, I can't help her if I don't know what she took."

Michael flopped back against the wall of the ambulance. He could feel the engine's vibration. He pulled at his shirt collar and struggled for a deep breath. The antiseptic smell was cloying. The air, cotton.

The paramedic turned back to the girl. He moved the teddy bear that was beside her and raised her arm. He checked her pulse noting it on the clipboard.

"Okay, look, she seems stable. Heart's good, breathing's regular. What's her name and date of birth?" The pen poised over the clipboard.

"I think...I think she wanted her awake... when she did it...," Michael exhaled.

Or maybe he didn't speak. He wasn't sure.

The paramedic strained to hear him. "Who? Who did what?"

Michael stared at the man, trying to concentrate.

"And whose blood is that on you?"

Michael wiped his lip and pulled out the front of his shirt, tried to make sense of the red splotches.

Couldn't.

Struggled to remember what he was asked.

"Jessie," he whispered. "Cooper. She's my sister." Michael checked the ambulance's driver. "Is he gonna... start driving soon? Get some fresh air?"

"Yeah, in a minute. But what are you saying? Who did what to her?"

Michael tried to track the doctor who moved in slow motion, his face a streak as if trying to catch up with itself.

"She's six…. like, maybe open… a fucking window, okay."

He felt drugged himself. He closed his eyes to stop the spinning. But flashes of Ruby Everheart, snarling and spitting, erupted without warning, her contorted face inches from his own. He remembered running, hanging, pulling himself up, falling…stabbing…

Michael struggled for breath. His lungs strained to pull in what wasn't there.

"Hey!" The medic checked Michael's pulse. "Whoa! Jesus, kid. Lie down!"

To the driver, "Larry! Hey man, time to go!"

…the fire and Jessie's picture and the cop…where was the cop…. and Jess dragged in the woods…and the light, the knife…the shining knife... what… what did I do…

Michael was thrown back and forth as the ambulance pitched through the underbrush, vaulted onto Highway 50. Full siren.

"What's your name, son? Your name?" The paramedic braced himself against the lurching of the ambulance, leaned over, and stabbed Michael's arm with a needle.

"Breathe slow kid. You're hyperventilating, okay. Slow down, relax."

"Name's M…. I…"

Can't breathe…can't breathe…

Michael flailed, fighting the undertow until he no longer heard the punching yips of the siren.

Until the beautiful, insistent swirl of white dots overtook him.

If he'd known it would all end up this way he would've gutted Ruby Everheart years ago.

The little brown man known as Pitic used the ambulance's retreating siren to cover the noise he made by ripping aside a blistered wall panel and scrabbling up into the back of Ruby Everheart's burned-out husk of a house trailer.

He had little time. Now, right now, he had to find Everheart's stuffed bear. Without that, he was fucked. They all were. Without that, he may as well just drive south, disappear, lose himself in some Mexican backwater. With the fire out they'd be sending the whole white-smocked forensic team to sift through the detritus of the sick, sordid life of Ruby Everheart, wanting to know every filthy secret of the worst child killer in California history.

Pitic crabbed past the charred couch and tried not to think how he'd made an abysmal mess of the whole Ruby-minding business. Oh, yeah. Make sure Ruby Everheart never got out of hand, like the old days, he was told. That was his job. His only job. And, strict truth be told, he had failed.

Still, how the hell was he supposed to know Everheart would grab the Cooper girl and drag her into the woods. Pitic believed those dark, dirty days were over.

Judging by the digging the police were doing, he was wrong.

They were all wrong.

He took a few steps in the dark. Something crunched underfoot. He struck a match and froze.

"Shit!" Staring up at him were the burned remains of scores of black-framed pictures of little kids, the frames well baked, glass broken, the ghostly faces barely recognizable.

A light flashed outside. He peered over the couch.

Except for the lone cop he'd seen sitting in the squad out front and some aged Chinese lady walking her mutt, the place was deserted.

The Everheart shell of a trailer, blackened and half-melted, squatted at the forgotten end of the Sunshine Vista trailer park. The park's residents, eager to see all the excitement, had crashed their way through the scrub and brushwood of Olive Park and were now sequestered behind police lines watching cops, paramedics, detectives, diggers, as they dealt with the untidiness that Everheart had left.

Minutes ago, pretending to be one of the milling curious, he'd been close enough to see what he feared and loved the most - Everheart's bagged body dragged out. They hadn't zipped the bag up all the way because they needed to leave room for the two-foot piece of oak sticking out of Everheart's chest.

"What?" he whispered. Holding still. Listening.

Child killer Ruby Everheart had the shit creepy habit of sitting in the dark, like a spider, waiting. But Pitic was certain Ruby Everheart was on the way to hell, primed to be the right hand of Satan.

"Freeze and don't move a goddamn' inch!"

Pitic jumped up, banged his back hard against the overturned couch.

"I said don't move a fuckin' inch! Down! Down now, on your face. Let me see them hands."

Even with the flashlight in his eyes, Pitic could see the cop was big. He filled the door frame. There was no getting around him.

Pitic lowered himself down, settling into the swampy mess, slipping the pictures beneath him as he did so.

"Hands out! Arms out! And what are you doing hiding shit underneath you when I'm standing right here."

Pitic didn't move.

"What is it that you got there?" The cop stepped forward.

"Don't shoot man," squealed Pitic in his best Mexican imitation. "I een do nothing. Just lookin' man. Stuffs all burnt up, man."

The cop pressed his boot against Pitic's head.

"Shut up. Just tell me what you got under you. It's not a gun is it?"

Pitic tried to turn his head.

"I said don't move. Tell me what you've got under you."

Pitic, his mouth smeared into the slop of sodden ceiling tiles, managed, "Ees nothin' man. Nothin'. Jus' need to find somethin' for my kid, man. She sick."

"What? I think you got a gun under you. Looked like a gun to me."

Pitic shook his head under the cop's boot. "Nothin' man. You know, my daughter, she's sick."

The cop quieted. Pitic heard the rattle of handcuffs.

"What a load of taco bullshit," scoffed the cop as he moved behind Pitic and straddled him while he fumbled with the handcuffs.

In one move Pitic rocked forward onto his chest, kicked back with practiced precision, and jammed both steel-toed boots into the cop's crotch.

The cop doubled over and fell backward.

Pitic jumped up, snatched the flashlight, and made it to the door before the cop took his first breath. He grabbed hold of the jamb and looked back into the trailer.

The goddamn bear!

He swung the light wildly.

The light found the cop, helpless and wheezing.

Pitic touched his knife.

The voice that screamed in his head was not that of Ruby Everheart but one much darker, one screaming with ghastly insistence.

Do it!

For a second he weighed his messed up life. The cop's life.

He stepped forward. His fingers flexed along the hilt.

The cop, gasping, raised his head. One eye lit by the flashlight. A hand fumbled for a gun.

Cursing his existence, Pitic turned and took off running.

Even before he jumped into the waiting limo's passenger seat, Pitic knew how he would lie.

He slammed the door and turned to face the presence in the back seat.

"Dead. It was the cops I think. But those kids had something to do with it, I-"

A hand shot out from the back seat and seized Pitic's right hand. The empty spot where Pitic's middle and ring fingers used to be glowed stark white in the glare of the trailer park's overhead light. He tried to pull away but was held fast.

The voice when it came, was guttural darkness itself. "Where is it?"

Pitic grimaced with the tightening on his wrist.

"Gone. Couldn't find it."

Pitic cried out as one of his fingers was bent back the wrong way.

"It's gone!"

Way back.

"It's GONE!" he yelled as the tendons stretched and tore.

When his hand was released he grabbed for the lifeless finger, cratering it, and whispered, "Trailers… burnt up. Everything's burnt up. It's… gone."

Impenetrable silence from the back seat.

"Burned up," he repeated. "I swear. All burned up in there. All burned." Pitic dry-swallowed.

"You… fucked this up. Now… you'll fix it."

"All burned," Pitic whimpered.

"That's a start."

PART ONE

CHAPTER ONE

"Identify yourself."

All heads in Sacramento Police Department's press room turned as the man in the back row lowered his hand and shuffled to his feet. He acknowledged the other reporters' stares with a smart-ass grin.

"Bobby Mazen. I have a blog. You know, 'Mazen Jars' dot com. Yeah, well, I've been perusing your carefully worded handout here, which by the way, doesn't give us any details and I seriously wanted to know exactly how do you spell transsexual? Or…"

He paused, drawing out the moment, collecting an audience, "Or, do you go both ways on the spelling?"

With his hands clenched on either side of the podium, Detective Stan Wyld stood alone, waiting for the laughter to die.

This was supposed to be an informative back-fill of the Olive Park case, not a full-blown free-for-all press conference with asshole bloggers.

And now, before he even started, young Mr.-white-teeth-and-California-tan near the back row was preening, proud he'd shot the first question and garnered a laugh.

Stan glared and was silent. He had requested no cameras. True to their word, the TV camera tripods at the back of the room were empty, though the number of cell phones aimed at him from the assembled group of local and national reporters resembled a smartphone commercial. Not surprising given the attention of the case. And the still harsh, red emotion.

No one else followed up with a shouted question. Or a joke.

Mr. California Tan looked to either side of him for further support. Finding none, he sat down quickly and pretended to be busy examining his shoes.

15 years in Sacramento Police Department's Major Crimes unit had given Stan plenty of practice sparring with the press, and especially after resurrecting and solving the Olive Park murders, where he was the lead detective and primary public messenger for all that had been right and wrong with Olive Park.

This morning, he stood alone.

Neither of the other two On-Going Investigation team were here. His partner, Detective Jake Steiner, and their IT expert, Mallory Dimante, had begged off. He didn't blame them and didn't push it. All three had had enough of Olive Park.

Dimante, still coming to terms with the red scar that decorated the right side of her face from scalp to jaw, loathed being seen by anybody.

Jake, Stan believed, was more affected by the kids they uncovered in the woods of Olive Park than he let show. Right after they wrapped the case and filed the mountain of paperwork, Jake disappeared only to reappear late one Tuesday night, rooting around in the archives, searching out their next cold case.

As for himself, he and Bea had gone to Carmel-by-the-Sea. He'd spent a few days letting the wash of the waves and several quarts of scotch erase what couldn't be erased - nights in the woods uncovering graves, skeletal arms raised in begging supplication, a small desperate hand holding two quarters.

Of course, former detective, now Captain of the SacPD, Carruthers wouldn't show. Afraid to address questions on why the investigation he headed 17 years ago into the worst serial child killer in California's history had gone nowhere. It had always been a wonder to Stan that, even treading on the short-term memory of Sacramentoans, it was near miraculous the way Carruthers had resurrected his career, to rise from flailing, incompetent detective on the original Olive Park case, to making Captain. Carruthers never publicly acknowledged Stan and Jake's success in bringing Olive Park to a close, which pissed off Jake and was a personal affront to Stan.

Hey, we completely did your work for you, you asshole.

Stan cleared his throat. The wall clock read just after 9 A.M. Stan didn't want to be standing up here past 9:30.

The press, representing the rest of the good and decent people of California, eager to learn the gory details, was not to be denied though, slobbering to learn all the gruesome bits of evidence uncovered that were held back as the investigation proceeded.

He recognized a few reporters and was glad to see Phil 'Quid Pro Quo' Ginger, front row center. Their quiet history of information trading over the years had benefitted both of them.

Ginger, now freelance, gave an exaggerated glance at his watch. He mouthed up to Stan, "Let's go Mitchum!" using the sobriquet that Stan had tolerated for years. Detective Stan Wyld, with his slicked-back hair and drooping eyes, sonorous voice, and dry sense of humor, resembled the late actor. There were worse people to have as your lookalike, Stan knew.

"Okay. Now," Stan announced, staring down eager beaver in the back row. "Let's get started. I'm Detective Wyld with Sacramento's OID, the On-Going Investigation Division. I was the lead detective when the Olive Park case was re-opened. You all know the gist of the case and because of the intense interest, OID felt we needed to fill in some of the background of the case. To put to rest some rumors and set the record straight, as it were."

This was a lie, but he sold it well. Neither Stan, nor Jake, nor Mallory felt they needed to rehash anything. For anybody. But those that oversaw the funding for OID, Stan's fledgling division handling cold cases, insisted.

Solving Olive Park was a bright success for Sacramento PD. And Stan foresaw the case being milked like a weary cow until it was sucked dry and couldn't stand.

"For those of you who want to make sure you have everything straight, the handouts at the back of the room have the case summary. The overview is that in 1997, the bodies of three children were found in the woods of Olive Park. As most of you know, thousands of man-hours were spent on the investigation. There were a few false leads but no arrests. The main thrust of the investigation continued for well over a year. Afterward, it was reviewed yearly but there was little, actually, there was nothing, new that would've demanded a full re-opening of the case.

"When Detective Steiner and I began looking full-time into cold cases, we decided to start with the Olive Park case."

Another lie.

Neither of them wanted to start with a big case. Rather they wanted to get their feet wet with something simpler, but their IT whiz, Mallory Dimante had, for personal reasons, seen that the Olive Park murders were their first case.

"By re-looking at the case, we believed we had the advantage of some of the newer forensic tests and databases that weren't available to the earlier investigating teams. And utilizing those improvements and with some luck, mostly luck, we made progress. The result, you know. During the apprehension of the Olive Park killer, Rudolph Rendell, or Ruby Everheart as he was known, was killed."

A gross prevarication.

Sure, he and Jake and even Dimante, actually especially Dimante, were closing in on the sick bastard but it was Michael Cooper, the brother of six-year-old Jessie, the next intended victim, who did the deed. Stan and Jake and Dimante showed up in time to see Rendell's steaming corpse on a pile of dirt in the moonlit woods of Olive Park. Between the three of them, they decided that the Cooper kids didn't need the life-long badge as the killers of Ruby Everheart, so that part of their report was rewritten.

As far as everyone knew, Michael and Jessie Cooper were near victims who escaped.

The tentative hand of Mr. Bright Teeth rose. Stan stopped him.

"I'm going to take questions in a minute, but I want to say something first."

Stan studied the wood of the podium. He'd thought about how to address what he would say. In bed, restless at 4 A.M., he still hadn't been sure.

He raised his head and addressed the group.

"We, Detective Steiner and myself and Ms. Dimante and the entire Sacramento Police Department extend our sympathies to the families of the nine additional victims that were uncovered in Olive Park."

Any movement among the reporters stopped. No one breathed.

"It is to our everlasting regret that this case could not be solved earlier, but it is a certainty that building on the efforts of hundreds of professionals who had diligently worked on this case over the years, we have prevented the deaths of any more children at the hands of Rudolph Rendell. Today, we will be releasing the names of the victims as a matter of public record. If we could, we would not do so. These families have suffered from not knowing the fates of their children for so many years. Now, they will be living with the knowing. We, as a department, ask you to respect their privacy now and in the future. At some point, if they want to address you publicly, they will do so on their own. Now, is not the time. Any harassment of these families will be prosecuted without exception."

Stan scanned the room, searching out each face, sealing the deal.

"Now," he sighed. "Questions."

Every hand shot up. Stan called on Ginger.

"Stan, why so long to release this information?"

Stan knew Ginger would start with a softball, something to which he already knew the answer.

"We needed the time to properly identify the victims and notify the families. Identification was completed last week and all families were notified as of three days ago. We delayed these few extra days to give the families time to adjust before we made the names public. One more thing, I will not go into detail on the specific condition of any of the victims, so do not ask."

"Yes?" Stan pointed to eager beaver in the back. He looked contrite.

"So, what about this Rendell, this Everheart? Was he or she or both a transvestite and a transgender type or what?"

"The psychologists who have done a cursory examination of the case don't believe Rendell was either a transvestite, that being a cross-dresser or transgender, that being somebody who identifies with a sex different than which they were born. It is thought that Rendell was masquerading as a woman to deflect suspicion. From his history, it was apparent that he was very adept at changing identities, using as you all know, the traveling carnival known as JOYLAND to lure victims. He was then, as he was until his death, working out of a house trailer, pretending to be the female fortune teller, Ruby Everheart."

Another hand.

"How exactly did Rendell die? It wasn't in any of the reports. He burned up in the trailer fire?"

Stan shook his head. "The fire burned the trailer where Rendell lived. The second trailer next to it, the fortune-telling business, was not burned. Rendell wasn't in either when the fire happened."

Here Stan paused. He had wanted to avoid retelling the gruesome aspects because it could not be done dispassionately. These were the juicy bits that everyone wanted to know. However, once known and assimilated, horrific aspects of any case become the baseline. The Manson killings in L.A. The Clutters in Kansas. Jonestown.

Olive Park.

There is a need to know what the worst one human can do to another, Stan believed. Not to understand in the truest sense, but with which to measure one's own life. Yes, doors get locked when a neighbor is murdered by person's unknown, fliers inspect their fellow airline travelers, schools go into lockdown and anyone who does not look like you is suspect, but measured by the worst, there is much good in life. Still, the morbid desire to know the worst remains.

Stan kept as straight a face as possible when he finally formed his answer. "There was a struggle during Rendell's apprehension. He fell on a broken shovel handle and was impaled."

No one will ever find out that young Michael Cooper was holding the other end of the wood handle, thought Stan with some satisfaction.

Impalement was hot and new to the assembled group. All of them made notes and all hands went up but most didn't wait to be called on.

"You mean like a vampire?"

"Was it a stake?"

"Through his heart? Like a werewolf you mean?"

"Who did it? Was it you?"

Stan used both hands to quiet them.

"During a struggle, Rendell himself fell on a broken shovel handle. That's all. The unofficial cause of death, according to Danni Harness in Forensics, was a rupture of the heart."

Stan sighed and could easily picture headlines and TV leads tomorrow. All would somehow work in 'vampire' and 'stake through the heart' he was sure. He looked to Ginger who had a big grin on his face as he made notes.

"Can we have pictures?" shouted from the back row.

"No."

"Stan, C'mon!"

"No! Sorry."

"How big was the stake?"

"I told you, it was a broken shovel handle."

Stan continued to deflect the question of pictures. Of course, there were pictures taken that would never see the light of day. One Stan would not forget.

When he'd first arrived on the scene, the image of Rudolph Rendell on his back in the cold blue moonlight, draped over a mound of dirt with a stick erupting from his chest had the disquieting effect as if Satan's staff had been shoved up from hell to capture the best prey the devil could find.

While everyone else scribbled notes, a singular hand emerged from the group from someone Stan did not recognize.

"Yes?"

The man rose to his feet. Stan instantly had a bad feeling. There was something rehearsed about the way the man stood, the way he waited until he had everyone's attention before speaking. The way he was dressed way too uptown to be dogging a story.

"Detective, I want to ask you one question." He paused as if gathering thoughts, but it was a ruse. The man already knew what he would say.

"Wouldn't you agree the Sacramento Police Department is culpable for the deaths of the nine additional victims that were murdered and horribly tortured by this maniac while for seventeen years the police did nothing?"

The question hung in expectant silence. Heads turned from the man to Stan.

Before he could summon a reply, a woman seated on the aisle, jumped up and pointed at Stan.

"Yes!" she shouted. "Yes! They are! They killed my baby. They did nothing! My baby was killed and they did nothing!" The man who asked the question smiled, satisfied.

The woman was thin and trembling. Coarse brown hair haphazardly pulled back, revealed a face flushed with indignation and rage.

To Stan's astonishment, she started down the aisle.

He looked to the door. There were no officers present. Why should there be? These were supposed to be vetted reporters, who had gone through security to get in. No need for any protection.

As she came forward, no one stopped her, out of respect for her loss. She reached inside her black vinyl purse as she came closer.

Stan stiffened.

To his relief, she pulled out a sheaf of papers and held them high as she turned, first to the group, then back to Stan. To Stan, they looked to be legal papers. Serve me, he thought. She's going to serve me legal papers suing us all for the death of her child.

"You killed my baby!" she hissed as she thrust the papers toward him. "This is for you, you bastard!"

Stan nodded and reached for the papers.

Too late he realized what they were covering.

In slow motion, he saw her hand come up from behind the papers. Her finger already pressing down.

The pepper spray hit him full in both eyes. He flailed in the air, trying to block the stream, and reeling, slammed back against the podium in squirming agony.

She kept advancing and spraying until Ginger and a few others knocked her down and pinned her to the floor.

She never stopped screaming about her son.

Her son, one of the last victims murdered by the Butcher of Olive Park.

CHAPTER TWO

Jake Steiner examined the pictures scattered over the conference table in the middle of OID's glass office. The pictures were all 8x10s. They all depicted the unluckiest day in the lives of the victims of Ruby Everheart. Full-on face shots, some eyes closed, some half-open. Their life essence fully drained, they lay on different morgue slabs or, as in two photos, at the site where they were discovered. They were commemorative photos, like birthdays or anniversaries or college graduations only these were all taken on their very first day of being discovered.

Now, they were being gathered for the last time. A sad fraternity ready to be boxed up and moved to the archives, soon to be forgotten except for those who remembered them as they had been.

Stan moved next to Jake, lifted up the sunglasses that protected his swollen eyes, and with practiced precision, matched up all the bottom edges of the pictures and then carefully slid each one so the edges were within a half inch of each other.

Jake sighed. He pushed back his sandy hair, leaned in, and studied the images.

"They're not in chronological order," he murmured.

Mallory Dimante adjusted the volume down on her iPod, pushed both men aside, reached in, and re-arranged the pictures in their correct order. After which, Stan moved in again and adjusted the bottom edges in an even line and the spacing back to a half inch.

All three studied the faces in the photos. All three wished they could've done more even though they knew what they had done had saved additional victims. It still wasn't enough for the twelve before them.

Jake gathered the photos, stacking them in order.

The grating screech of metal scraping against metal interrupted Jake and echoed in the cavernous building.

The front door to OID was pulled open and four people came in. The door squealed as it closed.

"Whaddya know," muttered Stan. "I knew the asshole'd show up here one day."

Both Jake and Mallory looked up.

Stan moved away from the conference table that dominated the center of the office and sauntered over to his desk, subtly palming the bottle of Speyburn scotch off his desktop and returning it to the bottom drawer.

Mallory removed her earbuds, shut off her iPod, pushed her blonde hair out of her face, and slipped on her shoes.

Jake sat down on the conference table, a bemused look on his face, fingers flexing, kneading an unseen tennis ball.

Sacramento Police Captain Ash Carruthers filled the doorway to the glass office and looked up to the clerestory, four floors above the atrium.

"Well, well, so this is our crystal palace, huh?"

The three people behind the Captain stopped short and dutifully looked up into the atrium's openness. One of them was Samuels, Carruthers' toady. The other two, a man and a woman were strangers.

Stan too, involuntarily looked up. It was an impressive site, one he lived with every day and took for granted. Now, with the late afternoon sun streaming down, reflecting off their four glass walls and lighting up the whole of the OID office space like a floodlit crime scene, he saw it again from an outsider's perspective.

The four-story Rogers and Sons Cold Storage building, the corbeled brick fortress that, as of late, housed almost all of SacPD's evidence and record archives and the OID, had long ago been converted to furniture storage. Now, after last year when the furniture boys went belly up having hidden their imported meth in every conceivable piece of stored furniture, from armoires to

Chippendale davenports, the building fell into the hands of the City of Sacramento who wisely skirted the need for making a sizeable outlay for a new building and practically for the price of a major drug decontamination, had more than enough space to let SacPD expand their archives.

No one really vetted the warehouse as a place to center the OID. That was obvious because the only real office in the old warehouse was four sides of clear glass panels, six-foot-high, centered under glowing clerestories in the middle of the ground floor atrium of the massive structure.

Even with his own desk and files and his workplace organized the way he liked, it still took Stan months to accept catching his own reflection out of the corner of his eye, and those of Jake and Mallory too.

It was at once confining and deliciously open.

"Captain," Stan said, not bothering to extend his hand. "About time you came over."

His lack of enthusiasm obvious.

Carruthers reached out nevertheless and grabbed Stan's hand and shook it as if they were estranged brothers and then did a short wave to Mallory and Jake. "Good to see you all."

"Impressive Stan. Damn impressive." Carruthers' voice trailed off as he stared up into the sunlight streaming into the building.

"You know, I saw pictures of this. I mean they keep giving me pictures of the progress they're making over here with the archive units and everything, but I guess I never realized how…how goddamn bright it is here. No wonder the construction boys been calling this our crystal palace, eh."

He looked down at Stan with faux concern. He put a hand on his shoulder.

"And no security, Stan. There's nothing to stop anybody from walking in here."

"You're right," Stan agreed. "Just anybody can walk in here." But the sarcasm was lost on Carruthers. The man was varnish.

Samuels, second in command, sidled up to Carruthers. "Security system's being installed here shortly."

Carruthers nodded approval but turned again to Stan.

"Seriously, detectives, how do you get any work done?"

Stan stepped back to let the rest of the group enter their area. "A little odd, but we're used to it."

"It's damn crazy stupid if you ask me," sneered Samuels

The other two in the doorway, a man and woman, were dressed in similar dark suits. The woman stifled a yawn but, the man, a short stubby creature, radared in on Mallory and the two open buttons of her blouse and the way her tight jeans molded her ass.

Samuels gained their attention when he rapped on one of the glass walls with his knuckles.

"What is this? Half inch glass? I mean this is crazy."

He stared up again. "An office of all glass walls stuck in the middle of the ground floor of a warehouse. And no roof on this place. An office with no roof!" he exclaimed. He looked at the Captain and the other two for some support.

Stan, Jake, and Mallory said nothing. Their unspoken feeling was if they would only stay quiet and still, these assholes would leave.

"All right, Samuels," the Captain snapped, waving him down. He turned quickly and held out a welcoming arm to the other two people who so far had remained silent and seemingly unimpressed with the glass offices of OID

"Stan, and people, these are our new facilities consultants we've just brought on. Margaret and Tony from ExecuSpace."

Stan nodded. He didn't remove his sunglasses. Mallory offered a weak smile which Tony answered with a direct leer. Jake said nothing and didn't bother to get up.

"Margaret and Tony, this is our OID, our Ongoing Investigation Department."

"Division," muttered Stan under his breath.

When Margaret and Tony did not react, the Captain added, "They work on the unsolved cases for us."

Tony spoke up. "So. Hey! You were the guys who solved that thing with that crazy transvestite vampire. Stake through the heart. Read about it."

Stan looked to Carruthers to see how he wanted him to answer. Instead, the impatient look on Carruthers' face signaled the Olive Park case held all the importance of an overdue parking ticket.

"Yes, well," offered Carruthers, "We're only really here to tour the archive installation progress. Don't want to bother you guys."

Carruthers summoned up a faux smile and turned to Tony.

"Tony, maybe ExecuSpace can do something about getting these good detectives a real office. Someplace normal. Some place they can get some real work done without having to deal with all this…light. Possible, yes?"

ExecuSpace Tony pursed his lips, looked at Margaret, then did a slow take around the office, lingered on Mallory, then turned back to the captain.

"Absolutely. I calculate the savings in utility costs alone should easily justify the cost. Rather criminal, shall we say, to let all the heat escape, absent a roof."

Tony from ExecuSpace couldn't keep a hint of disdain out of his voice.

Before Margaret could nod her assent, Mallory spoke up in a clear voice, not bothering to hide her derision.

"You don't know what you're talking about."

This got a sharp look from the captain and another raised eyebrow from Tony.

Jake merely tilted back in his chair with his feet on the conference table, his hands clasped behind his head.

Stan sighed.

Mallory slid off the conference table and addressed the short little ExecuSpace man who had trouble keeping his eyes on her face.

"There are no heating costs," continued Mallory. "It's always seventy, seventy-five degrees in here. So, you're not gonna save a dime closing us in."

Stan jumped in, addressing Tony as if speaking to one who didn't understand English.

"This place was built in the 1800s as a refrigeration storehouse. The place has insulation. Cork and rock wool to be exact. Walls are four feet thick. Temperature never varies. That's what she meant. That's why this building was selected to house the archives."

Stan turned back to Mallory and narrowed his eyes.

She ignored him, settled back on the conference table, not giving an inch.

Still, Samuels had to pipe up.

"Yeah, well, we should rip out this glass playpen of yours and put in something normal," he snipped. "You can't be a part of the department and not have a regular office for chrissakes."

Stan didn't need to look at Jake and Mallory. He knew what they were thinking.

Samuels had one last shot. "Completely ridiculous you know!"

Stan shrugged as he followed them. "I don't know Samuels. If you'll notice, we as the cold case division of SacPD, have immediate access to all the old files we need."

Stan gestured to the completed evidence archive units that now occupied two of the four floors above them. Even down here the new paint smell lingered.

The Captain laughed. "He's got you there Samuels. Look at this place."

The group gathered immediately outside the glass office.

Carruthers cupped his hands like a little kid and shouted "Heeelllllooooo!" from the floor of the atrium, waiting. The echo came back to him from all floors.

"Love it!"

He turned back to Stan "Thank you, Stan. Thank you all. Sorry to interrupt."

Carruthers waved and Mallory did a half-hearted, dismissive wave back.

"No problem. Anytime," Stan said.

Before he turned to go, Carruthers leaned into Stan, smiling and probing. "So, how are the...you know." He pointed to the sunglasses. "Better?"

"Docs are talking operation," Stan managed with a straight face.

Carruthers drew back. "Oh!" His smile disappeared and his eyes glazed as he momentarily calculated medical and legal costs.

He gripped Stan's shoulder. "Oh, I'm sure it won't come to that." Carruthers turned. "Okay people, let's move on!"

The entourage had taken a few steps toward the archive office, still an unmanned, patched together, temporary repository of the archive inventory, when Carruthers said a few words to the ExecuSpace people. Then with his hands on their backs, ushered them forward.

When they had safely entered the temporary archive office, Carruthers turned and approached Stan with a slim file he pulled from his briefcase. He started to hand it to Stan who reached for it, but the Captain didn't release it. Instead, Carruthers turned and made sure everyone had entered the archive office.

"Captain?" asked Stan, not understanding why the man wouldn't let him have the file he held out to him. Both had a good grip in a subtle tug of war.

There was no smile now as he released the file to Stan.

"Here," he said quietly.

"What's this?"

Carruthers licked his lips, tried a smile.

"You're doing me a favor."

"I am?"

Carruthers raised his chin toward Jake and Mallory. "You and them. A quick follow-up. You three. I know you're busy, I can see that. And you're still recovering. But, this won't take long."

Stan studied the man's face, hard set with a touch of uncharacteristic nervousness blended in.

"Something that for now doesn't leave this office, got it?"

Stan held back, reluctant to agree to anything. Twenty-six years dodging the office minefield bred cautiousness. One thing he was sure of; it was always better to be the askee than the asker.

"What is it?"

"It's a missing person, Stan. Simply a missing person."

"Okay. But, what does this have to do with OID?" asked Stan, not wanting to hear the answer.

"Nothing. You're doing me a favor, here. You and…" He waved through the glass at Mallory and Jake.

"This isn't a cold case," complained Stan, knowing the argument would go nowhere. Still, he felt obligated to defend his turf. "We're cold case. You say it's only a missing person."

The Captain affected an instructor's upbraiding. "You're on-going, right? On-going cases? That's your group here, right? That's the basis on which we granted you some temporary funding. So you could handle the ongoing cases, no matter how you like to describe them, cold or otherwise. So this is a missing person and it's on-going. You guys are handling it. So that's it."

The phrase 'temporary funding' hung like a sharp axe over their conversation.

Stan tried again. "Wouldn't this be better handled downtown, maybe with Fitch and Rodriguez?"

"Piss on Fitch and Rodriguez," hissed the Captain. "Screw 'em. This is a personal favor for me."

Again, the attempted smile.

Stan opened the file. He expected to see a standard case file cover sheet with the summary atop, and paper clipped to, further descriptions of what progress had been made on the case. Instead the only thing there was a small yellow sticky note stuck to the inside back of the folder. On it was a single name.

Stan looked up.

"Who is this?"

"Just what it says. James Marston, Junior. He's our AWOL."

"But, there's nothing here."

"James Marston Junior. That's all you need. Everyone knows him. Someone reported him missing. Just find out, you know, where he is. It's that simple."

"Oh boy," Stan ventured without enthusiasm, already making plans to dump this off on Mallory.

The Captain wiped his upper lip and appeared to relent. "Look, I know this a nothing thing to you three. But, Marston's a bit of a queer duck, if you know what I mean. Not queer queer, I don't think, but like a black sheep. Loner. Money. He's got a house here in Sacramento. Whole thing got bumped to me because whatever. Doesn't matter. I already sent two uniforms up there to the house to check on him. Wait, see if anybody shows. Place is locked up tight. Nobody there. Now, it's your turn. Do what you do. Check his phone, his houses, friends, business associates, vehicles, travel plans, his whole operation. You know."

The Captain rapped his knuckles against Stan's shoulder. Buddy-buddies.

"How long has he been missing?"

"Not sure. A week or two is my guess."

"Already!"

"Maybe more."

The Captain put his hand on the file as if to say tag-you're-it. "I guess you could say this is already a cold case, eh?"

Stan shook his head. "This is crap."

Carruthers wasn't listening. "Without a lot of hoopla, okay. Let me know how you're doing on it tomorrow. An email status update for starters."

He did another little wave to Jake and Mallory, who exchanged uncomprehending glances with each other.

"I wanted my best guys on this. And, according to the press, that's you and the group, Stan," he growled. "You're stars now, right?"

Carruthers dug in the briefcase and pulled out last week's front page of the Bee. "There."

Stan groaned. Under the headline, 'OLIVE PARK MURDERS SOLVED!' the sub-head read 'New Cold Case Group Takes Only One Month to Solve 17-Year-Old Mystery'.

They'd had to shut off the phones. Hundreds of relatives of past victims who thought their cases were lost in the bowels of obscurity now saw Stan and his crew as wunderkinds. They flooded OID with demands to solve their personal mystery.

Carruthers spread his arms taking in the whole glass office. "The goddamn On-Going Investigation Department. Whatever you guys need to do this, all right? Shouldn't take you more than a day or two. Probably stone dead or off cocking around in the south of France, you know."

Carruthers appeared to reconsider what he said.

"Look, just find him. And no going to the south of France. I don't want to see any of that shit on an expense voucher, you hear me. You and whoever can do it all from here."

Carruthers turned and started back to the archive office.

Stan fingered the sticky note.

Best my ass. You want secrecy. You want us to find this guy's sorry butt and drag it back here and put him back where he belongs with no one the wiser. And the family that much happier.

Carruthers, over his shoulder. "It's like a bike, Stan. I know you're supposedly cold cases, but you never forget how to handle a missing person!"

He gave a derisive laugh and closed the archive office door.

"Division, not department," Stan threw the words after him. "On-Going Investigation Division. And we're not supposedly cold case, we are!" But there was no one to hear him.

After a moment's reflection, he realized what the whole sham of a visit was about. It wasn't to show ExecuSpace flunkies how well the archives were coming along and it wasn't a surprise inspection of the OID.

"Son of a bitch."

Outgoing Captain. Rumors of eventually running for statewide office. Probably this Marston or his family were potential financial contributors. Nice. From slipshod detective to police captain to Governor.

Jake joined Stan. "I thought you'd locked the door, partner. Keep the low-life out."

Stan handed him the file.

Jake opened it, fingered the sticky note. "What's this? What's going on?"

"Shit. Tumbling downhill."

Stan realized that OID's isolation had made him complacent. Jake and Mallory too. They forgot they were financially tethered to SacPD; a small part of a whole.

Stan shrugged his shoulders. "Yeah, well, we have no lock on our door. This place is an open spillway for all manner of crap to float in."

He shook his head in grudging admiration, realizing that Carruthers had more than enough sleaze to make a damn fine politician.

CHAPTER THREE

Mallory flipped her blond hair out of her face and stuck her hands into her tight jean pockets.

"What gives?"

Four stories above them the sky had darkened and rain began spattering against the glass skylights. A sudden September Sacramento downpour with bursts of hail mixed in. So unusual, they all looked up at the sight.

"Rain. Figures," Stan said, as he resumed his place at his desk.

Sacramento Valley's crops grew on pumped irrigation and were not dependent on manna from the skies. And September's brought less than a half inch for the whole month. By the sound of it, they knew the runoff was already spilling out from the downspouts into the parking lot, the hail decorating their windshields.

Already the air felt close.

"So. What is it?" asked Mallory, taking the file from Jake. "Something important?"

"No. Only a project for you. Thought you could use something different to do."

Jake smiled to himself. Stan looked away, hiding his own smile.

She opened the file and saw the yellow note.

"Wow! Marston! What about him? This is for me?"

"You know who he is?" asked Jake, surprised.

"Sure. Who doesn't?" replied Mallory. She set the folder back on the table.

Jake looked at Stan with an uncomprehending stare.

Mallory looked from one man to the other. "Kidding, right?"

She realized they were clueless. "James Marston! You guys ever go to the movies? I mean, did you ever go to the movies, you know, like back in the Sixties and Seventies?"

Jake pretended to look hurt. "Jesus Dimante! How old is this guy? And how old do you think we are?"

"How 'bout the Eighties and Nineties?"

"So, who is he?" asked Stan.

Mallory held out her hands. "Movies, you know. Molten Pitchers! The production company?"

Nothing from either man.

"C'mon! You don't know *Alien Inquisition, March of The Rodents, Heil to My Martian Master, Naked Nubians from Neptune*?"

Mallory started in earnest. "You guys! Molten Pitchers Productions. Used to be JAM Productions when Marston's father started it. JAM was the group who started creating take-offs of the big screen epics or space movies or anything that was popular. Only, Marston had the twisted idea of adding a few masked slashers to the mix. Marston was right behind the big guys by a few months with his own version of the movie, with a few extra buckets of blood. And he did 'em on a shoestring.

"Then, in the '90s his son, Marston Junior took over, morphed good ol' dad's company into Molten Pitchers."

"Molten Pitchers, Motion Pictures," repeated Stan. "Cute."

Mallory stood with her hands on her hips and studied Jake. She raised her chin.

"C'mon. You never took some poor unfortunate girl to a drive-in and ignored the movie while you fumbled around trying to remove her bra?"

Jake smiled. "Sure, but there was no movie playing at the time."

"Figures."

"So, most of his stuff was years ago," Stan said. "Then how do you know of him?"

"Film raves. Weekend breaks where they dig up a whole series of his films. Like a twenty-four-hour bloody marathon. You can still get 'em on DVD or online."

"And you used to watch those?" asked Jake.

"UCLA, yeah. There was a group of us. It was a way to get our heads out of the books for a while, you know. So, okay, you have your Roger Cormans and such. They're grade-A schlock. Marston and Molten, not so much. Still, he's a big deal in the world of celluloid B grade shit. The guy's really famous."

Stan and Jake were silent.

"Anybody who's anybody has heard of him," chided Mallory. "His stuff is still on everywhere. Japanese love him."

Stan looked to Jake. "Well, now, if the Japanese love him…"

"Sheesh," she said, finally in exasperation, giving up. She pointed to the open file. "So, what? Why did King Tut give you a file folder with Marston's name in it?"

"Obviously, he wants us to deal with it. As a personal favor. The guy's missing, evidently. I thought it would be perfect for you."

"Me? Why doesn't the LAPD handle it?"

Stan sat down at his desk, opened his desk drawer, and retrieved the Dodge's car keys.

"Well, he's not in L.A. Marston lives here in Sacramento."

Mallory let her chair fall forward. Her feet hit the floor with a thump.

"Get out!"

She put her hands on the conference table as if to steady herself.

"He lives here? In Sac? Where?"

"Has a house here. Shouldn't take you long to find out."

"Here? In Sacramento?" asked Mallory, still trying to get her bearings. "I don't believe it."

"Look. It's not like he's royalty or anything," drawled Jake.

"To you, maybe," Mallory said as she slipped into her seat and tapped her keyboard.

"Shit, I didn't know this," she muttered.

She looked up at both. "So, what? He hasn't been kidnapped or anything has he?"

Stan looked at her sharply. "Why would you say that?"

"You have to see his movies to know. Grabbing some poor helpless schmuck, usually female, in any of his movies was his m.o. Then, of course, chopping her to bits in wonderfully imaginative ways was sort of his signature, you know. I just figured…"

"Well, no such luck." Stan turned and looked back at the closed door to the temporary archive office. "He's only reported missing."

Mallory kept tapping her keyboard, no longer listening. "No shit, here it is. Marston. Out on German Road, northeast of town. Way past Rancho Cordova."

Mallory read off the address then shut her laptop and retied her tennis shoes. "We going right now?"

Stan realized how easy it was to lead her on. He'd had his fun and now guilt surfaced. He really had been planning to give this wholly over to Mallory and let her play with it until he heard the Captain had already sent two uniforms to the house and they'd struck out.

"You don't go. Jake and I will cover it. You track down the family and find out who called in the missing persons' report."

Mallory ignored him. "Stan! I'm going with. Hell, this is James Marston. I'm going. I'll never get a chance to meet him otherwise. Assuming he's really there and not missing, just unfound. I can do background later."

Stan and Jake gathered their things. Neither answered her. Neither bothered to state the obvious. She was civilian. Regardless of the stuff she pulled in the Olive Park investigation. As much as she would like to believe she was more, she was an assistant. Not a cop and especially not a detective. And not trained in any kind of field work.

The connection and balance between the three of them since Olive Park had settled into a symbiotic collective, like mariners, alone together in a dinghy on the high seas with Jake as the oarsman, Stan, the captain, and Mallory as the energetic, eager lookout. A lookout who stayed in the crow's nest and never ventured ashore.

"Stan?"

Both men exchanged looks.

"Come on!"

"You're starting to whine. I hate that. Go on then. Go with Jake. Don't make an ass out of yourself and make us look bad when you meet him. If you meet him."

"Thank you, Detective Wyld," Mallory replied politely. "I'll try not to drool."

"Just tell him you're from the Department of Sanitation, there to check if he's recycling correctly."

Except Mallory had already sprinted out the door.

"Thanks. *Partner*," Jake said.

Stan gave a wave. "Anytime."

Stan checked his watch. Late. As usual.

CHAPTER FOUR

The waiter stepped aside and let Stan settle onto his chair.

"He'll have the four-cheese macaroni and cheese," Beatrice stated. "I'll have the mushroom burger, well done. With onion rings."

The waiter nodded and left.

Stan slipped off his sunglasses and regarded his wife. "I hadn't really decided, you know."

She was about to answer but laughed instead. It started small but grew.

"What?"

"Your eyes. Your face."

"They're fine." Stan slipped the menu onto one of the extra chairs and adjusted his knife and fork, lining up the bottoms of each in a straight line.

"Tender still."

"Makes you look, young and earnest. Like the man I married. Good news, though. The wrinkles are gone. You have that healthy freshman glow."

Stan reached up and explored the skin under his eyes before he replaced the sunglasses. He'd never been pepper sprayed before and while it had been a few days the tenderness lingered. And, evidently, the 'healthy glow' remained.

"You never told me who she was."

Stan stopped probing, remembering touching the area did little good. When it happened he'd been blinded and almost worse, had inhaled a straight shot of the OC spray. Couldn't breathe, couldn't see. He'd bounced off the podium, flat on his face with his hands covering. He knew from long ago training that rubbing made it worse. Still, it was impossible not to succumb to the natural reaction when a stream of liquid chili fire seared into your eyeballs. Someone, he thought it may have been Phil Ginger, guided him across the hall to the bathroom and stuck his head under the running water. Whomever it was had held Stan's hands so he couldn't rub it. Turning his head, so the water flowed over one eye, then the other.

One minute he was about to console a grieving widow, the next he was being waterboarded trying to flush burning sand-laced acid out of his eyes and off his face. Two officers from down the hall had pulled off his jacket and ripped off his shirt both of which were fully soaked. They led him down the hall to the locker room with the shower, shoved a chair in the shower, and sat him down. With his head back they ran the shower and with a substantial mixture of dish soap and water, they flushed his eyes and face and finally his hair, knowing the only thing that cuts the oily residue was the grease-fighting abilities of liquid dish soap.

"Name was Cradwell," he answered Bea. "Eloise or Ellen Cradwell." Stan shrugged. "Her son. The last one."

Bea nodded but didn't pursue it. The subject of Sacramento Police, the State Patrol, even the California legislature, being responsible for the additional nine victims because they'd let the case go cold was keeping the Op-Ed pages of the Sacramento Bee hopping. Then there were the scathing commentaries on the local cable channels and the Crime blogs on the Internet were all still banging on the story. Righteous anger over the failed responsibilities of the entire department for not going after Rudolph Rendell from Day One. There was little mention of not enough manpower and budgetary cutbacks.

A few lone voices challenged the complainers. You can have police respond to your domestic violence calls, your accidents, your murders, and assaults, your break-ins, your robberies, or you can pull them off the street and work on a singular case until it's solved.

Both. The people wanted both.

Higher taxes then was the answer.

We won't pay higher taxes.

Well. There you go.

"What happened to her?"

Stan moved his water glass closer to his napkin, then refolded the napkin.

"She was charged with assaulting a police officer. They made a big show, held her overnight, but given the circumstances-"

"Her son being dead and you being alive…" Bea looked away, then fumbled with her hands.

"Exactly that," said Stan, ignoring for the moment the pill case she pushed his way. "They'll let the charges drop in a day or two. Of course, they're all blaming me for it."

"Who is?"

"Upstairs. Not directly. They wouldn't come right out and say they think I screwed up."

"What? By taking Mace in the face?"

Stan shrugged. "What do you want them to do? They look for a scapegoat when things go into the shitter. I was the only one up there. The only rep for the department. So…"

The salads arrived. Stan started in on his, but Bea pushed hers aside. Stan could see she was peeved.

"So, first they think you guys are heroes because you solved the biggest case in this state's history, but now they're tossing you under the bus because you didn't solve it sooner?"

"No." Stan shook his head. "Because I didn't object to her claim-"

He jerked. His heart jumped. Out of the corner of his eye, he glimpsed the hostess.

Carrying menus.

She had something under the menus.

He tensed, ready to run.

The hostess smiled as she passed by.

Bea continued, not noticing. "They explain yet how she got the pepper spray past their new security system?"

Stan worked on his Caesar salad before answering. He moved the lettuce around, covering his shaking hand.

"What? Oh, yeah. Pretty slick. And pretty determined. First, evidently, it was her lawyer who found out about my little press meet, when and where it was going to be. So, she got herself arrested the day before. Shoplifting or something. 'Course our security is set up to catch the guns and knives and your occasional nuclear weapon, not plastic pepper spray on a keychain. They held her overnight. When they released her, thanks to her lawyer, they returned her purse and personal things. She had the spray in her purse and hung out until she slipped in with all the rest. And why did you order me mac and cheese?"

"Because…" She avoided looking at him and busied herself, refolding her napkin. She finished brightly. "Because you love it. And…you know. What the doc said."

They held each other in unsmiling, knowing looks. Stan gave a short nod. "Yeah. Sure. Said I can't have anything that tastes good. Hmm boy." Stan gave a wan smile. "Mac and cheese, wow, it's the best."

"Exactly," Bea answered. She followed up quickly. "What about that attorney? Isn't he at fault? Didn't he help her?"

"Says he had no idea what she was going to do. Says they had only arranged for him to ask the question."

"Jesus, they're a slimy bunch." She tapped her fork on the edge of the salad plate. "Okay, forget that. So, what's next for my hero of Sacramento?"

"You ever hear of a film director or producer by the name of Marston? James Marston?"

Bea poured more of the wine, nodded. "Mostly a lot of bad movies, I think."

"How does everyone know this guy but me?"

"How many kids did you nurse at 3 AM when his stuff was on?"

"Anyhow, Carruthers wants us to find him."

"Find him? Is he lost?"

"I think Carruthers is somehow scared of us. Or jealous. Acting funny about it. This is a piddly little job. A favor he said. But, I think he's unsure of how to deal with a department that suddenly has more visibility than he does. And, maybe he is lost, we're not sure."

"Carruthers?"

"No, Marston. I've sent Mallory out to his house to check it out. Evidently, she's a fan. Used to watch all his stuff."

"You sent her by herself?"

Stan shook his head. "Nah. And Jake wasn't thrilled about it either."

CHAPTER FIVE

Jake and Mallory wound their way through two subdivisions before unexpectedly emerging at a remote crossroads. They were beyond civilization, it seemed. North of the city where low furze covered the hills and eucalyptus saturated the air with heady warmth.

"Which way?" asked Jake. He tapped his fingers on the steering wheel. "What's that say?" pointing to the silent GPS mounted on the dash. Its display showed the last turn they'd made a mile back. But the thing had not updated. The sweet, mechanical voice hadn't uttered a word since the previous command.

Mallory flicked the side of the little box. The electronic map stayed stubbornly centered on where they'd been a mile ago.

"Screw it." Mallory flipped open the glove box. She rummaged around and pulled out the dog-eared owner's manual for the Dodge, a map of Oklahoma, a box of Kleenex, and several condoms.

"Really?" She looked at Jake who ignored her.

The last item was a ragged map of Sacramento and environs.

She turned the map 90 degrees and refolded it smaller and after a minute of tracing their route, she decided.

"Left," she said. "The map says this is German Road."

'Prepare to turn left in point four miles,' piped the GPS, as it attempted to catch up.

"Too late shitbox." Mallory reached over and pulled the navigator from its cradle and tossed it into the glove compartment.

Jake powered them left down the increasingly narrowing road. Golden fescue grasses crept from the side of the road over the surface as if no one was looking. Invading blackberry vines threatened to snag the unsuspecting. They scratched along the side of the car.

"Jesus, where are we headed?" muttered Jake as he tried to glimpse anything through the underbrush and the thick growths of eucalyptus.

They swept past a big green mailbox and a dirt driveway leading to a seedy white house.

Mallory glanced at it. "That can't have been it. Keep on."

Jake strained forward. "Can't be too many more places on this road. Gets any narrower, we'll be walking."

He one-handed the car around what turned out to be the last curve in the road and came to a sharp stop, braking in time so the car didn't plow through the double iron gates that hinged off of two vine-covered stone pillars.

A standoff. Idling Dodge and iron gates.

Jake looked at Mallory.

"Yeah. Okay, let me get it," Mallory said, grabbing the passenger door handle.

Before she could get out the gate crept open on its own with an unhurried whir.

"I'd say we're here," nodded Jake, indicating the tarnished brass plaque screwed to the right pillar.

MARSTON.

Above the name was a crest, an aged shield in the middle of which was a rose.

The pillar left of the gate had a matching rose and there was another plaque below it, but it was hidden, covered by a tangle of twisty vine and a profusion of red bell-shaped flowers until Mallory pulled the creepers aside revealing an unblemished brass plaque.

CRIMSON PARK.

Mallory surveyed the drive up as far as she could see. Nothing indicated why Marston, producer, director of slasher films, had thought to name his property Crimson Park, except maybe blood. He'd done a whole cavalcade of 'Crimson' films. This house was the last in the series evidently.

"Figures," mused Mallory as she watched the gate finish its torturous swing. She got in, closed the door as Jake put it into gear, and accelerated through the pillars up a seemingly unused drive that had once been pristine. A grey line of cracked concrete, lined with moss-covered stones, wound up past a field of brown grass that transitioned to an orchard filled with Red Delicious apple trees. Beyond the orchard, about a quarter mile ahead, they could see the dark outlines of a massive, grey slate roofline, then multiple roof lines merging and angling into each other. The closer they got to the top of the ridge the more manicured and dressed were the grounds.

Mallory lowered her window and inhaled the smell of the apples, many still on the tree, some ripening on the ground. The orchard was bounded by a low stone wall, after which were gardens, neatened and well-watered, alive with a suffusion of crimson.

As they crested the ridge they could see the entire structure. Grey-brown stones rose up against a bright blue sky. It was a magnificent castle-like, two-and-a-half-story stone imposition. The structure's 'L' shape enclosed a semi-circular drive, a sea of shiny exposed aggregate multi-hued stones. The drive was bordered by a stone curb, behind which were foot-high hedges enclosing a stunning blend of landscaping. Every square foot of ground was covered with distinct vermillion hues and textures, set off with their green leaves - roses, salvia, azaleas, cockscomb, carnations, camellias, begonias, tulips, and a riot of unrecognizable varieties.

"No shit, Crimson Park."

The drive entered a gentle roundabout that surrounded a fountain with birds of paradise flowers and orchids, variations of red hues, and plants with an overpowering fragrance that Mallory couldn't name. They rounded the circle and pulled to the entry, a stone portico centered between the two massive wings of the house.

Much of the first floor of the left wing of the place was ivied, with the vines erupting up between the casements, then spreading out above the windows.

To the right of the entry was a jutting crescent of stone and cathedral windows, maybe a library, with a stone-railed balcony above. The rest of the right wing was a crenelated fortress ending in a two-story, all-glass atrium. The graceful outline of twenty-foot palms and outsize fronds could be seen behind the atrium windows, dripping with condensation.

It took your breath away. The house, the grounds, the presentation, the site with the structure dominating the hill it sat on; it was one living, breathing, stretching, gazing, lovely and gentle and kick you in the balls house.

This wasn't money, thought Jake, at least not solely money. This was a different level of living. Instinctively, he knew what it would be like inside. The feel, the smell. The solidness of the flagstone floor, the indirect lighting behind a soaring fireplace, the kitchen that invited guests on its own, the different levels, up or down to match your mood. Water features. And glass. Glass everywhere, forcing you to admire the view.

Some architects believed that western architecture was rough floors and raw wood poles sticking through mudded adobe walls and so they took your basic Pueblo hut and made it gargantuan. Except, this wasn't that.

Jake looked up at the house again. This was California. Really rich California. When everyone else, everyone from the endless, freezing fields of North Dakota, the littered streets of South Philly, or the swelter of Georgia in August, when they all thought of life in California, when they imagined themselves living like Hollywood royalty, this little shack is where they imagined themselves living.

California. Where money goes to learn how to be money.

"Honey. I'm home," Mallory said, as she opened the car door and stood up, stretching.

Jake stepped out onto the smooth rock drive and rested his arms atop the Dodge.

"So, slasher movies pay pretty damn well."

"He didn't only produce blood and guts, you know. But, yeah," she said. "He seemed to keep his head above water. Hope he's home."

They both admired the house. The front façade stretched in both directions and seemed to go on forever with everything ordered as if the landscapers had recently stepped away.

Except for Officer Mazurski, leaning up against his squad at the far end of the circle, there wasn't a thing out of place.

Mazurski put out his latest cigarette and dropped it into the pile of squeezed off ends of butts piled in a litter around his feet and began his King Shit saunter toward Jake.

"The hell you doin' here?" challenged Mazurski.

Jake pulled down his sunglasses and peered over the top at Officer Billy Mazurski. Both he and Stan knew Mazurski from their days downtown at Robbery-Homicide. He was the walking example of conduct unbecoming, constantly playing on his knee injury, suffered a decade earlier in the futile effort of chasing after a carjacker he had no hopes of running down. It was why he was always drawing the toilet assignments: Traffic. Funerals. And crap like this.

The limp was even more exaggerated this morning, probably because he didn't want to be standing around all day smelling the cloying riot of red tea roses that flanked the front entrance.

"Hey, Billy. Looks like the leg's all better."

Mazurski had never reckoned to Jake's sarcasm.

"Huh? I'm stiff like I got bees crammed into the knee," he said with all sincerity.

As if Jake gave a shit.

"What are you doing here?" asked Jake.

Mazurski shrugged. "Hell if I know. Willstein and I got the call late yesterday. Check the premises. Didn't even tell us who owned the place. See if anybody's home, la-di-fucking-da. Same drill. We didn't make it out here 'til today. I mean what the hell. Place isn't goin' anywhere, right?"

"I can see you're on top of things as usual."

"Damn straight. Just me now. Let Willstein bail."

"Did you guys go in?" asked Mallory. "Is he home?"

Mazurski ignored Mallory.

"Place is locked up tight. Nobody in or out, like I said. We swept the perimeter made sure every entrance, doors, and windows, was locked. Me and Michael, Officer Willstein. Took us about three hours to climb through all these goddamn bushes. Big damn place. They say there are almost 100 acres here."

"And? Anything?"

"Nope."

"Nothing unusual?" continued Jake.

Mazurski smiled. "Look. Lights go on and off. We could hear music comin' on, goin' off. That kinda shit. We looked in all the windows, knocked on the doors. 'Bout drove us batshit crazy until we figured out they've got this place wired on fucking automatic pilot. Everything happens by computer probably. You know, programmed to look like somebody's home.

"But, nobody answered the doors. Nobody seems to be around, although the place is in damn nice shape. You going in? You got keys?"

"What..." Jake started to say but was interrupted by the sound of an approaching vehicle. They all turned and watched a small beat-up flatbed truck, with lawnmowers, rakes, garbage cans, and five Mexicans in the cab, round the circle and come to a stop quickly when they saw the squad and Jake in his detective suit.

Limp forgotten, Mazurski marched toward them, but Jake waved him off.

"I got this."

Jake watched the five Mexicans crowded into the cab start a conversation in earnest. He could see them behind the cracked windshield. The truck was still idling and Jake was sure a few were urging the driver to back up and take off. The only thing one could do when you had no papers was to smile and pretend you didn't understand. No Senor. Si Senor.

Jake made a slashing motion against his throat and the driver reached down and cut the ignition. The truck rattled on for few more seconds then gave it up.

With his badge in front of him, Jake motioned for them to exit the vehicle. When they had all filed out, they stood beside the truck, avoiding eye contact with Jake. Their demeanor was restive but subdued as if waiting for the first shot of the firing squad.

"Who's in charge here?" asked Jake.

When he got nothing but bewildered looks he switched to Spanish.

"¿Quién es responsable?"

The five looked at each other as if no one had ever asked the question before. Finally, one guy, the oldest one with a droopy mustache, tentatively raised his hand.

"Sí."

It took Jake and Mazurski, who wandered over, two minutes to shoehorn the useless answers they needed out of the groundsmen.

No, they didn't have keys to the house.

Yes, they were here three days a week.

No, they saw no one else around.

Turned out, Mazurski was reasonably fluent in street Spanish so Jake let him do the grilling. Harping on whether they'd ever seen anyone about as they tended the grounds. No senor.

"They don't know shit," stated Mazurski turning to Jake after the back and forth. "They get paid by Eastern Hills, some landscape company. They've been doing this place for a few years, always the same days."

Mazurski looked around and spied Mallory trying to work a window open. "Hey! What are you doing?"

Mallory saluted him with one finger.

"She's with me," stated Jake. "So, in two years, they never saw anybody here?" continued Jake.

Reluctantly, Mazurski turned back to the Mexicans. "That's what they say. 'Course…" He left the rest unsaid, meaning he personally wouldn't believe anything Mexicans said anyway.

Jake handed the group leader his card. The man took it, not sure what to do with it.

Jake pointed to his card. "Tell him if anyone grows a memory about seeing anyone here, it's important they call me."

Mazurski hesitated but relayed what Jake said. Jake held up a hand to the side of his head in the shape of a phone.

"Telephone."

The group leader nodded.

"Yeah," scoffed Mazurski. "Right."

Jake waved at the group, still lined up in front of their truck.

"Tell them, no work today. Cut 'em loose."

The Mexicans could not back their truck up fast enough.

Mazurski looked at Jake. "Hey, unless you've got more Mexicans you need questioned, you don't need me. Place is all yours. Adios partner."

He scattered the butts with his foot before he drove off.

CHAPTER SIX

Mallory and Jake waited until Mazurski's squad had passed through the pillars at the bottom of the hill before approaching Marston's front door.

They looked at each other.

Jake shrugged. "May as well try it."

Jake pushed the button on the intercom box. A small red light came on next to a small hole, the camera.

No sound was heard from inside.

They waited and after half a minute the red light extinguished. Jake pushed the intercom again. The red light came on again. This time Jake held down the intercom button. He leaned in and spoke into the box.

"Sacramento Police. We need to speak to Mr. James Marston." He released the button and stepped back.

Nothing.

"What about this?" Mallory pointed to the little white metal sign that stood discretely to the side of the entrance. 'Coliseum Security'. "Kinda pretentious."

"Call 'em. See what they know."

Jake studied the security company's sign. A memory stirred but he couldn't dredge it up.

Before Mallory could hit send on her phone they heard another vehicle approaching.

They watched the U.S. Mail delivery truck come up the drive.

"Busy place for nobody home," muttered Jake.

The mail truck came to a stop behind the Dodge.

They watched as the mailman flipped through the mail in his bin, grab what he needed. Seeing Jake and Mallory, he smiled and held up a finger then dug into a different metal container and came out with a clipboard.

The small, wispy-haired man slipped out of his van and approached Jake.

He handed Jake a bundle of mail, bound in a sturdy rubber band, then held out the clipboard.

"Finally. Somebody to sign for this."

Mallory looked over Jake's shoulder. The clipboard had a registered letter addressed to James Marston under the clip. Stuck to that was a little yellow slip with a large X where the recipient is supposed to sign. He handed it to Jake.

"Good thing. This was going to be the third and last time I tried for your signature. Gotta send it back to the sender after three attempts, you know. Though sometimes, I give it a fourth try."

Jake held up his badge and handed the mail back to him.

"Sacramento PD," Jake said.

"Oh. Oh! Guess you can't sign then." Though he didn't sound too sure. "Trouble here?"

"When was the last time you saw anyone around?" asked Jake

The man didn't take a second. "Never. Never been anyone here to answer the door. Oh, sometimes the gardeners, you know, but nobody else. Nobody to sign in person. Nobody to take packages when they came. Nobody. In three years I been on this route, never seen a soul."

"You just leave the packages?"

The man smiled and tilted his head toward the house. "Place like this seems pretty secure. I leave 'em at the door. They're gone the next day."

Jake handed the clipboard back.

"What do you do with the regular stuff, that doesn't need a signature?" asked Jake

"Push it into the slot there," the man said, pointing. "That one, attached to the wall. It's secured. Soon as I close it, it must drop in some place inside. I can hear it. If I open it again, it's gone. I put mail in, it's gone the next day. Never before had to have anybody sign for something, you know. So far, no dice."

He shrugged. "That's all I know."

Jake and Mallory watched as the man opened the cover to the mail slot built into the wall. He slipped the bundle of mail in and closed it.

"That's all there is to it. So, is this Marston in trouble?"

"Not that we know of," Jake said.

"Okay." The man climbed back into the truck.

Jake followed him and leaned into the open passenger side of the truck.

"How long have you been trying to get a signature on this registered letter?"

The man buckled his seat belt and started the vehicle. He picked up the clipboard. Checked it.

"'Bout a week or so."

He backed up his truck, pulled past Mallory and Jake with a wave, and was gone in a cloud of friendly propane exhaust.

"That registered letter was from Motor Vehicle," Mallory said.

"Impound," Jake added. "The red border on the envelope. It was from the impound lot."

Mallory sighed and surveyed the house again. It was tough to get over the size of the place. "You know, I think this place was used in one of his films. I'm sure of it."

Jake tapped the Dodge's roof. "Your hero's out of town, otherwise he would've taken care of his vehicle or had the chauffeur do it. Or, the assistant chauffeur. Carruthers said he had multiple properties. He could be anywhere."

"Maybe he's never here. Or, maybe he's always here and nobody can see him," mused Mallory. "Like Howard Hughes."

After a moment Jake yanked open the driver's door. "This is ridiculous. Let's bag it."

He got in.

"We're leaving?" asked Mallory.

"What do you want me to do?" asked Jake.

"You're just going to leave? You don't want to know where he is?"

"Don't give a shit. It's no crime to not be home."

Mallory leaned in on the passenger side and gave him the look. "Don't you need to…know?"

Jake smiled. Jesus, she knew what buttons to push. He leaned back in the seat. "You want me to bust in? Or you want to try and get a warrant?"

"A warrant? Good idea!" agreed Mallory missing the cynicism.

"For what reason? 'Cause, the guy didn't sign for his mail? Didn't bail his car out of impound? Is on vacation?"

"Stan's gonna ask."

"Do not play the Stan card here, sweetie. Stan knows this is a bullshit assignment."

"Yeah, but he'd still want to know." She paused. "So do you. I think."

Jake started the Dodge and jammed it into gear.

She was right.

Like footsteps leading to the dark cave entrance. Like a golden glow from a half-opened treasure chest. Like a man missing. Yeah, he'd enter the cave, open the chest, search for the guy. Of course, we'll search for the dumb bastard. Of course. Because we have to know.

He glanced once more in the rearview mirror as he pulled to stop at the pillars and waited for the automatic gates to open, half hoping to see Marston or someone running down the drive, waving, yelling, 'Sorry. I was on the shitter when you rang.'

Nothing.

"Look, bastard's probably screwing his nuts off in Turks and Caicos drinking gin fizzes from some hooker's shoe after he comes up for air."

Mallory didn't speak to him but took her time slamming all the crap she'd pulled out back into the glove box, one item at a time.

Jake stole a glance. "Okay, listen. We'll have Stan try to get us into the house. Must be somebody who takes care of the great film director's property. Satisfied?"

Mallory tried not to smile.

"And you," continued Jake. "You search to your heart's content on your laptop. You're so eager, you find him."

Neither spoke until they turned onto the highway.

When they hit Sacramento limits Mallory turned to Jake.

"You ever wonder what happened to those two kids?"

Jake pretended not to know who she was talking about.

"You know, those two kids."

"Which?"

"Jake! What do you mean which kids? Michael and Jessie Cooper. C'mon."

"What about them?"

Mallory turned away and watched the flow of traffic coming into Rancho Cordova.

"I don't know. It's been a couple weeks. Merely wondered how they're doing, that's all. Wondered if you wondered."

"No," Jake lied. "They're kids. Kids are tough."

After another few blocks, Mallory sighed. "Anyway, pretty sure it's rum."

"What's rum?"

"Pretty sure they drink rum out of the hooker's shoes down in Turks."

CHAPTER SEVEN

Jake slid into his chair and put his feet on the conference table. He pried the lid off of his morning latte and blew along the top.

Stan studied him. "Yeah? So, how's Marston?"

"Still AWOL," Jake said, tendering a sip.

"Tell me."

Before he could begin Mallory swept in.

"Okay, I brought both doughnuts and caramel rolls," she offered. "Which do you want?"

She pried the lid off her coffee as the two men exchanged glances.

"Neither!" they both said in unison.

Stan meant to soothe the surprised and hurt look on Mallory's face. He patted his stomach.

"You're making me too fat as it is."

Mallory shrugged off the slight. "Jake?"

"Nada, darlin'. I don't want to grow up and look like Stan."

"Okay. Tough. *Darlin'* will eat 'em herself. I'm ravenous when I wake up. I could eat anything."

She avoided looking Jake's way as she pulled apart the outer ring of the caramel roll and snaked it into her mouth.

"Right then," continued Stan. "Marston."

Mallory let Jake recount their strikeout and Mazurski and the Mexicans and the mailman.

When Jake was finished, Stan smiled. "So, you're saying he's not home. In absentia. Vamoosed. Poof."

He made a poofing gesture with his fingers before he poured out some coffee for himself then added a healthy dram of Speyburns.

"I had three irritating calls from dear Captain Carruthers wondering what's taking so long. I don't want to talk to the bastard anymore, so Marston's all yours kiddo," he said to Mallory. "You find him."

"What? Me? Jake and I did our duty. He's not home, you know. I'd have loved to find him and talk film with him. He's a great producer-director. He just isn't home right now."

"You'll never find him," Stan continued. "This was a fairy goose chase from the beginning."

"What do you mean? And what's a fairy goose chase?"

"Look," Stan said, moving on. "How quickly can you get Elton John on the phone?" He appeared deadly serious.

"Elton John?"

"Or, Justin Bieber? Or Elvis for that matter?"

"What are you talking about?" asked Mallory confused.

"Point is," offered Stan, taking a small sip. "Any of these people, excepting Elvis, want to be found, want to be seen, fine, they're all over the goddamn news. But, if they don't want to be found, there are seventeen layers of people and bullshit you'd have to go through and in the end, you wouldn't succeed. They want to be found, they will be. They don't, they won't."

"Same with your film guy. Doesn't want to be found. Won't be."

Jake raised one finger and continued with Stan's train of thought.

"I predict," he stated. "Mr. Academy Award is holing up in the basement making porn or tearing off mattress warning labels and we'd never know it. Or, he could be in a villa in a cute little town in France. Or, he could be escorting Lindsay Lohan to the premiere of his latest smash and gash movie. Or, he could be in Turks and Caicos. Who knows?"

"Turks and what?" asked Stan.

"Never mind," grumbled Jake.

No one said anything after that. Without acknowledging it, after Olive Park, they all welcomed the benign fun of searching for a reclusive film director.

"Okay, look," started Jake. "I think we should get into the house."

"What?! You flip-flopper," muttered Mallory. "Not what you said yesterday."

"On what grounds?" countered Stan.

Jake shrugged. "Hell, I need to know. Guy's missing for a week, maybe more. Nobody cares. Nobody misses him, except one anonymous person who calls in. Why? Maybe he's injured and can't come to the door. Can't answer the phone. Can't get his car out of impound. Music goes off and on. Maybe that's a signal. Besides, I'm intrigued."

Stan thought about it. "You're right, partner. I'm in."

"Now *you're* in?" Malloy exclaimed, wide-eyed.

Stan smiled. "For sure he's rat bait moldering in his gold-tiled master bath but, as the great detectives we are, we should check it out."

Mallory checked back and forth between the two men. "You two should take this act on the road."

Jake pushed back from the table and was about to comment when he stared at Mallory.

He spoke before he could stop himself.

"Glasses? When did you…" He paused, finally realized he had to finish the sentence. "…start wearing…glasses?"

Mallory reddened. "Got them yesterday. Helps me read," she said to cover her embarrassment. Without thinking, she reached up, re-adjusted the glasses, and touched the top of her scar that ran down the side of her face, then opened her notes. "You know your staggering powers of observation never cease, do they?

Jake looked to Stan for help but got nothing.

The scabbed-over wound was a nasty one; red and raised and running from her right temple to her jawline. It had been a couple weeks since Everheart attacked her and still it dominated her face. The slash had missed her eye socket but, Jake surmised, it must've affected her vision. Hence the glasses.

"You didn't have them a few minutes ago...I think…did you?" asked Jake, digging a deeper hole. "Well, you look good. Scholarly-like," he added lamely.

He turned away and pretended to pick up something off the floor.

Mallory blushed again and compounded the awkwardness by not responding to it.

Stan coughed. "Mallory, write up what you have and get it off to Samuels. Let him know the Marston guy doesn't want to be found and after we check a few more things tomorrow, we'll keep it active, la la la, bullshit, bullshit. Make something up. Then contact any gendarme in the jurisdictions near all of Marston's fine homes around the world and have them knock on the doors and see if he's home.

"Meantime, I'll make an effort to get us into the house, maybe find some Marston flunky, as yet unknown to me, who has a key. Jake'll check on Marston's car at impound. After picking up whatshisname."

Jake smiled and saluted.

"That's right," Mallory said, brightening. "Cool. We get our fourth partner tomorrow."

"We all good?" Stan asked.

Jake raised his paper cup. Mallory nodded.

"If we strike out, and we probably will," continued Stan. "You tell Samuels we've got our best girl on it, that's you."

"Gee. Thanks. How come I'm always 'the girl'?"

"You were born lucky," smiled Jake

"All right," huffed Stan. "Let's get busy." He got up.

"Oh, wait." Mallory turned to the front of her notebook. "They're starting to install the video surveillance stuff for the building today."

"Terrific," Stan said with tired indignation. "Brand new security system. Probably cost more than all three of us make in a year, yet, they can't find the scratch to give us a new vehicle."

Mallory looked at her list. "They'll be mounting cameras, they said. Putting in the new security door."

Jake laughed. "We wouldn't want anyone breaking in and walking out with our secret files on the JFK assassination."

"Whatever. Somebody's got to be here all day."

She looked expectantly at Jake then Stan.

"For the workmen."

Neither responded.

"Swell. Great. You'll know where to find 'the girl'."

CHAPTER EIGHT

There were six in the crew, all wearing identical powder blue shirts and black pants. Most had cute little tool kits. The oldest one, the supervisor, commandeered part of the conference table in the middle of the glass office He spread out the plans for the security system, camera locations, wiring channels, control box.

Because she was the only one there, he attempted to explain to Mallory what they would do, how it was to be configured, and where the controls and the monitors were to be located.

She lost interest when he said, 'You probably won't understand any of this...'

"You're probably right. I'm simply a woman."

He started to agree but stopped when his mockery detector went off.

"Have at it," she said as she slid back to her desk. "Let me know if you need help."

"Yeah. Sure, little lady."

Mallory glanced back at the man.

I could drop you where you stand, you prick.

She smiled though, remembering her year-long goal; to reduce by half the snide and sarcastic comments she made to others. A laudable goal, though she wasn't planning on beating herself up about it if she didn't come close.

Or if she didn't even try.

She picked up the office phone and realized there was no dial tone. She flashed the button a few times.

"Internet's okay but landlines gonna be down for most of the day," said the supervisor with a wide smile. "Sorry."

Right where you stand, buster.

She swiveled in her chair and using her cell, called Los Angeles.

While she was on hold, Mallory continued her search for Marston's properties on her laptop. She had also dragged Jake's computer over next to hers so they were side by side and on which was running one of her favorite old Marston films. She turned the sound down so she could barely hear the tacky organ music mixed with a moaning wind.

Blood and Honey was classic Marston. It was a perverted homage to Hitchcock and some of the Blaxploitation films of the 70s. About a gnarled old beekeeper who lived in the rugged hills above L.A. and made a special honey from bees who pollinated flowers that grew in the graveyard.

Sick. Twisted. Classic.

On her second screen, she pulled up the satellite map program and zoomed in on a house in L.A. in Hancock Park. Kind of a snooty area she assumed. Obscenely large houses on gargantuan lots. Movie star size. All protected behind walls and hedges and security gates and CCTV cameras. She zoomed in closer so she could make out what kind of cars were in the driveway. A Lexus and some military-looking thing, probably a Hummer. Even from the satellite, she could see their tops were shiny with waxed care.

Someone inside this house had answered her phone call and put her on hold. Were they walking the halls from the bedroom to the salon, or maybe running out to the pool looking for Virginia Marston Armwell, James' sister? Or stalling so she'd go away?

Just as the beekeeper was reaching down under the counter to bring out some of his special honey to serve to an unwary group of college students, the phone clicked.

It was the same bored male voice who had answered the phone.

"You say you're with the Sacramento Police Department?"

"Yes, my name is…"

"Mrs. Armwell will call you back to confirm. You understand I'm sure."

Trust. It was in no shorter supply than L.A. where no one was who they purported to be.

"If she must," sighed Mallory.

"What is the main department number?"

Mallory sighed again. "You can't get me through the main number. I'm in a special division. The OID. The On-Going Investigation Division."

"I don't know…"

Mallory rolled on the bullshit. "We don't deal with the general public, only those who need special consideration and tact. I'm sure you understand."

"Oh. I see. Of course."

"Mrs. Marston, I mean, Armwell, will understand and appreciate our handling this in this matter."

"And this is about Mr. James then?"

"Yes, it is. Have Mrs. Armwell call me, unless of course, she feels comfortable talking to me now without going to that trouble."

"Yes. Well. I'm sure. What is the number then?"

Mallory cursed to herself then gave him the direct number to OID.

"Thank you. Umm. Actually, I'll just check with her and explain the situation."

Again on hold.

The beekeeper was now in an aerie, a little room at the top of his house. He had installed close circuit cameras and was watching the hapless college students as they turned on themselves and morphing into something akin to vampires, only instead of blood they sort of leaked bloody honey.

Again the phone clicked alive.

"Is he dead then?" The woman's voice was strong and direct.

Mallory fumbled with the phone.

"Hello? Is anybody there?" The woman sounded less sure of herself.

"Is this Mrs. Marst- Armwell then?" asked Mallory righting the phone on her shoulder.

"Yes. Who is this? And what about my brother?"

"Mrs. Armwell, this is Mallory Dimante with the Sacramento OID, we're…"

"What about my brother?"

"Well, we're investigating his disappearance and we were wondering…"

"You mean he's not dead?" asked the exasperated voice on the other end. She sounded disappointed.

"He's been reported as missing, so far."

"My man here said this was important. Why are you calling me?"

When Mallory hesitated, Virginia Marston Armwell raised her voice.

"Get on with it child! What do you want?"

"We're trying to find your brother who's been reported missing and we were wondering whether you could help us."

"Me! Help you find James! I didn't report him missing. Who did?"

Good question thought Mallory. If we only knew.

Before Mallory could continue, Virginia Armwell sputtered on.

"If he's missing, you find him. He lives up there, somewhere in a big gaudy thing close the Governor's place, I think."

She was on the verge of closing out the conversation so Mallory hurried on.

"Mrs. Armwell, Mrs. Armwell, please, when was the last time you saw your brother?"

The laugh that came down the line surprised her. It was sharp and spiteful.

"Not since he was carted off to the hospital after that hoopla with whatshername and the incident in his office. And that was God knows how many years ago." As an exclamation point, she added. "We're not close. Now, is that all? I really must go."

Mallory could hear background noises all of a sudden. Children and splashing. She must be sitting out by the pool. Mallory glanced at the satellite photo and shifted her eyes to the pool. It was kidney-shaped with a diving board at one end. There was a smaller pool or hot tub attached to the pool. Maybe she was sitting in the hot tub with a tray of olives and cheeses pissed at having her day interrupted by a civil servant asking about her brother, about whom she gave not a shit.

"Really, Mrs. Armwell, we're simply trying to find…"

The voice on the end of the line dropped and softened. "Look, officer, detective, whatever. I have no blessed idea where Jimmy is. No one in our family communicates with him, you see. As you know, he travels, so you should probably start there. Now really I have to go."

And she was gone.

Mallory circled the words 'Other Houses' on her notepad just as the crazed college students broke through the beekeeper's door and with a hearty heave-ho tossed the beekeeper out the window and down three stories so he landed full onto his precious hives. Like lemmings, the college students then jumped after him, destroying the rest of the hives in their falls. Long pull back from the gory scene with the end titles floating out of the hives like angry hornets.

She tapped her pencil against her teeth.

Where oh where have you gone, Jimmy Marston?

CHAPTER NINE

Jake didn't really need to think about her question.

"It's time," he said in answer.

"What's time?" The young girl checked her watch.

Jake ignored her. "Look. I already have a plant. Two actually. An orchid, a Cymbidium actually, and a nasty little bushy thing with small thorns."

The girl, named Shawna according to the small blue-bordered name tag pinned to her striped smock, affected a concerned look.

Jake met her stare with an equally determined look. She was cute in an earnest schoolgirl way and he didn't mind staring.

Shawna sighed, realizing that the guy standing before her probably didn't get it. That, plus she didn't understand what he meant by 'it's time'. But, with his leather jacket and his sandy hair pushed back she thought he was kinda cute for an older guy. Reminded her of a sexy, seasoned Bon Jovi.

She affected a stern expression and began to repeat what she always said to eager animal adopters. "Okay," she said. "Look. There's a whole process we go through here at Willowood. You know, we're not just a shelter, but also an animal hospital so we have to be very choosy about who gets our animals. It can take weeks. There's paperwork to fill out. I mean you have to qualify and stuff. I mean like how many hours will the animal be alone during the day, stuff like that. Then you have to choose an animal and spend a few sessions here bonding with the animal…"

The double doors opened behind Shawna and from the back room swept Helen Pinsky, a short, commanding red-haired woman swaddled in an orange smock. She waved a file folder in her hand.

"Detective. Come on back, he's all ready to go. Had his shots yesterday. We're all shipshape."

She turned to the young girl. "Thanks, Shawna. The detective has been here before. He's done the paperwork. He's adopting Admiral."

Shawna's eyes widened. Jake couldn't tell if it was from the mention of his being a detective or whether she didn't believe he deserved Admiral."

"He gets Admiral. Aww," cooed Shawna. "That's great." She gave Jake an approving look.

"Course the good detective gets to name him himself. Come on. He's ready."

Helen Pinsky did an about-face and pushed back through the double doors. "She's new here," she said over her shoulder.

Jake followed her down a short hallway past what looked like an examination room where a very sad Bassett hound was submitting to an examination of his undercarriage. Through another set of doors and past cages filled with longing and hope in the form of beagles and boxers and labs and coonhounds and dachshunds. All attentive with eyes on Jake. All with grand expectations.

Jake acknowledged each dog as he passed their cages. He always believed in being as honest with an animal as you were with a person. If you weren't planning on giving them a home, there was no sense in giving them false hope. It was better to meet their stare and move on. They would understand.

A few, those that had been residents for some time, lowered their heads as Jake left the room.

The back room was set up like a family room. There were two L-shaped sofas, a large threadbare carpet, and a few thrift store side tables with lamps. There were no cages. Instead, four doggie beds had been placed around the room. Three were now filled with dogs leashed to mini-stanchions. All three dogs stood up when Helen entered, but only one dog wagged its tail.

Helen checked her paperwork again and moved to the young Weimaraner.

"Here he is. You're lucky he isn't one of the real excitable ones. Some of the Weimaraners we've had in here can get pretty rambunctious."

Jake looked at the dog who now sat down formally and looked up at him.

"Still, you know he needs exercise every day. They're an active breed." She opened the folder and consulted one of the sheets, then looked at Jake over her glasses.

"It says here detective that you wrote he won't be alone during the days. Is that correct?"

"It is."

Helen took off her glasses. "Does that mean he'll be with you at your work?"

"It does."

"Is that wise? I mean with what you do?"

Jake knelt down in front of the dog and ruffed him behind the ears. "He'll be with me all the time. He'll be fine."

"You're sure?"

Jake stood. "Mrs. Pinsky, I work in a very quiet environment. I hardly ever chase anyone at high speed and my gun hasn't been fired in years. Frankly, I'm afraid he'll be bored. But, at least he'll be with me. We can be bored together."

She looked slightly mollified.

"Okay. I need to make sure. He isn't a police dog, you know. Not like a shepherd or lab mix."

Jake smiled as big as he thought he needed to. "He'll be fine."

Helen checked her watch. "Alright. I've got your bag of goodies out front. You know, dog food samples, a few chew toys, and a doggie blanket. Your paperwork will be stapled to the outside. Check with Shawna."

"Thank you for all that. It's not necessary." Jake pictured all the dog stuff he'd purchased over the last week and sat piled in his living room.

"No thanks necessary. We're overloaded with the stuff from the manufacturers. You should see the storeroom. Anyway, here's my card. Call if you have any concerns."

She looked from Jake and then back to the dog, probably still wondering whether letting a cop adopt a dog was a good idea.

"Oh and by the way, have you thought up a name? We've called him Admiral, but he seemed to be a bit ambivalent about it."

"I have a name."

"Good." She opened the folder and took out her pen. "What is it?"

"His name's Jake."

At this, the dog stood up and slowly wagged its tail.

Helen looked over her glasses again. "But, isn't that your…"

"His name's Jake." Jake unclipped the tether and clipped his own leash on the dog.

"C'mon Jake, let's go."

Together they headed back to the main lobby, back past the cages with Jake doing his four-footed walk of pride as he left his fellow inmates behind.

When they re-entered the lobby, Shawna gave them both a big smile.

"Bye Admiral," Shawna said, as she held the front door open. She handed Jake the bag which seemed laden with mini plastic bags of dog food samples. At the bottom was a smallish blanket that said 'Love Me' on it.

"You know you can call anytime." Shawna handed him another adoption center business card.

Jake was about to hand it back and let her know that Helen had already given him one when he saw there was a handwritten number on the back.

Jake smiled and followed Jake who already sensed freedom.

"See you sometime," Shawna called. Then with an embarrassed afterthought, added, "Admiral."

CHAPTER 10

Jake opened the passenger door to the Corvette and Jake jumped in. Jake had already installed what was generously called the 'canine vehicle restraint system', a seemingly simple confluence of belts and harnesses. Jake slipped it over Jake's head and lifted his legs and tightened it. The dog looked at him with a slightly embarrassed look.

"I know. Don't be a baby about it, okay?"

Jake sniffed and turned to look out the front windshield. Eager to be gone. Eager to be moving. He took a crack at standing straight up in the bucket seat and shaking off the harness. Found he couldn't really do it and sat looking out the window.

Jake backed out of the parking lot and headed out. He watched Jake to see how well he would adjust to riding in the car. So far, the dog seemed to have settled in. Maybe it was his imagination, but the way the dog was sitting reminded him of one of his old partners, Siminski. Siminski who also used to sit up at attention with his focus always out the windows.

"Actually, you look a lot better than Siminski."

Jake gave him a quick glance and a lick of his chops but returned his attention to the passing cars.

They drove a few miles in silence.

"You like music?" When the dog didn't even turn his attention away from the front windshield, Jake laughed to himself.

"I'm talking to a dog."

He turned onto French Avenue and then turned into the small lot that serviced the impound lot. Why have a sizeable parking lot when most patrons didn't drive here to pick up their towed cars but had a friend or a cab drop them off?

Sacramento impound looked like a fortified convenience store in the foulest part of town. The building was small with bars on the windows and tinted film over all the windows. Only sorely pissed people showed up here wanting their car back after it had been 'unfairly' towed or repossessed. It was good to be ready for any wild show of retribution.

When Jake pulled in there were no torch-carrying hordes, just an empty parking lot.

Jake looked at Jake.

"Okay boy. Welcome to the force. Be professional now."

But, Jake wasn't listening. The car had stopped and he was ready to get out. His head moved back and forth from door to door. Which way?

Jake released the harness and Jake shot past him, past the steering wheel, out onto the gravel parking lot, and right to one of the concrete stanchions in front of the building. There he lifted his leg. It was a long piss and he looked back around balefully at Jake while completing his business, making sure Jake knew he had been holding it a while.

"Point taken."

When Jake was finished, Jake attached his leash and they entered the building. He'd been here before. The 'Vette had been towed when Jake had gone overtime with a certain blind date that had worked out marvelously well, except the towing part.

The room Jake entered was small, at least the public's portion was. Two small glass-covered windows with tiny openings through which the cashiers could communicate were also covered with a louvered grill. The glass, Jake surmised, was bulletproof.

The large lady behind the glass saw Jake and Jake. "You can't bring no dog in here."

"He's a guide dog. He's a police dog."

"Yeah? Which is it? You don't look so blind to me."

"Police dog then."

He held up his badge. She seemed unimpressed.

"Let me see what ya got."

She shoved open a drawer that bumped Jake in the stomach. He placed the Marston information, which he'd written down on the back of his grocery list, in the tray and watched as the drawer slammed shut.

The woman studied the paper. "Skim milk and what the goddamn is q-u-i-n-o-a?"

Jake waved his hand and she turned the paper over.

It took five minutes before she returned to give him the news.

"Looks like your vehicle is scheduled for auction. You're out of luck. Clyde'll be up in a minute."

She looked past him to the guy behind Jake.

"Can I help you?"

The guy moved past Jake and attempted to explain his problem. She cut him short.

"Let me see what ya got."

Just as the drawer opened again, another real door opened at the far end of the room. Jake could hear two deadbolts thrown and the door pushed open. Jake stood up and stood next to Jake.

"Detective?" asked a small little mustachioed man that reminded Jake of one-quarter of a barbershop quartet.

"Name's Clyde Fellows. This way."

He held the door and made sure it was bolted behind him as Jake and Jake went through.

Clyde led them down metal steps that hugged the building then out into the impound lot. Jake looked at the place. Metal corrugated panels, eight feet high, ringed the perimeter. Scores of tire rims had been bolted to the panels as some sort of trophy wall.

"She's still here I think. Ever since Joey quit I'm all by myself. 'Bout a week behind getting these things cleaned up for auction, you know how it is. Only goes to auction when the owner doesn't claim it after 60 days or so."

Jake knew all this. His 'Vette was a recovered drug dealer's ride that sold cheap 'cause most of the bidders thought it still had meth in it, but it was totally clean. Maybe thanks to Clyde.

Clyde worked a plug of tobacco between his cheek and gum and studied the paperwork.

"Think it's still over here. Joey had a bad habit of moving these around. Took us hours to find a guy's Lexus the other day."

They moved slowly down a row of cars. It was then as they approached the BMW that Jake realized that his dog was hanging back; still moving forward but with a wariness that straightened the leash.

Clyde stopped at the back of the car and rested his foot on the back bumper. "Here she is. Been here a while. Kinda dusty."

But Jake was looking at Jake who had gone rigid.

"Jake?" asked Jake, unsure of what was wrong.

"Dog okay detective?" Clyde asked.

Jake, distracted, said, "I'm not sure." He knelt down in front of Jake but the dog would not meet his gaze. Instead, he stared over Jake's shoulder at Marston's BMW.

"Jake?" Jake asked again in a quiet voice.

Jake still would not avert his gaze to him but Jake detected a low growl, more like a guttural whine coming from his dog.

Clyde, looking at the dog, addressed Jake. "I ain't got any keys, so I'm just gonna pop it, okay?"

"Sure. Fine," Jake mused, but he continued studying his dog.

Clyde pulled out his police authorized flexible pry and started toward the vehicle.

Jake had still not moved and the whine increased.

"Stop!" Jake yelled. "Don't touch it."

Clyde froze. "What? What is it?"

Jake stood and surveyed the vehicle. A dark blue BMW from what he could tell. Dark tinted windows. The dust was typical Sacramento. Except for few sporadic spatterings where raindrops had hit, the dust was coated evenly all over the vehicle. It was obvious the car had not been disturbed, except where Clyde had recently put his foot.

"You say you have no keys?"

"Naw. It was locked when it was towed here."

"Master key?" asked Jake.

Clyde looked at him. "Hey, you know how many cars and models there are? Most are programmed these days. 'Sides this is all the master key I need for most of 'em." He held up the pry.

Jake handed Jake's leash to Clyde. "Okay. Wait a minute."

Jake moved forward and inspected the car on all sides, squeezing between the front bumper and the corrugated fence. All of the windows were dust-covered. He could only discern an outline of what looked like brown cardboard boxes on the back seat, nothing on the front seat. When he got back to Clyde he indicated the pry bar.

"You haven't opened this before have you?"

"You kidding? I got enough to do around here than opening cars. We only open 'em if we gotta move 'em or when we're prepping for sale. And like I said, this one came with no keys."

"Hang tight onto the dog."

"He don't look like he's going anywhere," replied Clyde.

Jake sidled along to the back window on the driver's side and lifted the edge of his jacket. With a strong quick swipe, he cleared out six inches of dust from the window. With his penlight, he searched the back seat. Four or five cardboard boxes were on the seat and he twisted around so he could read what was written on the closest box.

'Clothes'.

There were additional articles of clothing, what looked like coats and down jackets partially covering some of the boxes and drooping down to the floor of the backseat.

He moved to the front window and cleared another patch of dust. The penlight traced over the entire front seat and dash but there was nothing he could see.

Jake returned to Clyde and recovered the leash. Jake had still not moved but the whining had stopped. Still, the dog wouldn't look at Jake even when Jake gently called his name. The hairs on the back of Jake's neck stood at attention.

He turned to Clyde. "Okay, here's what you'll do. I need you to open this vehicle but first, tell me how you do it with that."

Clyde hefted the pry. "Simple. Slip it up and over the driver's window and lower it to hit the door release. Hopefully, there's enough juice left in the battery that she'll open. Hopefully."

"What if there isn't?" asked Jake.

Clyde scratched his head. "Shit. It's a nice car. Normally I'd get the big rigid pry and we'd force the door open. Doesn't make me any friends with people who own the vehicle. Kinda chews up the door. Or we break the window. Or, in this case here, since it's a nice motor vehicle, we'd probably wait until we could get a programmed key for it. Have to search back through the plate and the VIN to get the code. Take a while."

Jake made a decision. "Let's try triggering the door lock. Let's hope there's enough battery."

Jake held up his hand. "But when you do it I don't want you to touch it. I mean try not to touch the vehicle unless you have to. Okay?"

Clyde looked at him. He twisted the pry in his hands. "You think something's in there?"

Jake shrugged. "I don't. But, he does."

They both looked at the dog who was still staring intently at the car.

"Gotcha," Clyde said. And he moved to the driver's door. "Probably left some McDonald's half-eaten fast food in there, you know what I mean. Dogs smell 'bout thousand times better than we do, you know. Probably fast food. That shit'll last forever."

Clyde Fellows stood by the driver's window and shook out his arms like a magician showing nothing up his sleeves. He worked the flexible strip over the window, careful not to touch the car.

The metal strip snaked its way down the height of the window, flapping forward and backward as Clyde twisted it. It wavered above the door release just missing it. Clyde readjusted his feet, taking a more determined stance, and twisted it again, this time advancing it inch by inch.

When the release clicked the dog jumped back against Jake's legs and moved behind him.

Clyde looked at Jake. "Okay. She's unlocked. Want me to open her?"

Jake hesitated. He didn't want to disturb anything but they had to move this along. Besides, Clyde was probably right; fast food. A molding half-eaten fish sandwich. Probably. These precautions were likely over-cautiousness. But, the fewer people that touched the car the better.

"Go ahead and lift the handle with this." Jake reached into his jacket and handed Clyde the card Shawna had given him.

"Place it under the bottom of the latch so you don't touch anything."

Clyde took the card, slipped it under the door latch.

And opened the door.

The smell knocked Clyde backwards. The foul, sweet stink of death burned his eyes and throat. A sick, sweaty sheen broke out on his forehead.

The preliminary report, done hurriedly by Jake that afternoon, indicated that the boxes labeled 'clothes' actually covered human remains. All except a head. The head had been lodged, unseen, between the front seat and driver's door, and when Clyde popped open the door, the head of James Marston Junior fell to the gravel with a dull thud.

Lifeless eyes and a bloody maw implored Clyde to do something about the putrefying stench leaching from the backseat.

But Clyde turned away and threw up his eggs and toast and orange juice that his wife had prepared for him that morning. He retched until he could heave no more.

The dead head of James Marston watched him without comment.

Jake launched a pitiful howling and turned in circles, wrapping Jake's legs in a tangled leash. Every revolution he'd stop and look up at Jake clearly wondering what the hell he'd gotten himself into.

Jake knelt down and put both hands on the dog's muzzle. "Hey, it's okay," he whispered. "The first one's always tough."

CHAPTER 11

"Yeah Captain, it's probably Marston. It's his car. It's his head, I think. The rest of him appears to be in the back seat."

Stan rested his ass against a midnight blue Thunderbird convertible as he continued. "You know the press is gonna be all over this, you understand? It's a helluva lot more interesting than whether it's gonna rain tonight. As soon as somebody spills it, it will be the lead for tonight and all of next week. So, I'm telling you, this won't stay quiet." Stan ended the call and shoved the cell back in his pocket. Memories of life in the Major Crimes division came rolling back. OID had only been going a short time and now here they were temporarily back in The Show with this.

Still, the lure was there. Right there on the ground. It had fallen out at their feet. He hated to admit it after all his work to get OID going, but he wanted this. Listening to Jake describe opening the door, seeing the head drop out, seeing him now pacing, he was sure that Jake wanted this too.

Besides, thought Stan, practicing his rationalization, it was a cold case, albeit a hot cold case.

The whole thing was sad and funny. On the ground next to the BMW, Marston's severed head, lit up under the lights forensics had placed around the scene, beckoned them.

Stan laughed out loud.

"What?" Mallory watched him.

"You know," Stan said. "Except for his screwed-up face and the molding flesh, it's easy to imagine that he's been buried in the sand with only his head out to greet passers-by. Like a prank on the beach. Something you did with your kids."

"Jason Grey. Patrol officer." Jake read the note on his clipboard.

"What?" asked Stan, realizing he hadn't been listening to Jake.

"He wrote it up. Officer Grey wrote it up as abandoned and called for a tow."

"Where?"

"Jones Road. That sharp section."

"Did you talk to him?"

"He's off shift tonight, I left…"

"Call him at home. We need to know what he saw when he was there."

Jake smiled his big college-boy smile. "Hey, Stanley. I said I left a message at his home. I left a message on his cell. Short of trolling the streets of the city, that's about as good as you'll get."

Stan finally smiled at Jake. "Shit. Know what we're doing here partner?"

"Hell, yeah. We're either hoping for Robbery-Homicide to come and relieve us or we're hoping they don't show and this is all ours. Kinda feel like we should keep it. We opened the can, probably should drink the Kool-Aid."

Despite the projected nonchalance, Stan knew Jake.

"Yeah," Stan agreed. "This is definitely above Rodriguez's comprehension level. He'd try but he'd find a way to screw it up."

"Undoubtedly."

"You know what Carruthers said to me yesterday?"

"What?"

"He said, 'It's like a bike Stan. You never forget how to handle a missing person. Haha'."

"Witty guy."

Jake appraised the BMW secured by the yellow crime scene tape. Immediately outside the tape's perimeter milled the antsy forensic crew, led by Danni Harness, anxiously waiting for the photographer to finish so she and her crew could move in. It was then he noticed that Danni Harness had dyed her hair.

Jake leaned over to Stan. "Look at that. She dyed her hair. It's jet black."

"We don't call it dyeing anymore," Mallory said, appearing at their side. "Dyeing was what your mother did. Dyeing is probably what men have to do to their greying pubic hairs. Danni has performed a color enhancement."

"My ass," muttered Jake. "She dyed her hair black as roadway tar."

Mallory held a cardboard tray holder with three coffees. The fourth position held a large plastic cup of water. She handed the tray to Stan, took the water around behind Jake, and knelt down before the dog. She took the lid off and held the cup while the dog lapped it all up in short order.

"Thanks," Jake said, sounding embarrassed he'd already neglected his dog after only having him a few hours.

Mallory petted the dog. "He was thirsty."

Stan sipped his coffee and studied the dog.

"Okay, so this is your dog, eh? With all this, we haven't been properly introduced."

Stan knelt down and looked back up at Jake. "What's his name?"

"Jake," Jake said.

"Jake?" exclaimed Stan and Mallory in unison.

"The dog's name is Jake?" laughed Stan. "A joke, right?"

Jake shrugged and smiled. "Name's Jake.

The dog sat up straighter when he heard his name spoken and looked Stan in the eye when Stan turned back to pet him.

"Hey, Jake. How ya doing?"

Jake acknowledged Stan's strokes.

"It's okay, dog. We're all sorry he gave that name, but we won't hold it against you, okay, boy?"

With all the attention suddenly on him, Jake let his tail swish back and forth in the dust and looked from Stan to Mallory then to Jake, evidently expecting something besides, blah, blah, Jake, blah, blah.

Stan rose and stretched. "I'm sure there's a joke somewhere about the owner and his dog having the same name."

"Frankly, it's the height of narcissism," Mallory quipped. "You had to drag this poor animal into your life so he could be your water boy carrying the rest of the ego that doesn't already fit in your inflated skull."

Jake tightened the leash and brought Jake close to him.

"Say what you will, it was Jake who found the body. Hadn't been on the job an hour and he solved the missing person's case. Didn't you Jake? Just like a good ol' Jake."

Jake, happy that people kept saying his name, wagged and repositioned himself in front of Jake.

Stan sighed. "From a simple missing person to this. Thanks a lot, dog."

The forensic team was changing places with the photographer. Gloved and masked, they moved in, three of them, each starting on one side of the vehicle.

"Crap. Couldn't they at least close his eyes?" Mallory asked. "He looks like he's winking at me. And to cut my poor guy's head off. Somebody was royally pissed. That's like hard-on vicious."

When neither detective offered an opinion, Mallory continued on. "So, what do we do now?"

Stan gazed back toward the setting sun, sorry it wasn't dark already. Seemed like this day would never end.

"Maybe, in about two minutes Rodriguez, or somebody else from Robbery-Homicide, will be here to relieve us. If that doesn't happen…" He left the rest unsaid.

After an uncomfortable silence, Mallory turned to Jake. "No one's coming from Robbery-Homicide to relieve us are they?"

"Doesn't seem like it."

"Didn't think so. So I ask again, what do we do now?"

Stan studied Mallory through squinted eyes. She looked so eagerly earnest and she had so much damn energy it was at once tiring and enervating. Instead of answering her, he turned to Jake and smiled.

"Well, partner. Know what this means."

Jake lowered his head in mock resignation and smiled. "Yup."

"EOS," they both said in unison.

Mallory swiveled back and forth between the two men. "What?"

Jake studied Danni and her crew as he explained.

"EOS. Means, Embrace it. Own It. Solve it. Murray, the captain we had in Robbery-Homicide years ago, used to stick this red-bordered sticker on the outside of the case files as he dropped them on our desk. 'EOS'. Meant the case was ours whether we wanted it or not."

"EOS," repeated Mallory. "So, we're committed. We've got this then."

"Got it 'til the end," Stan whispered. "Right 'til the end."

Mallory clapped her hands. "So, let's get started. What's first?"

Jake regarded Mallory-the-fireball. It was charming, her enthusiasm. Like a puppy. He took a moment before answering.

"Well, assuming it doesn't rain, Danni should be able to work the outside of our BMW in a few hours. Knowing her, she'll have it dragged back to the shed and they'll work the inside tomorrow.

"Tonight, maybe tomorrow, we should have positive I.D. from her on Marston."

"It's his car isn't it?" asked Mallory.

"Registered to James Marston," Jake said. "And if it is him, it means he's been festering, unfound, in his BMW in police custody for some weeks. If it's not him..." Jake left the rest unsaid.

"Oh," Mallory said, understanding their search for Marston would now be tangled with solving who this headless 'Harvey' was.

"Yes," added Stan. "We sincerely hope this is our boy. Probably is."

Stan and Jake exchanged glances.

"Probably," affirmed Jake. "And you know what this means?"

"What's that?" asked Stan.

"You'll have no trouble getting a warrant to search Marston's house."

"True enough."

Clyde Fellows, who looked lost and useless, wandered up to Jake.

"Detective, if you don't need me anymore, I'd like to get on home."

"Clyde, only a few more minutes," Jake said. He turned, indicating Stan. "This is Detective Wyld. He's the lead detective on this. This is Clyde Fellows. He runs the yard here."

Clyde cast his eyes down. "Well, I wouldn't say run it exactly."

"Mr. Fellows," acknowledged Stan, taking the man's hand. "I understand you were here and helped open the vehicle."

"Mr…I mean Detective Stoner and the dog, here. We were all here. The three of us. I used the flex jimmy I got. Slid it over the driver's window. Lucky we had enough juice to pop her."

"Tell me, before we got here, or before Detective Steiner arrived, how much did you touch it?" Stan asked.

Clyde scratched his head. "Steiner, yeah. Umm. Hell if I know."

"It's been here a while. I would think you would've inspected the vehicle."

Clyde gave a slight smirk. "Like I told Detective Steiner here, I don't got a very liberal schedule. We don't touch these cars, none of them unless we gotta get them ready for sale. We got 'nough to do, you know."

"So you never went near it?"

Clyde scrunched up his mouth in thought. "Well, when it first came in, I guess I cleaned the dust off the driver's window so I could see. Played with the door handle some. See if it was really locked. Secured and all. I probably leaned up against the door, you know."

"You never entered the vehicle?"

Clyde shook his head and looked to Jake.

"Not 'til the Detective and me opened her up this afternoon."

Danni and one of her techs approached them.

Jake spoke up. "Clyde, this nice lady here's going to get your fingerprints."

Clyde hesitated for a second, nodded, and followed the tech to the forensic van.

Danni remained.

"This your dog?" she asked, looking at Jake. The head of SacPD forensics rarely came out on site anymore unless the situation was something she knew her team had never dealt with before. Severed head falling out of a car evidently was one of those. Barely over five foot, she commanded her troops like a little general and kept them in line like a second-grade teacher with a sharp ruler. She suffered few fools, detectives included.

She didn't wait for Jake to answer.

"Weimaraner, eh?"

"Just got him today," Jake said, patting the dog.

"What's his name?"

Both Mallory and Stan groaned.

"Jake," Jake said.

"Jake!" exclaimed Danni. "You named the dog Jake!?" The guffaw started deep down and rolled up until she had her head back and was hooting to the sky.

The dog joined in.

"Bwaahaahaa," howled Danni." She punched him on the shoulder. "You are too much!"

"What?" she rolled on. "When you go to call him, you check your badge for your own name?" She thought this was very funny.

"'Here Jake, here Jake'," she mimicked.

At this Jake sat up and wagged his tail.

"Oh look! He responded!"

That set off another round of laughter. "Jake! He calls his dog Jake!"

She waved to Jake and wandered away, still laughing. "Steiner, you're one crazy sonofabitch!"

The two Jakes watched Danni walk back to the BMW. Jake wanted to ask her when OID would get her report but he was sure it would set off another round of derision.

Instead, he turned to the dog.

The Jakes stared at each other.

From behind them, came a sudden high whirring sound. Through a crack between two panels of corrugated fencing erupted rapid flashes.

By reflex, both Stan and Jake spun, dropped low and separately, each held out an arm trying to shield Mallory, at the same time pushing her backward. She fell over the dog, scrambled to her knees, and held onto him.

A moment later, a drone, with camera and flash already strobing, rose above the fence.

"Shit," exclaimed Stan.

"I'll deal with this," Jake shouted as he took off running.

Mallory found herself trembling with the sudden adrenaline rush. Or maybe it was the dog. Maybe both of them.

"Stan? What is that?"

Stan was already on his phone.

"Hey, tell him lids off... Yeah, I'm sure. A photographer I think. Probably from the Bee. But, I wouldn't be surprised to see News5 or some other station overhead in about fifteen minutes."

Stan listened to the response. Mallory saw his shoulders slump. He scuffed his right shoe in the dust.

Stan didn't want to hear any more. He took the phone away from his ear and spoke into the mouthpiece. "Okay, let Franklin know I'll call him later with what we want to do." He ended the call and shoved the phone back in his pocket.

"What was all that?" Mallory asked again, indicating the fence where Jake had gone. She was petting Jake who was the only one shaking now.

Stan knelt to pet the dog too. She saw Stan's hand wasn't as steady as hers.

"Reporters, hopefully only one, sent up a drone with a camera. The news. The public's right to know. Probably getting a nice close up of our friend on the ground."

He looked up. "Everyone is going to have this story, if not tonight, then when we issue some statement tomorrow. We're lucky we've kept it quiet this long."

"Stan, it's only been six and half hours."

They both turned and watched as the drone began a series of chaotic gyrations, finally hurtling back toward the fence. It crashed headlong into a tire rim from a '76 Pontiac and fell to the ground, flopping hopelessly in a mechanized death spasm.

Stan smiled. "This is going to be a rather sizeable story."

Mallory sank back with the realization of it all.

Stan continued to give his attention to the dog. "Yeah, News at 11. Headless corpse discovered by a dog after weeks in police custody. That'll play."

Mallory brightened. She gave Stan's arm a slap. "There you go. And just wait 'til we tell 'em who it is."

Stan studied the lone head on the ground. "Yeah. That's what worries me."

CHAPTER 12

Jake pushed open the metal door to the tarred roof of the OID building and propped it open. The lock was broken on the door. In fact, the handle was missing, but neither Jake, Stan, nor Mallory trusted much about the old building's doors, and the thought of being locked onto the roof and the resulting embarrassment made propping the door second nature. Especially when they all gathered up here at night.

Jake followed Jake, bounding over the threshold and making straight for the low half-wall that marked the perimeter of the roof. Unexplored territory! He snuffled all along the wall, making a complete circle before spying Mallory and Stan and making a beeline for them.

Someone had jury-rigged a ramshackle lean-to of sorts, complete with chair and table. Jake suspected a disgruntled night time security guard of the former tenants of the OID building, had used this as a retreat and escape from the mind-numbing monotony of guarding other people's shit.

Jake had 'remodeled' what Johnny Security Guy had started. Chateau OID was now twice its original size and sported three chairs and a larger table. Jake had one day hauled a mess of 2x4s and some plastic sheeting up the five stories by himself, liberating the materials from the construction pile downstairs. He not only bolstered the tacked-together structure but added what amounted to a sun porch, at least if this had been a house, it would have been a sun porch. Jake had even run an extension cord so they had power.

Already, in the last hour, Stan's phone had insistently vibrated three times with unrelenting messages from Samuels on Carruthers' behalf.

"Good you could join us," Stan said. He brightened as he reached for the dog.

"Hey, Jake!" He scratched the dog behind his collar. Jake's back leg started a phantom scratch in response.

"Nice night," Jake said. The roof was dark, some street lights escaping over the edge of the roof wall, the lights of Folsom glowing as a distant white, unkempt fire.

He looked up. Sacramento did not always allow their residents to view the stars at night. Too much crap in the air most times. But when the warm wind was just so, like this night, the growing starlight offered its good graces to all of middle California.

Jake set three beers down on the table and dropped the paper he'd been carrying in front of Stan.

"Been waiting for this. From Danni. It's Marston all right. Dentals match. She rushed this and has another set coming tomorrow as a double check. Guy had more than one dentist. Go figure."

Jake wagged his way from Stan to Mallory, then settled next to Jake's chair. His head on his paws, his eyes followed the conversation.

The cone of light from the shaded gooseneck in front of Stan reflected his pen, a silver thing, flashing as he spun it. He studied the copy of the forensic email then made a notation in the margin.

It was time, past time, for them to get a handle on James Marston, Junior. Now that it was officially OID's case. Carruthers had made that clear with the announcement to the press yesterday.

Stan surveyed the meager notes he'd made and turned to Mallory, "So, neither Missing Persons nor anybody from Robbery-Homicide did anything with this before we got this, did they?"

"They didn't do jack," Mallory replied. "Because, they said, they didn't even know about it. At least the guys I talked to. Somehow, Carruthers got it then threw it to us. So no, nobody over there did anything."

"And there was no name on whoever called in about Marston missing in the first place?"

"Who knows? As I said, they're clueless over there. That, and they don't really give a shit about helping us."

Stan nodded. Missing person reports, he knew, especially of an adult, were given scant attention. People are free to come and go as they please. Just because one person can't locate another doesn't mean the person is missing. Husband doesn't want to be found. Wife on the lam. Businessman has had enough and bugs out to Vegas for a week.

Free to come and go.

And a report wouldn't have been taken seriously unless the caller gave their name and a boatload of other personal information.

It was only with the connection of Carruthers with Marston it gained any credence.

Jake opened the beers and passed them around.

"Been twenty-four hours so let's talk out what we've got. I need to get my brain sorted out on this," Stan said."

"I'll start with what we know," Jake said. He took a deep breath and tapped on the table.

"Really early on a morning in May, the 13th I think, according to our dear Captain, dispatch gets an anonymous call about a broken down car and a woman standing by it over on Jones Road.

"Uniform doesn't get there until a few hours later. Officer Jason Grey. He told me he saw nothing unusual. No one around. Car locked up tight. Assumed it's abandoned. Has it towed it to the lot on French Street. Impound calls and mails the owner, listed by way of the tabs to be a James Marston, Jr. Nothing happens. Marston never responds. Everybody drops the ball.

"Now, it's our turn. We check the house. No one home.

"We grill the gardeners. Have they ever seen anyone around? Nothing. We see the mailman has been trying to deliver this registered letter to Marston. It's about the car, which as we know is about to be sold.

"In our brilliance, we, that is my faithful Jake and me, have the impound guy pop it, and Jake here discovers Mr. Marston Junior, though slightly disjointed."

Jake sat up, expecting mention of his name to bear fruit, as in a treat from Jake's pocket. It didn't.

"So, that's up to today."

"Background," Stan said turning to Mallory.

She flipped over the top page of her notes. Cleared her throat.

"Okay. First, Marston's family doesn't appear to give a good goddamn where he is, as in 'don't call me again'. And they sure don't care that he's deceased. Positive it wasn't the family who reported him MIA in the first place."

"Yeah," Jake drawled, trying for a nonchalant recovery. "Who was that who called in?"

"Good question," Mallory said, continuing on. "Marston has, besides the Sacramento house, a townhouse in London and a house in Miami. Had a small production studio and office here in Sacramento for a few years handling all the residuals from his movies, but it appears that closed down a year ago."

"No Turks and Caicos?"

Mallory ignored him. "Marston has not been to the London house in over a year, according to the housekeeper. In Miami, I was shoved off onto this whiny guy who mans the gate in the guardhouse at the entrance to the fancy-schmancy enclave that's called the Coastal D'Argent. He was useless. So no idea on Miami."

Mallory took off her glasses. She folded them, slipped them in a case, and put the case under some papers, out of sight.

"That's all I have really."

"Nothing else?" Stan asked, making notes without looking up.

"Yes. While waiting on hold for-ever, I was able to watch *Blood and Honey*, a true Marston classic. And, for good measure, I downloaded two of Marston's best old movies, *Assault of the Sewer People* and *Insect Spasms* onto Jake's laptop."

"Swell. And what did you learn from watching movies all day?" Jake asked.

"Do not try and make friends with a queen bee that looks like a squash. She'll only break your heart, then eat it and crap on the rest of your internal organs."

"Jesus Mallory" Stan sighed, annoyed.

"What? You think I screw around all day?"

Jake leaned down and patted Jake. "She said it, didn't she boy."

Jake wagged in agreement.

"Zip it, Steiner. I also worked up a timeline."

She handed a color-coded legal sheet to both Stan and Jake. "It's accurate as of ten minutes ago. And, I worked up a cursory personal and professional history of my Mr. Marston."

She handed these to Stan and Jake.

"And, I started the casebook."

Mallory set a black notebook onto the table. She opened it. Stan and Jake could see the cover sheet with all the contact names and numbers of persons mired in the case. There appeared only about five other pages, so far. She sat back and regarded Jake.

"And so, what did you two do? Anything?"

Jake leaned over to Jake. "That's called sarcasm. It flows like acid from her pouty lips."

Jake lifted his head, but put it back on his paws when he realized 'sarcasm' didn't mean 'treat'.

Stan ignored her. To Jake. "What about prints and hair or fibers?"

"All I got from Danni was a 'don't bother me'. After we left last night they dragged the car over to Forensics. This morning they vacuumed the hell out of it. Course, it rained the night it was abandoned and it's rained a few times since, so they'll be concentrating on finding prints on the interior. That, and working to verify that the head is Marston's, which they just did."

Stan held up his hands. "Wait a minute. Back up. So, our friend is whacked, chopped in two, stowed away in his car, then while his parts and pieces are being driven to God knows where, by person unknown, and then whoever's driving breaks down in the rain. The only person to see it evidently is some anonymous Joe who calls it in."

Stan pointed to Mallory who nodded. "Again? I already checked. They know nothing."

Stan continued his stare.

"Okay, okay tomorrow. I'll bug 'em until I get it."

"Thank you.," Stan said, continuing on. "And when our uniform gets there he doesn't see a damn thing, calls it in for a drag to impound and there it sits. This whole mess happened weeks ago. So this Marston goes missing and no one else reports he's gone and no one misses him?"

"Some guys have no friends," Jake said as he sat down. He reached down to pet Jake.

Stan looked to Mallory for confirmation.

She sighed and held up the timeline.

"Correct. Weeks gone and not a crooked soul missed him. From what I've found, and it wasn't much, my Marston was kind of a recluse. Rich as a bugger, but never socialized. Not even with any of the old Hollywood crowd. Least not as I've found out."

Stan looked at Jake. "What do you have to say?"

Jake shrugged and looked at his dog. "Aw shucks, Stan," Jake drawled. "Jake and I are done, aren't we boy." Jake lifted his head. "This was, a missing person. My faithful hound and I found the guy. Our job is done."

"Hah!" snipped Mallory. "Your dog found the guy. You were on the stupid end of the leash. Your dog brought you along out of sympathy."

Jake smiled. "We're a team."

"Yeah. Like Timmy and Lassie."

Mallory switched her attention to Stan. "Hey! Marston was a great, and I do mean great, producer-director, always in the spotlight. He got tired of it, probably. Dropped out. No one is gonna miss the man who wasn't there."

Both men directed their attention to her.

"What did you say?" asked Stan, though he had heard well enough.

Mallory sat up straighter and turned her beer round and round. "Look. I said how are you gonna miss a guy who nobody ever sees."

Stan continued to marvel at their young addition. "Good point. When was the last anybody saw him?"

"A regular Howard Hughes," Jake added. "Like Hughes, though, he's gotta have his Melvin."

"Yeah," agreed Mallory. "Good point. We need to find our Melvin."

"I feel stupid asking, but who's Melvin?" asked Stan.

Mallory rattled off the information while studying the last page of the casebook.

"*Melvin and Howard*, early '80s film. 'Bout a guy, some hoo-hah Vegas yokel, who hangs out with Howard Hughes and who supposedly has a will where Hughes left him a chunk of his dough."

"Well," Stan sighed. "We have no Melvin. What we do have is a lot of speculation that's gonna hit the fan tomorrow, if it's not already on the net. So, I called Franklin in PR this afternoon. He agrees. We're going live with it in the morning."

"Already?" asked Jake.

"Impound is a leaky faucet," countered Stan. "Somebody's got the story and probably with pictures if our voyeur was able to get a decent shot."

"So, now what?"

"We shake some trees, see what fruit falls." Stan spread his hands. "Somebody had to have seen something. A hundred cars must've passed that way before Jason whatshisname arrived. We know because it was called in."

"Still, that was weeks ago," Jake said.

Stan got up and gathered his notes.

"In the middle of the night," Jake added.

"Seriously, I guarantee somebody knows something. This James Marston Junior didn't live in a vacuum. Let's find someone who hated him and who had the opportunity to chop his Hollywood producer-director head off and leave it where everyone could find it."

"Stan," Jake offered. "Media isn't gonna be really excited unless you give them something else besides an abandoned car."

Stan smiled. "You want to give 'em the head?"

"You don't mean the actual head head, do you?" Mallory asked, sitting up.

"Not yet. We'll hold the headless part back for now," Stan said. "Unless of course our photographer from last night already has it. Don't we have a picture of Marston? With his head?"

Mallory hunted through the second file. "Maybe."

Jake held up a hand. "So what? We announce to the press that we have a dead film director and we've had him actually for weeks but because of police cockups, we really just found him?"

Stan shrugged. "I don't care. We're OID. On-Going Investigation. This has been on-going and now we need the public's help. We couldn't reveal details before because, well, we simply couldn't. Hell, we're heroes. We have credibility, so let's use it. We don't have to give reasons for what we do. Besides, he was Hollywood. Everyone loves to hate Hollywood."

"You want to do this before we get the prints from the car and autopsy stuff back from Danni?" Jake asked, still not sure going public was right.

Stan thought. "Yeah. We need to move this along. It's already old and cold. We have a positive I.D. Now we need witnesses. I want this out while we have control of what gets out. If this is going to leak out by tomorrow anyway, we'll get the jump, and do it our way."

Mallory stood. "I see what you're doing, what's Boy Wonder here doing?" She shot Jake a look. "Sorry. I mean Dog Wonder and his faithful companion."

Jake looked down at Jake. "That was sarcasm, boy"

Jake dog ignored him. Sarcasm did not mean treat.

Jake turned serious. "Stan. Sure you want to be doing the press thing so soon after what happened at the last one? I could do it."

Stan waved him off. "I'm good. I need you to get some of Rodriguez's crew and anybody else downtown'll give us. Get 'em banging doors on Jones. See who saw what."

"Won't be much."

"Probably nothing. Not much out there near that part of Jones, people or houses. After the press conference, I'll be doing important stuff," smiled Stan.

"What's that?" asked Mallory.

"Following the money," said Stan. "If it wasn't revenge, if I'm all wrong, we'll soon know it. Your movie guy had dough, judging by his spread," Stan continued. "Somebody's gonna make out. We need to see who."

"Right."

"And you need to find out everything about your Hollywood hero. Where's he been these last few weeks? What'd he do normally? Who'd he hang out with? Phone records. Who'd he talk to? His life for the last month."

"Yeah, yeah, okay. What about the head?" Mallory asked, with lurid interest. "We gonna show it?"

"Only attached to Marston. We'll make this as simple as we can. Find a picture of him and the car and a diagram of Jones Rd where it was found. Tomorrow, I'll make it sound like we've been working on this for weeks. OID kept Marston's death quiet until now because his death was still under investigation. Now we need the public's help and so on. That should do it."

"I don't know," Mallory said. "I still really like the idea of giving the press guys a close up of his head." She sighed. "They'd cream their jeans for sure."

CHAPTER 13

"Good morning everyone." Rick Franklin, the beefy ex-cop, now PR mouth for SacPD, looked out with some annoyance at the gathered group of reporters and media bloggers still milling around, loathe to find a seat.

The crowd was larger than normal, mainly to see who was going to be pepper sprayed this time.

And there was grumbling about the extra security they all had to endure to gain entrance. Carruthers had sent down orders from on high - there would be no distraught family members present, no one was to approach the dais and all liquids and aerosols, especially pepper spray, were confiscated. There would not be a repeat incident that would embarrass the department and highlight the glaring deficiencies in the building's security.

One by one, as they straggled in, they placed their microphones or digital audio recorders on the lectern, the top of which had been modernized last year to accommodate everyone's audio gear.

The TV crews already had five permanent audio lines running to the back of the room where they were set up. But, even the cameramen from the three broadcast stations weren't paying attention. They were trying to sort out their Starbucks order.

Stan, seated on the platform behind Rick fiddled impatiently with his cards and scanned the assembled group. He didn't expect to see another Louise Cradwell, but then again, he still felt some tenderness on his face and was taking no chances.

One thing that hadn't changed over the years was Rick Franklin's inability to launch these things on time.

"Rick," whispered Stan, urging to get started. "Let's move it."

Rick gave him a quick glance and scowl but rapped his black granite rock, which actually resembled a gavel, on the lectern. The resulting bass notes had an effect. The mumbling quieted and asses slid into seats.

"Okay. Couple things. Regular department briefing will be as usual at four o'clock today, assuming there is anything to talk about. Second. I need you guys to clean up when you leave here. Don't leave your trash all over the place. I'm getting holy hell 'cause some of you are just plain slobs. Some aren't, but some are. And if you don't think you are, go ahead, ask the person next to you. They sure as hell know."

It was standing room only with every seat filled, amazing for a group that eschewed any serious activities before 9 A.M. There were familiar faces but also a large intrusion of new ones, decidedly younger and with a perpetual skepticism etched into their features, which was good considering all the bullshit they had to listen to every day.

Stan purposely avoided looking at Phil Ginger. He could feel Ginger's eyes boring into him, trying to get his attention and wondering why the hell Stan was back up in front of them. Probably asking himself what cold case could be so important that they had to drag everyone's butt down here now.

"...second, the department is asking for the public's help with an on-going case. The details are in the handout up front here."

No one moved. Miffed, Franklin moved on.

"You all know Detective Wyld from OID. He'll fill you in. Stan."

Stan stood and passed Rick. The TV guys slid their earphones in place and readjusted their cameras. Red lights came on. Those in seats, while not attentive, at least stopped talking.

Even if they weren't regulars, they all knew this was the guy who had headed up the Olive Park investigation and solved it. And was pepper sprayed the last time he stood up before them.

Stan put on his reading glasses. He knew he looked younger without them and Bea would probably give him hell or pester him with aging jokes for the next few days, but he needed to see what he'd be reading.

"Some of you know me-"

The group as one broke out in laughter.

Stan held up his hand. "For those who don't, along with Detective Steiner and our assistant Mallory Dimante, I'm part of OID, the On-Going Investigation Division…"

"That's cold cases isn't it?" interrupted someone in the back.

Stan smiled and addressed his answer to everyone.

"OID handles any case that is 'on-going'. Sometimes that means working cold cases, sometimes it just means a more current case that has not yet been solved. Which is the situation here today."

"But, doesn't…" The guy in the back tried again but Stan ignored him.

"Questions after.'

He studied the guy in the back to see if it was the asshole who asked about transsexuals the last time Stan stood up here, ready to toss his ass. Satisfied it wasn't him, Stan continued.

"May 15th, a car was abandoned on Jones road, approximately 2 miles south of Elverta. It is believed the driver was having car trouble and was asking people to stop and assist. This was approximately 2:30 on the morning of the 16th.

"We're asking for anyone who saw the car or witnessed the driver or spoke to the driver to please contact the OID. In addition, we know someone called in to 911 about the vehicle without leaving their name. We'd like that person to come forward as well, and give us what additional information they might have."

Stan looked up. No one was exhibiting much excitement. From the back, he saw Mallory slip into the room. She seemed overly animated and actually waved at him, then put her hand back down when one of the TV guys looked over at her.

Stan frowned.

Franklin flicked off the lights and lit up the overhead projector.

Visuals! The TV crews snapped to attention and focused on the screen. The younger reporters sat up. The veterans had yet to be convinced this was anything at all. Ginger, Stan saw, didn't even have a notebook out. Merely sat with his legs crossed.

"This is a map of Jones and the "X" indicates where the car was." Stan looked up.

Nothing.

Franklin moved to the next slide.

"This is a representative picture of the car. A BMW. Specifically, a 2012, burgundy, 750 series BMW sedan. Similar to the one pictured."

"Similar?" asked Ginger from the front row. "Why similar? Where's the real one? Is it missing? Are we all just here for a stolen car?"

Ginger's last questions were voiced loud enough for everyone to hear. There were titters from some of the younger scribes but the older ones were quiet. Something was up.

"So where is it?" persisted Ginger.

Stan didn't answer Ginger directly but moved on. "Being a traffic hazard where it was on Jones and because the owner could not be located, the car was eventually towed to police impound, per procedure."

And there he paused.

Mutterings of 'what the hell' and 'so what' rose between the rows.

Front the front row, Ginger continued on, "And, the owner was found…?" His voice rose in inflection, trying to coax from Stan the rest of the story.

Stan saw Mallory wave again but this time with both hands as if she was standing in the middle of I-5 trying to stop a barreling semi. Stan ignored her. Instead, he nodded and Franklin moved to the last slide. It was a picture of James Marston.

"The owner of the vehicle, James Marston, Junior, was found yesterday. In the vehicle.

"He had been dead about a month."

The surge of shouts and questions flooded the room, everyone seeking Stan's attention. Those reporters who had no idea who James Marston, Junior was, tried to mine their neighbor for details without notable success. When they couldn't get answers they fired up their phones.

Stan saw Ginger smile and shake his head. Affirmation that Stan still knew how to hold a press briefing.

Without the pepper spray.

"The handouts at the front here have all the information including a brief bio of the deceased…"

To Franklin's chagrin, everyone now scrambled forward to grab one or two or three press releases.

Stan looked around, pleased with himself. It was one thing to hold a press conference. It was another to get people jazzed about what he had to say and communicate the help they needed. And reporters were the toughest gatekeepers. You had to move them, to motivate them to inform their readers, listeners, their audience. Least kick 'em in the ass.

'If it ain't screaming, it ain't worth it.' It was Ginger's favorite phrase.

Well, they seemed to be screaming now.

In the back of the room, Stan glanced up in time to see Mallory yank open the conference room door and leave.

"Stan! Stan!" The hands were insistent now.

"I'll take questions now. Yes, Phil?"

"I have a couple questions," drawled Phil Ginger. "First, what condition was the body in?"

Stan started to answer but Phil wasn't finished asking.

"Second, why did it take so long for the police to discover they had a dead body in their possession…"

The cries of "Stan! Stan!" swelled again.

"Third…" Ginger held up his hand so he could be heard.

"Third, is it true that your OID team tried to confiscate pictures taken by our photographer the other night?"

The last question quieted the crowd. This time, like jackals sensing weakness, they eyed Stan.

"Is that it?" asked Stan of Ginger.

"For the moment."

Stan nodded. "Okay. Two nights ago, at a crucial phase of the investigation, a member of the press illegally accessed a secure police facility…"

"Stan, Stan he was at the fence at county impound," quipped Ginger.

"…and took some photographs with a drone that might have detailed an important part of the investigation we're not revealing yet. As a consequence, the camera was confiscated-"

"Wrecked you mean."

"-and with the cooperation of the photographer in question, the images were digitally erased."

Stan looked at Ginger pointedly. Ginger smiled. Stan knew, and Ginger knew, that before they could be erased, the photographer had emailed them to the photographer's own email account.

"As to why the body was only recently discovered. When it was found on Jones, it was written up as an abandoned vehicle by the officer who called for a tow. It was a hazard where it was and the officer needed it moved. It was locked and he believed it disabled and that the owner had gone for help and would find his or her way to police impound when they discovered it had been removed from the roadway.

"Impound attempted on numerous occasions to contact Mr. Marston, but obviously that wasn't possible."

Stan stopped and called on one of the TV women from a middle row when Ginger spoke up again.

"Third question was what condition the body was in? What did he die of?"

Stan could see Ginger was waiting to see Stan wriggle out of this.

"What condition was he in?" repeated Stan.

Ginger nodded.

"Dead. The man was dead and had been for two months. The condition of the body was indicative of someone who had been dead two months."

Without waiting, Stan called on Virginia something from the local ABC affiliate.

She never got her question out because Ginger interrupted again.

"Cause of death?" he asked.

"We're not releasing the specific cause yet. Yes, Virginia."

"You sure the body is that of Marston?" she asked.

Stan nodded. "Forensics matched the dental records."

After that Ginger remained quiet and another twenty minutes of questions were repeats that Stan patiently answered.

Finally, Franklin, leaning up against the wall spoke up.

"Stan why not review what help your team needs again."

It was a signal they were done. Stan ran through the three slides again, but most of the group had gathered their recorders and things and, under the pointed surveillance of Rick Franklin, most cleared their trash as well.

Stan found Mallory in the hallway, waiting for him and she didn't look very happy.

"What were you doing in there?" he asked. "Waving your arms like that?"

"Trying to protect my partner from making an ass of himself."

"What do you mean? It went well," he answered, trying not to sound defensive.

"Yeah, right up until the time you named Marston as the dead body."

"What? What! Are you telling me Danni's wrong? Is it Marston or not?" fumed Stan.

Mallory motioned toward the stairs that led to the basement where Forensics held court.

"Stan!"

Neither of them heard Phil Ginger come up behind them. Stan didn't know how much he had heard, but it didn't matter.

"Stan! Beer? Blue Moon? Six-ish?"

Stan hesitated, but only for a second. "Make it seven."

Ginger waved and headed back down the hallway.

Mallory regarded the retreating figure of Phil Ginger. She turned to Stan.

"Who was that?"

"Never mind! Listen, is it Marston or not?" he hissed. "I thought the dentals matched!" He was already dreading having to retract the identification. A credibility-crippling admission. Tough to spin it any other way.

Mallory parroted the question. "Is it Marston?"

She hooked one arm through his.

"Come on big fella. I've got something to show you."

CHAPTER 14

As Stan and Mallory exited the elevator in the basement, they could see Danni Harness, the head of SacFor, Sacramento Forensics, at the end of the hallway. Next to her, stood Jake and Jake. Jake was tied to the leg of a stainless steel embalming table that had been shoved into the hallway. The dog kept turning and pulling, testing the leash, unhappy with the mournful mix of formaldehyde and death stink that permeated the basement.

Stan, wasting no time, squeezed past the coffee pot kiosk with the five-hour old coffee baking in its carafe, pushed past the copy machine and two locked metal cabinets plus four swiveling office chairs that had been unceremoniously shoved against the hallway wall.

He confronted Danni. "Well?"

Danni regarded him over her reading glasses. A big smile broke out across her face.

Stan hated it when she smiled. It led to nothing good.

"Don't screw with me, Danni."

Danni rolled her eyes, turned, and started back through the main Forensic office.

"You guys and your cases. The shit you bring me. You never really know what you've got do you?" She laughed.

"What's so funny?" asked Stan, moving quickly to keep pace. "Danni! Just tell me it's Marston in the car and I can die happy."

"Some detectives you are," cackled Danni.

"What do you mean?" Stan persisted. "And what about this case?"

Danni kept walking but held up her hand. "Not to worry. I've already called National Geographic and Guinness World Record people. They should be here any minute. You'll be going down in history with what you've found."

She turned and faced them. "And you don't even know why."

"Why?" asked Stan and Jake together.

Danni laughed again. "Because of what was dumped in your lap, you idiots. C'mon."

She pushed open the double doors to the autopsy room.

The exhaust fan was running full blast but still, the bouquet of months-old death pervaded the large room with a sallow stillness. The two shiny metal autopsy tables held the remains found in the BMW.

One table with the torso.

The other with the lonely head of James Marston, Junior. 'Where's the rest of me?' the head with the vacant stare really seemed to be asking.

Stan took one look at the headless torso which, though it was highly decomposed having baked in a nice warm car for two months, was obviously untouched by Danni's Forensic team.

"You haven't even started the autopsy yet. What gives? Why are we here?"

Danni held up both hands. "Whoa, Stanley. First, we've been busy as shit, okay. We had your car to deal with yesterday. And I have two techs still working on the inside right now. Plus, you're not the only customer we service, you know. You can't just snap your fingers and we give you the answers you need. Solve your cases for you. You guys are cold case, right? There's no urgency with your stuff. But, now you bring me this!"

Danni smiled now and positioned herself between the two autopsy tables. She was beaming. "This is beautiful. Before I fired up my buzz saw and tore into these, I wanted you to behold…the missing link."

She extended both hands out, pointing to the head on one table and the headless torso on the other.

Stan and Jake looked at each other.

"What link?" asked Stan

But Mallory piped up. "What's missing?"

Danni faced Mallory, pointing her finger straight at her.

"Ahhhaahh. That's good, Melanie. What's missing, she asks."

Danni turned to Stan then. "You know she should be running your OID. I like the way she thinks."

Mallory reddened.

Danni rattled on. "Good question, Melanie, nice try, but nothing's missing. However, you're on the right track. In fact, it's the opposite. No, I mean this could've been the missing link that anthropologists have been searching for for years, except..."

Neither Stan nor Jake understood nor did they want to ask. They knew they'd find out.

Danni waved her hands in the air. "Okay, okay. Question. How many vertebrae are in the human spine?"

"Anyone?" Danni looked at them expectantly. "Thought not. Thirty-three. All mammals, except a few weird ones, have thirty-three. Human spine. Thirty-three."

"Danni, come on," started Stan.

Danni waved his interruption away. "Okay. Your Mr. Marston here has thirty-five vertebrae. Two extra."

She stood back and looked from Jake to Stan to Mallory.

"Pretty cool, eh?"

"Is that possible?" asked Stan.

Danni sagged a little. "No, of course not. But, don't you get it?"

No one answered her until Jake uttered, "Oh shit."

"Exactly! He gets it," indicating Jake.

"What?" asked Stan.

"Tell him," demanded Danni, almost hopping out of her shoes from excitement.

Jake took his time but turned to Stan.

"Our head, here, doesn't belong to our body, there."

Stan and Mallory studied the two tables in silence.

"What you have here is a head..." She indicated the head sitting incongruously in the center of the gleaming left autopsy table.

"And, over here is a body." She looked up at Stan. "Just not the body that matches that head."

She stepped back a step so Stan could make his own survey.

"Who is he? I mean the other one," asked Stan.

Danni frowned, disappointed Stan was not seeing the humor.

"Well, you're right the head is Marston, James Junior. Got a second set of dentals about an hour ago. Confirms what I told you after I examined the first set."

"Thank God," sighed Stan, knowing he narrowly avoided stepping into the dung hole of public embarrassment.

Danni moved to the other table.

"But, this dude. I have no goddamn idea. We're able to get a partial print. Somebody messed up his fingertips with crazy glue and glommed them together. Had a bitch of a time pulling them apart. We weren't very successful, but I think we've got enough to work with. If he's in the system, we'll find him. May take a while."

Idly, she twiddled the drooping skin on two of the fingers with her gloved hands as if remembering the trouble they'd had trying not to damage what was left of the tattered skin.

"I can tell you he's probably Caucasian. Don't know yet. Two months baked in a luxury car will change your complexion."

She moved over to the table that held James Marston's head and put her gloved hands on top, mussing the hair.

"Thirty-three complete vertebra with that bad boy there." She indicated the headless body.

"And two with our torso-challenged friend here. That's thirty-five. And no matter how good I am I can't put these two Humpty-Dumptys back together."

She smiled. "Damn, but you guys bring me the best stuff."

Stan, Jake, and Mallory gathered in the crowded hallway.

"What do you think?" asked Stan. He was looking at Jake.

"I still think her hair looks like roadway tar," replied Jake.

"What?" asked Stan.

"I think we wait until she finishes with the car."

Before Stan could answer, Jake continued.

"Also, we're going to need some help."

"I agree," Stan said. "And we need to keep this low. No need to broadcast we've got another one in the backseat." He turned to Mallory. "Can you get that red-headed kid or somebody else from the IT section to lend a hand?"

"I know someone else. Sue Spruance. She's good."

"Jake, see if we can steal a few more bodies from RH for a few days, maybe tomorrow to help search Marston's place, after they get done working the neighborhood where the BMW was. Shit, it's been weeks already, so we won't expect too much. Anyway, we'll plan on a room by room crawl over the whole place soon as we can round up some bodies. I don't want to do it piecemeal."

"Did you find keys?" Jake asked.

Stan chuckled. "Yeah. His attorney has some. Guess who his attorney is?" Stan answered before Jake could speculate.

"Saunders. Michael Saunders," beamed Stan.

"Squinty?"

Stan nodded.

"Figures. We'll need a good-sized crew," Jake said. "The place is a big mother. I'll get some people, most likely Rodriguez's guys and whomever he can shanghai."

"Well, the place is not going anywhere."

Both Mallory and Jake set out punching numbers into their phones.

Stan shifted his attention back to the autopsy room. Somewhere out there was another head and torso each with not enough vertebrae. Maybe, out there, in some other car, waiting to be discovered by some housewife or eighty-year-old grandmother some fine morning, is a rotted head, which will drop at their feet. Messing up their day.

Through the glass of the Forensics' double doors, Stan could see the head and drooped and cloudy eyes of James Marston staring at him. He didn't look at all happy to Stan.

Yeah. Join the club.

CHAPTER 15

The bar was dark and Mallory nervously drummed her fingers on the table. She was in a back booth. The place was called Rhinos and she liked the joint. It was like a Red Robin for adults crossed with an English pub, a little kitschy with the tin ceiling, dark wood, wrought iron railing with a brass top rail surrounding some of the tables. Little two step-up levels led to the booths around the perimeter. Most of all the lighting was subtle, flattering. And there was just enough quiet, unidentifiable music coming from overhead to cover most conversations.

She also found she liked sitting in the last booth. Back to the wall. Have a view of the entrance. She smiled to herself. Stan and Jake's influence was coming out in unexpected ways.

Always watch your back. Always.

Susan was running late and Mallory didn't want to be on a second gin when she arrived so she busied herself with other things. The little white paper doily under her drink was fair game and she proceeded to rip it to shreds, one small strip at a time. She used the sweat from the glass to soften the paper then scratched it with her fingernail, an inch at a time.

"Hey. You started without me. What is that, gin or vodka?"

Mallory didn't look up. "There's a difference?"

"Both clear and 80 proof and you can murder olives in either. So, yeah, you're right."

The woman sat down opposite Mallory, took off her sunglasses, and fluffed her long dark hair.

"You pouting?"

Mallory looked up at her. "Kids pout. I'm drinking." She tore up the rest of the doily, gathered the remnants into a pile, and dumped them in her empty glass.

Susan looked good as always. No, not good, terrific. Susan Spruance had taken Mallory's place in the IT division of SacPD when Mallory left. Actually, it was a stroke to Mallory's ego because she was replaced not only by Susan but also with another geeky kid named Simon. It took two of them to do what Mallory had been doing for Sharon Ollestad, the battle-ax who ran IT.

The waiter came and regarded the mess in front of Mallory without comment. She reckoned he'd seen worse.

Susan batted her eyelashes at the waiter. "She'll have another I guess and I'll have whatever she's having and a few extra of those paper things if you have any left."

After the waiter had cleared off Mallory's glass full of paper shards, Mallory fiddled with the lamp made to look like a fake candle. She twisted the shade and flicked it off and on a few times.

Susan glanced up, then back down at the table, not wanting to stare. "Nice glasses. Thought you had contacts?"

Mallory shrugged. "Didn't take. Felt like acid-laced sandpaper. Couldn't see through the tears."

Susan held up her hands, framing Mallory like a portrait artist. "Well, those frames make you look…"

"Scholarly?" asked Mallory with sullenness.

"Well, yeah. Scholarly. Like a Rhodes scholar."

"Swell. Great. That was the look I was going for."

Mallory leaned back as the waiter set down two fresh ones. Before he retreated, he made a point of setting a small pile of paper doilies between both women.

"So. What's up?"

"How's Ollestad?"

Before Susan could answer, Mallory shook her head. "I withdraw the question. I don't really care."

"To answer your non-question, your old boss is the same. Actually better. She has a boyfriend, I guess. Must berate him at home, because she's eased up on us. Least compared to last year. Only screams at Simon, the redheaded kid. I figure he's the surrogate for the boyfriend at work."

Mallory nodded, not listening.

"So, if you had to cut somebody's head off, how would you do it."

Susan opened her mouth, but the surprise was momentary.

"Well, assuming I was on my knees, I'd hold his ass real tight with my two hands and bite really hard I suppose."

Mallory kept a straight face. "Wrong head. I mean the big thing above your shoulders."

"That's what I was talking about."

Both women laughed and sipped at their gins.

Susan continued. "I guess it depends on how long you've been dating him."

"Not so much," replied Mallory. "Dating is not happening. I mean James Marston. Rather James Marston Junior."

"Figured as much. Heard you guys had been handed that. What's Danni say?"

"She's still working it. Dribs and drabs. Stan and Jake are going nuts. Official report is days away. One thing she did say…"

"Yes?" asked Susan.

"Stan hasn't released this yet. Maybe tomorrow, maybe never, I don't know."

"Well, what?"

Mallory gave a little smirk. "You know the head was found in the front seat and there were remains in the back."

"Know that, yeah."

"Well, the head and the remains don't match. Two different people."

Susan put down her drink. "W. T. Fuck! Then, why are you guys still handling it?"

"You mean why hasn't it gone to Robbery-Homicide?"

"Hell, yeah. No offense to Stan and Jake, but sounds like this all belongs with Rodriguez and his merry band."

"Agreed. Word came down from on high-"

"Carruthers?"

"According to him, Robbery-Homicide's too busy, blah, blah and we're the best team for this and since we started it blah, blah. Bullshit. We didn't start it. Carruthers gave it to us like it was a great big present. Something fun to do while our cold cases drag on."

Mallory, then Susan, started in on destroying doilies.

Mallory sighed. "Stan's not sure how he wants to use it," continued Mallory. "Doesn't want the two bodies' information out, but I'm sure some jerk in Danni's office or upstairs will let it leak probably tomorrow."

Susan stirred her drink. "So why would somebody go to all this trouble?"

"Cutting their head off? Revenge is Stan's pet theory. I don't buy it. Marston, man, he'd have to have done someone really wrong for she, or he, to return the favor."

"You see it? The head?"

Mallory smiled, nodded. "Saw a movie once, Blackbeard, The Pirate with Robert Newton. Jeez, I loved that guy. Treasure Island, Jamaica Inn, then he did a TV series playing Long John Silver. Best, pirate, ever. Anyway, last scene. The last scene showed Blackbeard buried up to his neck in the sand as the tide came in. Marston looked like that. Looked like he'd been buried and was waiting for the incoming tide."

"Lovely image. Stan pissed that OID has this?"

Mallory shrugged. "I think he feels like he's going backwards. This was supposed to be an easy missing person, this favor for Carruthers. So easy, he was planning on dumping it in my lap. You know, 'Hey Mallory, run out to Marston's place and check, see if this guy's there, if not, make a few calls'."

Mallory shook the ice in her glass.

"Now look what we have."

Susan emptied hers and signaled for another.

"So," she probed. "How's Jake feel about it?"

"Jake? Why?"

Susan shrugged. "Curious."

"Curious?" Mallory leaned forward. "My ass. You're curious how big his hands are."

"I like introverts."

"Yeah? Well, he can be a real asshole."

"Like those too."

"Forget it," said Mallory, sharper and more possessive than she meant to.

"Damn," said Susan. "Sure you don't want to come back to IT? Switch places? You can play your old head games with Ollestad and I can play with Jake."

Mallory tore at another doily. "Funny. But, hey you can help us out. See what you can dig up about Marston, his life and times, you know. I'd appreciate it."

"Sure. I'll deliver it personally. Which one is Jake's desk?"

Mallory ignored her comment. "If you can make time, I'll probably have other stuff you can help with, especially if we get some witnesses to come forward."

The two women sat silently without speaking until Mallory cleared her throat.

"Listen, I know this is going to sound silly…"

"Probably," said Susan, indicating Mallory's empty glass. "You're already ahead on points. But go ahead, whatever you say won't be used against you."

Mallory leaned forward and dropped her voice. "I think someone's watching me."

"You lucky." Susan kept the smirk on while she awaited the punchline. When there wasn't any, she moved her glass out of the way.

"I'm sorry. You're serious?"

Mallory looked around at the other tables, nodded. "Yeah, pretty much. Pretty sure."

"Like following you? Stalking you?"

Mallory shrugged.

"The hell! What did Stan and Jake say?"

Mallory held up her hand.

"What? You mean you didn't tell 'em?!"

"Look, it's just a creepy-crawly feeling. I was shopping at Arden Fair Mall the other day getting something for Stan's birthday. Anyway, there was this guy. Short guy. I swear he was shadowing me. He seemed to be interested in every store I was interested in. Always stayed some ways behind me."

"Okay…?"

"Then, I saw him again in the parking lot. Pretty sure it was him. Seriously, how many ugly, dark-skinned little guys are there always walking behind me? I mean, I know I stand out with this," she fingered her scar. "So maybe only ugly guys are attracted."

"Cut that shit out."

Mallory adjusted her glasses and looked back down at her drink.

Susan scanned the restaurant. "You see him again? See him here?"

Mallory shook her head. "Just that feeling, you know."

"Yeah," mused Susan. "Know that feeling. Okay. Listen, what do you have for protection?"

"Still have my Mace and I still remember how to use my car keys."

"Not good enough. You know how to shoot a gun don't you?"

"No. Yes. Sort of."

"Swell answer, Mal."

"I know guns, kind of. My father had one. He used to let me clean it. Left it to me when he died."

"What? Father-daughter bonding?"

Mallory looked up. "When my brother disappeared, I was the only one left to do projects with. It was tough for him. He wasn't used to thinking up things to do with a daughter."

"Yeah. Sorry."

"So, I know 'em. Just never shot one. Last year though, I even went as far to get a carry permit."

"You already have the permit and a gun? Well, screw it. I'll teach you myself or my dad. My dad owns a range and he's an instructor and stuff. But, in my opinion, all men get too excited when playing with a firearm. I mean, look. You've got something hard at your waist, that when you squeeze it, it jerks and shoots stuff. Come on."

"And it can kill too," added Mallory.

"Another bonus."

Susan took a healthy slug and twirled the ice with her tongue.

"Now, we've got you squared away on that, and speaking of ejaculate, you getting any?"

Mallory gave small smile, shook her head.

Susan leaned forward. "Nothing?"

Mallory sighed and scoured the sides of her glass free of condensation. "It's been so long since I've had sex, I've forgotten who pays whom."

CHAPTER 16

The Blue Moon lost hundreds of loyal (and occasional) customers when Sacramento moved the police headquarters out of the old Fisher building. 'Old Fish', as it was called, was named for one of the first police chiefs of Sacramento, back in the days when the state charter was still wet and the town was alive with gold seekers. Old Maurice Fisher had his work cut out for him with the thousands of gold seekers who 'seeked' but did not find. They resented anything that looked prosperous. He was the only police chief ever shot while in office in Sacramento.

Apparently, in Sacramento, it takes death while on duty to get a building named after you.

These days, the Blue Moon's façade had the forlorn look of having watched life pass it by. The Fisher building across the street was only half re-rented and it seems the business people that worked there couldn't match the drinking habits of Sacramento's men in blue. And especially the detectives.

The atmosphere was no better inside. The interior exuded a tired air of stale beer and lonely corners. Perfect for an out of the way get-together.

Stan took a moment to adjust to the dimness, then moved past the unused dartboard and the vacant pool table to the next to last booth where Phil Ginger was slouched.

"You know why they keep it so dark in here?" questioned Phil as Stan slid into the seat opposite.

"Yeah. Saves on cleaning costs."

"That too. I once worked in a bar. Sorta like this one, back in South Dakota. Once a month we turned all the lights on and up full to clean the place. Found a dead cat in one of the corners."

"Didn't stink?"

"Stunk bad. Only you couldn't tell it from the ripeness of the pig farmers and all the slop they had all over their jeans and the pig shit they'd drag in on their boots."

Phil waved at the beer he'd bought for Stan.

"There you go. There's your beer. Now, who the hell is this James Marston? I mean besides an old reprobate film guy from L.A."

Stan didn't answer right away. He replayed in his head the scene in Forensics. Danni Harness, giddy as a schoolgirl, with two different dead guys on her hands.

As usual, he weighed his words to Ginger. Their relationship was always quid pro quo. He wasn't sure Ginger could give him anything that he needed. Hell, he didn't even know what he needed.

"And why the press conference this morning?" Ginger locked his eyes on Stan, the reporter's trick to weigh evasiveness.

"And why the guy with the drone?"

"Stan, c'mon. Doing our job. We have a right to know what's going on." Ginger turned his beer glass around a few times. "And shit, you didn't have to destroy it, you know."

"You want to know why the press conference? We figured if this Marston story was gonna break thanks to your guy violating a crime scene, we thought we'd be the ones to break it. Maybe get some good citizen to come forward and solve it for us."

Stan set his beer down and looked back at Ginger to see if he bought it.

"That's bull, Stan. Our guy didn't violate shit. I've seen the picture."

"And?"

Now Ginger looked away and studied the sweat on his pint. "We didn't run it because we didn't know what we had. Besides, we decided to hold it anyway 'til after we heard what you guys had to say."

He smiled up at Stan, conspirators.

"As I said, I've seen the picture. We're the only ones who know about it."

"Know about what?"

"C'mon Stan. Give. We know about the car and that Marston was found in it. And that it's been there, in police possession I might add, for what must be weeks."

"Oversight."

"Some oversight. Car gets dragged to impound lot and the tow guy doesn't see anything unusual. Whoever ticketed the thing in the first place and called it in didn't see anything?"

Stan shrugged.

"Tells me he was well hidden, probably in the trunk. Am I right?"

Stan didn't reply.

"And if he was out of sight then he probably didn't crawl into the trunk and pull it closed himself. So, this was death by nefarious means as they say. How'm I doing?"

"You're the reporter," Stan said not committing anything.

"Yeah. And you're giving me jackshit."

Ginger waved his last words away and continued on, trying a new tack. "Okay, this Marston was a big deal I heard."

"Thought you didn't really know who he was."

"Aw. Got one of my gals to look him up. Movies. Money. Nutso. Lived by himself, apparently. Spreads his dough around. Political. The Arts. That kinda shit. Right?"

Stan mulled over what he wanted from Ginger that he couldn't get himself. There wasn't much. At the moment.

He didn't delude himself. That a dismembered body was found in police impound would be out soon, if it wasn't already. In reality, secrets like a prominent citizen found beheaded sooner or later found their way to light. Usually sooner.

He decided to give Ginger a head start then smiled at his own joke.

"Tell me what your guy's picture showed," asked Stan.

"What?" asked Ginger, confused for a second by the change in subject. "What do you mean?"

"You say you've seen the picture. What did you see?"

Ginger started squirming. He shifted in his seat and pursed his lips. No sense in perpetuating the bluff.

"I don't know Stan. Kinda blurry, you know."

"Too bad."

Ginger perked up. This was some of the dirt he came for.

"Okay, what am I supposed to see?"

Stan finished his beer. "You'll owe me."

"I bought you the damn beer."

"I said you'll owe me."

Ginger nodded. "So? What you got?"

Stan didn't answer directly. "Have your guy blow up what he took last night. Doesn't matter how blurry. You should be able to make out something on the ground next to the car."

Ginger leaned forward. "What? Drugs? What? The guys in the trunk and there are drugs on the ground? That what you're saying'? Maybe a brick of cut Mexican blow? What?"

Stan stood up. "You'll owe me."

Ginger shrugged assent.

"I mean it."

"I got it, Stan. I'll ink it on my wrist for chrissakes."

Stan smiled. "You like movies, Phil?"

"What do you mean? Yeah. I like the movies. What am I supposed to be seeing that I'm not?"

"Like Peckinpaugh? Sam Peckinpaugh movies?"

"Peckinpaugh? Yeah. Sure, so what?"

Stan patted Ginger on his head.

"You know what my favorite is?"

"Tell me."

"I've always liked *Bring Me the Head of Alfredo Garcia.*"

Stan chugged his beer as he got up to leave. He could see the wheels spin in Ginger's head.

At the door, Stan didn't need to look back. He knew Ginger was already on his phone.

CHAPTER 17

Jake made the turn about the twelfth hole of the Ancil Hoffman golf course he figured, on the northern arm of the American River Park. Someday, he'd like to try golf. Now, it was enough to keep up with his four-pawed bundle of energy.

While they ran he calculated the age difference between them. Dogs were seven years for every one of his. That meant his thirty-eight years were keeping pace with a ten-year-old. Who was pacing whom exactly? And how fair was that?

They passed several sand traps with Jake showing no signs of tiring.

Jake watched his dog. He knew Jake probably wanted to stop and smell up everything since this was his first time running the route, but he kept on with the run. Both knowing they needed the exercise.

It had been a helluva day with Danni throwing another body into the mix and his crew of door bangers comin' up empty. Actually, he hadn't expected any results. Who sees anything at 2:30 in the morning. And the spot on Jones Road where the BMW was found was not a populated area. A few homes set back from the road. The only residential development nearby was accessible by hacking your way through an intimidating tangle of underbrush, which they decided wasn't worth it.

Jake realized the BMW couldn't have broken down in a worse spot. Not only was it a traffic hazard at the curve, but anyone looking out their front windows from any of the nearby houses would not have seen anything. 2:30 A.M. or not.

He and Jake made the turn back up California Avenue.

He could see the dog checking him out as they jogged, keeping pace and keeping on track. Every time Jake would speed up, Jake would match him. It wasn't until Jake really slowed the pace, about two blocks from the condo that the dog really gave him a WTF look.

"It's called cool down, boy. Someday you'll understand. Someday you'll have lungs that scream at you to slow the fuck up. Someday you'll have a body that says, please dear God, stop this shit. And that's what we're doing. Okay?"

The dog matched his slower pace but pulled ahead on the leash to let Jake know he still had plenty of gas and that he wasn't the one who was gumming up the works.

"Yeah, well you're only ten years old, relatively speaking. Quit showing off."

It was near eleven when they finally loped up to the condo. It was then Jake realized how hungry he was and how neither of them had eaten since before lunch.

He leaned against the front door of the blandly named Smithson Towers to catch his breath. They were neither towers nor owned by anyone named Smithson. Jake knew that because, first, the building was only five stories, and second, he owned the building. And his name wasn't Smithson.

Rumor had it randy ole Cyrus Smithson, (1888-1933), ran the first hardware/software store back in the '20s. Seems, if his customers had the 'hard'ware they could find the 'soft'ware in the beds on the second floor. And if their tastes ran more to the bizarre, there was some 'apparatus' in the basement that would restrain the most energetic of clients and their guests.

Even though Jake had gutted the whole place, he could never remove the eyehooks from the basement walls. They were now covered by the tenants' numbered storage units.

And, he'd kept the name of the building. It was always good, he felt, to honor in some small way the city's pioneers.

He entered the door code. "You're not even winded are you?"

The dog didn't look at him, only waited for Jake to open up.

"Didn't think so."

They both jogged up the stairs to the top floor.

Jake dragged his leash ahead to the condo's door and sat waiting for Jake to open up. Another condo was on the same floor as evidenced by the door with the number 52 on it at the end of the hall. It was smaller and the view wasn't as good. And it was vacant because Jake kept it for guests. After six years, he was still waiting for the first guest.

The dog made a dash for his bowl when they entered but found it empty. Lapped up some water out of the water bowl and then sat determinedly next to his empty bowl.

Jake turned on the lights and the TV and went to solve the food problem. He'd burned through all of the sample food he'd been given and now he had to decide on the stuff he'd already purchased.

"What d'ya want?" asked Jake. "A handful of nuggets or some manly food, meat by-products that smell like they've been dipped in hog sweat and nicely aged in somebody's nasty coffin? Which?"

The Jakes looked at each other.

Jake licked his lips.

"Okay. The manly crap it is."

Jake spun open the can and ladled a healthy helping of liver and pork dog food simmered in obscene gravy into Jake's bowl.

"I hope you like this because it smells…"

But Jake ignored him and moved him out of the way with his nose and wolfed it down.

"Easy guy. We don't want that stuff to come back up now, do we?"

Jake ignored him and kept grabbing at chunks and tossing them back.

"I'll answer that. No, we do not."

Jake was finished even before Jake could open his Anchor Steam. He looked up expectantly at Jake.

"No way. You're gonna have to learn about pacing. Maybe a treat later."

Jake knew the word treat. He wagged his tail in anticipation.

"Later. Maybe. If all that good yummy stuff you scarfed stays down. Got it?"

Jake followed Jake to the living room, a sparsely furnished room with a leather 'L' shaped couch in front of a fifty-two-inch flat screen with a Bose sound system.

Jake settled back in the center of the barge-sized couch with his beer. Jake jumped up beside him and rested his head on Jake's lap.

Jake watched his dog. Watched his dog as he burped, expelling an airy reminder of what he'd just eaten.

"That's it, right? Nothing more is coming up is it?"

Jake licked his lips and swallowed once. It was an answer of sorts.

He lifted his head when Jake moved through the channels and paused in the rotation. "That's Oprah," Jake said in his best explaining-to-a-child voice. "We don't watch Oprah. Men don't watch Oprah. So, we don't watch Oprah."

"There," Jake said, still explaining, as he settled on the channel previewing Sacramento King's and their chances of putting on a decent showing this coming season.

"There. Men watch sports. We watch sports. Usually. But not tonight. Tonight we try to find an epic movie by our dead guy, Mr. Marston. What d'ya say. Something with zombies or blood-sucking aliens. Sound good?"

The dog settled down again on Jake's lap and stretched out taking up the left half of the couch. Jake tried not to notice the emptiness of the right side of the couch.

Spawn of the Cradle was the Marston classic he found on cable. Kids with fangs turning on their parents, turning them into gelatinous masses. The special effects, with the goo running down the legs of the parents, wasn't bad. Being in black and white made it even better.

Jake slid down a little lower on the couch. He looked at his dog. He looked over at his two plants, his orchid, and his thorny thing. Then back at the unoccupied right side of the couch.

"We'll see how it goes, okay?" he murmured to Jake. But the dog was already asleep, his eyes roving in a dreamy chase after some younger bitch.

And that's how they woke in the morning.

On the couch.

Together.

CHAPTER 18

Mallory punched her phone, disconnecting, and shoved it in her pocket.

"Bastard."

"What?" Stan asked.

"Jesus, when you look up 'shithead' in the dictionary, his picture has gotta be right there."

"Who?" asked Stan.

"Samuels."

Stan continued to look at her waiting for more information.

"Aw, he was pissed with my report on Marston."

"What report? I never saw it."

Mallory shrugged. "You told me to get back to him on our progress, so I did."

"What'd you tell him?" Jake asked.

"Told him we were on it. Bastard wanted more."

"And I didn't see this report," Stan said.

"'Course not. I never wrote a report. I told him we were on it. We were working it. Shit. It'd only been a few days. What do they want?"

"That it? Can I continue with this now?" asked Stan, annoyed. "You dragged us out here and my morning coffee is still sitting on my desk, probably not even lukewarm."

The three of them and Jake dog stood outside the OID building clustered around the security touchpad for the new security door. Stan fingered a business card on the back of which he'd scrawled the directions for setting the security code for the door.

Mallory avoided answering him. "Well, they weren't really happy about the press thing. I think the Captain wanted this solved by goddamn osmosis. Maybe use the 'think method' and somehow divine what the hell happened without calling attention to it. Sensitive guy, the Captain."

"Guess it's a good thing we didn't put an 8x10 glossy of the head out there, eh?" offered Jake.

"Well, we would've gotten a good response," continued Mallory. "People tend to take notice of a guy who has come unglued from his body."

"Yeah, well, c'mon let's finish this." Stan started in again on the instructions. "All right. Third. Hold down the- "

"You'll have to start over," Jake said as he peered closer to the digital readout. "Looks like it reset itself while Mallory was whining."

"Swell." Stan handed the card to Mallory. "Here, you have better eyes."

"Not sure we all have to be out here," suggested Jake. "Let's go in." He gave a tug on the handle but it wouldn't open.

"You have to wait until I set the code. It's not going to open until I do."

"It opened earlier this morning," Jake protested.

"There was no code set this morning Sherlock. Now, that we've started the process, it thinks you're trying to break in. Let me finish."

Mallory shot her sleeves as if she would be spinning the tumblers on a casino vault.

"Room, boys. Give me room."

She read the directions, mouthing the words silently.

"Okay." Her tongue settled between her front teeth in concentration.

She punched a few numbers, checked the card, hit a few more, then put the card between her teeth and with two fingers pushed two buttons simultaneously.

"It's ready," she declared. "What do you want the code to be?"

Jake looked at Stan. Both shrugged.

"Come on! Or it will reset again."

"How 'bout 6969," offered Jake.

"I would've expected nothing less, Steiner."

"I don't know," said Stan, grinning at Mallory. "Seems easy to remember."

Mallory turned and looked at both. "It is true what they say about men isn't it?"

"I guess," said Jake with mock sheepishness. "We're merely simple creatures. Right, Stan?"

"Affirmative."

The security pad beeped with a five-second countdown to reset. Mallory punched in 6969.

"There you go. Now we've made it easier for any male who tries to break in. It will be the first code he tries."

"Nah," scoffed Stan. "It's too obvious." He tugged on the handle. It didn't budge.

He held up his hands in frustration.

"I think we're out here forever," Jake said. "You want the dog to try setting the code?"

Mallory's phone rang. She covered the mouthpiece. "Hey, big guy. I just set the code. Now you have to enter it. You both remember it, don't you?"

Stan stepped aside. "After you," to Jake.

"This is how it's done." He entered 6969 with a flourish. "Open Sesame!"

They heard a subtle click and Jake swung the door open. Jake dog led the way.

Mallory followed them in, phone to her ear.

"Well, give me the bad news first."

All three made their way back to their desks.

"Nothing? Nothing on 911 or dispatch?"

Stan and Jake watched her. She looked up and shook her head.

"You're sure? I know 911's got everything recorded but I heard dispatch isn't always the best at record keeping-"

Mallory cradled the phone as she pulled her legal pad closer.

"Ask who was on duty that night," Jake suggested.

Mallory waved him down.

"All right. Yeah. So on the dispatch side, can you find out who was working that night?"

Mallory made a notation. "And you checked with her?"

Mallory held her cell away from her ear as the caustic reply could be heard by all of them.

"Enough. Okay, got it. What's the good news?"

Mallory listened.

"Just one, huh."

Mallory moved the mouthpiece. To Stan and Jake, "Just one witness that sounds credible for that night."

"That's something," Stan said. "Given how long ago this went down."

"Let me have it," said Mallory, back on the conversation. She filled a few lines.

"What was she doing?"

Mallory concentrated, made a few notes, and hung up.

"Okay. Nobody seems to have any idea who called it in initially. Either into 911 or dispatch. They can't find any record of a call referencing Jones road, or a woman in distress, or a broken-down vehicle on the night of the 16th."

"Maybe we're wrong about the 16th," Stan suggested.

Jake slipped his hands behind his head and leaned back. "Is there nothing on the 15th, the 17th, or the whole week?"

"Nope."

"They can't find it, or it doesn't exist?"

"Doesn't matter," Stan said. "Look, they've never been the best at paper trails. Be surprised at the shit that gets lost over there."

Mallory looked perplexed. "Aren't they trained to document or record everything? Anonymous calls, heavy breathers, old ladies looking for someone to talk to at 2 A.M.?"

"Yeah. But no. Not in this case, evidently. You're thinking of 911."

"So," continued Stan. "Okay, we have no copy of a call to dispatch- "

"Why didn't it come into 911?" interrupted Mallory. "I mean I know Carruthers told Stan it came in to dispatch but, you know if you see someone in trouble, their car's busted, it's the middle of the night, you don't want to stop, wouldn't you think to call 911 instead of directly to dispatch?"

"Maybe Carruthers was guessing. And why call the cops anyway on somebody broken down on the side of the road unless there was trouble?" offered Jake.

Both Mallory and Stan considered it.

"Regardless, whoever called in was probably drunk, high, or maybe not thinking straight," Jake continued. "I mean, really it was probably a woman."

Mallory zinged her pencil at him. "Funny."

Jake addressed his dog. "Do you believe that pal? Seems information about this abandoned car simply floated into brother Carruthers' arms. Landed on his desk, delivered by messenger fairy. What do you think?"

Jake settled on his paws. He had no answer.

"Maybe it came from our witness," Stan suggested. "Called it in and got lost in the mix."

Mallory appeared determined. "If it's there, I'll find it. I know people."

"Good luck. And what about our witness?" Jake asked. "She good or a crackpot, looking for attention?"

Mallory read from her pad.

"She said she saw the car and was pretty sure it was the 13th of May since she was coming back from the airport that night." Mallory gave a thumbs up. "She also mentioned the woman standing by her car."

Jake's phone vibrated.

Stan's phone vibrated.

Jake read the text and looked up at Stan.

"Danni."

"What's she say?"

"Progress."

CHAPTER 19

Jake and Jake dog came down the hallway same time as Danni was leading Stan past the garage where the crew was working on the BMW. Danni looked askance at Jake, then back up to Jake.

"Don't want any dog hair in any of my stuff, understand?"

Jake, seeing the attention was all about him, wagged his tail, looked from Danni up to Jake.

"He only sheds when I tell him to," Jake said. He looked down at Jake who sat next to him. "Don't shed."

Danni didn't crack a smile but turned and started down the hallway.

Stan looked to Jake for agreement on Danni's mood.

Danni smiling was bad, laughing even worse. Not smiling was uncharted territory.

"What?" Jake mouthed.

Stan inclined his head toward the retreating march of the head of SacPD Forensics.

"Yeah," Jake nodded. "Her hair still looks like road tar."

Stan shook his head. "She's pissed."

"Maybe she doesn't like her dye job."

"C'mon."

They got to Danni's office door as she plopped into her chair behind her desk and swiveled back and forth.

"Close the door," she commanded.

Jake pulled Jake into the confining room and closed the door.

Danni tilted back, lit one of her stinky home-rolls, and shook her head as if she was a regretful executioner.

"Okay, here's what we've got." Danni Harness slipped from one page to the other then back to the front of the pile. Her flippant manner from yesterday was gone.

"And, it's a lot. A lot of strange shit."

Jake and Stan stood shoulder to shoulder in her office. There was no place to sit. Every spare surface was claimed by boxes and files of current cases. There was scarcely enough room for Danni to sit at her desk and maneuver.

Jake dropped the leash and watched as the dog made a circle near the door and curled up.

"First. Marston." She handed the pictures up to Jake.

"Head was garroted as you know. Not a very clean job. Lots of stop-starts, tentative cuts. Sort of like whoever didn't want to start on the job or they weren't sure or they just wanted to take their time."

"What did they use?" asked Jake, glancing at the close-ups of the underside of the skull then passing the pictures to Stan.

Danni sighed as if there was something larger pressing on her life. "We thought at first it was a straight piano wire type garrote. Anybody can make these, two sticks and some piano wire. The pros use ones with comfortable wood handles. 'Course you have to be strong and you have to have the subject taken by surprise…"

"Or there have to be two of you and one of him," suggested Stan.

"Or that. But, here's what we found when examined the neck bones."

Danni swung around in her chair tapped twice on her keyboard and fired up her 20" by 30" digital monitor. It had replaced the backlit lightboxes and transparencies that Danni used to love.

"Yow," exclaimed Stan when he saw what came up on the screen. "Detail is amazing."

She couldn't keep the pride out of her voice. "Yeah, well, cover your balls. Watch this".

Waving her hand over the screen, she highlighted an area and enlarged the view. Then two more times, zeroing in on one of the cuts in the C2 vertebrae which was easily seen. The details remained sharp and lost nothing with the zooming.

Jake put his hand on the back of his neck and traced his own vertebrae. What a piss-poor way to go.

The mouse pointer moved around in small little circles.

"See those?"

Both Jake and Stan leaned forward putting their hands on the desk.

Stan put on his reading glasses.

The magnified cuts the garrote made on the bone looked like white canyons in desert rock with bits of other stuff Stan didn't need to know about. Enlarge something enough it goes abstract and loses its context, like anything when examined too closely.

"Looks like reflections off something," Jake said. "Some metal caught in the bone cuts."

Raked into the cuts and stuck in the bone were small glints of light, sparkles.

"Not metal." Danni's eyes closed, like a kid about to reveal a confidence. "Diamonds."

"Diamonds? Diamonds?" asked Stan.

"Yeah, I'm afraid boys you're looking at the grindings off someone's engagement ring."

"It's what?" asked Jake.

"Kidding, Steiner. It's from diamond dust. Dust collected after shaping the raw stones, probably when they were shaped for industrial cutters."

She looked at Jake. "Not engagement rings."

"This leftover dust is heat-fused, like 1200 degrees, with the metal wire. Gives you an edge with tens of thousands of little razors. Slices and dices with less effort."

Danni swung back in her chair and pulled out a print.

"Got this off the internet. Called a daiishka, something like that. Middle East in origin. Israeli diamond cutters must've had a slow day when they invented this. Thing is black-marketed mostly in Russia and Eastern Europe."

Stan looked at Jake. They both studied the printout. A coiled garrote appearing longer than normal with what looked like bicycle grips on either end.

The writing was Czech or Russian, Stan guessed.

"What does this mean?" Stan pointed to a list of Russian words in a column next to the daiishka.

Danni laughed a short quick laugh. "I looked it up on the translator. Seems you can get your diamond-studded killing wire with black or red handles."

"There's no domestic outlet for these?" asked Jake.

"How should I know? Try the CIA or men from black ops or Assassins Inc. These things aren't legal anywhere as far as I can tell and not available except in the backrooms of some of the finest of Europe's illegal weapons emporiums."

Danni continued in a more conciliatory tone. "Listen. Important to note that whoever used this still didn't have the brute strength to do this in one swipe as it were. The sawing patterns on the bone suggest that even with this fine weapon, the severing wasn't done quickly."

"You mean, what, in ten minutes? Twenty?"

"Or more."

"No shit." Jake settled back against the wall. His imaginings were all too clear.

"Which meant probable cause of death is a tossup. But, I'd vote for bleed out. When this baby, this daiishka, hit the carotid and other main blood vessels there would've been your standard hemorrhagic eruption and he would've lost it."

Of course…" Danni sat back with a creased concern. "He could've drowned in his own blood. Or if his spinal cord was severed early he would've been paralyzed.

"Anyway, somebody wanted his head off and there you go. It would help if you two detectives would find the rest of him. If that's not asking too much."

Stan wasn't listening to Danni. He struggled to assimilate what they knew about Marston. All he could arrange was a jumble of unrelated, disparate facts that had no common pattern. No similarities. The sheer number of 'whys' made his head hurt.

Some cold case.

He needed a drink.

"That's Marston. Now, second thing. According to our mechanic, your BMW was perfectly fit to drive. My guy called me this morning. She cleared her throat and affected a Minnesota accent, 'That there Beemer. Well, t'weren't broke. Runs goot.'"

"Ahh, hell," exclaimed Stan.

Danni picked up her sheaf of papers. "Okay. That was number two. Moving on." She hesitated, actually looked as if she didn't want to continue.

"Before we get to the car, and you're gonna love this. Our second guy bumming a ride in the back seat is one Peter Berlin- "

Stan started. "Berlin? Peter Berlin?"

Jake turned to Stan. "You know him? Felon?"

"No," answered Stan. "Cop. Used to be. If it's the same Berlin."

"SacPD?"

"Yeah. He was okay. He worked with Carruthers for a while, back in the day. Got out and opened up his own private shop. Was doing really well, I think. Wives who needed their husbands followed or found, or bailing rich teenagers out of trouble. Like that."

Danni nodded. "You're right. He had a PI license, timely renewed each year. Seemed to be in order. My guess is, you check upstairs, you'll find a missing person on the guy. Address and all that. And lucky you, you guys get to do the next of kin."

She handed Jake a picture. "Here's his picture from when he got his license."

Danni paused. "Oh, yeah. Listen. Tell 'em upstairs that the crack team of Wyld and Steiner found part of him so only the top half is still missing."

Her hard smoker's laugh segued into a smoker's hack. Still, she tilted back in her chair, more than pleased with her own humor.

Jake studied the small headshot, then held it down so the dog could see it.

"Toxicology?" Stan continued.

"I don't know. Won't be back for days and probably won't give us much after this amount of time."

Jake spoke up. "What about time of death?"

"You mean how long had they been dead before the car was opened?"

"That would help."

"Sure it would Detective Steiner, but I can't really tell you. There is only a limited amount of data on bodies that've been baked in a car in our Sacramento sun for a month or so. I can say that given the almost complete absence of any bodily fluids in the car, on the seats or floor, that they were dead well before they were dragged into the car. By days, probably."

"Great," sighed Jake, not hiding his disappointment.

"I can tell you that they were definitely not killed at the same time, but a week or two apart."

Jake looked at Stan. "Practice? Think our guy was practicing on this Berlin before starting in on Marston?"

Stan shook his head. "Could've been Berlin was in the wrong place but this is a big-boy piece of hardware and it sounds as if it was in the hands of an amateur."

Stan moved his hands back and forth.

"Just sawing with my daiishka."

Daiishka. It sounded so funny both men laughed. Black humor with an uneasy, nervous bravado. They avoided looking at each other, both sensing an undercurrent they couldn't name. As if making eye contact would confirm what they both felt.

"Except," sniffed Danni. "It was the other way 'round. Marston, our front seat head was severed well before our backseat passenger. I can at least determine that much."

Stan managed a ragged breath. "Okay, Danni, please dear God tell me you found fingerprints in the car that tells us all we need to know about who the hell we're looking for. Tell me you know their identity and home address, shoe size, and what they had for breakfast and you're going to give it to us to make our grand and glorious day complete."

Danni sighed.

"We found a lot of partials on the outside, as you would expect. The cop, whatshisname."

"Grey."

"Yeah. And the tow guy. Even Marston. Nothing we can't identify, however."

"What about inside?" asked Jake. "You must've found something."

Danni held their gaze. "We hit the mother lode on the inside. Interior was riddled with prints. Except, out of all of them, we found prints of only two different… people."

"Two? Only two?"

"Crazy, eh?"

"C'mon Danni. You have an ID, right?"

She nodded. "One anyway. It was easy. A convicted felon."

Stan smiled at Jake. "Now we're cooking'."

"We ran a quick check this morning. She was released not long ago from Central California Women's. They should be able to give you her address."

"She?" said Jake and Stan in unison.

"Yeah. A she. Name's Ilsa Pokovich. She's forty-eight years old."

"Pokovich," Stan exclaimed, animated. "Pokovich. Sounds Eastern European."

"Stan," Jake exclaimed. "She's forty-eight."

Stan waved the fact aside. "Okay. She's forty-eight. Kinda old but it fits. So, look, okay she was royally upset about something. Got out of Women's Correctional, headed right for the man who done her wrong. Probably had this daiishka thing her daddy gave her as a sweet sixteen present stored away. Or got it with airline points, I don't know, then found Marston and slowly sawed his head off. Then Berlin found out and bingo, bango, head's gone too. Piled 'em in the car for a little joyride to who knows where. Abandons the car. There you have it."

Jake and Danni stared at Stan.

"Have what?" Jake asked. "We have what exactly?"

"What? What's wrong with that?"

"Once again, she's forty-eight years old," stated Jake. "Even if she's involved, she couldn't do this by herself."

"So? She's a convicted felon, just released. I'll bet there's a connection or she made some connections in the pokey. Probably got a gang up of female Ed Geins and Marston and Berlin's gooses are cooked. Never mind. Let's go. We need to be picking up this Pokovich broad, slapping her in a chair, grilling the shit out of her 'til she folds like a bawlin' baby."

Danni tilted back in her chair. "I shiver all over when he talks cop talk."

"Tracking a released felon," said Stan with uncharacteristic enthusiasm. "Perfect job for Mallory." He stepped into the hallway punched in Mallory's cell.

"What about the other print?" Jake asked.

"Nothing yet, cowboy." Seeing Jake's expression, Danni rocked forward and stood. "Hey, gimme a break. We're working as fast as we can. Girls gotta take time for some sex now and then."

Jake did not want to go there.

CHAPTER 20

Stan checked his watch.

2 PM. Exactly on time.

He exited the elevator and seeing there was only one way to turn, pivoted right and entered the frosted, double glass doors into a hushed world of plush under his feet and tasteful art on beige, rattan walls illuminated by subtle, lighting. An immaculate woman with a futuristic headset smiled as he entered.

She whispered, "Good afternoon."

It was so quiet it made Stan's ears hurt. For a moment he wondered if anyone else was in the office.

"I'm here to see Squinty...I mean Michael Saunders."

His voice sounded overly loud.

The woman smiled. "Of course and you are?" she inquired with solicitude.

"Detective Wyld. I called earlier."

Without missing a beat, she maintained the smile. "Of course. I'll let Mr. Saunders know you're here. Espresso? Evian?"

"What? No, I'm fine." He guessed visitors on a not so friendly visit to the lawyer's office needed all the expensive hydration they could get before viewing their bill.

Not waiting for his answer, she had punched in the numbers for Saunders's office.

"Detective Wyld to see Mr. Saunders," she whispered again. Without waiting for an answer, she smiled at Stan. "His secretary will be right out to take you back."

Stan wandered over to the nearest piece of artwork. It was modern, Picasso-esque. Not something he'd have on any wall, but the muted swirl of colors was pleasant. Not great, but pleasant. He peered into the tacked-on brass plate on the frame. The artist was a Penelope something and the painting was called 'Anna'.

His phone rang to the tune of 'Green Acres' TV show. Bea was always fooling with the ringtones. It sounded loud and raucous in the polite waiting area.

He saw it was Mallory.

"That was fast. You found Pokovich?"

"Found where she was supposed to be. Sacramento General."

"Supposed to be?"

"Was. Ilsa Pokovich checked herself out this morning."

"Mallory, I don't care what kind of release she got, compassionate or conditional or what I don't care, but her somebody must know where she is now."

"Motored over to where the parole officer said Pokovich is supposed to be. No one home. Left three messages."

"What messages?"

"Slipped my card under the door, stuck one between the door and jamb. Gave one to a neighbor. You want me to do a citywide alert too?"

"You can't do that but I can."

Mallory wasn't about to argue and reveal to Stan her complete computer abilities, so she simply agreed.

"Good idea, boss."

"Don't call me that."

"Detective. This way," came a sweet voice from behind him.

"Gotta go."

"Me too. I've got to do this thing," answered Mallory, but he didn't hear her.

He ended the call as a well-coiffed woman with marvelous legs gestured for him to follow. He was only too happy to follow behind her.

The hallways were a continuation of the lobby. Money was plastered to the walls in the form of more signed oil paintings. Along the hallway, there were little plaques below each painting that listed the name of the painting in fancy script, the name of the artist, and now the price. Evidently, Whitfield, Marsh, and

Stansfield's walls doubled as a consignment art store. Nice scam. Display a boatload of expensive art for nothing probably take a cut of every sale.

It seemed a perfect place for Squinty Saunders to be holed up.

"Detective," said the legs in front of him as she stopped and turned, indicating an office entrance. "Mr. Saunders."

She was right. There was a brass plaque that read 'Michael Saunders' on the wall next to the door.

"Thank you," Stan said and he meant it as he watched her disappear down the hall.

"Detective, come in."

Michael 'Squinty' Saunders didn't rise from behind his desk. Or maybe he did, Stan wasn't sure. Challenged in both height and gravitas, Squinty Saunders appeared to be an old kid playing at being an attorney. Stan even wondered if his feet touched the ground while he swiveled in his chair.

"Hey, Squinty." Stan slid into the leather chair in front of the desk. The office was as colorless as Squinty. Only the 16th story view out of a large window brought any life into the room.

"Detective," answered Squinty. He waited for Stan to say what he wanted even though he and Stan had spoken not two hours ago.

Stan studied the man. He hadn't changed in the ten years Stan had known him. Still the same dark, pudgy man with fat fingers. Eyes so sunken into a round, shiny face that Stan was never sure if Squinty could see anything. It was only if he got excited did the folds of skin separate enough that Stan could tell there were eyes there.

"Marston's will. Where are we?" asked Stan.

Squinty tapped the file folder in front of him. "I have it right here, but…"

"But…what? Tell me. It's a series of trusts, annuities, stock, futures, real estate, off-shore oil reserves, Swiss bank accounts, Cayman Island cash? I don't need to know all about that. I need to know who profits from Marston's demise. Who gets the dough?"

Saunders smiled. "It's not that simple…"

"Look. I know you haven't made it public yet. Notified all the heirs, but time is important. I need a list of who gets what before it goes to probate or whatever you do."

Saunders started to say something more but shrugged instead. "Okay." He opened the folder before him and withdrew what couldn't have been more than five sheets of paper bound together.

"But, I don't think this is going to help you."

Stan took the will, hefted it and noted its lack of substance, and quickly read through it.

When he got to the last page with the signature of Marston and the witnesses he turned it over to see if there was more.

"What the hell?"

"Told you. Wouldn't be much help."

"This is the latest? There's nothing else?"

Squinty Saunders hesitated for a second. "This is the official will of James A. Marston Junior. The last Will and Testament."

Stan flipped to the last page again and checked the date. Two years ago.

"Nothing since this one?"

Again Squinty hesitated. "This is the last official Will and Testament."

Stan wasn't picking up on what Saunders was not saying.

"But, this just leaves his dough to about ten, eleven charities. That's it? No people? No person to get the bulk of the estate? Nobody but…" He flipped to the third page. "Red Cross, Planned Parenthood, Hollywood Actor Development Foundation, Studio Motion Picture Producers Guild and so on."

Squinty smiled a big smile. His eyes closed tighter.

"In varying percentages. That's what it says."

Squinty settled back in his chair, scooching his butt back like a little kid.

"You let me come all the way down here for this?"

"Well…" Squinty drew it out as long as he could. "There was a draft. A beginning of a draft of a new will. But it was never finished and never signed, so it really…"

"Where is it?"

"Detective Wyld, it was only a draft and not recognized by law. Merely a draft. Not official.

"Yeah. Got that. What does it say?"

Squinty Saunders settled back and tented his fingers. "I can't let you read it, officially, but in the interest of furthering your investigation into the death of Mr. Marston..."

"Yeah, yeah. What does it say? Who is to get the dough?"

Squinty smiled, at least Stan thought so.

"Wait. Please don't say Ilsa Pokovich."

It was Squinty's turn to be surprised. His catbird smile disappeared as he studied Stan.

"How...?" stuttered Squinty.

"Stan shook his head. "I'm psychic. How much?"

Squinty shuffled some papers, settled on two buff-colored sheets.

"Ilsa Pokovich was destined to inherit approximately two-thirds of Mr. Marston's estate, the remainder to be divided up between the non-profits you see listed there in the official will."

"Ilsa Pokovich? Two-thirds?"

"Yes, she-"

Stan interrupted. "She's a felon. She just got furloughed from Women's Correctional."

Squinty Saunders smiled at the detective's joke. "Sure. A felon."

Stan sniffed. "Squinty this is for real." He didn't bother mentioning that her fingerprints were in the death car and she was rapidly shooting to the top spot of the I-Beheaded-James-Marston club.

Saunders squinted tighter, his eyes disappearing.

"What are you telling me? She's a crook?"

Stan shrugged. "She was in for assault, we know that. Just not the details yet. We're checking."

Squinty's hands moved automatically to the Marston file spread out before him. "I..."

"Jesus," exclaimed Stan. "How can he leave...how much are we talking about?"

Squinty looked to the ceiling and appeared to be deep in thought, trying to figure all the sums in his head. But, Stan knew the squat little guy knew almost to the penny what Marston was worth.

"Estate's in the neighborhood of forty-two million, six hundred and twelve thousand dollars, depending on the final value of the properties. The house here in Sacramento and London and Florida."

Stan did the math.

"So two-thirds is somewhere north of twenty-eight million."

"In the neighborhood," confirmed Squinty.

"So, he was gonna do this because he knew her how?"

Squinty pulled himself up to the desk and attempted to regain some dignity. He intertwined as best he could his fat little fingers.

"I have no idea. I didn't ask. Wasn't my place. And besides detective, it was a draft. Nothing came of it. Nor will anything come of it. It's moot. Moot."

Stan got up and wandered to the window. He couldn't make out where he was in this mess. He hoped that Jake was making progress and that he'd found a neighbor that miraculously remembered a lady pounding on their door at some ungodly hour, pleading that she'd broken down and explaining why there were two people chopped up in her car.

Or, maybe Mallory right now had Ilsa Pokovich pinned to the sidewalk and was calling for backup.

Or why some film producer was planning on leaving lottery-like money to a felon?

Now it didn't matter because the draft will was purely that, a draft. All of Marston's dough still goes to all the charities. But, what did the woman have to do with anything?

"Detective?"

Stan turned. "What?"

Squinty cleared his throat. "I have some other appointments."

"Yeah, right. By the way, we're going through Marston's house tomorrow or the day after, whenever I can round up a good crew, and I need access."

Squinty looked up. His eyes opened as wide as they could. "I represent Marston, you know."

"Your client is in the morgue," Stan said. "Pretty much anyway." Stan smiled to himself.

"I still represent the estate," said Squinty, sitting taller.

"Great. I need you to join us. With the code or keys so we won't have to beat that pretty front door to a pulp."

Squinty Saunders sighed and pulled his calendar toward him. "Fine. But I don't want any property damaged. Here." He stood up and held out the will.

"Here's a copy of the Mr. James Marston Junior's will for you. I will file it for probate shortly."

Stan took the folded up legal sheets and stuffed them in his jacket. He stopped at the doorway.

"There's no way Ilsa Pokovich will receive a dime from Marston is there?"

Squinty shook his head.

"There is no way."

Stan stood on the street in front of Squinty's building. He rubbed his stomach, trying to soothe the acidic burble. He needed bicarbonate of something that made sense. Something wasn't right. He could feel it. Sometimes the bad juju just rolls out of control. And you can feel it before it hits you full on.

If you're lucky.

CHAPTER 21

Mallory could feel Murphy's eyes sizing her up. The moment she pushed through the double set of doors to Murphy's Guns and Ammo, he'd been all over her, butter to his toast. Started and ended with her chest, as usual.

Overt roaming eye evaluations had been flattering for her first eighteen years. Since then, annoying. Now with her scar, she'd just as soon keep the focus elsewhere.

There was no formal greeting. She could see he was military all the way. Crew cut, weathered, sinewy, and short on words and with hooded, almost shy eyes that missed little. She knew the demeanor, the attitude, and it no longer intimidated her. She liked it, in fact. It was simple when you knew what you were dealing with.

He raised his chin. "You're the one Susan sent over, eh?"

Mallory held out her hand. "Mallory. Dimante. OID division of SacPD," she added for some gravitas. "Is she here?"

"When isn't she?"

Murphy took her hand and gripped it with both of his.

She gave him her best chicken choker grip. She watched as he assessed her forearm sinews and biceps.

"I pass?" snipped Mallory. She let her hands fall, wondering what he was evaluating.

"You'll do," he stated without enthusiasm. "Little wick of a thing, aren't you? What are you?" he asked. "5'3"? 5'4"?"

"Nearly 5'5."

"Hey, there you are," Susan said, breezing in from the back room. "Don't let him start his cross-examination. You'll know it when he checks your grip and asks for your vitals."

Mallory rubbed her arm and hoped no one noticed. "I believe we're past that."

Susan slapped her father on the arm.

"Cut it out. She's a friend, not a recruit. I told you she's SacPD, in OID."

"Where do we start?" Mallory asked as she made a hurried inspection of the place.

Under the Scarlet and Gold Marine banner, two walls were covered with caged-in handguns and rifles. Another caged and locked case held boxes of ammunition. On the far wall were peg-boarded displays of accessories, mostly protection gear, Kevlar vests, sights and scopes, and a colorful arrangement of tactical eyewear. A table next to the counter featured a layout of written material. Everything was neat and in military order.

Sort of like Murphy himself.

Susan had not exactly warned her but had felt it necessary to describe Murphy and his history to Mallory before she arrived.

Marine Corps, then cop with LAPD. Moved to Sacramento after being wounded. A dealer's so-called assault weapon in a drug raid had made mincemeat of one of his feet.

Now limped, but still walked.

That was Murphy, said Susan. Grinding bone on bone tough.

Murphy's was the unspoken supplier for many of SacPD's employees. No yellow page ads, no internet website, couldn't find him on Google, but he was known.

You wouldn't find his place unless you knew where it was, or if someone had already taken you there, or if a friend had scrawled it on the back of a Rhinos cocktail napkin. There was no address on the building, except for the standard small blue number address sign, required by the Fire Marshall.

A set of double security doors trapped you until you were eyed by Murphy on the security camera and buzzed in through the inner doors.

Murphy's. You had to fight your way in.

"C'mon. Let's see if you know anything." He turned and led her through two swinging bar doors to a workroom. A man in a leather apron with a lighted loupe headband sat hunched over one end of the workbench carefully filing what looked like a firing pin.

Murphy preceded Mallory to the far end where he had an assortment of handguns laid out, both pistols and revolvers, in a variety of calibers and sizes.

"I brought my own." Mallory reached into her purse and pulled out her father's Glock.

With a practiced hand, she slid back the slide to confirm the chamber was clear, then released the slide and set it on the counter.

The young man with the loupe stopped what he was doing and gave a sideways glance. It was as much praise as she was bound to get.

Murphy remained unmoved. "Now, can you take it apart?"

She pointed the unloaded Glock in a safe direction and pulled the trigger then, using both hands, she undid the slide lock, removed the slide, and set the grip on the counter next to the magazine.

Cradling the slide, she expertly popped out the recoil spring, set it next to the body. Without pause, she turned the slide over and removed the barrel, and set them both on the counter. When she was done, she felt like OCD Stan as she arranged all the pieces, evenly spaced out on the bench.

"This was my father's favorite," she said, standing back to admire her work.

"Cop?" asked Murphy, eyebrows raising an inch.

"Accountant," shrugged Mallory. "But, he liked to be prepared."

"Huh."

Mallory sighed. "Look Murphy...can I call you Murphy?"

Loupe laughed but a sharp squint from Murphy cut him off.

"Look, Murphy, I was a teenager when I cleaned my father's guns. He showed me how to do it and I thought it was cool. I liked to do stuff for him. But, he never took me shooting, okay. I've never shot a thing."

Murphy's unflinching expression gave nothing away. Likely he had not seen such a creature who knew the innards but who had never felt the recoil or even aimed a firearm. Usually the other way round. Too many shooters must be trained in how to break down and maintain a firearm.

Loupe put down his file. He couldn't help himself. "You never shot a thing?" he asked. "No squirrels? No targets?"

Mallory ignored him. "Look, Susan said you were the best at training shooters. So, what the hell, here I am."

Mallory checked her watch and fidgeted.

"Nervous?"

"No. Just want to get on with it."

"Why?"

Mallory looked out at the range then back to Murphy.

"I think someones… Look, I want to be prepared. I want a good defense."

"You do, huh?"

"Yeah." Mallory returned his steady gaze.

Murphy re-assembled the weapon without looking. He paused for a moment, then handed the Glock back to Mallory. His face was impassive but his eyes crinkled at the corners.

"Well, then," he said. "We better get started."

"Thank you," exhaled Mallory.

Loupe shook his head and resumed his work. "Good luucck.," he drawled under his breath.

Mallory tensed as Murphy put both hands on her shoulders and turned her around. Then back around.

"You righty-righty?"

"Right-handed," replied Mallory.

"What about the dominant eye? Right or left?" asked Murphy patiently

"They're both pretty good."

Murphy shook his head. He made her form a triangle with her hands at arm's length.

"Look up at the clock. Both eyes open."

Mallory sighted on the face of the cat clock with eyes that moved back and forth in opposition to the tail.

"Close your left eye."

She did.

"What happened?"

"Clock's gone."

"Right hand, right eye then. And what the hell is OID?"

"On-Going cases. Cold cases."

Murphy pulled open the back door, grabbing a box of ammo on the way out.

"Cold cases. Then, you're not usually in many shootouts per day are you?"

"Depends on my mood."

Murphy's range was open-air with a partitioned covered area for the shooters. He handed Mallory goggles and a special set of ear protectors. She slipped both on.

Murphy donned a small headset with a microphone.

"What's that for?" asked Mallory speaking too loud.

Murphy keyed his mike. "So you can hear me?"

His voice came through with a clarity she didn't expect.

"Where's my mike? I can't talk to you without shouting."

"Then don't."

"Not loaded," shouted Mallory.

"You're not ready."

Murphy spent the next few minutes reviewing safety rules, ticking them off on gnarled fingers.

"One, assume all guns are loaded. Two, never point a gun at anything you aren't willing to destroy. Three, keep your finger off the trigger until your sights are on the target. Four, know your target and what's beyond it."

Mallory nodded. "'Course."

"So, before you shoot add another step. Be sure. Before you squeeze, be sure."

Mallory nodded again, but Murphy held up a finger to get her attention.

"Be sure. Only one chance."

"Message received," Mallory said. "Got it."

Murphy sent out a target.

"Okay, Annie Oakley. Load 'em up and I'll show you how to shoot the shit out of whomever you think is hassling you…" He checked his watch. "In about 50 minutes."

Murphy smiled for the first time.

Susan, who had joined them, gave her a thumbs up.

After nearly an hour of having something hard recoil in her hands, Mallory realized how she had muscles she never dreamed existed and how they hurt like fuck.

Moreover, she understood the power she possessed. The way it expressed her will with a slight squeeze and an explosion of determination. The way she felt it throughout her body.

She understood a lot now.

CHAPTER 22

Mallory set the gun on her entry table and double locked her door. This was gun number one in her life. She couldn't imagine getting another. She wasn't into collecting and had no love for the damn thing.

She wouldn't be going hunting. She had no desire to kill and eat her prey.

It was enough to know how to use her tools. And that's the Glock, another tool. Know how to change a tire. Know how to shoot a gun.

She didn't want to spend any more time at the range than she already had, but Murphy had told her in classic Murphy-speak that it wasn't enough to just know how to shoot the 'fucking weapon, but you gotta be good at it and that means fucking practice'.

He had actually grinned when he told her she'd be back.

Meh. Probably right but all she could think about now was hoping she had the energy to turn the shower handles and wash the lead dust from every part of her body.

Mallory stripped off her clothes, dropped them on the floor. Then, pretending her mother was standing in the doorway, picked them up with what momentum she had left, folded what was clean, and tossed the rest into the hamper.

She let the water from the shower pound into her shoulders for ten minutes, advancing the temperature a notch at a time. Her head rested against the tile as she used a rough washcloth to scrub her hands and arms clean of any memory of even holding a gun.

Smelling remarkably like lavender overlaid with a touch of gun range, she pulled on her faded UCLA tee shirt, turned off the light, and slid under the sheets, relishing the feeling of clean sheets.

Mentally exhausted but unable to fall asleep after ten minutes, she realized she'd been staring up at the crisscrossing lines in the wallpaper on her walls. Wallpaper that had been there since the Revolutionary War, she guessed, judging by its ability to yellow and curl. Wallpaper she'd been too busy, really lazy, to change out. The thought of scraping that shit off and the ugly layers below that represented a mountain she was sure she'd never climb. And even then, if she actually went through with it, she'd only have a bare wall and she'd have to do something creative with it. That made her head hurt. She barely had the drive left at the end of the day to get excited about creating something new and wonderful on her walls.

Paint it out.

Sure. But what color?

And all those lines.

Screw that thought. Ain't painting. Ain't peeling. The lines stay. They give the room an antique look, which she surmised, was as good a look as any she could envision.

She propped herself up with a few pillows. The lines had reminded her of roads. And roads reminded her of a map. And what was bothering her.

She opened her laptop and pulled up the map program.

She zeroed in on Jones Road and located the sharp curve where Officer Jason Grey had found the abandoned BMW. She tapped the screen with the eraser end of her pencil.

Yeah. Right there. So what?

She pulled her legal pad in front of her and started to make notes. A throwback to her days at UCLA. Write it down. See it in front of you. Order your thoughts.

Something the three of them hadn't done. So much had been happening in so short a time, details had floated away in the mist.

The lines on her wall. Roadmap.

The car.

The car was marked with an 'X'. And 'X' denoted stuck, busted, not moving, but that was wrong. It should've been marked with an arrow showing what direction it was going. On Jones Road.

Now that Danni determined it hadn't ruptured a camshaft or threw a rod, whatever those were, they knew it wasn't a random abandonment. The car was headed either to the mansion or away from it. This wasn't a case where somebody had a hankering for chocolate ice cream at 3 A.M. and their precious BMW broke down. Or the baby's colic was acting up and someone had to make a run to the all-nighter pharmacy and their BMW ran out of gas. This motor vehicle was dropped deliberately.

At that time.

At that spot.

She moved the mouse, erased the 'X', and inserted a red arrow that pointed both ways where she surmised the car was found, based on what Officer Grey had noted.

She constructed the timeline.

'??? Car breaks down.'

She crossed out Breakdown.

'??? Car Stopped.'

Okay, when was that? Before 4:18 A.M. when Dispatch gets a call.

She tapped her pencil against a tooth. She did it all the time according to Stan. It drove him crazy.

Tap, tap, tap.

"Dispatch gets a call," she repeated.

"Or did it...?"

She fell asleep before she understood what it all meant. That would come later.

PART TWO

CHAPTER 23

Dr. Patrick Avery's stockinged feet were the first thing fourteen-year-old Michael Cooper saw when he pushed open the door to the psychologist's office. They were atop Avery's desk, knocking back and forth in beat with some unheard rhythm. White cotton, running socks. One had a hole.

"Your feet. You airing them out?

"And, it's good to see you too, Michael."

"Too many upset patients threatening you about all the dough you're charging them making you nervous? Feet sweat?"

Avery took his feet off the desk, pulled himself up to the desk, and settled into a more formal pose.

"Have a seat."

Michael plopped down at the front edge of the red leather chair in front of Avery's desk. He didn't settle back but fidgeted. He tapped his fingers on the armrest. He examined the room, noting the quiet.

"So, how's Michael?"

"First rate. Never better. A-1." Michael studied his reflection in Avery's picture of his kids. "Just can't lick this not sleeping thing."

Avery was silent for a moment.

"You've been through an ordeal."

"I guess."

"Even though the newspapers didn't name you two, I knew who it was, especially when they mentioned your trailer park. The whole thing's hard to believe."

"You're so gullible, Doc. You can't really believe everything in the papers. Or maybe you do. Maybe everybody does. Like the internet. It's always true. Every word."

Michael yanked Avery's desk phone handset.

"Dr. Avery's office," Michael said into the dead mouthpiece. "Michael Cooper, killer-for-hire speaking." He pretended to listen to a phantom on the other end.

"No. No. I wouldn't do that," he continued. "Speaking from personal experience, I've found that the best way to stop a sick fuck from killing your sister is to first slice his neck open with a shovel blade. Now, while you may think this will disable him, all it will really do is piss him off. So, then, when he comes at you with what looks like a Samurai sword, what you need to do is to break the shovel handle in two and simply let him fall onto it. Easy. That's how you deal with an asshole who previously just hung you from a flowering chestnut tree."

He listened, concerned. "What?"

"No the watery sound you'll hear is not from the piss running down your leg because you're scared shitless, it will be the gurgling of the blood trying to escape from the massive wound you've created in said asshole's chest cavity. It is a strange sound, but you'll get used to it."

Michael looked Avery in the eye, keeping the phone to his ear. "I did."

Michael replaced the phone, then brought it back.

"Oh. And for that useless psychoanalysis that will be $4,000, please. Otherwise, my feet start to sweat."

Michael shrugged, got up, and stepped to the window overlooking South Point Park. He fiddled with the window latch.

"I told you, don't believe everything you read. Of course, then again, maybe it happened just the way they said. Doesn't matter."

"How's your sister?"

"Lucky."

Avery was quiet, studying Michael. "Lucky you were there, you mean."

Michael spoke to his reflection. "No. Lucky the asshole drugged her. She hardly remembers anything. Like a dream she says. What she remembers is not really real, I think. It's crazy, but she still thinks of the old bitch as a nice old lady who was taking care of her. Seems she doesn't remember anything bad."

Avery nodded. "Your sister was being groomed."

Groomed. Michael had heard the word. He remembered Jessie's picture in one of Everheart's identical black picture frames. Jessie was smiling. Jessie was also sitting on Everheart's lap. Michael shuddered.

"Still, it was fortunate you had the presence of mind to do what you needed to do."

Michael's own reflection in the window was replaced by Ruby Everheart's contorted, painted face. He could see the hate. Feel it, even now. He closed his eyes.

"Whatever."

"I called your aunt when I heard. She never got back to me." Avery continued in a softer tone. "And I never heard from you."

Michael opened his eyes. The vision of Ruby Everheart was gone. Nevermore. Just like dear old Dad. Maybe they've teamed up in hell. Probably.

"Yeah, well. She's been...busy."

"I thought maybe if I saw you both, you and Jess, it might help. Thought you might want to talk."

Michael scoffed. "Sorry, doc. No more court-mandated psycho visits for me anymore, or Jess. Aunt Jane says she's out of dough. Now no healthcare either. Seems Aunt Jane, good old AJ, had a bit of a tizzy at her work the other day over all this. They suggested she no longer work there."

"They fired her?"

Michael nodded. "Out on her ass."

"Sorry to hear that. How can I help?"

Michael turned to Avery. He realized no one had asked him that directly how they could help. Everyone was always dancing around the question. The 'incident' shouldn't ever be mentioned.

Michael swallowed twice, still finding it tough to speak. His eyes filled.

"Help? You want to help?"

Avery got up and shoved his feet in his moccasins and slipped his sports jacket on. "C'mon. Let's get some air."

Michael wiped his face and made himself presentable.

"Yeah. Okay."

Neither spoke. As if by silent agreement, they headed across the street to the park. Their old bench was empty.

"What's Jessie doing today?" asked Avery, as they shooed the two pigeons off and took possession of the bench. "She with your Aunt Jane?"

"Babysitting."

"She's only six, isn't she? A might young."

"She's running herd on good old AJ. They went grocery shopping."

"Keeping your aunt company then."

Michael turned to Avery. "No. She's babysitting Aunt Jane. Really. The old bat's teetering. Jess is the one who should be wandering around in the middle of the night unable to sleep. Instead, it's AJ. Found her the other morning plunked on the couch turning the TV on and off. I don't know how long she'd been at it. When she saw me, she started to apologize again. Over and over. Sorry, sorry, sorry. Shouldn't have put you with that devil. Same old. She'd been bawlin' her eyes out, I could tell. It's pretty depressing."

"You think she needs help?"

Michael picked at a piece of the bench. "You're the doc. But she seems to be able to function. She only needs a weeklong coma to get over it all."

Michael went quiet and used his fingernail to pick at part of the wood bench.

"So," Avery started quietly. "Tell me about it."

Michael shrugged, picked some more. "You know. It was your standard psycho taking it out on a little kid. It was as you said, she was being groomed. She fooled Jess."

Michael breathed a big sigh.

"Shit thing is… she or he or it... fucked me over too. I thought she was just an old lady. Okay, weird, kinda dodgy, but… I never figured that shit out. Not till I saw her dragging Jess."

Michael tried to smile.

"And *it* wasn't even a woman! Jesus, I was stupid, so fucking stupid. I left my sister alone with her…it. I… I don't know what I thought."

Avery touched Michael's arm.

"You saved your sister. You saved yourself."

Michael looked at Avery. He couldn't help the tears that ran down his face.

"You did good Michael."

Michael allowed himself to be pulled into Avery's side. He tried to stop the sobs that heaved through him but no one had asked him before how they could help. How it had been. Now he was blubbering into the only one that seemed to give a shit.

Avery let him go on.

Only when the struggling sounds of roller skates came their way did Michael look up. Two pretty girls on skates swooped precariously by. Both Avery and Michael watched them until their short shorts were no longer discernible.

"So, how are you physically? How was the hospital?"

Michael wiped the snot off his face. "Yeah, that was a trip. My arm was kinda bunged up. They had to fix that a bit. It was Jess. First, they had to like transfuse her to get all the shit she put in her. I kept checking on her. They kept me right next to her. We had connecting rooms. So, it was kinda funny…but really good she doesn't remember much."

"What did you tell her," asked Avery.

"I said to myself, 'what would good ol' doc Avery do'. What would he tell her?"

"And?"

"I told her the truth. Pretty much. I said the nice old lady who had been babysitting us went wacko and tried to hurt us."

"What did she say?"

"She said, 'like in the movies when someone turns bad?'"

"Yeah, I said. Like we're in a goddamn movie and now it's over and we're okay and the bad lady isn't around. She asked me if she was dead. I told her yes, she was dead."

Michael settled back against the bench. "All she said then was, 'Huh.' That was that."

"What about your plans to move? Arizona?"

Michael brightened for the first time. He sat up and smiled. "Yep. Why I wandered down here to your part of town. Just came to say adios, doc. We go pronto. This bullshit state threw a lot of bullshit paperwork we had to fill out. I had to help AJ through it. CPS lady kinda came through. They're supposed to be super inefficient but, I don't know, she sorta got it done. Against her better judgment though, she said. So we're off to see the wizard – my mother's cousin, a Shippen Travers. Kind of a goofy name, but he sounded cool on the phone."

"How do you feel about leaving your aunt right now?"

Michael looked away. "How do I feel? Pretty fuckin' good, tell you the truth. You know, time to reap. Time to sow. Time to go. Besides, my aunt will probably be much better without us."

"Even so, maybe there would be a better time- "

Michael stopped him. "My mother used to say, nothing is ever perfect. She always said it. Like a friggin' mantra. I kinda know now what she means, though. Means I can't wait until everything is better. Until AJ is up and running on all cylinders. Until the bad dreams stop. Until the birds chirp and the squirrels are laughing."

He shielded his face from the sun and smiled at Avery.

"Can't wait doc. Gotta go."

"How's Jessie with all of this?"

"The move?"

Avery nodded.

"She's great. Really. We both are." Michael scanned the park, the fountain, office workers eating lunch, kids playing. He studied the scene as if he'd never see any of this again.

"We just need a quiet place," he continued. "A new place. Start over, you know. Yeah, I'm pretty sure she's right on target with this."

"You want me to talk with her before you go?"

Michael scoffed. "No offense doc, but I'm not sure you'd do any good. You're a nice guy and all, not a pervert or a child rapist, but as far as a psycho doc who can solve other people's problems, I don't know. All you and I did is talk, talk, talk and I'm the same after it all. I think we'll both be fine as soon as- "

Michael's phone rang. He checked the I.D. and answered it.

"Hey, what's up?"

Michael turned away, listening, not smiling.

"I'll come get you, okay? Where?"

Avery could hear sobs come through the phone, even from where he sat.

"Jess," Michael shouted. "Where are you?"

"M! WE'RE ARRESTED! WE'RE IN GROCERY STORE JAIL!"

CHAPTER 24

Michael had the passenger door open before Avery came to a stop. He hung onto the door until Avery slowed enough for him to land on the parking lot asphalt.

"Michael! Wait!"

Michael dashed between the Rancho Cordova and Sacramento County squad cars parked at the entrance to Safeway. They were empty, motors off and no flashing bar lights.

"Maybe it's okay. Maybe it's all right, then," panted Michael as the automatic doors slid open. "At least there's no ambulance."

But in the door's glass reflection he saw an ambulance arriving, pulling up behind the two squads.

"Great. Just great."

Past the deli, he saw the sign for Customer Service and headed that way but stopped when he realized all he had to do was to follow the two paramedics who breezed past him.

The two tall, white-shirted guys with murmuring walkie-talkies headed for the back of the store as if they dealt with people in grocery store jail daily and knew where to go.

He quickened his pace and fell in behind them. When they pushed open the double doors that led to the warehouse portion of the building, Michael was right behind.

One of the paramedics glanced back at Michael but Michael looked so purposeful in his walk, nothing was said.

The two medics motored on toward a back office, but Michael pulled up short, his attention grabbed by what he saw on a monitor being watched by the two cops in an adjacent office.

It was security footage of the store's produce section. The round display in the center of the monitor featured tomatoes. The sign on one side said 'Organic', the other side 'Roma'. That's where Aunt Jane was.

"There sound on this?" asked one of the cops to the harried guy next to them who appeared to be the manager. He shook his head.

But really there was no need for sound, Michael saw because the action was riveting.

First, it was simply Aunt Jane standing at the tomato display. Michael saw Jessie, holding two apples, approach her aunt and appear to ask her a question. Aunt Jane ignored her and stared at the tomatoes. The Romas. Michael could see Jessie look from her aunt to the tomatoes, then around the rest of the store.

Aunt Jane was still as stone. Then she leaned in.

Time seemed suspended, almost frozen.

Michael saw Jessie tense.

Without warning, Aunt Jane threw her head back, stuck her arm out, and with accusing forefinger appeared to be lecturing the vegetable. Getting no response, her body spasmed, her hands clenched, and came down full on the poor Romas. With machine-gun precision, crazy Aunt Jane yanked every tomato off the Roma side onto the Produce floor and stomped on them. Squished tomato guts and seeds sprayed everywhere.

Jessie tried to grab Aunt Jane's arms. Hardly breaking rhythm, Aunt Jane swept her aside, sending Jessie backwards where she slammed up against the fresh corn display sending ears of yellow corn cascading down.

And the howling continued. And the stomping and squishing. Juice and seeds and pulp everywhere, staining the floor, the display, Aunt Jane's legs, covering her shoes.

As if in slow motion, a hapless produce man in a white apron appeared in view and like Jessie had done, tried to secure Aunt Jane's arms. Without even turning, she rotated a fist backwards and hit the guy square on the nose.

Michael couldn't help it. He laughed because it looked so robotic and cartoonish.

The cops too.

"Well, she got him there I guess," exclaimed the County cop.

"Guess that's it," said the other one.

"I'm pressing charges, officer," erupted the manager. "I want her out of here. In jail. Never to come back."

"Yeah, well…" drawled the County dude.

"She's crazy and I won't have my customers scared out of their wits, possibly assaulted, nor any of my employees roughed up by her. You get her the hell outta here."

With that, he left the two cops and headed back out to the store.

The County guy turned to Rancho Cordova. "I got this."

"All yours. Just passing by anyway," the other said.

They both turned to go. Michael stood in their way.

"Hey! Kid! What do you want?"

"Where you taking her?"

Both cops assumed an armored stance, exchanged glances, creaking leather, and narrowed eyes.

"Who are you?" demanded County.

"She's my aunt. Where are you taking her?"

"You shouldn't be back here," stated County. "We'll let you know."

"Piss off, asshole. Just tell me."

"Hey!" spit County, rising an inch. "No lip kid, hear me?"

"Yeah? Well, fuck you if you don't have the smarts to answer a simple question."

Rancho held out a restraining arm against an increasingly agitated County.

"Your aunt's sick, son," said Rancho in a suppressing tone. "We'll have the medics look at her and she'll be escorted down to Sacramento General for observation." He looked up, searching the back of the store for another adult. Not finding one, he turned back to Michael.

"Are you here with her?"

"No."

"Where do you live?" interrupted County.

"Why? You want to see my papers, Gestapo?" It was something he read about in school. Innocent people being stopped in World War 2 all the time and being asked for their 'papers', having to prove their existence, their innocence. It was also a recent attitude with all cops it seemed.

"How did you get here then?" sighed Rancho, ignoring the rest.

"He's with me," said Avery as he pushed through the double doors. "He's with me. We came as soon as we got the call."

"You are?"

"Dr. Patrick Avery. I'm a psychologist."

Both cops studied Avery - moccasins, shirttail out, hair mussed.

"I'm with the family."

County looked from Avery to Michael. "I can see why." He backhanded Rancho on the shoulder. "I'm gone. Have fun."

He pushed between Avery and Michael, making them both step back.

"Asshole," muttered Michael.

"How is she?" asked Avery.

Michael didn't wait for a response but set off following the paramedics' trail to see for himself.

"What's with the kid?" asked the cop.

The only words Michael heard of Avery's reply, "He's been through a lot…"

Yeah, thought Michael, a lot of asshole cops.

Michael found the two medics in the manager's office kneeling down in front of his aunt, their kits opened on the floor next to them. They had placed a blood pressure cuff on her arm and were speaking quietly to her.

She sat slumped like a rag doll plunked onto the hardback chair against the wall. She was pale and didn't seem to want to stop shaking her head. It was obvious she wouldn't or couldn't answer any of their questions.

Jessie was sitting in the office chair behind the manager's desk. She looked paler than his aunt. She still held an apple in her hand.

Michael hustled to her and Jessie leaned into him and with profound seriousness whispered, "She went crazy M! You should've seen her."

"Yeah, I caught the show. You okay?"

Jessie rattled on, needing to tell the story. "It was all at once. We were standing getting some fruit and stuff and she started this like wolf howl. I thought she was hurt or something, you know. Then she started yelling at the tomatoes, M. The tomatoes! She pulled them all onto the floor, was calling them names and, and,

and trying to squash them." She paused, looked at Michael, seeing him and understanding he was right there in front of her.

"What's going to happen? Are we arrested?"

"What? No." He glanced over at his aunt. "They're taking her downtown. Check her out. Probably give her some drugs to calm her down. She'll be fine."

Jessie looked at her brother as if *he* was crazy. "No way. M, she freaked!"

"It'll be fine. Trust me."

Just then the manager appeared at his office door. He addressed the two paramedics.

"She has to pay for what she did. You have to make her understand she has to pay for all that produce she destroyed and the time it's taken my guys to clean up the mess. She has to pay."

When the paramedics ignored him, he confronted Michael and Jessie.

"You were with her," accused the manager, pointing at Jessie. "You helped her wreck my tomatoes. You'll have to pay for what you did!"

Michael got between him and Jessie. He held his cell phone up to the man's nametag.

"What are you doing?" blustered the man, stepping back.

"I'm recording you falsely accusing a seven-year-old girl of store destruction. And I've got your name now and when we leave, I'll get a good clear picture of the storefront and I'll have it all online in a few minutes. Good publicity."

"Give me that!" The manager reached for the phone.

Michael jumped back and smiled. "And now I just got that too."

"Why you- "

Avery grabbed the manager from behind and spun him around. The paramedics turned from their work to watch the action.

Avery reached into his pocket, brought out his wallet, and stuffed a hundred-dollar bill in the man's apron.

"Here you go…" He glanced at the man's name tag. "George." To Michael and Jessie. "Let's go, kids. We're leaving."

Jessie didn't move. "Are you arresting us?"

Michael pulled her up out of the chair. "Naw. He's okay. He's the doc."

They started to leave the office when the manager spoke up.

"The apple." He indicated the apple Jessie still held. "$1.49. A pound."

All three turned. Michael held up the phone, aimed it at the manager.

After an awkward silence, the manager managed a grimace.

"She can have it."

They pulled up in front of Aunt Jane's trailer.

"I'm worried about you guys," Avery said. "Who's going to look after you?"

Michael and Jessie piled out of Avery's Volvo.

"Aww. We're fine. We've got a nosy Chinese lady next door who likes to mother us."

Jessie's eyes widened.

"Well, I'd like to stay, make sure you're okay, but if you're sure. Maybe I should check with your neighbor…"

Michael shrugged. "Not really necessary. She's watching us right now. Wave to that trailer right there."

Michael pointed to the next trailer over. Lights were on and someone could be seen in the window.

Avery waved.

"Besides," added Michael. "It's only for a few days. We're leaving."

"Still? With your aunt in the hospital? Is that wise?"

"We can't do anything for her. She's probably better off without the hassle of us being around anyway. The place'll be okay," said Michael nodding toward their trailer.

Avery handed Michael a piece of paper and a business card. "The medics gave me the number for you to call to check on your aunt and here's another of my cards." Avery held up his extended pinky and his thumb to his ear, like a phone, and mouthed 'Call me.

Michael rolled his eye but took them and started Jessie down the walk. He turned back to Avery.

"Hey look, thanks for what you did. You know. Sticking up for us. Getting me there and everything."

"Of course. Look, here's some money. You know, in case." He held out what looked like to Michael a few $20 bills.

Michael hesitated for a second. "Naw. That's okay. We're good. We're ready to go."

"Sure?"

"Positive."

"One more thing, Michael. You know what PTSD is, right. I want you to see someone when you get to Arizona, okay?"

Michael laughed. "You are one big box of goofy doc if you think I'm goofy. I'm fine. We're fine."

When Avery didn't return the smile, Michael relented.

"Fine. I'll look someone up who's as crazy as you are."

Avery seemed at a loss for words and uncertain about leaving.

"You go," Michael urged. "We're good."

Avery smiled. "Proud of you Michael."

Michael bit back adolescent smartass. Instead said, "Thanks doc. Maybe see you in Arizona."

With nothing more said, Avery turned the Volvo around and waved as he drove off.

Jessie confronted her brother. "That's not the Chinese lady's house, M."

"So?"

"And she doesn't even like us. She's not going to look after us like you said."

"No. I will."

"M! What about money?"

Michael took the paper Avery had given him, balled it up, and stuck it in the dirt of the planter by the front door. He took out his key and unlocked the front door.

CHAPTER 25

Michael Cooper lifted the two white silk blouses from the dresser and tossed them in his aunt's suitcase. He wasn't used to packing for someone else and really, he wasn't used to packing at all. For anybody. Yet, here he was.

He checked out the window. Just beginning to get light. They still had a few hours to get all the important stuff packed. Including themselves.

He hadn't slept well. All night he'd imagined footsteps outside the trailer. One time he thought he smelled smoke but convinced himself it was leftover bad memory juju from when Everheart's trailer had gone furnace.

"Hand me some shoes," he said, pointing to the six or seven pairs of shoes that rested atop each other in the bottom of the tight closet. "Not the high heels. Tennies'll do fine. I don't think she's going on any formal dates in the nuthouse."

"You said nuthouse."

Michael wedged the shoes on either side of the suitcase. He paused to glance at the walls of his aunt's bedroom. Every inch of the room, walls, and ceiling was covered with newspapers, all detailing the events of the Olive Park murders.

Like Dr. Lecter was her exclusive interior designer, everywhere you looked, headlines shouted 'Transvestite Child Murderer…Children Buried Alive…Gruesome Find in The Woods…California's Worst Child Killer' and more and more, all glued over each other. A pastiche of slaughter, a visual shitstorm of death. And the pictures. Even worse were the pictures. Good old Aunt Jane had painstakingly excised with a razor blade newspaper photos of Ruby's trailer, Ruby, both male and female from the old days, the detectives, the six holes in the woods, the forensic team, and hundreds more. A glued up mishmash of a massacre.

Michael took a sweater from his sister, jammed it in the suitcase.

"She just had it," he said. "I think we did it to her. She didn't go crazy, just got stressed. With all that happened..." He shrugged. "She felt guilty."

"No, M. She went crazy!" Jessie emphasized each word.

He was always surprised at his sister's intensity. For a little kid, she'd seen way too much. Too much of the warped side of life. Her life balance was undoubtedly skewed. Her memory of recent events was like Swiss cheese. Every day, since what happened, he felt like a parent with the responsibility to get her re-established on an even keel, as his mother liked to say.

'Balance in life, like in a boat, depends on an even keel.' She'd smile. 'An even keel.'

He pretended to straighten up the layers of clothes in the suitcase but really, staring into the suitcase, all he could see, all he could remember was flashes of the last few weeks. Still, it was getting easier now, to block out all the shit that had rained down.

He shook his head, clearing the dark stuff.

"Okay!" He closed and latched the suitcase.

"Now, let's get us squared away."

"Do you think she wants her pillow?"

Jessie was staring at a lacy chintz thing on her bed. It was embroidered with his aunt's initials, JM.

Michael turned his sister around and pushed her toward the living room. "Naw. They have pillows in the nuthouse, right?"

"M, you said nuthouse."

"Yeah, well. C'mon."

He guided her from the small bedroom that occupied one end of the trailer, down the narrow hallway, to the mobile home's 'living room' that served as their bedroom ever since their aunt took them in. The pullout couch was now piled with everything they owned. It was a small pile.

Jessie held up a shirt. It had long sleeves and was 60's tie-dyed. She'd done the tie-dyeing herself, with help from Michael. The '60s were her current favorite decade. She loved it. Started listening to Herman's Hermits and the Turtles, and recently, much to Michael's relief had glommed onto the Beatles. Yesterday, she'd asked him about 'free love.'

"It's sex you don't have to pay for I guess," Michael had ventured. "Hence. Free love."

Jessie had considered this. Finally accepting. "I guess it's okay. For old people anyway. Think I'll skip sex altogether."

Jessie turned the shirt around. "How hot is it in Arizona?"

"Hot. Mostly. Like the desert, I think. You need water all the time."

"I won't need this probably, but I think I'll take it anyway."

"Look. Take everything. You never know what the ranch is like. I mean, this Shippen Travers sounds okay and his kid sounded cool. But, maybe they'll make us sleep in the barn or something."

"With the pigs?"

"I don't think they have pigs. Only cattle."

"Cows?"

"No. Not milk cows. Cattle. Like for hamburgers and steaks."

Michael opened up the two other suitcases he had dragged from the garage. They were his aunt's which is why they were matching pink and white with yellow flowers formed in decorative masking tape on the side.

"We're packing in those?" Jessie made her scrunched up face.

"Like what else do we have? She never drove us back to the house to get our stuff. Everything of ours is probably hauled to Goodwill or the Shriners or something by now. I didn't have time to find any suitcases when we left. So, we'll use hers. She's not going to need 'em."

Jessie looked at Michael. "M, they're pink."

"Beggars can't be choosers." Another of his mother's favorite phrases.

"Are we beggars?"

"No. Not yet. But, we sure can see the soup line from here."

"Where?"

"Just pack up. There's more stuff in the garage. I'll be back."

"I'll come with."

Michael, for what felt like the millionth time, stopped and tried to remember what Jessie had been through. This must be what it feels like to be a parent, he thought. Ever since Olive Park, Jessie would not be alone. Even when she went to the bathroom, she made Michael stand outside. Standing guard.

Every now and then, she'd call out. "M? You there?"

"No. I've left. Paul McCartney invited us over for tea and I left about ten minutes ago. Too bad you couldn't go."

"Okay," was always the reassuring response.

Now, he turned and looked at his sister.

"I said I'll be right back, okay? Only going to the garage."

"I want to come. You know, check for my stuff."

Michael opened his mouth to make fun of her. Call her scaredy-cat, but he didn't. He knew he should say something. Something to get her over her fear. He just didn't know what.

Dr. Avery would know what to say to a seven-year-old who had been dragged into the woods by the psycho kid killer, Ruby Everheart, and had her head bent back, and had a knife held to her throat and was seconds from buying it. Good old Dr. would know what to say.

But he didn't.

"Yeah come on if you have to."

Jessie slipped off the couch and followed him close to his heels.

"You know, you can't always go where I go," he said over his shoulder. It was the best he could think of.

"Yeah," came the quiet reply.

The garage, which was only a carport Aunt Jane had closed in, had only space for a single car. Unfortunately, the diminutive VW bug of his aunt's left plenty of room for her to fill up the space with a ton of crap.

Boxes of stuff, labeled and re-labeled sat under the fake Christmas tree. Some hooks on the wall held gardening tools and baskets and buckets. The tiers of shelves had an impressive and poisonous array of garden fertilizers, bug killers, weed killers, wasp bombs, surrounded by a plethora of dirty mismatched gloves and boots.

Half raided bags of grass seed and mulch and planting soil sagged next to each other on the floor.

Set off from everything else was a cardboard box with the letters 'M / J' scrawled on the side. It was their stuff, Michael knew. Confirmed by the clear plastic bag of Jessie's clothes.

The bag still had its police evidence tag on it. Inside the bag, he could see a dirty jumper. At least he thought it was dirt. Ruby Everheart had bled like nothing he'd ever seen on TV. It had gone everywhere. Afterward, he'd tried to clean Jessie up best he could. But...damn. It *was* everywhere.

He picked the bag up with two fingers. As he lifted it something inside the bag clunked.

"Jesus!" he dropped it back onto the box.

"What is it?" Jessie screamed. She clung to him and peeked around.

Michael licked his lips and tried to calm his pounding heart. He sighed as he spied the red tennis shoe Jessie had been wearing that night. There was only one in the bag. They had never found the other one.

"It's all right. Just a shoe."

Jessie straightened up but said nothing.

Michael picked up the bag again and tossed it atop the grass seed bag to be left there. Reminders of the night in Olive Park would not be coming with them.

He opened the box. "Let's see what's left."

"Is this ours? Our stuff?"

Michael leaned into the box. "Yeah. I think this was the stuff we had at...you know. Up there."

He didn't need to point. He knew she knew or thought she did. He was never sure what she remembered and where the fear lay. But he felt it wasn't good to say the name 'Ruby Everheart'. He thought Dr. Avery would approve.

"These are our things they brought back from there. Been sitting out here since...you know. See if there's anything we want."

"M, I don't want anything from there." She pivoted and walked out of the garage.

Can't blame you, he almost said, grabbing the first thing he found, a coloring book, half colored.

"Well, here's your coloring book," he muttered to himself. "Probably don't want it." He tossed it aside. Pulled out a pair of red and white striped socks.

"Don't need 'em."

His fingers touched something scratchy and furry. He pulled it out of the box. Michael stared into the mismatched glass eyes of a stuffed bear.

"You're kinda porky for a little bear, you know."

His brown furze covering was still the golden-brown fleece of soft comfort except for a small half dollar sized scorch on one of his legs. Michael almost tossed it down with the rest of the rejects until he realized Jess'd probably want something to cuddle with where they were going. If this little guy made it through the fire, it must be a testament to something. Maybe a desire not to be left behind. Maybe a need to find a new life somewhere else.

Michael took a sniff. Not bad. "Ah, what the hell." He stuffed it in the backpack.

It was only then he heard the knocking on the trailer door.

CHAPTER 26

"Who is it?" asked Michael. He had parted the curtains and could see a large woman with a briefcase and a clipboard. It wasn't the emaciated Mrs. Finch from CPS that was supposed to take them to the airport.

The woman spotted Michael.

"Hello. I'm looking for Mrs. Cooper."

"We don't want any."

The woman leaned away from the door so her head was close to the window.

"No, dear. I'm from CPS. I'm here to see Mrs. Cooper about Michael and Jessica."

"Where's Mrs. Finch? She's supposed to be here."

The woman looked uncertain. "I'm not sure, hon. I was just given this assignment to come here and…." She hesitated. "Is your mother there?"

Michael almost blurted out the truth. That his mother was dead. That she'd had her head bashed in by his father and Michael had not been able to stop it.

"Let's see some ID," he said instead.

The woman held up her identification on a lanyard around her neck. She only lowered it when Michael opened the door.

"Thank you," said the woman as she entered and scanned the trailer. "Where's your mother?"

Jessie took her place on the edge of the pull-out couch and put her hands between her knees. Michael stood before the woman, not allowing her any further into the room.

She saw he had a backpack in one hand.

"We live here with our aunt. Did live here. Mrs. Finch is coming to take us to the airport. We, my sister and I are moving to Arizona. She should be here soon."

"Your aunt isn't here?"

"She's at work."

Jessie raised her head, her mouth opened.

"Works night shift sometimes," Michael added.

Jessie slid down lower on the couch, working her way to invisible.

"But, it's okay," continued Michael. "We already said goodbye to her. And it's Miss. Miss Cooper. Not Mrs. She never, you know, married."

"Oh." The woman tapped the clipboard against her generous thigh. "Oh," she repeated. She checked her watch.

"Can I call her?"

"They don't allow personal calls where she works unless she's on a break."

"I…see. And you two are here alone?"

"It's okay. I'm fourteen. And we're only waiting for Mrs. Finch. From your office. What do you want?"

"May I sit down while I make a call."

Michael moved out of the way and the woman placed herself gingerly next to Jessie.

She cradled her cell phone against her shoulder while she consulted her clipboard.

Michael looked at Jessie. She was hunched over. Shrinking.

"Victor. Olivia. I'm at the Cooper residence. The guardian isn't here and I can't reach her at work, and I…"

Her eyes shifted to Michael as she listened.

"If you think so."

When she ended the call she placed her cell on her clipboard and flicked the edge of the top paper on the clipboard.

Michael had a bad feeling. Anything out of the ordinary was bad. This was out of the ordinary. It had taken him the months since he arrived, since his aunt had had to take them in, to arrange the transfer to Arizona to his mother's cousin, Shippen Travers. He'd had to forge some papers, lied to his aunt, had to convince good ol' cowboy Travers that his aunt was suffering financially, trying to care for him and Jessie.

Then there was the paperwork from the great state of California which had seemed reluctant to let them go. Maybe they were hoping they would stay, grow up, and become taxpayers.

It had all come together in the last week. Mrs. Finch had called with the good news. She had received the final final paperwork and the two first-class plane tickets to Phoenix. But Michael knew the whole scheme teetered on the edge of failure, that a breath of doubt could easily topple it into the morass of bureaucratic delay. For Jessie's sake, especially, this move had to happen.

'I'll be by around six to take you two to the airport', Mrs. Finch had said when Michael had lied and told her that his aunt had to work. That was the same day the great state of California had also decided that they'd had enough of the craziness that his aunt was exhibiting and had requested she 'rest' for a bit in the Hollydale Center over in Pasadena.

Michael hoped that the court records wouldn't find their way to CPS before he and Jessie left. As of ten minutes ago, he thought they were home free.

Now, someone had let in a sharp, dark wind. An unsettling disturbance in the force.

"Your name is Michael?" the woman asked.

"Michael Cooper. My sister, Jessie. Where's Mrs. Finch?" Michael didn't want to hear the answer he knew must come.

The woman placed both hands on the clipboard.

"Mrs. Finch isn't coming. I'm Olivia Warner. She was supposed to come but she couldn't…"

"Our flight leaves in a few hours."

"Yes. Well…"

"Is this about my aunt?"

"Your aunt? No. Why would you think that?"

"We're due in Arizona. We have to go." He said it, but the 'oh shit' vibe spread like black tar.

"There's been a change of plans. I really should speak to your aunt. It seems that Mr. Travers is in the hospital. I understand there was an accident of some kind."

She gave what passed as a compassionate smile.

"What? What does that mean?" Michael sat. Stunned.

Mrs. Warner looked away. "Without a relative, someone…ambulatory, to look after you, an adult on the other end, I'm afraid we can't release you. I'm sure your aunt understands, or will."

He grasped at anything. "You're sure? Your office coordinated everything with him in the last few days. He can't be not ambulatory. Couldn't be. Everything's set for the move. Everyone approved it."

"I'm sorry. Truly."

Olivia Warner checked her watch again.

"I would imagine that in a week or two, Mr. Travers would be in touch with your aunt and our office and then we can see where we stand. I don't suppose there's a Mrs. Travers."

Michael stood and turned away. He looked out the window toward the rest of Sunshine Villa.

"There is no Mrs. Travers," he muttered.

Olivia dug out a business card and placed it on the coffee table.

"If your aunt has any questions, she can call."

She stood and moved toward the door.

"Will you two be okay until your aunt gets home? Would you like me to stay?"

Michael shook his head. "We'd like to be alone."

Sounding more relieved than she meant to, "Okay, now. Again. I'm sorry. I'm sure in a few weeks, or so, when Mr. Travers has recovered, we'll be back on track."

She gave Jessie a brief wave and left.

Michael watched her back out of the short driveway and speed off.

"M, what do we do now?" Jessie asked. "What does this mean? Are we still going to Arizona?"

Michael spun and kicked the hassock as hard as he could, burying his foot inches into its side.

"Arrrggggh!"

He slammed his fist into the top of the hassock.

"M!" cried Jessie.

"Shit, shit, shit!"

"M!" she yelled with a quivering chin.

"We were so close! So damn damn close!"

His chest heaved. It was all so wrong. So life-wrecking wrong. All of it. His father. His mother. Their screwed up existence now. The light that was Arizona. And now, what did they have. Piss and nothing that's what. A few weeks, a month, a year. Didn't matter.

"I don't know. I don't know what we're going to do."

"M, we'll be okay, won't we? When Aunt Jane comes home?"

He studied the green vinyl of the hassock and the shininess his tears had left.

"She's not coming home. Not for a while."

"What are we going to do? Are we staying here? Do we have food?"

He sat back down on the floor his legs around the hassock.

"Yeah."

"Do we need the soup kitchen?" Her lower lip quivered. "Is a soup kitchen bad?"

"Soup kitchen," Michael muttered. He looked around the trailer. At the pile of their stuff. At the half-packed flowered suitcases. At the quiet.

"No. No soup kitchen."

He spied the stuffed bear peering out at him from the backpack.

"What are you looking at?"

CHAPTER 27

Jake and Jake dog stopped before the entrance of the Chapman Towers building, an aging three-story office edifice in downtown Sacramento.

"Towers, huh?" Jake addressed Jake dog. "You can tell this used to be a nice place because it has two big planters which used to be full of live flowers on either side of the entrance. That's how you can tell."

Jake stared up at Jake, unmoving because he hadn't yet heard a word he understood.

"So, because they provided planters for you, you need to relieve yourself here, before we go in. I don't want to hear any whining after we get in there."

Still staring.

"You can pick right or left planter. Your choice where you do your duty."

The dog looked to the right.

"Right it is." Jake moved over next to the round, exposed aggregate planter full of lethargic geraniums. Jake followed with his head down.

"Don't tell me you don't have to go. I saw how much water you drank."

Jake looked back up at Jake to verify what was required.

"Go on. We have work to do."

Resigned. Jake sniffed the planter's base on all sides before adding to the watery collection.

Jake finished and looked back up at Jake.

"That it? Or is there more?"

The dog looked toward the building's entrance.

"Good. Let's go."

Jake held one of the glass entry doors for Jake and they settled before the building directory.

"He's on three. Well, his office is. Part of him is downtown."

Jake pushed the call button and addressed the dog, who sat next to Jake on the warped floor.

"This your first elevator ride?"

Jake snuffled and shifted.

"Of course it is. Nothing to it. Follow me."

When the doors opened Jake and Jake entered, followed by a woman and a young child. A boy about eight, Jake guessed, dressed in a little man's suit, grey with a white shirt. They had an appointment somewhere where the kid had to look presentable, at least credible. A lawyer's, Jake surmised. Divorce. Custody. Only child. The woman had done a passable job dressing the boy except the boy's shoes were brown and scuffed. You judge a person by their footwear Jake wanted to tell her. A person's history is reflected in his or her shoes.

"What a nice dog," the woman said.

Jake nodded. "He knows it too."

She was about to ask to pet him when the boy balled up a fist and raised it over the dog's head. The dog shied. Jake caught the boy's fist in time. Then one of the boy's legs reared back ready to deliver a crippling leg smash.

"Billy! Behave yourself!"

Jake jerked Jake's leash, pulling him out of range.

The woman grabbed the boy's other arm as the doors opened on the second floor. She dragged him out of the elevator without a word or glance at Jake. They turned left. Jake heard the woman down the hallway. "I can't trust you, can I? I will never trust you. Just like your goddamn father."

Before the doors closed Jake saw the directional plaque that pointed to the left. It led to the offices of the Wilson Child Psychology clinic.

"Better hurry," Jake muttered.

The doors creaked closed again and Jake reached down and gave him some reassurance as the elevator gave a jump.

"Now, we have to deliver some bad news to Mr. Peter Berlin's staff."

After a moment. "And I have to stop talking to you as if you're going to answer."

Before the elevator stopped on three, Jake reviewed what they'd been able to find out about Peter Berlin.

Berlin's cop record showed he'd put in twelve years, and only two as a detective, his last year working with Thompson and Carruthers on Olive Park. Right after the case was abandoned he bailed, leaving the force at 47, claiming ill health but no health claim was ever filed.

Wasn't until a year later he surfaced, having formed his own PI agency. Rumor was, Carruthers was supposed to retire as well, bring some hefty client friends and he and Berlin were to go, partners, just like Sam Spade and Miles Archer. Seems Berlin waited a year for Carruthers to join him.

Never happened. Evidently, Peter Berlin had to fend for himself.

The third floor was all carpeted after a fashion, Jake saw. He avoided tripping on the loose wrinkled rills that crisscrossed the hallway as he made his way to the suite of what was supposed to be Carruthers and Berlin. Except there wasn't a tasteful sign with 'Carruthers and Berlin' in gold lettering relief gracing a double glass-doored entry. Instead, a business card was thumbtacked to a dark wood door.

Jake leaned in.

'Peter Berlin – Investigations'

She was bending over, watering a plant on the lower tier of an ornate metal plant stand when they entered.

Instead of interrupting, Jake let her finish all the plants on the lower level.

She took her time.

Straightening and turning, she saw both Jakes.

"Oh! Hello!" She tugged at her skirt and blew the stray hairs that had floated in front of her face. She wasn't the plastic eye candy he usually found in the high buck offices. Her eyes didn't have that no-ones-home look and her nose was not pointed northward.

Before Jake could say anything, she'd abandoned the watering can and was advancing toward the dog.

"What a cutie! Can I pet him?"

"There no eight-year-olds running loose here is there?"

"What?"

"Sure. Go ahead. He loves women."

"What's his name?"

"Treat."

"Treat?"

Jake barked.

"Funny name," she said as she ruffed behind his ears.

"I don't know. He always seems to come when I call."

"I'll bet." She gave Jake a tender muzzle crush and rose. "If you're here to see anybody, you're out of luck." She shrugged. "Actually nobody is ever here. Did you have an appointment? No, I know you didn't because I would've made it and I haven't opened the appointment software since we had to schedule the annual Fire Marshal inspection of our fire extinguishers two weeks ago. So?"

Jake dug for one of his cards and handed it to her.

"What can I do for you...Detective Steiner." She turned the card over as if she expected to find an imprint from the 'Jolly Fake Card Company.'

"Mr. Berlin, does he have a family?"

She studied Jake for a moment, vetting his seriousness. She sat back on the edge of the reception desk.

"Not sure. Pretty sure he doesn't. I'm a temp here. Christine Carter, almost Attorney at Law. Been here three months, with one week to go and I can tell you I've never received a call from anyone claiming to be a family member and there are no pictures on his desk. People or dogs. And I've only seen him a few times and so I don't know him all that well."

From the cop file, Jake knew that while he was on the force Berlin hadn't been married. Circumstances could've changed.

"Any idea what case he was working on?"

"Not a clue. I can hardly describe the man." She stopped and eyed Jake. "What's wrong? Someone die?"

"Berlin."

"Are you kidding? Shit! This was the best temp job I've ever had." She indicated the disarray of books on the desk. "Going for my JD and this was ideal."

"Which is Mr. Berlin's office?"

She indicated the one to Jake's left.

"That one? With the open door?'

"Yes. It's the only one. The other door's a closet."

"I'd like to take a look."

She looked wary. "My orders from Mr. Berlin were to never let anyone anywhere near Mr. Berlin's office and to always say he was out on a case and that he'd be back tomorrow."

"Still…"

"I'm sure there are some canon of ethics about disobeying a standing order from a dead boss, but I don't know what they would be, so if you have a dog biscuit, let me have it."

"Biscuit?"

"Yep."

Jake took a dog biscuit out of his pocket and handed it to her. She threw it into Berlin's office.

Jake dropped the leash and the dog took off after it.

"Oops. I better go get my dog."

"That was my thinking." She smiled a knowing smile. "It's a big office. You may not find him right away. Call if you need help."

"Any trouble for you?"

She shrugged. "Hell no. But, I demand that you go round up your wild animal which is loose in Mr. Berlin's office. I insist you take your time and do it safely. Then per the instructions from my now deceased employer, you will have to leave rapidly. Go find your dog."

Jake found Jake nosing in Berlin's trash, having already downed the biscuit. The office itself was in muted light as the gauzy inside drapes were pulled closed and the heavier curtains were only partially open. It was a sizable office with a couch and a translucent etched glass table off to the side. A few low Italian leather chairs were pulled up to the table opposite the couch as if the last thing on Berlin's agenda in his office was a conference with several visitors.

"Jake! I mean Treat! Here boy." Jake threw another biscuit. "Knock yourself out."

The desk was a dark mahogany battleship. Behind the desk was a standard office chair and behind that was a matching dark wood credenza. It was clean except for the tray of full liquor bottles and four clean glasses.

Jake took out his phone and careful to not touch anything, shot pictures of what was on the desk. Most interesting was the desk blotter which Berlin had used a scratchpad. Doodles of large spurting penises and naked women were intertwined with phone numbers, various dates, and time.

A transcript of what appeared to be a telephone wiretap sat open on the left side.

"Naughty, naughty, Mr. Berlin. On whose phone have we been eavesdropping?"

Jake scanned it but could make out little in the dim light. He took two flashes, the top page and a little of the second.

There appeared to be nothing else of interest. True to Christine's word, there were no pictures, no family, no dogs or cats, merely a leather embossed pencil holder with gold initials stenciled on the side and a stapler.

Jake moved to the side of the desk and with a well-executed ankle flip, tipped over the trash can.

"Dammit Jake, look what you did."

The dog gave Jake his attention, but with no more biscuits forthcoming, wandered out of the office, back to reception.

"We'll have to clean all this up. Paper by paper."

Jake took out his phone again and without taking time to read anything, placed each sheet atop the trash can, snapped a picture, and let the paper fall back into the trash.

"Hey," called Christine from reception. "Come get this vicious animal before he gives me rabies or foot and mouth disease."

"Coming."

Twelve sheets in all. And a lot of candy wrappers.

With his foot, Jake maneuvered the waste can back into position. He took a final scan around the office. Best he could do.

"There's my vicious dog," Jake said as he came back into Reception. Jake didn't even turn. He was getting a great back scratch.

"Did you know you can make a dog love you if you scratch him right here," Christine said, indicating the area above Jake's haunches. "It's the one spot they can never scratch themselves."

"I think it works with people too."

"It might." She smiled, concentrating on the dog.

The short silence was filled by a blushing Christine.

"How'd he die?" she asked. "Berlin."

"Unpleasantly."

She gave Jake a few final pats, stood, and studied the desk on which her few textbooks and notebooks were strewn.

"This was the perfect job, you know. Nobody's ever here."

"Anybody ever show up or call and threaten Berlin?"

"No heavy breathers with Brooklyn accents if that's what you mean. And practically the only one who poked his head in was the mailman who just wanted to ask me out."

"Did you?"

"Um. No."

"Let's see his recent mail."

Christine indicated the unopened three envelopes in a red plastic 'IN' basket. "Two weeks' worth. Have at it."

Jake flipped through. "Just utilities."

"Told you this is no hotbed of activity."

Jake picked up Jake's leash. "Well, if you need a study partner, you have my number. Jake and I would be happy to help. Well, I would anyway."

"I thought his name was 'Treat'?"

"Nickname. Anyway, when you need help memorizing Miranda, call."

She held up her left hand. "Fully booked."

"Last chance. I have handcuffs."

"There's never a cop around when you need a good cuffing." She handed him back his card.

"Goodbye detective. And 'Treat'."

Jake barked again.

"C'mon hound, wrong office."

CHAPTER 28

Jake took the duct tape and wrapped it around the two 15 foot lengths of bamboo he'd found left over in the back of the OID warehouse. Combined and secured together, they gave him a 30-foot reach. He took his pocketknife, slit one end of the bamboo down twelve inches, and spread the ends apart.

"That should do it don't you think?" asked Jake. But his dog wasn't interested in this craft project. He remained with his head on his paws and it was only his eyes that followed Jake.

"Not impressed. I understand. But watch this."

Jake drained what was left of the coffee in his Starbucks cup and shook it out, then wiped it out with a napkin. He pushed the empty cup between the two split fingers of bamboo. It held.

"It has to hold it securely, but not too tight you see."

The dog yawned.

Jake walked to the other end of the bamboo and picked it up like a fishing rod.

As it rose, so did the dog. He sat up and looked back and forth from Jake to the captured coffee cup at the other end. This was new.

"The hell are you doing?"

Mallory stood at the office opening. She slipped off her coat and patted the dog when he came over to greet her.

"Just a moment." Jake didn't turn to look at her. He kept his concentration on the far end of the pole.

"This…is…a…very…delicate…operation." Jake had the end with the cup well above the top of the glass walls. The pole was flexing up and down, threatening to dislodge the cup so he slowed the ascension to dampen the oscillations.

"Is this some sort of game? And if it is, don't you have something better to do? Like napping."

"You will thank me in a moment. I am securing our freedom."

"What are you talking about?"

"I'm mad as hell and I'm not going to take it anymore," Jake said, smiling.

"I'm so glad, Peter Finch."

"Hey, this isn't Orwell's 1984. There is no reason we have to be in this prison, under the all-seeing eye of Big Brother," said Jake, his concentration fully on the cup as it rose to the second balcony overlooking the atrium.

"I don't…" said Mallory, craning and twisting to follow the cup. Then she got it. "Oh. Oh!"

She moved to stand behind Jake. "You're too high, bring it lower. Lower."

"I can see."

"Steady, now."

"Thank you so much."

Both held their breath while Jake shuffled forward, feeling his way, guiding the cup home.

"Now!" shouted Mallory. "Now!"

Jake gave a little shove and the cardboard coffee cup slipped onto the lens of the brand new security camera mounted on the second balcony. With care, Jake slipped the bamboo fingers off of the cup, then with a slow flick of his wrist, he made the fingers whap the bottom of the cup, pushing it further on and guaranteeing its permanency, blocking half of the work area. More importantly, it eliminated Jake's desk from downtown's view.

According to the installers, it was a 50/50 bet their OID work area cameras were being recorded by the security voyeurs at their Star Wars control room in SacPD headquarters. But given the state of financial cutbacks, it was a tossup if they were monitored at all. If they were, then Jake should get a call in the next few days, or a grumbling, uniformed IT tech would make the trip down to fix one of the newly installed and now malfunctioning, cameras.

"That should do it. Free at last."

"Easy for you to say," said Mallory glancing up at the other two cameras. "Looks like Stan and my misdeeds are still at risk."

Jake handed her the pole. "Here you go, except we're all out of coffee cups."

"You have a gun don't you?"

Jake slid into his seat and opened his laptop. "Destruction of company property is strictly off-limits. Besides, I'm not that good a shot. Where've you been?"

"So, what's Danni's progress?" countered Mallory.

"What? Oh, yeah. A daiishka. She said it was a daiishka."

"I thought it was a BMW."

Jake made a two-handed choking mime. "Daiishka. The garrote. A diamond-studded garrote. That was what removed Marston's head.

"Diamonds?"

"All good assassins have climbed on board the daiishka bandwagon. Cuts cleanly, assuming you know what you're doing and according to Danni allows you to die one of three ways, with bleeding out being the leading candidate."

"Jesus."

"And the car, the BMW, was not broken down. It was perfectly drivable."

Mallory opened her laptop and took out her glasses. Her hand brushed her scar. "Yeah. Got that."

"Oh, and she made a tentative I.D. on the other guy. The prints were skewed, but you know Danni. Until the guy sits up and introduces himself, she won't say for sure."

"Any relation to Marston?"

"Don't think so. Some private investigator. Former cop."

Mallory turned toward Jake. She gripped the back of her chair. She had that feeling. That feeling as if you've heard the words before they're spoken. "A former cop?" she whispered, but she didn't hear herself speak. The rushing in her ears was too great.

"Who?" was all she managed. She closed her eyes.

"Berlin. Peter Berlin."

Mallory let out a cry. "What?!"

Jake jumped up. "What's wrong?"

Mallory shook her head side to side. "I… don't believe it." Tears welled up.

Jake moved in front of her. "Hey, what's going on? Mal? Talk to me."

After a moment, she wiped her nose with the back of her hand. "Is Danni sure?"

"I think so, really. Mallory, what's the matter?"

Mallory looked up. "Jake…" She blinked as tears overflowed, dripping off her chin. "Jake, he was such a nice man."

"You knew him? You knew Peter Berlin?"

Mallory nodded and let out a sniffle.

"How?" Jake asked softly.

Mallory raised her chin and tried to will the tears to stop. She shook her head. Looked right at Jake.

"He…Jake, he worked for me."

Jake's eyes widened. "What?"

"Jake, Peter Berlin was the man I hired ten years ago to find my brother."

CHAPTER 29

Jake watched as Mallory made her way back from the bathroom and sat down opposite him. His faithful dog followed her in, licked her hand, and then curled up next to her feet.

"He's a good dog, Jake. I think he knows things." She reached down and scratched behind his ears. "I know he feels things."

"Like dog, like owner."

Mallory gave a quick smile, then let it slide. Her face was pale, make-up free. The only color came from the scar which pulsed a dull red, reflective of her turmoil.

Jake cleared his throat. "I have some things I want to show you," he said, indicating his laptop. "But first tell me about Peter Berlin."

Her voice was clear and steady. Jake realized she'd done all the grieving she would do.

"My father..." She took a breath. "You remember my father was arrested when they thought he had done the Olive Park killings. Well, of course, he wasn't officially arrested, but he may as well have been the way they treated him."

Jake remembered. When Mallory had revealed who her father was, Jake had gone back and reread all the newspaper accounts of the early days of the investigation. The hysteria and outrage and the pressure to find the killer and torturer of three children were like nothing California had ever seen. There had been serial killers before, but the age and innocence of the victims, the horrific nature of their deaths, and the callousness with which they were buried hit with an urgency for serious retribution. No one was immune, least of all Highway Patrol and SacPD investigators. There was a contagion of avengement and it resulted in wholesale rousting of anyone who had ever dealt with children. As its focus narrowed, they believed they had found their man.

A child photographer. One who specialized in portraits of children of exactly that age. Parents and kids liked him. And he liked them. Too much, thought the lead detectives, Carruthers being one, though there was never any evidence he had made any untoward advances to any of his subjects. In fact, at all of his photographic sessions, he insisted the parents be present.

The spear in the side for Mallory's father was the unfortunate and coincidental fact that he had actually photographed one of the victims some years before at a charity event.

He was hauled into the bowels of SacPD. The press picked up the story and eager to be the first to break the news, discovered and released his name.

He didn't emerge from police custody for a week and only after it was discovered that it was physically impossible for him to have committed any of the crimes. The police issued a small statement saying he was being released and no charges were being filed. Of course, they had to add the phrase, 'at this time'.

Except, as Mallory related, his life was over. The family's life was over and done. There was a divorce. He could obviously no longer go near a child alone, let alone photograph them. He was able to eke out a living as a landscape photographer. Houses, trees, hills, and sunsets never make accusations.

But vengeance is never far away and some believe what they want to believe.

Roger Dimante was killed in an 'accident'. While photographing scenes of Big Sur from the Pacific Highway he was run down by a car driven by the father of one of the Olive Park victims. No charges were filed.

And the Olive Park case remained unsolved.

"After the funeral, after the news of my father's death was released," continued Mallory. "I was back at UCLA by then. One day, at a coffee shop, a man sat down across from me. He told me he was a private investigator. He gave me his card and showed me the missing person's flier that our family had filed years ago on my missing brother. He said, no family should have to suffer as ours had, with my brother missing and father killed. I couldn't help it, I broke down and cried right there in front of him. It was the first indication that anyone gave a damn about my brother. We had gotten zilch from Sacramento or Highway Patrol in all the years since he went missing. And now, this man, this kind man with a gentle voice, said he would find my brother.

"That was Peter Berlin."

"How was he planning on doing that?" asked Jake.

"He was working on other missing children cases and he thought there might be a connection. He was cryptic. I didn't care to ask anything more. This was the first person to come forward and offer help, so I didn't care how he did it."

"He was doing this for free?"

Mallory paced. "I told him I had no money to pay him. Any of my father's life insurance had already prepaid my tuition. He smiled. Said, 'Buy me a cup of coffee and we'll call it square'. That's how he was."

"He never told you his background?"

"Periodically, I'd get a note, a voice mail, saying he was still working on it and to take heart. Even if he never found my brother, he gave me hope Jake, and showed me that there were some people that cared."

Mallory smiled. "It was much later, years later, that I thought to look him up on the Internet and saw that he'd been one of the investigators on the original Olive Park case. He had been one of the officers who investigated my father. He admitted he felt tremendous remorse about how my father was treated and his part in it. He said that was why he wanted to help."

"And, he thought there was a connection between Olive Park and your brother?"

"Yes, but…"

"What?"

"There was something more. He hinted that he wasn't happy with the original investigation."

"But he was on the original investigation."

"How better to know," said Mallory as she stared up at Jake's handiwork. The paper cup didn't look like it would ever come off. "I think he felt there was something…fishy."

Jake swiveled slowly back and forth. "So, he was the one who gave you the idea that missing kids were connected to Olive Park?"

"Yeah." Mallory looked away.

Jake could tell she wanted to apologize, yet again, for miring him and Stan in the Olive Park investigation. He didn't want to hear it. She had rolled the dice so to speak. She had lied to sandbag them. But the case was solved. She won. And lost. Either way, it was over. It was past.

"When was the last time you heard from him?"

Mallory roused herself. "A few weeks ago. He left me two voicemails after what happened at Olive Park. Condolences about my brother. I never got back to him. You know, we were busy. Over the years, he would ask me random questions now and then about my brother. The last time we met, it's funny, but he asked the same thing Stan asked. Had my brother's bike ever been found? So, maybe he was close. I don't know."

Mallory pulled her hair back and tied it. She sat down on the conference table. "But Jake, what connection would he have to Marston? Unless he was working on a case and this is all a coincidence. The two of them together."

Jake pulled his laptop around so they could both see the screen. "I'll show you. Look at this.

"I got into Berlin's office," Jake continued. "I've never seen anything so clean. Like he was never there. Never worked. If he did, he was the most fastidious of men. Hardly anything out of place, except on his desk. All I could do in the time I was there was take some pictures. On Berlin's desk blotter, hidden under some junk mail, he had written this."

Jake used the mouse, grabbed and enlarged the left side of the blotter. Hidden among and surrounded by curlicue doodles, swirls, and adequate renderings of various breasts with erect nipples were an abbreviated series of dates.

5/14!
5/22 F&S Who?
5/24 Gone!
5/25 check WST
5/27 G Rd.

5/28 G Rd. C! WTF?

Mallory studied the list.

"Tell me what you think," smiled Jake. "Before I tell you what I think they mean."

"Well," drawled Mallory. "I would think they were appointments or part of a to-do list, except-"

"Except for the fact that it was on the 14th that Olive Park went down, right?"

"I thought you wanted me to do this without you interrupting?"

Jake pushed away from the conference table. "So right. C'mon Jake. We need a walk!"

Ten minutes later, Mallory had pulled her own laptop over and was intently studying the screen.

"Well?" asked Jake.

"Shit! You scared me. I didn't hear you come in at all."

"Sorry."

"Damn, I miss that old door. At least you could tell when someone was sneaking up on you."

"I didn't sneak. Well?"

Mallory put her feet up on the conference table and propped her legal pad on her legs.

"Okay. The 14th, we know. Then, a little more than a week later we have F&S. I made a guess it was a company, and-" Mallory checked her pad to make sure. "I came up with two. F&S stationers, like a Hallmark store. The other was Franklin and Sons. A mortuary. I chose the mortuary. And I'm guessing that was where one of the services for one of the victims was except none of them were from Sacramento. Berlin wrote 'Who?' so he didn't know who it was either. So, short of calling the funeral home and pretending I'm some grieving relative, I'm working the media outlets to see what funerals were covered that day."

"Don't bother."

"Why?"

"Just go on, I'll tell you when you finish. I want to hear your take."

"Look, if you've already done this, why let me?"

Jake took Jake's leash off and rolled it up. "As much as Jake there hates to admit it, he told me the other day that he feels you sometimes have a unique way of looking at things. I grudgingly agreed. So, go on. I want to hear what you think."

Mallory studied him. Compliments were rare. Sarcasm was the norm. She stared hard, waiting for a breaking smile, but he seemed sincere. Wow.

She checked off F&S on her pad and continued.

"Two days later, on the 24th, something was 'gone'. Haven't a clue on that one. But there's an exclamation point, so it was important-"

"Or surprising."

"Or surprising to him. WST on the 25th. WST. That's like saying Acme. That could mean anything. It's gotta be a business, not an area or a person I think. So, I'm still working on WST."

"Okay."

"Since we're looking for a Marston connection, I'm betting 'G Rd' is German Road, where Marston lives. Lived. Evidently, Peter was there twice, on the 27th and the 28th. The 28th he was surprised. Something went wacko since he wrote 'WTF'."

Mallory tossed her pad on the table, brought her feet down, and turned the laptop toward Jake.

"All right genius," said Mallory, crossing her arms. "Impress me."

Jake slipped into his chair. "First, it took me an hour to figure out F&S. So good on you."

Mallory tried not to look smug and caught herself before throwing some smartass his way.

"And you are right. Franklin and Sons, funeral home. But you're wrong about the service for one of the victims. And Berlin wasn't uncertain about who it was. He knew."

"Who was it?"

"Franklin and Sons handled the body of Rudolph Rendell. Ruby Everheart."

"Shit! I would've gotten that. Should've."

"What Berlin wanted to know, I think, was who paid for it. And who took the ashes. Or the body."

"Body? I thought it would be cremated and the ashes dumped in the nearest landfill. But we don't know who came and collected whatever they collected?'"

Jake shook his head. "I'm not that fast, but we'll get it."

"I'll get it."

"We'll get it."

Mallory shrugged. "Sure."

"I'll skip the 24th and WST on the 25th. I'll come back to it. I'm sure we're correct on German Road. Seems Berlin cased Marston's place on those days."

"You're sure? How?"

Jake picked up six clipped together sheets and set them on the laptop keyboard.

"Cell phone records."

Mallory ran her finger over the report. "How? These take time to get."

"When the account holder is dead and you're doing an official investigation," Jake smiled. "And you know somebody."

Mallory flipped to the last page and studied it.

"This says…this makes no sense. According to this, he kept calling his own number. Over and over. I don't get it. Wouldn't you get your own voicemail?"

"Sure. Your Mr. Peter Berlin was one smart cookie though." Jake moved to the next screen on the computer. It showed a map of Sacramento. There were over twenty red dots marked on the map.

"The cell phone report shows not only who he called but also the GPS of the tower or towers that picked up his signal. That's how I know he was at German Road on those days. Most tracker programs can give you real-time tracking, most of the larger services have archived data which details the history of someone's locations. In this case, Berlin was taking no chances or didn't know how cell phone records worked. He kept calling himself, which registered his phone call and locked in his location on a permanent record."

Mallory studied the map. She looked up to Jake. "And you only do that if-"

"If you were afraid. Afraid you might never be able to tell someone what you were doing or what you had found."

"He wasn't a paranoid guy, Jake."

"Then he knew what he was getting into might be illegal. Or dangerous."

"Okay, what about WST?"

"Once I had these," said Jake, indicating the cell phone records. "It was easy to narrow in on who or what WST was. And the 25th was also the first date that Berlin made a call to himself. On that day, he only did that only once from…" Jake reached around Mallory and pointed to an industrial section of Sacramento. "From here. No residences here, so I ruled out WST being a person. And there was only one business, according to the map software, that comes close to WST and that's Westside."

"Westside what?"

"Just Westside."

"No Westside T something?"

"Nope. And as far as the 24th, I haven't a clue what 'Gone' means."

Mallory studied the map. There was something familiar about the area, but it wasn't clicking. She scanned the surrounding streets and looked at the businesses tagged. Nothing jogged.

Jake walked to the whiteboard and pinned up the name Peter Berlin next to the BMW.

Mallory flipped back to the picture of Berlin's desk blotter. "There's no notation after he was at German Road on the 28th. That was the last entry."

"But," said Jake turning. "It wasn't the last call he made to himself. That was on the 29th."

Mallory flipped to the last item on Berlin's cell record.

"I see the GPS coordinates, but where was he?"

Mallory looked at Jake. There was something he didn't want to tell her.

"Jake?"

"He was right here Mallory. Peter Berlin was right outside our door."

CHAPTER 30

Stan surveyed the scene before him. There were three squads, one behind the other, in Marston's circular drive, with the six officers milling around, waiting for Mazurski.

Some idiot had brought the Forensics van to a halt partially onto the manicured lawn, knocking a few of the curb blocks askew and pinning one of the prize azaleas under the front bumper.

Someone had also ordered an ambulance, though Stan had no idea who might have done it or who they planned on saving. The two bored EMT's sat in the cab, both fiddling with their individual phones.

"Mazurski!"

"Yeah, yeah," he puffed as he limped up to Stan.

"Well?"

"Nothing. Still locked up tighter than a virgin's…" He shrugged catching his breath between wheezes. "Still locked. All the way around."

"Same as yesterday?"

Mazurski nodded. "Yeah. Only this time I went out further. There's a nice little like gazebo thing with a fountain and a square garden like one of them English gardens, plus they've got a construction trailer out there aways. I think he's planning another fountain or maybe another gazebo. When you've got the dough, I guess you never stop."

Mazurski brightened. "Hey! You know that glassed-in plant area- "

"Conservatory."

"Yeah, the conservatory has automatic sprinklers watering the plants. You can look in the windows and see it. There's music too. I think the guy plays music to his plants."

Stan's phone buzzed. The screen said it was Jake.

"Go rest Mazurski. You've had a whole day's work in fifteen minutes."

"Damn straight," answered Mazurski, still not understanding sarcasm.

Mazurski wandered off to be replaced by Michael 'Squinty' Saunders at their side.

Stan held up a finger and answered his phone. "Jake. What've you got?"

"Rodriguez's guys report nothing. Nobody who lives out on Jones saw or heard anything. Pretty much what we expected. It's been six weeks."

"Figures. You headed here?"

"No. There was some interesting stuff in Berlin's office. Mallory is going to be following up. I've got the witness coming in, the one who called in about seeing a woman next to the car."

"Good. But listen, finding Pokovich is priority. Remind her."

He ended the call and Squinty was right there.

"I don't like this," asserted Squinty, now hovering next to Stan.

"What's not to like?" Stan asked. "You're his attorney. Was, anyway. We have a search warrant. You have keys. Seems like a perfect match."

"Still, I understand Mr. Marston is allegedly deceased- "

"Allegedly? Squinty, his head fell out of his car the other day. And the rest of him was not attached."

"I've not seen the coroner's report," he said defiantly.

"Look, I can make an appointment for you with Danni Harness in Forensics. She can reacquaint you with Mr. Marston's head."

Squinty sagged. "Okay, okay. So he's probably dead, but I'm still the attorney of the estate too."

"Which is why you're here. To open the goddamn door so we don't have to break it down."

"Okay, okay. You can go in. But don't touch anything."

Stan laughed and slapped Squinty on the shoulder. "That's the spirit. Now open it up."

Stan moved aside and let Squinty's rounded form toddle up to the front door.

"Wait," Stan said. "Isn't there a code for an autolock or something? You just have a key."

"You're right. That's all I got. Detective, it is an autolock, but it opens with a key. What can I tell you."

Squinty fumbled with the key ring. The man had sausage fingers and a puffed-up face that appeared to close off his vision. Stan wondered how he could see anything.

'Squinty' Saunders kept smoothing out what was left of his thin black hair at the front of his head. It was already plastered down with sweat, but every time he got to another key, the hand would come out and try to flatten it further.

Before he found the key, the whole assemblage turned their eyes skyward as the Bell Ranger from the local ABC affiliate came into roaring view. It circled twice then remained hovering. Even the six uniforms stationed outside the residence turned to look at the uncommon sight. This was Sacramento, not L.A. There wasn't enough news here to fly over, usually.

"Now what," muttered Stan, as he watched two Highway Patrol cars race up the driveway, leaving black skid marks on the shiny exposed aggregate drive when they skidded into place. One officer from each jumped out of their vehicles and approached the group at the front door.

"What is this?" asked the first CHiP, challenging the group. Since he was outnumbered, he left his sunglasses in place.

Stan sighed. "I'm Detective Wyld. We're executing a search warrant."

The CHiP looked around at the rest.

"Big group. Expecting trouble?"

"Nope," Stan replied. "Big place. Expecting the search to take a long ass time."

CHiP sniffed. "Alarm company called. Seems when a vehicle sits in the drive here for more than 15 minutes, it gets their attention. When they can't get their asses out here, we get the call."

"I guess you can call 'em then. Tell 'em everything's okay up here at the ranch," Stan continued.

"Yeah. If we had the number," replied CHiP, purposely not looking at the blue-bordered white sign for Coliseum Security stuck in the lawn ten feet away.

"Mazurski!"

Mazurski tossed his cigarette down and ground it out.

"What?"

"Call the alarm company. Tell 'em everything's dandy here."

"What's the- "

Stan pointed to the sign.

"Oh. Yeah."

With a wave of assurance, Mazurski pulled out a cell phone and punched in the alarm company's number.

"We'll be on our way, then." Both CHiPs turned in formation, got in, and backed down the drive. They gave up halfway and backed onto the grass to turn around. They drove the rest of the way down the drive but had to stop at the gate.

Stan glanced down to the pillared entrance to the property. His mood soured as he watched two TV microwave vans try to bluster their way past the two CHiPs.

"Roberts, drive down there and close the gates. Make sure none of those boys get close enough to see anything."

When Roberts left, Stan turned back to the attorney.

"Come on Squinty. You want me to do it?"

"I'm responsible for this property. As legal advisor to Mr. Marston, and with him absent, I'm in charge now."

"Squinty, you sound like Alexander Haig," Stan said.

"Who?"

"Never mind. Open up."

Squinty was about halfway through the keys on the ring when he gave up.

"Okay, here. You try. But I'm coming in too," stated Squinty. He handed the keys to Stan.

"Fine," Stan said. He traded the keys for a pair of latex gloves. The lawyer examined them, then held them out with two fingers as if they were infected with the plague.

"I don't need these. I'm a lawyer," puffed the little man. "Why do I need these? This is not a crime scene."

He jerked his head up from trying to put the gloves on his fat fingers. "Or is it?"

Stan sighed as he slipped the first key into the lock. He hated most lawyers. It was a visceral loathing.

"Look, Stan, I'm doing my duty here. I represent the estate of the late James Marston Junior. This house, his financial interests or rather the estate's interests, are now my responsibility. You know this."

"Don't you go touching things just because you're a suit. Got it?"

A line of sweat broke out on Saunders's brow. He shifted his leather briefcase from one hand to the other. The latex gloves dangled, half on, half off each meaty hand. He appeared almost offended.

"Of course," he snipped.

Stan flipped to the sixth key on the ring. It fit.

"Bingo."

He grasped the knob and pushed open the heavy wood door.

As soon as he stepped inside Stan heard shrill beeping coming from the hidden keypad.

"You have the code?" asked Squinty.

Stan pulled the slip of paper from his pocket. "Yeah, I've got it. Where's the keypad?"

Squinty took another swipe at his brow. "How should I know? You know as much as I do, detective."

Shit. He didn't want to have the code but not be able to enter it because he couldn't find the damn keypad.

Stan moved into the foyer, turned, and looked up. It was a two-story entry with dim, filtered light coming from the one tinted massive skylight above.

He moved over to one of the panels of a small triptych that showed a stylized view of the surrounding grounds as if viewed from a higher vantage point. He tugged on one of the panels and it came off the wall in his hands.

He dropped it on the floor.

"Hey, hey," cried Squinty. "Watch it!"

The beeping quickened in warning.

The second panel also came off in his hands. Behind it was nothing but wall. He dropped this on the first.

"Detective!"

The beeping went into overdrive and then erupted into a series of banshee screeches. Squinty stepped back and eyed the front door as an emergency exit.

"Mazurski!" screamed Stan.

When Mazurski looked up, Stan shrugged his shoulders, held out his hands. What about the alarm?

Mazurski held the phone away from his ear and shrugged. "Still on hold," he yelled.

The other uniforms Rodriguez had sent over to help with the search watched Stan's struggles with bemused expressions.

All tough guys. None of the uniforms covered their ears against the screaming wail.

Stan pulled at the last panel which swung out on hidden hinges.

Stan held up the paper with the alarm code on it. He could see his hand was trembling.

He entered the code.

The alarm ceased.

It was as if the air was sucked out of the world when the alarm died. The sounds of real life rushed back in, including the annoying voice of Mazurski, "Got 'em. They said they'd shut off the alarm."

Squinty, meanwhile, gingerly lifted the panels off the floor, where Stan had dropped them and propped them up against the wall.

Stan ignored the gathering of Rodriguez's men at the entry as they waited for instructions. He stepped away from the alarm panel and walked to the center of the entry.

It was like none other he had seen or imagined. And it belied the weighty rectilinear outline of the exterior.

Here, in the home of James Marston Junior, everything was curves and bends and cambers all on multiple levels.

And it was open. And light.

Stan centered himself below the circular, gridded skylight and studied the beveled glass panels, held in place with a thin white frame. As he watched, the tinting of the glass lightened with measured grace. Sunlight steadily strengthened as did, Stan noticed, the scores of recessed lights, all responding to his presence.

The floor came alive too. Southwestern flagstones, filigreed with veins of ochre and muted crimson, were suffused with subtle crystalline flakes that glimmered in cadence with his movements.

Each floor stone was grand piano size and was outlined with bright white grouting. Placed at random locations, yet not really random, were four-man boulders that erupted from the floor. Mini downlights, hidden in the stones, defined their position and surface personality.

The walls appeared to be textured by hand, colored a relaxing sandy beige, the color of the beaches in St. Tropez or St. Barts or Wailea, Stan guessed.

As the lights came up, Stan could see the entry was really a hub from which three arms branched. Through thirty foot openings in each arm, he could see room after room in a winding dance of glass partitions, twisting walls, all enhanced with a perfect balance of radiance, at once both flattering and amusing.

Each room seemed to blend into the other. To his left, below the second level sweep of a curved balcony was a hint of a glass-sided dining area, beyond that, were manicured gardens and a small swimming pool with teak wood cabanas.

Ahead of him, up a few wide and rounded steps, was the quarter circle of a bar on one side of the room. On the other was what Marston undoubtedly called his living room. A subtle Feng shui arrangement of leather couches, chairs, ottomans, and low tables. Each table was of a different design and coloration, but each matched the chair or couch it was next to. Several flat screens were strategically placed to catch the eye of the person opposite.

To his right was, Stan surmised, the arm that led to the sleeping quarters. It was narrower, a snaking two-story hallway, colonnaded on one side with vine-like pillars. Diffused light seemed to come from everywhere in the hallway, especially the walls which glowed as if phosphorescent.

Stan inhaled and realized Marston was imbuing the air with a delicate and understated scent, a clean new-wood fragrance with a soothing hint of vanilla. Same as the Vegas casinos.

He felt happier already.

Stan turned and was about to instruct the cadre behind him on how he wanted the search to proceed when a gunshot rang out followed by a strangled, gurgling scream.

Everyone reacted as expected, each drawing their weapons and immediately moving to covered positions while at the same time scanning the area for threats or victims to determine who had either been shot or had shot.

Squinty stood stock still.

Above them, the face of the curved second level balcony came alive with different images. Onto seven different areas of the bone-white wall was projected a different movie.

The soundtrack, with the gunshot and scream, was coming from the middle movie.

Everyone relaxed and, with Stan, moved into the center of the atrium. All stared as images from seven different Marston movies were projected above them. A highlighted box in the upper corner of the middle projection informed them they were viewing *Spawn of the Cradle*. Beneath the title was 'Directed by James Marston, Jr'. As if there was any doubt.

Stan was about to turn back to the crew when a news-type crawl started along the bottom of the screen.

He watched in wonder as the up-to-date gross domestic rental figures of *Spawn of the Cradle* tracked across, followed by international grosses, listed by country. He had to watch the crawl come around again to verify that both grosses had increased in the short time they took to re-appear. Just as they did, the film looped and there were the same gunshot and the same shattering scream.

Richards nudged Stan. "Didn't this piece-of-shit Spawn thing come out like twenty, twenty-five years ago?"

"Got me."

"Think his shit films are big with the Japanese though."

"So I heard."

He nudged Stan again. "Look! Since we've been standing here breathing with our mouths open and our thumbs up our asses, this guy has made $1,380. In like half a minute."

"Appears so."

Richards turned away. "I'm gonna break something in here. Something worth $1,380."

Stan pointed to the screen.

"$1,552."

"Shit. This is unbelievable."

"Nice work, if you can get it," said Stan as he moved to the center of the group.

"Richard, take a few men, go that way." Stan pointed to what appeared to be the dining room, with the kitchen beyond.

"Can do."

"Rest of you left. I'll take straight ahead," Stan continued. "Squinty you're with me."

Stan gathered his own group and headed up a few stone steps into what appeared to be a hallway library to the sound of another gunshot, another scream.

He didn't look back, choosing to ignore the other six films that were spooling away, each with a separate crawl at the bottom, each earning dough while the rest of the world toiled.

CHAPTER 31

Squinty joined Stan as he pushed through the solid glass doors that formed an airlock into the enormous Conservatory.

"Holy shit," breathed Squinty. "I've never been in this part. This is awesome."

He sounded like a little-awed kid. No more puffing attorney. Stan could see why.

When Stan had appraised the Conservatory from the front of the house it only appeared to be a part of the right wing of the house and it seemed to match the height of the rest of the buildings. But when Stan entered Marston's version of a Brazilian rainforest he descended three steps on a broad, flared concrete stair.

And now the gridded side windows soared over two and a half stories high.

The roof was supported by colonnades of three-foot round pillars smothered with tended moss and trimmed ivy. The pillars lined both sides of the structure, allowing the entire central area to be open. Walkways extended forward and sideways each promising a verdant and peaceful stroll through a heady jungle of tropical and subtropical plants.

Adjacent to each pillar were Arabian-looking concrete planters, each holding a palm tree with brilliant fuchsia gracing the rest of the planter.

Bordering every exposed aggregate walkway was bed after bed of red flowers and buds and leaves. The sea before Stan shimmered crimson.

Stan fingered a three-pointed leaf and bent to smell. There was no bouquet from the plant but the humid air was laden with earth. It reminded him of quiet and peace and evermore.

Stan left Squinty on the steps and moved to one of the concrete benches. It faced the swell of splendor that was Marston's Conservatory, a gently swaying growth of seven-foot Golden Cane palms.

He stretched his arms out along the back of the bench. He tried not to dwell on how different this place, this sense of rightness was, in contrast to what he did every day.

With little persuasion, he could spend a lot of time right where he sat.

"It's like an art museum," whispered Squinty, coming up behind him.

"I wish Bea were here."

"Your wife?"

Stan nodded. "She'd know all the names of these plants. She'd never want to leave."

Just then the sun broke out, streaming through the thirty-foot windows, each window filigreed with arched grids. The shifting light patterns on the plants only highlighted their color and uniqueness.

Stan took a deep breath of the freshness and raised his head to the glass above just as a gentle mist fell. With a slight but insistent hiss from the overhead sprinkler system, rain fell in a gentle spiral spray.

Richards stuck his head in. Whatever he had been going to say instead came out as "Ho-ly crap. Look at this."

He took the steps down to Stan.

"Frickin' amazing. And automatic water too." He held out his hand and let the sprinkle cover his hand.

"Richards, what's up?"

Richards' attention came back to Stan. "We're done. You know there are eight bedrooms in this place. Each has its own bathroom, most of 'em have a separate dressing room. All of them have a fireplace and a what you would call a sitting area, a few have a bar."

"And?"

Richards shook his head. "Clean as my granny's fanny. Tossed the mattresses, box springs, bedside tables, bathrooms. You know there aren't any shower doors anymore. These showers are really like some Roman fuck station with tile and nozzles and jets of water coming out of everywhere. And you have to get through the shower just to get from the bedroom to the sitting area."

"A sitting area?"

"Yeah. And mirrors. The wife would never leave. Every time she'd turn around, she'd have to stop and admire her reflection."

Stan regarded the subtle sheen of the concrete beneath his feet. There wasn't a leaf, a blade of grass, a red petal out of place. Nothing disturbed the absolute orderliness and cleanliness.

"Pristine. Untouched," answered Stan.

"Well, not exactly. That's what I came to tell you. A guy's outside. Says he runs the cleaning service that cleans the place."

Squinty snickered. "And I thought it cleaned itself. Computerized, like everything else in here."

Stan brushed back his hair, letting warm water rivulets run down inside his shirt and down his back. "Where is he?"

"He made it past the gate…well, you'll see."

Stan followed Richards out to the circular drive where one of the squads was parked, engine running, Officer Sunglasses leaning up against the passenger door, picking his teeth.

Stan approached the car. "Where is he?"

The uniform nodded to the backseat.

Stan bent down and peered inside the tinted windows. A sullen and regally ruffled ruffian sat stiffly, centered in the back seat of the squad.

"Well, get him out," demanded Stan.

Uniform unfolded his frame and with laconic deliberateness opened the door.

The man scooted across the seat and stood awkwardly before stumbling into Stan. Stan caught him by the cuffs that shackled the man's hands behind him.

"You've got him handcuffed!"

The officer shrugged and delved into the cuff case on his duty belt, found what he was seeking, and unlocked the cuffs. With a practiced twirl, he spun the cuffs so they nested together, circle to circle. He slipped them in his rear pocket.

"All yours."

Stan, Richards and the man watched him head back down to the gate entrance.

Stan regarded the man. Big-shouldered and thick neck, close-cropped grey hair. He looked Slavic or German to Stan. Very well-dressed but he also looked like the type to grab his crotch and spit as he left the opera.

He was dressed in a black, one-button cutaway coat, razor pleated grey trousers, a dove grey silk tie, and a white shirt that Stan swore was starched.

Starch. Who uses starch? Stan hadn't seen a starched shirt since the last time he went to a funeral. And that was on the deceased.

The man rubbed his wrists and sighed. "Thank you, sir. I believe it to be rather unfortunate, being treated this way. I was only doing what was called for."

The voice wasn't British, but it had a European snootiness to it.

"Who are you?"

The man took a moment to adjust everything into a more perfect arrangement before answering. Finally, he looked at Stan and almost clicked his heels.

"Spiros. Anton Spiros. Proprietor of Belle Services. Maintenance and Preservation."

Anton Spiros readjusted a perfectly knotted tie.

Stan wondered if this was the regulation dress requirement of Belle Services. Must be damned hard to get down and scrub a toilet and keep the crease.

"Maintenance and Preservation? The hell is that?"

"I would think it speaks for itself." When Stan didn't seem to get it, Spiros continued on.

"We are simply in charge of maintaining and preserving the properties under our care."

"You clean houses."

Had the man been any taller he would've looked down his nose at Stan "No, sir. We don't clean houses." He sniffed and turned to face the expanse of the Marston manse.

"We clean these."

He turned back to Stan with a smile.

"Sir."

"Like I said."

Spiros let it pass but continued. "May I ask what has happened here?"

Stan ignored the question. "What are you doing here?"

"I am automatically alerted by the security concern when a door is inadvertently left open by one of the staff when they leave. If it should happen, if one of our staff fails to secure the property correctly, we are notified to come and rectify the oversight. I was informed that a door was open. I came to check and secure the property as our instructions dictate."

"Cars sitting here too long, doors open. This is a busy alarm company."

The man viewed the assemblage around him. "Seems so."

"These were Marston's instructions?"

"I believe the request we be informed came from the master of the house, yes."

"Marston told you this directly?"

The man shuddered. "I have never met Mr. Marston personally. All communications are done by FAX, or email, usually through an intermediary. There would be no call for us to interlocute with Mr. Marston."

Starch, cutaway coat, and now interlocute. That's not even a word, thought Stan.

The man's eyes darted away from Stan to Richards to the other members of Sacramento's finest. "I presume with all this…force, there has been some sort of altercation here?"

"What about your staff? I assume you don't do any of the dirty work yourself."

Spiros saw his question would not be answered. "Well, yes. I do oversee everything personally. Our clients would expect nothing less."

"C'mon Anton. Who works here with you?"

"I have a very small staff. As you might imagine, our personnel must be bonded and have a pristine history before we can take them on."

"Sure, I'll bet. Well, we'll need to find out the last one of your fine employees to see Mr. Marston during one of your cleaning soirees."

"Impossible. None of us have ever seen the owner of the property, Mr. Marston. We only arrive, rather we are only scheduled to be here when the owner is absent or is in another part of the estate."

"How are you scheduled?"

"We are here three days a week, Mondays, Wednesdays, and Fridays. If there are any changes, we are informed by email."

"From Marston?"

"From someone on staff, I believe."

"Staff? There's no one here."

Spiros nodded. "That's always been the case."

Stan ran a hand through his hair. "So, in the last say, six weeks, you've been here three days a week?"

"We strive to be dependable."

"In these last few weeks, has anybody bothered to change your schedule?"

"There has been no change in the last six months."

"What has the condition of the house been?"

"When we leave, immaculate."

"I don't mean that. I mean what have you seen?"

"I don't understand the question."

Stan didn't want to lead him. "What has been the condition of the house when you arrived? What do you see when you get here?"

Spiros affected a thoughtful pose. "If you mean to ask if we've seen anything out of the ordinary the answer would be, No."

"Nothing?"

Spiros turned to the entryway where Richard's men were coming and going like bees to a hive.

"If you would please ask your... *staff* to try and not sully our home."

"Our home?" said Richards in a surprised tone.

Spiros addressed Richards for the first time. "Our home. Yes. Of course. Belle Services treats all our clients' homes as our own. Wouldn't you want the same standard for your... home. Wouldn't you want the ones who service, who maintain and preserve your home to treat it and respect it as their own?"

Richards shook his head and walked away.

"Where can I reach you?" asked Stan, weary of this overdressed janitor. "Let me have one of your business cards."

Anton Spiros smiled a deprecating smile. "Our service is by referral only. We do not need to… advertise. I'm sure you understand. However, I will note my personal…" He looked up at Stan. "My personal and private number on whatever bit of paper you might have."

Stan retrieved a pen and one of his own business cards.

Spiros studied the front before turning it over on the back side and writing his phone number. He returned pen and card. Before walking back down to the entrance pillars, Spiros touched Stan on the arm.

"Best of luck in your endeavors. And please take good care of our home, won't you?"

CHAPTER 32

It was like a Hollywood entrance, thought Mallory. At least that was her first thought when the UPS guy held the outside door open as he was leaving. The woman ignored the courtesy and stood there, backlit by the late afternoon sun. She was a slim silhouette and in a dress sheer enough to confirm she was a woman.

She stood in the entrance, pausing long enough for anyone inside to take notice. Only Mallory noticed. Jake was busy screwing around with the video recorder.

Mallory had to hand it to her, the woman strode into the building as if she, not Mallory, belonged.

The woman stopped at the entrance to the glass office, one arm outstretched up the side of one of the glass walls. One leg coquettishly bent, in front of the other. It would've been comical if it hadn't been so damn effective.

Mallory tried to withhold judgment, but couldn't help hating her. Even though according to the information gathered when Samantha Barnes responded to the call for witnesses, she claimed she did charity work.

How do you 'do' charity work? Volunteer at the Mission handing out cookies and condoms? Empty bedpans at the VA hospital?

Mallory thought not. After viewing her, Mallory believed her version of charity was probably tossing a dime to the cardboard sign guy at the off-ramp from her Lexus.

With her arms full of two file boxes, Mallory approached the woman, who turned only slightly and gave the same acknowledgment to Mallory as she would a bug on the floor.

Mallory returned the deprecating smile thrown her way as she pushed past the woman into the office, noticing only the beautiful white teeth, the flawless face, and the arresting green eyes.

Addressing Jake, the woman spoke, "I'm supposed to meet Detective Steiner here, I think." Wide-eyed and with a slight twist to her mouth, she surveyed the whole office setup, as if she wasn't sure she was in the right place, but she really knew she was.

It was a nifty performance.

Jake, kneeling on the floor in front of the ancient video camera turned. His mouth opened and Mallory could see him pause. Whatever he had been going to say, he said instead, "That's me."

To Mallory, it sounded like a little kid wanting a popsicle.

The woman moved further into the room with a warm smile and extended her hand. "Samantha Barnes." She glanced again at her surroundings. "Not sure I was in the right place."

Jake rose and shook her hand. "You are. Have a seat."

Mallory let the two boxes drop to the floor. Jake shot her a glance in irritation. Samantha Barnes, however, never turned her attention away from Jake, who pulled out a chair at the conference table. Instead of sitting, Samantha Barnes moved to the center of the room, resting her pert behind, Mallory noticed, on the edge of the conference table.

She looked up into the atrium above.

"So, is this where they keep all the evidence from the crimes you're working on?"

"Some," Jake answered. "The floors above hold all the evidence from past crimes usually."

"This is fantastic. And," she said, pointing a coy finger at Jake. "I know who you are. You're the detective who solved that kid killer thing, aren't you? I recognized your name."

"I was one of them."

"When you're done with me," she paused. "You must show me around. I was fascinated by that case. Do you have all the gruesome evidence here? Pictures and stuff?"

"Well-"

Mallory cleared her throat. "I thought we were doing interviews at Freeport Avenue?" asked Mallory, trying to regain lost ground.

Jake turned to her with a what-do-you-want-now look. "Change of plans, remember. They're busy. Full up. They sent me this… stuff." He indicated the out-of-date video camera/recorder. "But thanks. I'm all set up here."

Mallory forced a smile.

Jake repeated his invitation to Samantha Barnes who sat down, set her purse on the table before her, and placed her hands together. It appeared as if she had a pronouncement to make, like the Chairman of the Board.

"I'm not sure I can really be of any help. I didn't really see much of anything that night."

Jake smiled a knowing smile. "Most witnesses feel that way. You might be surprised at what you can remember."

He turned and instead of making his witness move to the video camera, slid the tripod around the edge of the table.

Mallory couldn't take anymore.

"I'm outta here, then."

Jake, seemingly surprised she was still here, said, "Yeah. Fine. I've got this." Then as an afterthought. "If you're going to lunch, it's okay, I don't need anything."

Wasn't going to ask, asshole. "And I wasn't." Mallory pulled a few random files from the top file box for show and left.

What was it about men, she asked herself as she threw the files onto the passenger seat of her red Honda. But she knew that wasn't the problem. Men were men. Simple creatures who needed a sledgehammer to their nuts to make them understand. No, the man wasn't the problem. And it really wasn't the woman either.

For some reason, she had an urge to drive out to Murphy's and empty some clips into some helpless targets instead of what she was supposed to be doing, finding Pokovich.

Confused, Mallory lowered her visor against the setting sun, gunned the Honda past the sleek black Miata that Miss Green Eyes had arrived in, and attempted to put the woman out of her mind.

It would be a task that would prove impossible.

CHAPTER 33

Michael Cooper closed his aunt's old flip phone.

It was true. Shippen Travers was laid up. Both legs busted good, according to the nice nurse at the hospital in Phoenix.

Michael had used his aunt's cell phone and even though it was rather early, called the Travers house first, hoping to get Travers' son. All he got was the housekeeper who informed him through muffled sniffs that 'Mister Travers been helicoptered to Phoenix right after the accident.'

After some confusion with Michael imagining Shippen had been in a helicopter accident, the housekeeper kept saying, 'No, No'. In a slurred rush she'd told him the story of how some cattle fell over on him, or something. Or a stampede. And wasn't it terrible?

"Terribles not the half of it," said Michael. He disconnected while she was still babbling, still not sure how a cow falls over.

Lying in bed this morning, before Jessie was awake, he had harbored the fiction it could all still work. That somehow he could lie his way to Arizona. Get himself and Jessie to the Arizona ranch. Start over. Work with animals. Live in a ranch house or a bunkhouse. Riding horses. Driving feed to animals out in the field.

The dream lasted ten minutes before reality came calling in the form of the Chinese lady from two trailers down knocking on the door. He'd never learned her name.

Michael had opened the door partway.

"I wake you?"

Michael had realized his hair was sticking up at disparate angles and he made to smooth the pokies.

"No. I'm good."

"Where is Jane? She here?" The Chinese lady had craned around Michael, searching.

"At work. She's at work."

The Chinese lady's eyes had widened. "She at work? Today Saturday."

Michael had no answer but abruptness. "Don't know what to tell you. She's at work. I'll tell her you were here."

Michael started to close the door but the Chinese lady pushed a newspaper between the door and the jamb.

"Here! You in paper."

"We don't want a paper."

"No! You take it. Your picture there."

"What?"

"Little missy too."

Michael stared at the rolled-up paper.

"You take it," she beamed. "You sign for me later, okay?"

She pushed the paper into Michael's hand. He shut the door gently but firmly.

"The hell."

He unfolded the copy of the Bee. Frontpage.

"Oh shit."

Michael mouthed the headline to himself. 'Two Children Escaped from Killer'.

Below it and the article were two big photos.

"Why now?" He had no answer except someone must've held onto these until the price was right. And now these are the only two photos that have ever made it out into the world about that night. That night. He remembered and felt it and smelled it and didn't want to any longer. His finger traced the photos. He couldn't believe it.

Michael studied the one of him. In it, he was sitting, perched really, half on a rock. His head was lowered so you couldn't see his face. One of the detectives, Detective Wyld, Michael remembered, was kneeling beside him.

The second photo with Jessie in it was almost beautiful. He had no doubt this would be the image that would spin around the web.

With all the morbid interest in Ruby Everheart, Michael guessed there would be no one in the remotely civilized world that wouldn't see it, especially when the caption under her photo read 'Six-Year-Old Rescued from Serial Killer'.

Didn't matter Michael tried to tell himself.

Still, it was angelic, he realized. Mesmerizing. Backlit from the blurred light of the ambulances, it was Jessie being carried by Detective Wyld, her arms hanging nearly lifeless, except from one hand dangled a stuffed bear.

The two of them glowed as if walking into a great light.

Michael tossed the paper into the trash. Had Aunt Jane been here, he thought, she would've carefully cut out the two pictures and added them to her colorful wall of death.

"This is way beyond bad." He started random pacing around the room.

With Shippen Travers down for the count, with the neighbors snooping around and now with him and Jess splattered all over page one, it was obvious their chances of getting out of Sunshine Vista even staying in Sunshine Vista and living below the radar, would be short-lived.

Someday soon, like probably tomorrow if they subscribed to the paper when CPS couldn't get a hold of Aunt Jane, or the paperwork of her commitment found its way into the clutches of Mrs. Finch or the new Mrs. Warner, it would be over and their new adventure into the vast and thrilling world of foster care would begin.

Michael stared at his aunt's cell phone. How much does this cost per month he wondered?

He looked around. How much does the trailer cost? Is there a mortgage? What about food? Electricity? Water?

He hadn't a clue. He'd never cared before. His aunt had taken care of all that. And even if he'd asked her about it, about what the cell phone or the TV or the trailer space or the car cost, she wouldn't have told him. Even though he had helped her set up online banking with the used laptop someone had given her, she would've still dismissed him with a wave.

She was oh so friendly like that.

He only knew Shippen Travers had been their last and only hope of any kind of new life.

Michael felt his right jeans pocket. Without looking, he knew there was something like fifteen dollars there. Savings from a year of working for his aunt minus all the dough he'd had to put out the last few days.

He jumped as something banged against the front door.

"M, what was that noise?" asked Jessie as she emerged, yawning, from the bedroom.

"It was a zombie asking you to come out and play."

"Okay," came the listless reply. She turned around, headed back to bed.

Michael opened the door in time to see the mailman turning from the overgrown walk heading toward the next house.

In front of Michael was a package. Atop that was the mail, secured with a wide red rubber band.

Michael brought it in and set the mail aside because the box was addressed to him and Jessie.

The return address was in a withered scrawl.

'S. Travers. Bullhead, AZ. 86429.

Michael started to tear off the brown paper wrapping when he stopped. He should call Jessie. After all, it was addressed to both of them and it was from Arizona. But he thought better of it.

He continued to tear at the paper, unwrapping an old shoebox, bent down on one corner. But it wasn't a shoebox, more like a boot box from someplace called Boots by Espinoza.

He opened the top of the box expecting a shiny pair of cowboy boots. Probably two; one for him, one for Jess.

It was not boots.

Instead, nested together were two western hats wrapped in grey wrapping paper, used as padding. Atop the hats was an unsealed envelope addressed to Michael.

Michael emptied the envelope. Out fell a letter in which was wrapped two twenty-dollar bills. Old bills pressed flat with the corners straightened.

He unfolded the letter and examined it. It was written on the back of a paper menu from Slick Chick's BBQ, Bullhead City's Finest.

The handwriting was determined, written by someone not used to managing cursive.

Dear Michael,

Hope this reaches you in time before you leave. Just thought you two should have some hats. Sun gets pretty rich down here. You don't have some cover; you'll be a crispy critter. So, I'm sending two hats.

Hope they fit.

Cody wants me to tell you he's excited about you two coming to stay.

I guess I am too. Didn't expect it, but like I said on the phone, family's family. So, you two are welcome.

Remember this is a working farm. Like Cody, you'll be working. So you know, I've set aside some getting started wages for you down here. It'll be for both of you. Leave it to you to divide it up.

Guess that's it. We plan to meet the plane, so we'll see you when you get here.

It was signed just Shippen.

Michael could feel something else in the envelope. He reached in and brought out two pictures.

One was a school picture. He could tell by the standard blue background. It was Cody. Blond toe-head, crew cut, tanned with a generous face that looked ready to smile.

The other picture was Shippen.

Michael studied the picture.

Travers was a tall man, judging by the horse he was next to. Plaid shirt, dungarees, not jeans, dirt-covered boots. His hat was pushed back on his head revealing a shock of escaping grey. He was challenging the camera to hurry up.

Michael looked closer.

He would've been one to expect you to pull your weight, to keep up, to only rest when everything was done. He'd never tell you when to work or how long. He'd only shame you into keeping going because he did.

Michael could tell because of the eyes.

They were his mother's eyes.

Michael pocketed the money, closed the envelope with the pictures and the letter.

He took out the two hats and put the larger one on his head, adjusted the slant, and studied his reflection in the window.

Just an old cowhand.

He pushed the hat back like Shippen's picture and he watched himself watch himself.

A hat, some dough, and a picture. Welcome to Arizona. Not.

Michael turned away from the window but stopped.

Arizona.

Maybe he wasn't there. Maybe Shippen Travers wasn't in front of him setting an example of how to work the land, care for the livestock, provide for a family, but Michael at that moment knew what Shippen would do if he were here.

He'd get to work.

Damn straight.

CHAPTER 34

Lunch was Michael's famous peanut butter and jelly (with butter) sandwiches, which was all they had in the trailer, which was just fine with Jessie. After lunch, she wandered around, finally settling down with a book on the couch. Michael made her change books when she asked him what 'masturbation' was. He wasn't ready for that kind of parenting.

He did a quick wash-up of the kitchen, then conducted a thorough inventory of what was left in the kitchen cabinets. It didn't take long.

Tomorrow he'd have to dig into his Arizona stash, walk to the QuickMart, the only place within walking distance with food, and stock up. He could drive. He was sure he could handle his aunt's Volkswagen, but best not to get caught.

That was tomorrow. Now, right now, he owed it to Jessie at least to calculate how long they would be able to 'live low' in Aunt Jane's trailer before the dragon known as Child Protection Services belched fire and swooped in.

He half expected a SWAT team of foster parents to come barging through the door any second. His constant companion, paranoia, forced him to check and re-check the area in front of the trailer every five minutes for unmarked cars sliding up the driveway.

There was nothing but Sunshine Vista.

He didn't dwell on the view at the far end of the trailer court where the two Ruby Everheart trailers had been.

He was surprised to see that by the time he and Jessie were released from the hospital and reunited with a jubilant Aunt Jane, Ruby Everheart's trailer, which had burned to a pile of crap, had been further smooshed to rubble, picked up, and hauled away. The other trailer, the one where she had practiced her fortune-telling scam, 'Fortunes by Ruby', had been craned onto another semi at the same time, he'd heard, and both trucked away in the middle of the night. Even the rusted thirty-foot pole, with its gaudy neon sign that read 'Fortunes by Ruby' in red and green on both sides, he saw was gone.

Like she and her whole kit and caboodle, as his mother like to say, had never been there.

Still, no one from the trailer park ventured anywhere near there. It was as if the whole neighborhood had seen Carrie and believed the crookedy old hand of Ruby Everheart would erupt from below ground, grab their arms and pull them face to face with evil itself.

And even though Jessie recalled little of the bad stuff, he noticed she never even cast a glance in that direction, even when playing outside. And she wouldn't ride the bike that Ruby Everheart had given her. She'd made Aunt Jane buy her another one, though Aunt Jane was never sure why.

When it had first happened, for the first few weeks, cars by the dozens would cruise through the trailer park, confused when they couldn't find the burned-out trailer they'd seen on the news. They'd stop and ask anybody in the park where was the child killer's house?

After a time, Michael and most of the other residents would either ignore their inquiries or send them to some other development.

"You got the wrong place, friend. It's down the way 'bout half mile. Can't miss it."

At one point, traffic got so bad the homeowners association voted to change the name from Sunshine Vista to Regency Park. It passed overwhelmingly. They just hadn't gotten around to ordering a new sign. Not enough money.

Money.

Michael briefly thought about printing up something about what had happened. Sell his autograph by the side of the road. But it sounded cheesy after thinking about it for two minutes.

Now he almost wished he had because he sure could use the dough. But cheesy is cheesy. And the thought of having to answer all sorts of questions over and over made him sick to his stomach.

The trailer park, suffused with the faint but distinctive aroma of rusting metal and dead animals, was the only reminder of where evil had once had its lair.

Everything was gone except his and Jessie's personal crap the cops had returned to them.

All gone except a cute backpack, some dumb clothes, and a stuffed bear.

The red-bordered envelope, the final notice from the electric company, had shown up with the mail this morning. Evidently, not only had Aunt Jane gone bonkers in the produce aisle at Safeway while trying to decide which avocado was best by massaging each and every one, and then murdering the Romas, it also appeared she had decided to tell the utility companies to Suck Wind. According to the notice from PG&E, she'd severed all relations with electricity six weeks ago and they had decided enough was enough and were now giving her 48 hours to recant. And pay $562.56 to rejoin the grid.

What was next? Water? He went to the sink and turned the tap. It flowed but for how long?

Michael fired up the laptop. Last month, he'd helped his aunt set up her online banking, and even though she had somehow managed, on her own, to change the password later, he'd found the little booklet she'd started with all her accounts and passwords.

He logged on.

There's probably only ten grand or so left, he thought. Could be more, but judging how his aunt was living, maybe not.

He scanned the checking portion of the Bank of America account.

"Ouch."

$22.33. That was it. Plus, his hundred he'd saved. Plus, what Shippen had sent.

He knew her paycheck of $872.13 was deposited like clockwork every two weeks on the 15th. Even if she was bounced out on her ass, there should still be a last check, shouldn't there?

Two weeks' notice. Okay, here's your final check.

So where was it?

He flipped back a month, then two. Paychecks had stopped five weeks ago. Evidently, the powers that be at In-N-Out EZ Loans had no longer required her services weeks ago.

Great.

He hit the tab that took him to savings.

$39.11

Fucking great.

Michael decided to hold off raiding the savings account.

He was about to close out when he checked her email.

He'd read it was a federal offense, like a FEDERAL offense to snoop into somebody else's email account and read their private correspondence.

Well, with no feds in sight, he opened her inbox.

He scrolled down. The usual scams and promotions. Nigerian princes and weight loss and erectile dysfunction.

She must not have many friends, at least ones that emailed. There was, however, a ton from an Amber Condon.

Michael didn't recognize the name as a cousin or relative.

His finger hesitated over the entry, but only for a polite second.

It opened up into a series of over twenty emails grouped in one conversation.

He saw the header from Amber Condon's letterhead.

Cliff EDGE Productions. Los Angeles. California. Below the letterhead, it said Independent Film Producers.

Oh yeah?

He read the most recent email in the list.

'Dear Miss Murray, we're thrilled you want to move ahead with our project about the Olive Park events…'

What?

The color drained from Michael's face.

What??

He scrolled further.

*As we stated in previous correspondence, CliffEDGE
Productions has secured the cooperation of some of the parents
of the deceased children and, of course, we have the official and
media reports of those events. To make this production as
accurate and as true-to-life as possible we required the
cooperation of both Michael and Jessica. They needed to tell
their story as they lived it: their relationship with Everheart, the
events leading up to that night, the details of exactly what
happened in those woods and the aftermath, and their life now.*

The project could not go forward without their inclusion.

*And we are delighted to understand that you, as their guardian,
can guarantee their full cooperation, including participating in
extensive interviews with our staff, on and off-camera, and more
importantly, acting as principals in the on-location re-creation of
the murders in the Olive Park woods...*

Oh, God.

'on-location re-creation'?

'on-camera interviews'?

Are they nuts?

Like that'll ever happen.

Michael's head spun with the what-ifs.

What if good ol' Aunt Jane hadn't gone bugnuts?

What if he and Jessie had made it to Arizona?

And then he realized the sickening truth. His aunt had planned
to scuttle their move to Arizona at the last minute. She'd had to,
to make her scheme work. There was no way in hell she would've
let them go.

Now, with her out of the picture, they could go, except their
new Arizona guardian had played Who's-Your-Daddy with some
of his cattle.

Irony.

Michael thought of his mother. She would be embarrassed by
all this. The desperation, the scheming, the senseless deaths. And
now being asked to parade ourselves before everybody. Like
common trash.

He was about to close out when the last paragraph caught his
attention.

And he froze.

Not comprehending, then quickly not believing what he read.

Pursuant to our discussions, fully delineated in the attached contract, and encompassing the above points, CliffEDGE Productions will compensate you $200,000. $10,000 will be advanced upon signing of the contract, the remainder to be paid on completion of the project.

Michael glanced at the figures from his Aunt's checking account.

$22.33.

He dug into his pocket and freed his $114.22, plus the two twenties from Shippen.

'In for a penny, in for a pound', his mother used to say.

He took an hour to formulate his aunt's response to Amber Condon of CliffEDGE Productions.

Most of the time was spent practicing his aunt's signature which he needed to do before the power company turned off the lights.

PART THREE

CHAPTER 35

The morning sun was barely above the mountains as Stan stood at the half-wall that surrounded the roof of the OID building. The long light lit the splash of greens that made up the farms of the Sacramento Valley. Beyond that, the patchwork brown and green hills above Napa were alive with activity. Every year, every month, despite all they heard and read about California taxes, California crime, California cost of living, like lemmings, they poured through the mountain passes, streamed down the freeways, modern-day Okies seeking the warmth of the good life, or spiritual rebirth or to be discovered or to complicate Stan's life by clogging the grocery line or gumming up I-5 or not appreciating the paradise they've stumbled upon.

Stan held out his hand, palm down, and felt the sun warm the back of his hand, tan and strong.

He and Jake getting OID off the ground had done what Bea had been asking for for years. Get out of the field, she'd say. She never said it out of fear. At least not directly. But, the odds were never skewed in a cop's favor he knew. And she was right. And OID had been the answer. Still a cop. Still catching up with the assholes of life. Just not shooting at them or vice versa anymore.

He turned his face upward and took a deep breath. A medical blip will force you to appreciate what you have. A re-evaluation of even the small things. The very small things.

Mallory emerged from the stairwell, slightly out of breath, carrying a shiny black nightstick.

Jake and Jake followed.

They both looked like Stan felt; hit and run over by a case that had then backed up and run over them a second time to finish the job.

Even the dog looked disheartened.

Jake had the morning paper which he tossed on the table.

'OFF WITH HIS HEAD!' screamed the Sacramento headline.

All three had seen the picture.

"And then we have…" He dropped four more. "New York, San Francisco, L.A., and Chicago."

"Terrific," moaned Stan.

"Wait." He dropped two more, a tabloid from Britain and one from France.

No one spoke for a moment.

Mallory prodded the paper with the fat end of the nightstick. "I thought drones had better lenses than that."

"They do," sighed Stan. "But after Jake grabbed the controls I'm surprised they were able to capture anything.". Stan had marveled at what Ginger and his staff had to go through to enhance what was arguably a fuzzy, smeared shot. And it must've been the best of the lot because this is what made it onto the front page.

"But, it only looks like a blob," smirked Mallory.

"That's the problem," stated Jake. "Looking like a blob that may or not be a head gives it legitimacy. Makes it authentic. People are gonna believe it just because it is a blob. Like a picture of a UFO. If it looks like Mom's pie plate that someone threw into the air in the backyard, no one with an IQ above 75 believes it's real. But you show a five second, jerky video of streaks of lights or a blurred picture of a lighted orb and you have people taking to their shelters. They believe because it's not perfect."

After a moment of silence, Mallory spoke up.

"I shut off the phones."

"How?" asked Stan.

She laughed. "I suppose there's a master switch somewhere, but I simply went around to all our phones and unplugged them."

"It's not like we were using the landlines."

"Yeah, but the rest of the world doesn't know that. Before I shut them down, I answered one. Some guy said he was president of Marston's fan club in Japan."

"There's a fan club?"

"What did he want?"

"What they all want. Pictures. More pictures"

Jake slid into the third chair. He put his feet up on the table.

"Please," admonished Mallory.

When Jake didn't move, Mallory kicked off her tennis shoes and put her feet up next to Jake's.

"Sure. Why not?" Stan unlaced his, shucked them, peeled off his black socks, and added two more, albeit bone-white feet, to the mix.

No one said anything.

Well, they were up in the fresh air. Not staring at the whiteboards that showed not only their lack of progress but clearly illustrated their near total confusion. They were not answering phones. Not listening to the endless beseeching from the press. Not allowing either Carruthers or Samuels to disturb what little quiet time they had.

Stan sighed. "Look, I want to work the victim."

"Victims," corrected Jake. "Mr. Berlin."

"Yeah, victims."

Stan started slowly. "Okay, first Marston. We know where he lived and that the place looks like it's been sterilized thanks to the marvelous cleaning service. So, nothing there. We know where he was found- "

"And we have the witness's statement on video," smiled Jake.

"Which we'll take a look at in a few minutes. So, can we please get some answers!?" He avoided looking directly at Mallory. "And, let's begin with motive."

No one spoke.

Jake was petting Jake.

Mallory had her head tipped back trying to get some full-face sun. She was slowly thwacking the stick against her other hand.

"Right," Stan continued. "I know this looks like some slasher murder with a lot of rage because of the head, but if it wasn't- "

"You don't think revenge?" asked Mallory. "I mean with whatshername, our felon, being released."

"Why?"

"She had some history with Marston."

Stan looked at Jake. He shrugged.

"It's in the casebook," said Mallory, not altering her pose.

"Like we've had time," said Jake.

"Our felon, Ilsa Pokovich, white female, sentenced to 26 years with the possibility of parole after serving 12 years at Central California Women's Facility in Chowchilla. She was convicted in August of '95 of, get this, aggravated assault and attempted murder."

"Against Marston? Asked Jake.

"Of course."

"Well, so we know the guy was unpopular," Stan said with a dismissive wave. "I could've told you that. A film producer ranks right up there with rattlers and Ebola."

Mallory held up a hand. "I'm not done. She evidently worked for Marston-"

"Worked for him?"

"Yeah, she worked for him and one day snuck up and dumped a bucket full of battery acid on him. Or tried to. Studio security found her kicking him in his face as he shrieked on his office floor doing his level best to crawl away. It took four of them to pull her off him."

"That's aggravated."

Jake slid the casebook over in front of him. He opened it and paged through. "And, based on the fingerprints Danni found, she returned to finish the job."

"Pokovich was released from CCWF three weeks before our friend lost his head and your dog discovered him in his late-model BMW."

Mallory smiled proudly.

"How'd she get out?"

"Compassionate release. There was a note somewhere that she might've had stomach cancer. Released to the hospital and she pulled a vanish from there.

Jake looked at Stan. "Finishing the job herself, before she checks out?"

"Makes sense," agreed Stan. "But, she's how old again?" He looked at Mallory.

"She's forty-seven, forty-eight."

"She's forty-eight, maybe with cancer. She didn't do this by herself. If she was involved at all."

Jake found Ilsa Pokovich's page. He pulled out her picture. "Wow. That's a clock stopper." To Mallory "So, no idea where she went?

"I'm working on it."

"And I sent out a bulletin yesterday," added Stan.

"Okay," Jake sighed. "Motive. If not revenge, how 'bout good old money?" He looked to Stan who seemed lost in his own funk.

"You know, this whole thing could've been worse," Mallory offered.

"How?" asked Jake.

"I was thinking. If metro had popped the door right there on Jones Road a few months ago, there'd have been a freakin' frenzy. Cell phone videos on the net, telephoto shots of Marston's head on the ground then, helicopter shots of us running around. We'd be up to our asses fending off the hordes."

"Except it wouldn't have been us. It would've been Robbery-Homicide dealing with it," Jake countered.

Stan pushed his chair back and started pacing.

"What? What is it?" Mallory asked.

"You're right."

"About?"

Stan picked up a felt marker and used it as a pointer, angling to Mallory.

"Don't you see? You're right."

"Usually," Mallory smirked. "But how now?"

"The hoopla, the helicopters, the telephoto shots of Marston's head lolling on the ground next to his car, all of it."

Mallory looked to Jake who shrugged.

"All of that stuff," Stan continued. "All of that. That was what was supposed to happen. That was the plan. Their plan. They wanted that to happen. That's why they dropped the car out there. They expected Officer Grey to open the car and check it out, but they screwed up and locked the car."

He swung on Jake.

"Were the keys in it?"

"Yeah. In the ignition."

"Of course they were. They screwed up. Plain and simple. They had a plan to reveal a dead Marston to the world weeks ago, but they messed up royally."

Jake raised his hand. "Hate to bust your wonderfully constructed bubble, but who are 'they' and why? Are you talking about the dreaded Pokovich gang led by an aging cancer sufferer? Why not shoot the bastard if they wanted him dead and leave him lying on the side of the road? Or, run a stake through his heart and put him on a park bench? Why do this? Helluva a lot of work for the same result."

"Because it's revenge. Pure and simple. Yes, they could've just knocked him off and made it obvious somehow, but these people or Pokovich, whatever, wanted to satisfy themselves that he was not only dead but that he suffered and that the world would know it. They did it for themselves. They believe they are bulletproof. They think they can exact retribution and we won't get it. They think they'll never be caught, that's why they were so emboldened they felt they could chop the guy's head off and we wouldn't figure it out."

Stan stood back, flushed with accomplishment.

Jake and Mallory exchanged glances.

"Nah," both said in unison.

"What?" Stan leaned both fists on the table. "Stop thinking like yourselves. Stop believing every evil asshole has your sensibilities. Stop thinking they think like you. Of course, it would be easier to simply kill him, but try thinking like someone incensed with rage, hell-bent on getting back at Marston for whatever reason and letting everyone know you got even. Like this Pokovich."

Stan slid back into his seat. "We need to think on a whole different level. Dropping the car right there was a plan. They really gigged themselves by locking it."

"For revenge?" Jake questioned.

"An eye for an eye," Mallory said.

"Which leaves everyone half blind," added Jake.

Stan smiled. "Unless you're already blind and have nothing left to lose. Or have stomach cancer and nothing left to lose."

"Swell," Mallory said. "The Stan Wyld 'Blind looking for the Blind' theory.

"And," added Stan, pointing at Jake. "The motive doesn't appear to be money. As I said. Seven or eight charities are the only beneficiaries. Whole estate goes that way, divided up."

"What about Ming vases or gold bars in the basement?" Mallory asked.

Stan shook his head. "Nope. Nothing. Unless there's a secret door hiding the proverbial cache of Hollywood loot, there is nothing of beheading value in that house. And there is no basement. Went through it all. Eight bedrooms with sitting areas, bathrooms we stopped counting at ten, two kitchens, wine cellar, six-car garage, a few studies, a library, a huge greenhouse conservatory with all these huge planters and exotic plants and water that automatically sprits out when you least expect it."

He considered. "Artwork. Lots of film in the screening room. All goes into the estate according to Squinty. Still, now that I think about it, I should've stripped a few of the beds. I know Bea would kill for some of those linens."

"Okay," offered Mallory. "Revenge. But why? And how'd she do it herself?"

"With a daiishka," added Jake with a smile.

"Look," said Stan. "Until we find Pokovich and on the minutely slim possibility that I'm wrong about revenge, we still need to recreate this guy's life. What did Marston do every day? Who did he see? Who worked for him? How did he spend his dough? Where did he go? Did he use his passport? Was he threatened? Was he scared? Cell phone? Who did he call? Can we track the car? Did it have On-Star or something? I can't believe this guy was a vapor. That nobody saw him or interacted. You can't live in a place like that or have worked with so many people that nobody sees you."

Stan studied Mallory. "And the same with Berlin, though with the cell phone records on Berlin and what you two have done there with Jake rifling the office, we know more about a dead detective than we do about your famous Hollywood director. How are we on all that cryptic shit you found?"

"Workin' it," said Jake. "Mallory and I are."

Mallory gave him an appraising look.

"But here's the thing," Jake continued. "It appears that Berlin thought there might be a connection between what happened at Olive Park and Marston."

Stan gave him a sharp look. "A connection?"

"We're not sure," corrected Mallory.

"Berlin tried to get to us, well Mallory anyway, before everything happened. Before Olive Park, before Marston. His last stop was here according to his cell phone. And if we're right about the notes he left, he was snooping around Marston's place before all of this."

"A connection..." mused Stan.

Mallory slapped the nightstick against the casebook. "Meanwhile I'm tracing Ilsa Pokovich's background, her prison stay, who wrote to her, who visited her."

"Also," added Stan. "See if you can pull the original trial record. Find out who her attorney was. See who the witnesses were to this acid incident. Maybe we can find out what their real relationship was."

Mallory slapped the nightstick faster.

"What's with the stick?" asked Jake.

Mallory shrugged. "Just happy, I guess. There is one odd thing," mumbled Mallory as she tilted her chair back further.

"Yes?"

"You know where the car was found, out on Jones."

"Sure."

"You know which way the car was facing?"

"No clue."

"I called Officer Grey. It wasn't in his report. Why would it be? He clearly thought it was abandoned. Just called it in, right? No need to note details like that."

"So, which way was it going?" asked Jake, interested.

"North. It was headed to the mansion."

"Which means the crime scene was someplace else," said Jake.

"Yeah," drawled Mallory. "Good deducing."

All three pondered the significance.

"I don't know what that means, but we've got a witness, right?" Stan looked to Mallory for confirmation.

She rolled her eyes. "Ask the grill master there," she said, indicating Jake. "He put her through her paces."

"That I did."

CHAPTER 36

The video screen was filled with a close up of her driver's license. She held it long enough for Stan to read her name and address. The driver's license picture wasn't bad at all.

But he wasn't prepared for the beauty that was Samantha Barnes. When she took her license away from the camera and settled back in her chair, Stan let out a little 'Whoa'.

Jake, who was watching his partner watch the playback felt he needed to offer, "She's from L.A."

Stan nodded and watched as Samantha Barnes straightened her dress, then Sharon Stoned it and crossed her legs. She had on a dress that was both scooped neck up top and short in length, allowing a perfect presentation of all assets.

"I guess she is," agreed Stan.

There was paper rustling behind the camera as Jake prepared to start the interview. It appeared Samantha's eyes never left him and followed him around the room.

In the interview, Jake started in on the preliminaries. Name, address, phone number, marital status. Stan looked over to Jake when that came up but Jake remained staring at the monitor.

Jake could be heard off-camera. *"Okay, Miss Barnes, let's review what you told our assistant on the phone when you called, so we have it down."*

"Samantha. Call me Samantha."

"Fine. Okay, you were on Jones Road the night of May 13th, is that right?"

Samantha smiled. "Early morning. Yes, I was headed to the airport."

"That was early wasn't it? I mean early to be catching a flight?"

"I had an early meeting in L.A. so I had an early flight."

"Approximately what time was the flight?"

"The flight was first one out. Around 5 A.M. I think."

"So, you were on Jones about what time?"

Samantha did a little shrug. "3ish I suppose."

On the recording, Stan heard Jake move around behind the camera. It sounded like he shifted his chair.

Then Stan watched as the camera did a slow, smooth tilt down off the face of Samantha Barnes so it was now only showing her chest and legs. He looked over at Jake.

Mallory pushed the pause button. "Nice camera work buddy," drawled Mallory. "I didn't know we had air conditioning in here."

Examining the still frame of Samantha Barnes' chest, Stan could see why Mallory asked.

"I guess real women don't wear bras," murmured Mallory.

Jake started the video again. It was obvious he'd fixed the problem as the camera wobbled, then tracked up her body and once again settled where it started. Samantha seemed not to notice.

"I must've bumped the camera."

On the video, Jake asked her to describe what she saw on Jones Road.

"Well, it was raining. Not hard. I saw a car, a dark red car, I think."

"It was on the side of the road?"

"Yes. It looked like it might be having some trouble."

"What was its condition? Describe it."

Samantha hesitated.

Stan watched her hands work in her lap.

"Not sure what you mean."

"I mean, by trouble you don't mean it was smoking or on fire or anything."

"Oh, no. It had its hood up you know. Like someone was looking at the engine."

"Was someone looking at the engine?"

Samantha's hands worked some more. Stan couldn't tell if she was nervous or definitely acting for Jake. Nobody likes to be questioned, especially when they know it'll be forever on tape. Some react differently, but no one is comfortable.

"Of course. As I told your girl, there was someone at the car but they weren't examining it or trying to fix it."

"A person? Man or woman?"

"Woman. Pretty sure it was a woman?"

Stan sat up and looked at Jake. "She wasn't sure it was a woman?" asked Stan.

Jake paused the playback and froze the picture.

"Just wait," Jake said. "We get into that."

Mallory slipped into one of the conference table chairs and put her feet up

Samantha Barnes started up again. She had a flirty little frown.

"No. I said I wasn't sure when I called and spoke to your girl…"

"That must be me," murmured Mallory behind her hands. "I must be 'the girl'."

Samantha seemed to hesitate. "I told her I thought it was probably a woman, but…"

"But?" Jake encouraged.

"Well, this woman, if it was a woman, looked very mannish."

"Mannish? How so?"

"You know. No makeup. Kind of a severe face, not soft."

"Was there facial hair that would make you think it was a man?"

Samantha Barnes thought it over.

"No. There was no hair. It just looked like she could grow a mustache if she wanted to. Know what I mean?"

Mallory subtly ran her finger over her upper lip.

"I rolled down my passenger window and she sorta stuck her head in. It was raining and all and for a moment I thought she might try and get in. And she looked kind of mannish so I…"

"What?" Jake waited. "You what?"

Samantha affected a sheepish look and shrugged

"I drove off. I yelled to her that I'd send help, you know before I left, but, she kinda gave me the creeps. I'd only stopped because

it was raining and it looked at first like it was a woman. That's why."

"So you called 911?"

Samantha Barnes sighed. "Look I know you guys keep a tape of 911 calls, so I guess you know I didn't call it in. I know I said I would and I meant it when I said it. But, I...well, I wanted to be outta there. I was sure someone else would come. I'm sorry."

They could hear Jake shuffle papers.

"That's okay. So back to when she stuck her head in. You didn't let her speak. And you had no other conversation with her?"

"None."

"You never heard her speak?"

"Nope. I told you. She merely looked in my window like she wanted to get in and I was sure I didn't want that. Cops like yourself would recommend I not do that, correct?"

Jake shut off the tape.

"Wait," Mallory said. "I want to hear what a cop such as yourself, recommends that a woman in Miss Barnes' cleavage-filled situation do."

Jake looked at Mallory. A slow smile invaded his face. His blue eyes sparkled.

"I told her if that happened again to call me on my cell. Anytime."

"Cute," was all Mallory could think of to say.

Stan put the heels of his hands to his closed eyes and ground them in until the itching was gone and he was seeing stars.

"That it with her?" he asked.

"Pretty much. I went over it all again with her, but the story stayed the same."

Stan threw his pencil across the room. "And who is this woman at the car? Is it Pokovich? Or a wife? A lover? The one who de-headed Mr. Marston?"

Stan to Mallory, "Do we have some decent pictures of Pokovich we can show Miss Legs?"

"We have the booking picture from many years ago and the one we have from when she was released."

Stan checked his watch. "I have to go. Let's quit screwing around and find this Pokovich."

CHAPTER 37

It was well after midnight. Well after visiting hours. The nurse, Debbie Bridge, looked up as they exited the elevator, then looked away as she was paid to do always when 'he' came.

The nurse stole a glance anyway as he entered Room 227. From what she could make out, he was tall, well-built, well-dressed. Her sister would've said he was Mafia. Any well-dressed, collar up man with a bodyguard was Mafia, unless he was a celebrity.

This was no celebrity. No Mafia either. Though she couldn't see much, still, he had a coarse uncaring ruthlessness to him. It wasn't anything overt that he did, it was the actions of the others around him.

Deferential and scared. Not respectful, scared.

The other girls on the floor had coerced her into putting money into the pot, the winner to get it all. All the victor had to do was to positively identify the guy.

Having graveyard made her the leading contender as he mostly turned up in the dead of night. And she could sure use the dough. On the other hand, she was paid to never look, approach, or speak to the guy. Paid and paid well.

Still, $430 is $430.

And how tough could it be?

As before, the goon bodyguard, as she called him, stayed outside the room. He didn't stand like Presidential bodyguards stand, with their backs to a wall, hands folded in front, stoic expressions.

No, this guy looked like a small, brown piece of mean son of a bitch. He prowled the hall a short distance from Room 227, pretending to read the notices on the bulletin board, flicking the front paper when he was done reading, curling the edges of the papers.

Once he turned suddenly and caught her looking. Though she pretended to be reaching for a file, he saw. And she knew he saw. He had continued staring. It made her so nervous, she got up, grabbed a random coffee cup, and pretended to go to the backroom for coffee, which she never drank.

The woman in 227 was cancer bound. The chart said the last name was 78-4532. Debbie wondered what astronomical sum their itinerant quasi-physician, 'Doctor' Parker was being paid to shield the woman's identity, but like a good snoop, she'd discovered the X-Rays had the name Pokovich in the lower corner.

She'd searched the internet for the name, but there wasn't much, nothing that alerted her, nothing that would seem important enough to pay people to generate a wall of anonymity.

Which made it more intriguing.

Cancer. Started in her stomach, Parker had proclaimed. Like a good host, the metastases were welcomed now in the liver and soon the pancreas and that would be just about all she wrote. Not enough time to get to the colon and the marrow.

Based on the crap Parker had prescribed, the woman was sick as a dog, but it was obvious she was perfectly ambulatory. Not marathon-worthy, not even ready for a walk-a-thon, but many nights the nurse had seen the woman wander down the hall and out to the terrace to catch a smoke. Highly against regulations, but then again that's why she was paid to look away.

It was time for 227's midnight meds but there was no way she would dare go in.

Instead, she had three other patients who needed either medication or to be woken and checked or turned.

She arranged the meds for each room on her tray atop their prescription slips and centered the tray on the rolling cart. She rarely used the cart, but this way she could walk slower and maybe get a glimpse of the man in the room. See if she recognized him. It would be something to tell her sister.

She made her way down the hall. Finished 217, then woke and turned the bedridden man in 220, then went to 228 under the withering scrutiny of the little brown man. As she passed him, she didn't dare look at him but noticed instead his small fingers. She didn't know why but she almost laughed thinking what a terrible bodyguard he must be because with those little fingers he must have a lot of trouble even holding a gun.

She left the cart outside of 228, positioned across the hall from 227.

She left the door to 228 open a crack and made a show of waking and helping 228 take her meds and even helped her to the bathroom though she said she didn't need to go. After getting the woman back in her bed, she moved to the crack of the door and waited. The brown man would get suspicious if she was absent much longer.

But it was moot because her pager, linked to the call buttons on the floor, went off. Not simply vibrating, but with the demanding mechanical voice squawking, 'Arrest 202, Arrest 202.'

202's heart monitor was indicating a cardiac arrest.

She gave a backward glance at 228, turned and swept out of the room, and ran full into the man she'd been trying to identify.

She bounced off of him. And looked up into his face. His expression, Russian junkyard dog, didn't change, except his eyes narrowed, then went to her name badge.

"D. Bridge."

His voice was rough with age and menace and she would remember it and his ghastly, twisted, lipsticked visage right up until that little brown man ran a knife into her an hour later in the private parking lot of the Executive Repose Recovery Center.

CHAPTER 38

"Paper or plastic?"

"Both."

The Safeway clerk stopped pulling the items past the scanner. "C'mon kid, what'll it be?"

"I need one of each," Michael said. "I need paper 'cause we're trying to be friendly to the environment and I need the plastic cause my aunt's Depends diapers stink and I need to close them up in something."

The clerk hesitated but the seriousness of the kid's face stopped him from making a rude comment. The clerk turned his attention to Jessie who avoided his gaze and studied her shoes.

"Say, don't I know you? Weren't you here with that crazy lady awhile back?"

Jessie moved behind Michael.

"She's a mute."

The checker looked contrite. "Deaf and dumb, huh."

"Both," Michael repeated. "Both paper and plastic." He dug in and brought the last of the Arizona cash out. After paying, that left him with $7.02.

Jessie stopped him when they got outside.

"Why did you say that? About me and the paper and plastic?"

"Practicing my bullshit."

Jessie looked at her brother, not comprehending.

"Here, take a bag," he said.

Michael gave her the lightest bag, mostly boxes of ramen, macaroni and cheese, and toilet paper.

His internet survey of the cheapest foods that were wholesome encouraged him to consume whole grains, nuts, legumes and fruits, and vegetables.

His cooking experience consisted mostly of watching people who knew what they were doing in a kitchen and while he felt he should do what he could to keep both of them healthy, he didn't think anyone died from eating ramen and macaroni and cheese for any length of time.

He did get some apples and bananas and a bag salad and a tomato.

They wouldn't die he was sure. Much of it could be packed for traveling.

And he had no goddamn idea what a legume was anyway.

The dirty grey car with the CPS logo on the side was waiting at the curb in front of the trailer when Michael and Jessie approached.

The slim frame of Mrs. French exited that car, skinny legs first.

"There you two are!" she said. Traces of accusation swirled around the three of them.

"Where have you two been? I've knocked and called. Nobody answered. I can't get hold of your aunt. Her work number says she doesn't work there and then you two are nowhere to be found."

She ran out of steam.

Michael approached her with concern on his face.

"How are you, Mrs. French? We understand you were sick. We were worried the night you were supposed to take us to the airport."

Jessie's eyebrows elevated watching her brother pretend to be the ambassador of caring.

"Well…I was under the weather," the woman said. Then eyeing him more carefully and looking at Jessie, then back at the dark trailer and back to Michael's earnest face.

"Where's your aunt?"

Michael moved past her to the trailer door. "They decided to keep her one more night. Would you like some tea?"

"What?" asked the woman, following Michael to the door.

"Tea. Would you like some?"

"Tea? No! What do you mean keep her?"

Michael opened the door and all three went inside.

"Where is your aunt?"

Michael stopped and looked confused.

Jessie couldn't watch the performance any longer and hid her smile behind the paper bag as she unloaded the groceries.

"I thought Mrs. Warner would've told you."

"Mrs. Warner? Olivia Warner?"

Yes," Michael nodded. "Your temporary replacement while you were ill."

"You met Mrs. Warner?"

Michael made a show of pulling out the bananas and apples and the bag salad. He held the tomato in his hand as a symbol of a healthy diet.

"It was thoughtful of you to send her over. She was the one who gave us the sad news of my uncle's accident. She did a thorough inspection of the premises, spoke with Aunt Jane and everything."

Mrs. French struggled to regain her place.

"I didn't hear anything about that," she added without resolve.

"I don't believe she expected you to recover so quickly. You said no to tea?"

"What? No. Well, where is your aunt?" She eyed Michael again, boring in.

"As she told Mrs. Warner, she had to go into the hospital for an overnight to set her sprained hand. This afternoon, they decided to keep her another night, to be sure."

"So, you two are alone?"

Michael laughed. "Only technically. We have at least three people from the park here, looking in on us, including Mrs. Chan, I think you met her, from a couple doors down. We have more guardians tonight than we need."

"Well, I don't know."

"We've just been to the store. Getting supplies for my aunt's dinner when she gets home tomorrow. You're welcome to join us then."

Mrs. French consulted her clipboard briefly but there was nothing written there that would help her.

Sudden inspiration struck. "Sprained? Your aunt is incapacitated?"

Michael folded up the paper bag and tucked it under the coffee pot on the counter.

"My fault, I'm afraid."

"You hurt your aunt?"

"Oh, no. Nothing like that. It was an accident. She wanted to play catch and I was trying to teach her how to throw a football and she hit her hand on…Jessie's bike."

"My bike?" Jessie exclaimed.

"A bike?" asked Mrs. French. "Play catch?"

"Looked like it hurt like the devil."

Mrs. French tapped her clipboard against her thigh. Her bullshit-o-meter was nearing the red. She decided.

"I can't leave you kids all by yourselves. I'll have to call someone. You need full supervision."

Michael feigned a hurt expression.

"Well. Mrs. Warner approved it all. She said y'all at CPS were short-staffed and it would be better not to disturb everything by moving us for one night, especially with all the kind adults around here. But if you feel…"

Mrs. French moved toward the kitchen. "It's just that it's against regulations to knowingly leave minor children unattended…"

"Mrs. French," smiled Michael, recalling all the fake smiles he'd been subjected to over the years. "I know you mean well and are only thinking of us, we're fine. If you want, you can check on us by phone later tonight. All we're going to do is have dinner and watch some TV and go to bed."

Mrs. French's eyes flicked around the kitchen.

"What will you make?"

"Make?"

"For dinner?"

Michael turned away and moved to the other end of the small kitchen where one of his aunt's Ladies Home Journal was left open to a 'Featured Recipe' page.

"Salisbury steak, roasted potatoes, and salad," he read.

"I see."

The cell phone on the coffee table rang. It was Aunt Jane's phone. One she would not be needing where she was. Jessie and Michael had forgotten about it.

Jessie moved back further on the couch, away from it.

Mrs. French looked to Michael.

"Oh," he said. "I'd better get it."

Mrs. French watched him as he answered, listened, then awkwardly covered where he thought the mouthpiece was.

"Mrs. French," he whispered. 'It's the Travers family calling from Arizona."

Mrs. French straightened.

"They want to fill me in on the accident and all. This'll probably take some time. Can I have my aunt call you next week?"

Mrs. French studied the 14-year-old boy with a mix of distrust and polite sympathy.

After a moment she nodded, then as if noticing Jessie for the first time, knelt down in front of her.

"How are you doing child?"

Jessie smiled. "Just drenched in love."

Michael grinned.

Mrs. French tapped her clipboard twice then backed to the door.

"All right. All right. Good night."

She gave a worried look but closed the door.

Michael followed and watched as she backed out and drove off.

He and Jessie slapped hands as he left her on the couch, moved to the kitchen, and picked up the conversation.

"I'm here Mrs. Condon. No, my aunt has laryngitis but she's whispering to me that you can't start filming until she receives the money."

"What? That's right. The $10,000."

Michael listened hard and dry swallowed. His voice was strained.

"Mrs. Condon, what exactly is the problem with the contract?"

More listening.

"Uh-huh. I see. Let me relay this to my aunt."

Michael covered the mouthpiece and moved to the sheet with the cable TV listings. He ran his finger down until he found a good one.

HBO.

He uncovered the phone.

"Mrs. Condon. She says she doesn't think much of you and the rest of the people there at HBO. She says when you promise…What?"

Jessie could hear Mrs. Amber Condon's protestations from across the room.

"I don't understand," continued Michael. "Then who have we been talking to at HBO. She thought you worked with Mr. Turner at HBO? When he called he told my aunt the money from HBO would be forwarded as soon as she said yes."

Michael smiled as he held the phone away from his ear and the jabbering continued.

He pulled the phone back.

"So, there really is no problem, then?"

Purring assent from the phone line.

"My aunt will be glad to hear it. She always liked you and CliffEdge Productions the best."

Michael ended the call and rubbed his head. He had no idea spewing tale after tale was so exhausting.

CHAPTER 39

Jessie Cooper followed her older brother from room to room. The only respite he received is when he secured himself in the bathroom.

"M, what are you talking about? Who was on the phone? Moving on? Where?" she said, her cheek pressed to the door.

"I'm working on it."

"Arizona?"

"Maybe. Yeah, probably."

"But we don't know anybody else." Her lip quivered and her eyes filled. "Where else could we go? You said we needed money."

She hit the door. "And I'm not a baby anymore."

Michael exited the bathroom and studied her earnest face. "Yeah. I know."

He wondered if this was the face that his mother saw as a parent.

His sister's innocence was forever tainted but, like a patched wall, there was a new face of hope and belief and most amazingly, trust. In him.

Trust he knew she would never have with anyone else.

"We only know Aunt Jane." Tears spilled over. She wiped them away. "And she's not here."

Michael considered telling her about the money that should arrive later today, wired into his aunt's account from the TV production people. But then she would ask why they were getting the money and then he'd have to explain that to earn their money the documentary producer would want Michael and Jessie to recreate the night in Olive Park, which Michael would never do and certainly not let Jessie.

"I know she's gone, I know. But before she left, Aunt Jane left us some money which I just found out about."

It was a slight stretch.

"Really?"

"So, we're gonna be okay."

"Yeah?"

Michael looked away to the window. His eyes, as if drawn, always went to the end of Sunshine Vista where the Everheart trailers used to be.

He also found himself checking the driveway often, like a nervous tic, expecting pissed-off CPS kidnappers to come and drag them off to the Acme orphanage. Or worse, a semi-trailer from the Hollywood production company roar into sight and take up residence on the front lawn.

The clock was ticking. He figured he and Jess had maybe a day before the sand ran out. They were living on borrowed time. Somebody somewhere would soon come for them. At least they had food.

"Yeah, we'll do fine," he proffered with all the assurance he could front.

Jessie studied him, finally convinced.

"Okay. I trust you." She took her own place in the bathroom.

Trust. Michael faltered. He wanted to call her back and tell her they were leaving tomorrow. That the money he was taking under false pretenses he had rationalized was dough compensating them for what they'd been through. That it was time they got a break.

And if breaks didn't come your way, you had to make your own. That, he thought, is what adults had to do. And he was hating pretending being the adult. Really hating it.

The beep from his aunt's laptop drew his attention.

Email, from Mr. Huber at the bank. He was following strict instructions to email his aunt when the wired money arrived into the account. The email meant the dough had arrived.

Bingo.

"I'll be right back. Get packed up," he shouted as he bolted out the door, knowing they finally had some breathing room. He didn't wait to hear Jessie's reply.

Michael made it to the Quick Mart in ten minutes. He felt the need to hurry. He had that feeling when someone's watching you, or the hairs on the back of your neck stand up and scream 'Run' or that feeling you know when the next time the phone rings someone will have died.

That get-a-move-on feeling.

Even though he knew where they were headed he had only a vague idea of how they would get there.

They couldn't fly without an ID. They couldn't drive. Well, he could, but if they were caught it would be just as bad, no, probably worse, because it would mean CPS jail and they would undoubtedly split up the two of them.

So, it was either the train or the bus.

He'd checked the Amtrak schedule. Holy shit. Might as well take the bus the way the lack of tracks between certain cities kept you moving from train to bus to train and back to the bus.

So, Greyhound it was. There was a bus at 10:40 going to Phoenix. Transfer once in L.A. Do-able. This time tomorrow, he'd be ready to punch cows on Shippen Travers' ranch. Sure the guy had a busted leg or two, but it would heal. They'd be able to start over.

Like a life re-boot, he thought. He liked the idea. This was a good plan.

With the cash he was getting here at the Quick Mart, they'd be able to take a cab to the bus station. Get there early. Lay low.

No worries.

The East Indian behind the counter barely gave him a glance as he made his way to the ATM.

He realized he'd never used one, but he was sure it couldn't be any more complicated than a gym locker. Sheesh. People needed to get their money. If it was tough, the banks wouldn't be providing ATMs.

He rounded the last end aisle and found a guy in front of the machine. He had on a grey shirt and khakis, a worker for one of the utilities, cable or power.

Michael leaned around him, all the while pretending to study the soup labels on the shelf next to him. He watched as the guy slid in his card, entered a few numbers, and stabbed the screen a few times.

Michael could see he was only getting $300.

The bills fanned out of the slot. The guy grabbed them and turned and almost ran into Michael. He looked accusingly as he stuffed the bills in his pocket.

"Standing a little close kid. Back it up."

Michael shrugged innocence and backed up.

The guy swept past him and out of the store.

Michael removed his aunt's debit card from his pocket. It was another thing she wasn't going to need where she was staying.

Just like the cable guy, he slid the card in and removed it quickly.

"Enter PIN number," he said to himself.

7608 was his aunt's security code he'd helped her set up. It was Jessie's birthday in four digits. He entered it.

Then he had a choice. Make a deposit, withdraw, check his balance plus other stuff no one standing in a Quick Mart would need.

He punched withdraw.

He was left with a choice, $20, $40, $60, $100, $300. Or he could enter his own amount, in multiples of $20.

No problem. He wondered if he should check the balance first. But, why? He'd gotten the email from Mr. Whoever at the bank. The dough was there from the TV people.

Suckers.

He thought he ought to leave some in the bank. He could always access the balance when he got to Phoenix.

"Let's only do $5,000."

He entered the amount in, including the cents.

"Okay." Before he hit complete transaction, he tried to figure out how many twenty-dollar bills that would be. He was good at math.

Thank you, sir, that will be 250 twenty dollar bills we'll be sending your way.

He pushed complete transaction.

'Maximum Daily Withdraw $300' came up in front of him.

"The hell."

The same screen, showing the dollar amounts he could withdraw, came up again.

He tried $1000.

Same screen.

He raised his chin. Sweat trickled down his sides.

$500.

No go.

He went for the $300.

After a few suspenseful seconds, the money came out of the slot.

Michael took it and wandered up to the counter.

"How come your machine won't give out more than $300?"

"What? The ATM?"

Michael nodded.

"What are you doing with the ATM?"

"Getting my birthday money. Or trying to," Michael lied. It was getting easier and easier to tell people a story.

The guy softened. Leaned in. "Look, you can only get $300. That's not my rules. It's the bank, okay? You want more, you come back after midnight."

"Midnight?"

"New day. After midnight, you can get another $300. That's the way it works. You want more today, you go to the bank."

This was the shits.

It took longer than ten minutes for Michael to get back to Sunshine Vista. He ambled and tried to work out the alternatives. Having the ATM's parcel out $300 a day wasn't going to cut it.

Going into the bank was not an option. He was becoming an excellent bullshitter by necessity, but even he couldn't believe that a 14-year-old can get $5000 in cash from already suspicious bank people.

An uncaring, unknowing ATM was one thing. But people inside a bank, guarding all that cash, would probably even laugh at the Pope if his Holiness asked for $5000.

He needed to raise more cash fast.

$300 was a start. A small one. It would get them to Phoenix on the bus, and a few meals and that was about it. He used to disregard money. Money was money. Cash was money. And he used to take it for granted. It was always around when they lived in San Francisco. Not a lot, but it wasn't the big goddamn need it was now.

Now, the value of having folding paper in his pocket was all that mattered. That and the ATM card. The shit part was once the TV people realized he and Jess had bailed, they'd probably take back the dough, somehow.

As he shortcutted through the back of the trailer park, moving right past where Ruby Everheart's trailers had been, he attempted to figure out how many days it would take to liquidate Aunt Jane's account at the pace of $300 a day.

He counted on his fingers as he kicked and shuffled at the raked debris that was left of Ruby's trailers.

He'd just have to figure out how to get more—

"There he is!"

Michael looked up.

Who had yelled?

He leaned forward. And then he saw. And then he knew.

"Oh shit."

In front of Aunt Jane's trailer were four white vans. Even from this distance, he could see that light stands had been set up on the lawn. It seemed like an army of people were unloading metal cases and tripods.

And two of them were running toward him. A man and a woman.

A sudden terrifying thought jolted him.

Jessie!

He took off running toward their trailer. He ran right past the two production people coming toward him.

"Hey! Michael! Michael Cooper!"

He ran through the tangle of cords and the lights and up past the little porch and inside. People, strangers, were already inside. Inside!

He ran down the hallway and grabbed the handle of the bathroom door. It was locked.

"Busy," came a deep male voice.

He went the rest of the hallway to his aunt's bedroom. There was a woman outside the door. She had a clipboard and a pencil stuck in her hair. She turned to Michael.

"She won't come out."

Michael pushed her out of the way.

"Jess! Jess! It's me. Let me in."

The woman gestured a 'come here' to the cameraman who had been waiting for something, anything to happen.

After a few seconds, the door lock released.

Just then a bright light erupted behind Michael's head.

"In tighter," urged the woman.

Michael turned and drop kicked the cameraman in the nuts. With his eye to the viewfinder the guy never really saw it coming. He and the camera and the bright light went down in a groaning heap.

"Hey!" yelled the woman. "You can't do that!"

Michael turned the doorknob and slipped in and locked it behind him.

"Jess."

But he didn't see her at first. When he did, it broke his heart.

She was huddled on the floor between the wall and his aunt's bed with her legs pulled up.

Tears streamed down her cheeks.

CHAPTER 40

He wasn't even hearing the insistent banging on the door. It was happening, but he only focused on Jess.

Her face was all red and blotchy from crying and she was trembling. It took careful, soothing minutes before she was calm enough to talk.

He could hardly look at her honestly. He had caused all this and now he had to fix it. Somehow.

"They said my name, M. I opened the door and they said my name. How do they know my name?"

"You opened the door?"

"I thought it was you. I heard a noise. I needed to show you something. And I opened it."

Michael sat down in front of her. "I'm sorry."

"They came right in 'cause I opened the door. They were looking for Aunt Jane. They said your name, too. They were looking for you too.

Her lip trembled. "What do they want? Why are they here, in the house? Who are they? They have cameras and lights. They shined a light in my eyes. And you weren't here."

"I'm here now. I'll fix this."

"What do they want? Make them leave."

Michael sidestepped the question.

"Seems Aunt Jane… she made an agreement with some television show to talk about…what happened to us. And she didn't tell us."

"Why?"

"Why didn't she tell us?

Jessie nodded.

Michael hesitated. He was tired of fabricating stories and skirting the truth. And he really didn't want to lie to his sister. It wasn't good to alienate the last member of the team. He took a breath.

"She didn't tell us because she needed money. She wanted money. And she saw a way to make some dough by telling what happened to us."

Jessie sat up straighter.

"You said we would never tell anyone after we told the police what happened. We had all those people wanting to pay us money back then, just so we'd talk to them. You said we weren't going to do it. It wasn't right." She looked away. "Especially after what else they found in the woods. You know."

"I know. I still feel like that. I guess the idea was eventually too much for AJ. Maybe that's why she went cuckoo. I don't know. Sometime, recently I think, she finally agreed to this deal, and now here we are."

"Was she going to tell us?"

Michael shook his head. "Nope."

"Why? If she was going to talk to them about us, wouldn't that be fair?"

Fair? Michael looked back at the bedroom door still holding tight against the onslaught. Fair? There is no fair. When you're a kid you're at the bottom. Fair is way at the top.

"Here's the deal, Jess. She didn't tell us because she didn't make the deal for her to talk to the TV people. She made the deal for you and me to talk to them."

"What?"

"It's kinda worse than that. She made the deal for us to not only talk to them, on television but for you and me to take them on a tour of the woods and… you know, to like pretend it's all happening again."

Jessie shrank back. "I can't do that. I can't. I won't."

Michael gripped both of her arms. "You won't have to, okay. It will not happen. I won't let it."

"How do you know all this? Aunt Jane told you?"

Michael sighed. "No. I read her emails. It had all the details."

"And you didn't tell me? How come?"

"I didn't think they'd show up. Well, not really. I knew they'd show. I just hoped we'd be gone by then."

He stood up. The banging on the door had stopped but the noisy business coming from the rest of the trailer sounded much like the buzzing of pissed off wasps.

"We almost made it too. We'd of been outta here in a few hours."

"Can't we leave?"

Michael went to the window and parted the blinds. He watched a crew member arranging two chairs in front of a camera, creating an intimate little set on what used to be Aunt Jane's front lawn. Other crew members were positioning the lights, holding their hands out to see how the light looked on skin, then moving more lights in.

He had no doubt who the two chairs were for.

Beyond, someone had set up a rope at the front edge of the property. Inside the rope was the crew. Outside were, to Michael's alarm, a growing gathering of the neighborhood curious. The Chinese lady was at the front, her knees pushing at the rope, insisting, Michael guessed, on being allowed in to find out what her neighbor Jane was up to.

Jessie stood, wiped her face with the back of her hand.

"Well, tell them we aren't going to do anything. We don't care what Aunt Jane said, we're just not going to do it. Aunt Jane isn't here so we'll tell them no and they'll go away."

Michael closed his eyes and tilted his head back.

"Almost made it. Only another few hours."

"M, go tell them now to get off the property. Aunt Jane's not here. It's your job."

"Yeah. It is my responsibility. You're right Jess. Only one problem. There's a signed contract. Money was paid."

"Already? They paid Aunt Jane money already? Can't we give it back and tell 'em to forget the whole thing? We changed our minds."

Michael laughed. He reached into his pocket and pulled out the money from the ATM. He fanned out the fifteen $20 bills.

"I'll just go give this back shall I?"

"Where did you get that? Is that part of the money they paid?"

Michael stuffed the money back in his pocket.

"Down payment. There's a lot more. If I can get it."

"But if we take the money, doesn't that mean we have to do it? Do all the stuff they want us to?"

"It sure does," Michael sighed.

"Well," said Jess thoughtfully. "What if we kept some and only talked to them a little bit?"

Michael laughed. "First you want me to toss them out, now you want to negotiate."

Jessie parted the blinds at her eye level. "M, how bad would it be? Couldn't we talk for a little bit? Not do anything else. Not go into the woods. Not go near where her trailer was?"

"Jess," Michael began.

"How much money is there?" interrupted Jess.

"Jess, c'mon."

"How much? You got some of the money. Enough to get us to, you know, Arizona? Enough to buy food and other stuff?"

"It's complicated."

"M! How much?"

"A lot, okay. More than enough to do whatever we want. But we can't get it 'cause it goes to Aunt Jane's account and we can only get a few hundred every day. And besides, they don't want to negotiate. I think, no, I know they want the whole enchilada."

"Well, you tell me-"

The short, sharp chirp from the squad car's siren startled them both.

"Oh, crap."

Michael saw the police car with the two officers making their way through the gathering crowd. They stepped over the rope and proceeded through the lighted set when they were stopped by a crew person with a clipboard. This was a medium-sized clipboard which Michael thought probably meant mid-level bullshitter.

Michael watched as the first cop surveyed the disarray and began kinda waving his arms around, definitely taking in the whole enchilada.

The two cops meant to go around or through Mr. Clipboard, but instead, he pulled out a cluster of papers from under his mid-level clipboard and gave them to the officers. The cops exchanged glances and the first cop proceeded to scan the documents.

Clipboard turned away, believing he had proved his point, and shouted instructions to somebody at the front of the trailer.

Jessie whispered. "They're going to arrest us."

Michael didn't answer because, while having Hollywood on their front yard expecting them to do something they would not do, having the neighbors and friends of neighbors gathered to watch what they would not do, having the cops show up being thwarted in their attempt to stop the Hollywood crew from filming what they would not do, what was even worse was what Michael now saw at the back of the crowd.

The Laurel and Hardy of Sacramento CPS, skinny Mrs. French and waddle master Olivia Warner, were now shoving their way to the front, past the cops, and over the rope, blowing past Mr. Clipboard and heading for the trailer's front door.

"You can fool some of the people all of the time, and all of the people some of the time, but you cannot fool all of the people all of the time."

Jessie turned to him. "What?"

"Abe Lincoln telling us 'Time's up'."

Michael looked past the mussed up bed and the dresser to the other side of the bedroom. He grabbed Jessie's backpack.

"C'mon. I sure hope that window opens wide enough."

CHAPTER 41

Mallory pushed open the heavy door and entered the room. "Jesus."

It was as she expected, completely dark except for a dim fluorescent above the woman's bed giving off the only light. The digital EKG worked silently on its stand. The IV bag was nearly full with a milky solution, its drips implacably trickling into the plastic line.

Dress it up all you want with neutral color vinyl wallpaper and bright, nothing to hate colors, and scrub the ever-loving hell out of it, but a hospital room with its cloying warmth and medicinal overbite is a living coffin.

Mallory approached the bed. She let her fingers trace the starched sheets and the light blanket while she studied the woman's face. She brought out the picture she had of Ilsa Pokovich and held it under the fluorescent and then moved it beside the woman's face.

The old woman stirred. Her nearly bald head moved back and forth on the pillow. The yellow cast that was the hallmark of a deathly countdown masked the immutable rigidity of the woman.

"You're a tough old cunt aren't you?" Mallory muttered. "Nothing can kill you can it?"

She pulled out her phone but before she could call Stan, the woman spoke and raised her hand a few inches.

"Give me some water, will ya?"

Mallory turned and found the glass with the straw in it. When she turned back, the woman's face was up against Mallory's. The woman's death breath laced with some sort of custard gone bad and stale cigarettes made Mallory gag.

Before she could move away, the woman's hand seized Mallory's arm with a steel grip, slopping water onto the floor.

Ilsa Pokovich brought her face closer. "And who the fuck're you, dearie?"

The eyes, watery at the edges, were suffused with a sickly sallowness. Mallory was transfixed.

The grip tightened. "Aw Christ, you're a cop."

Mallory managed a nod before she could pull away. The woman fell back against the pillow.

Before Mallory stepped out of the room she thought she heard the woman whisper.

"You're dead, princess."

The laugh that followed was raspy with hacking fatigue.

Mallory moved down to what passed as a nurse's station. She leaned on the counter as she called Stan.

"Got her."

Mallory glanced around her in response to Stan's question.

"Place is private-run, like a halfway house for, I don't know, people recovering from surgery or hospice, something like that. Like one step down from a real hospital."

The male nurse lounging behind the counter, peeling an orange, nodded in agreement. "Word."

"How'd I find her?"

Mallory turned away and lowered her voice. "Got lucky. Oh, and I lied to the security guy. Dropped Carruthers' name a bit. Told the rent-a-sentry the captain would get him a cush job downtown if he let me look around. Still had to spend a wad of cash to get me in here for which you need to reimburse me... What...? No. She's not going anywhere soon. When can you get here and where the hell is Steiner? He's not answering."

Listening to Stan, she didn't see the person step from the darkness of Ilsa Pokovich's room and move past her to the stairwell.

CHAPTER 42

Jake watched Jake sniff around the bench leg. They had been in this part of Discovery Park a few times before, yet Jake always went to the same bench and checked it out. Made sure the bench was the same. Made sure the same smells were still there. Made sure whatever dog had left them was still leaving them. Satisfied, Jake lifted his leg and reaffirmed their connection. They had never met. But when they did they would know each other. Would know so much about each other.

Then, the dog was straining to run. It was one of those misty nights and Jake was tempted to let him slip the collar and go. Let him explore the areas he never could in the daytime. Sacramento's leash law was not only tightly enforced, ignoring it raised the wrath of all who saw the scofflaw.

What the hell. Jake knelt down and fumbled with Jake's collar.

"You're not going to let him loose are you?"

The tone was highly accusatory. Jake gave up loosening the collar. Jake seemed to understand but then wagged his tail slightly at the woman behind Jake.

Jake stood and turned.

"Do you know what it's like to step in dog shit? Seriously. And also, I don't know if your dog is friendly or gonna take a bite…"

She stopped.

"It's you."

Jake took only a few seconds to recognize Samantha Barnes. She was obviously not dressed for company. It looked as if she'd just thrown on a sweater and jeans and a raincoat and a fisherman's type rain hat. It was black covered with clear plastic and sparkled with the drops of gathering mist.

The dog she had, straining to get a sniff of Jake dog's ass, looked like a little rat terrier or some terrier mix that couldn't make up its mind what it was.

"Detective…Steiner, right?"

Jake nodded. "Miss Barnes."

"I'm sorry. I thought you were going to let your dog run. Sorry I said anything."

Jake smiled. "I was. Sometimes he needs to run and mark some territory he doesn't usually get to mark. He's cooped up all day."

Samantha lowered her eyes. "Well. It's late. I'm sure it's probably okay. Just, you know, pick up after. But you already know that. We better go, Max. C'mon."

But Max had a mind of his own and would not be denied checking out the competition. Jake stood stoically and watched the little dog get within a few feet of him. Both Jakes knew that Jake could take a fair chunk out of the backside of little Max if he became any more obnoxious.

Samantha tugged on Max's leash. "C'mon Max. Time to go."

Jake let out a little slack on Jake's leash and Jake wandered forward.

"Maybe they should get to know each other. Then they won't be quite so frantic," Jake said.

"It's only Max who's frantic, it seems." Still, she gave a little on Max's leash and the two dogs met nose to nose. Both tails stopped and they paused to see if the other was going to try something. Satisfied that wasn't the case, they circled each other and tangled leashes.

Samantha tried stepping over both leases and ended up next to Jake.

"What's his name?" She asked, trying to distance herself from him.

"Jake," answered Jake.

"Jake? Isn't that…" But she didn't finish.

"Well, this is silly. C'mon Max, settle down."

Jake knelt down and with Samantha stepping when needed, separated the two dogs and their leashes.

Samantha shortened up Max's leash so he couldn't go anywhere.

"Is he friendly?" she asked, eyeing Jake. "Oh, wait. This is the dog you had at your office."

"Seems to love everybody, don't you boy?"

Samantha ran her gloved hand over Jake's head. He moved closer as Max went into terrier hysterics.

"What is he?"

"A Weimaraner."

"Well, he looks intelligent, aristocratic."

"That's why I named him Jake."

Samantha laughed easily. Jake answered with a stern expression.

"Near the top of his graduating class. That's nothing to laugh at."

Samantha pulled on Max's leash. "Not like this one. Truthfully, he's a four-legged set of peeing vocal cords. When he's not barking, he's lifting his leg."

They both turned away from the river and headed back to civilization together.

"How long have you had him?"

"Oh, he's not mine. I'm simply dog walking for some friends who are out of town. They get Tuscany, I get the little poop machine. What about Jake?"

"'Bout a week, we've been together."

"You seem like a good pair."

They walked on, both dogs having lost interest in each other and like the horses turning for home, both strained, pulling ahead.

"You don't live nearby, I thought." Jake knew the address she gave was nowhere near this part of Sacramento.

"I wish. I love this park and the little neighborhood shops. No, besides dog walking, I'm housesitting. Seemed easier than keeping this mutt at my place. So, I'm around for the next few weeks."

She gave Jake a sidelong glance which he pretended to ignore.

"Looks like it stopped raining," Jake said as he examined the sky longer than he needed.

Samantha removed her plastic rain hat and shook her hair which had been bunched awkwardly into the hat. It fell to her shoulders.

Jake smiled. "This is where we split. I'm over toward El Camino.

"Well, it was good to see you again, Detective Steiner. If you're out here again, I know Max would love to see Jake again. I do feel sorry for both of these guys, shut up all day." She tilted her head. "You want some coffee?"

Jake hesitated. He knew the next part of the dance. And with any other woman, he would have played his part. He knew what Stan would say, that she was a witness in an on-going investigation. But, Jake would argue, not really a witness, witness, merely sort of an innocent bystander.

And really, isn't everyone a witness to something now and then? A question of timing.

He almost gave in, watching her shake out her hair and imagining what she'd want for breakfast. Before he could come up with something clever to propel him home with equanimity, she surprised him.

"That's alright. It's probably awkward for you. Sorry I mentioned it. I just thought you know. I don't know anyone around here and we have the two dogs…"

Jake shrugged. "Maybe we'll run into each other out here again."

She smiled. "Maybe. Anyway, it's good to see a cop as human. To know he has a dog and a regular life, picks up dog poop, and thinks about breaking the law by letting his dog off the leash."

She pulled Max. "Come, Max, before we're arrested and… handcuffed."

She started down the path. Over her shoulder, she tossed a final thought, "Don't forget, I have your card detective."

Jake watched them make their way along the river's path, never once wondering if there was some other reason why Samantha Barnes had turned up.

Before he turned back toward home, he looked down at the dog, who stared back.

"It's true what they say. You are a chick magnet, aren't you?"

Jake licked his chops and gave a short bark.

"Which way do we go, then?"

Jake looked up at him and evidently realized he had to decide.

"So which is it? Home or home with benefits?"

The dog held his gaze steady, then shifted it to the retreating figures of Samantha Barnes and the noisy rat.

Jake smiled and turned off his phone.

"If you insist, you randy mutt. Double time, then."

CHAPTER 43

Stan and Mallory stood in the doorway and regarded Ilsa Pokovich, propped in bed on her elbows, veins prominent and near breaking. Her face flushed.

"What the hell do you want of me?"

Stan was the first to move. He smiled and in one fluid motion grabbed a chair and pulled it up alongside her bedside.

"We're sorry to bother you..."

Mallory stared at Stan. Sorry to fucking bother you, my ass. This was their prize. This was the goddamn killer ghost they'd been after and she had found and he was apologizing for bothering her. They should be at least clamping her leg to a table. This was the first break they'd had. Sure, this broad was probably going nowhere, but she was also a felon recently out. Who knew what shit she'd pull?

Now, well past midnight, Mallory studied the woman. In the green glow of the unflattering fluorescent, Mallory could see Pokovich's bald head was now covered with hair, an auburn wig that was mismatched to her ragged face. She looked well over fifty, though she knew her to be late forties. Tallish. Maybe mannish. Maybe the description given by Samantha Barnes was right. Eastern European features with a strong nose and brow, no makeup. Her eyes were half-closed, mocking, pretending to be uncaring and untouchable.

According to what Mallory pried from the orderly on duty, she was riddled with cancer.

She definitely had the aura of some poor schmuck who just rolled craps.

And her hands. Mallory scrutinized the woman's hands. Age mottled skin covering blue veins and sharp bones, arthritic knobs where the knuckles should've been. These were not the hands that worked a daiishka back and forth and back and forth.

Stan pulled his chair closer. Ilsa eyed him like vermin.

"Miss Pokovich, we have been trying to reach you in connection with the death of James Marston. Do you know him, or of him?"

"Wait!" Mallory approached the bed, pulled the rolling table so it straddled the bed. She propped up her cell phone against a bedpan and started the video recording.

"We're going to record this," she said. It wasn't a question. She stated the date, time, location, and who was present. For the record.

Stan seemed surprised at the interruption but nodded.

Both Stan and Mallory placed business cards on the table.

Ilsa studied Mallory with a sly grin. "I don't mind. I've been beaten by secret police. I'm not afraid. Record me all you want."

Mallory watched as Ilsa sat up even straighter and angled her head to one side, raised her chin.

Jesus thought Mallory. She likes it. She's playing to the camera.

Ilsa maintained a bolt upright posture. Her pale face gave away little. But something, like a subtle breathy exhale, escaped her.

Ilsa sneered. "Movies for the movie man, eh?"

Stan ignored the comment. "Your name is…?"

There was no hesitation. "Ilsa Pokovich."

Stan tossed Mallory his phone. "Would you let Detective Steiner know where we are and that Miss Pokovich is here giving a statement?"

Mallory nodded and slipped out into the hallway.

She left a voice mail for Jake since he didn't pick up. "Jake, you slacker. We got Pokovich. Stan's taking her statement right now. We're at some Executive Recovery Center east of town. Maybe you can join us if you're not too busy." She hung up and resumed her place next to Stan.

"Miss Pokovich, would you like somebody with you while we take your statement?" Stan pretended to study his notes while he awaited the answer; the difference between stonewalled and progress. "An attorney, perhaps?"

Ilsa snorted. "I'm not afraid of you. I've handled tougher than you."

"So, you don't desire an attorney being present while we talk?"

"You might need one. I don't."

"Fine. Has this been your address since you were released?"

"No."

"Where else were you?"

She stared at Stan as if he were an idiot but didn't answer.

Mallory pushed forward. "Were you at the home of James Marston?"

Stan shot her a look and held up his hand.

"Where were you Miss Pokovich?"

Mallory got up and paced. Get to the point already.

Ilsa lifted her chin and stared at the cellphone lens. "I was not well. I was...convalescing. In a hospital."

Neither Stan nor Mallory said anything. Silence was a void that always needed to be filled. The weakest usually succumbed.

Ilsa shrugged as if it didn't matter. "Sacramento General. I was convalescing at Sacramento General."

To Mallory, Pokovich made it sound as if it was an exclusive spa and she was reluctant to tell anybody about it or exclusive club neither Stan nor especially Mallory, could ever enjoy.

"What were you in for?" asked Mallory, leaving out 'the hospital'.

Stan sighed.

Ilsa glanced quickly at Mallory, then back to Stan. There was a slight pause before she answered.

"Woman troubles."

"And when did you get out of the hospital?" asked Stan. "And move here. A few days ago?"

Ilsa shrugged.

"How long have you been here?"

"Long enough. The bill will be...more than I will pay."

"How will you pay the bill?" interjected Mallory. Stan put a restraining hand on Mallory's arm.

Fingering her gold lighter awkwardly in her hand, the woman swung around to Mallory and sneered. "I'm a charity case. Can't you see? You stupid taxpayers will pay all my bills. You will pay. I am free."

Ilsa gave a short laugh as she turned back to Stan. "Is this how you spend your time?" she asked, giving out another smokeless exhale. "You really wanted to find me so you could discuss my internal problems? Do you need to know what I ate there? How many times did I shit? Ridiculous and a total waste of my time."

"Never mind. We can check the hospital records," Mallory said impatiently.

Stan glared at Mallory, his mouth set.

"Not without my permission," stated Ilsa. It was obvious she would not give anyone leeway to shoehorn their way into her life, any more than she had to.

Stan resumed questioning. "Mr. James Marston, Jr. How do you know him?"

"Why would I know anything?"

Mallory rolled her eyes and settled back into one of the chairs, still keeping herself between Pokovich and the exit. There was a tenseness below the old woman's bravado that Mallory didn't trust.

"I'm an old lady." She gave a smile that said she was far out in front of Stan and Mallory.

"Your name has come up in our investigation," continued Stan. No reaction.

"Did you know Mr. Marston?"

Instead of answering, Isla picked up Stan's business card and threw it at him.

"You people are pathetic."

"Did you know Mr. Marston?" Stan repeated.

Mallory got up and stretched out her back. Tension always found its way to her lower back. She did not understand why Stan was pussyfooting around. Shit, they had her name, her record, her assault of Marston, her fingerprints in the car, probably all over the house too.

Mallory knew what she wanted to do. She imagined Ilsa Pokovich spread-eagled over an anthill or waterboarded or anything to shake the smartass complacency and annoying coyness. Anything to make her quit dancing around the questions.

A good bitchslapping would set her to rights. Cancer or no cancer.

"Mr. Marston," repeated Stan.

"What about him?"

"Tell me how you knew him?"

Straining, Ilsa reached into her purse on a side table and withdrew a cigarette.

"No smoking in here," stated Stan.

Ilsa sniffed and snapped the lighter open anyway.

Mallory reached around and took the cigarette, broke it in two, and tossed it into the trash can.

Ilsa gave both of them a 'fuck you' stare but put the lighter away. She exhaled as if she had taken a drag. "Everyone knows of Marston. Movies. Bad movies."

"And, how did you know him?"

Ilsa shrugged. "It was a long time ago," she said as if it didn't matter.

"What was your relationship?"

She closed her eyes. She appeared to be in thought or she was, in fact, sick and whatever it was, was now winning.

When she looked up, it was apparent her mantle of feistiness had died. A sadness borne of bone weariness was left.

"Detective. I was born in Gdansk, Poland a few minutes after midnight sometime in January of '65. I was born four weeks early after my father beat my mother one night. She delivered me in a sea of blood, then had the intelligence to escape my father by dying twenty minutes after my first scream."

The speech seemed to exhaust her. Her eyes drooped and the smile was full of false effort.

Mallory was amazed at the change in the woman. It was as if someone had crept up behind her and pulled a plug, leaking her innards.

But Stan wasn't buying it. He checked his notes and avoided eye contact.

"Let's get back to Mr. Marston. You said you knew him. When was that exactly?"

"I didn't. You said it."

"We know you were in James Marston's car recently and his house," said Stan putting aside his notes. "We have your fingerprints."

Mallory watched the woman's reaction to Stan's lie about the house, mixed with the truth of her prints in the car. For once, it was one of surprise.

Ilsa Pokovich took her eyes off the cellphone and looked at Stan. She appeared to be momentarily at odds. Her hand went fumbling for the lighter but stopped when she realized what she was doing. She gave a little shake of her head, then without warning, erupted.

"You are a liar!" she yelled. Stan and Mallory jumped at the explosion. "Just like all police! Lies! I've never been to James Marston's house and no idea what kind of car he has. If you say different you are a liar!"

"We have your fingerprints," restated Stan in a quiet voice, watching her.

Ilsa shrugged, immediately quiet again.

"You say you've never been to the house on German Road?"

"No."

"Never in his car?"

"I deny it."

"But you knew James Marston, didn't you?"

There was quiet defiance as she spat the confession. "Of course I knew him."

Mallory exhaled. She hadn't realized she'd been holding her breath.

Even Stan settled back in his chair.

"I knew him many years ago. I have not seen him in … a long while. I have not been to his house or his car or anywhere near him, since…"

Since you sawed off his head, Mallory wanted to blurt out.

Stan waited for more, but the woman sat staring into her lap.

"Since…?" prompted Stan.

Suddenly, she stiffened up and looked straight at Stan.

"Since when James Marston raped my daughter."

CHAPTER 44

Mallory looked at Stan who glanced back at her, then to Ilsa Pokovich.

Ilsa raised her head and said, "Water. Can I have some water?"

Mallory, wary of the woman, grabbed the glass with the straw and headed off to fill it.

Stan noticed Ilsa staring at the cell phone, then, as if seeing her surroundings for the first time, scanned the bare room, turning as best she could.

Stan studied her. It was clear she was suffering, but her eyes were bright with black intensity. They appeared to be the only thing of hers that was alive. They flicked around with purpose in an otherwise lined and haggard face.

He never knew what to make of Eastern Europeans. Or gypsies or Russians or Arabs. They all operated on a different value system from his. Their view of life, their value of life was baser. They were like sinew, the toughness under the fat. Never pretty but always there. Tough to excise. Tough to kill.

"Polanski was born in Paris; did you know that?" Ilsa's voice was stronger than the body it came from. Its clarity belied her condition. The accent was all but hidden.

"Polanski?"

"Yes. Polanski, the director. He was born in Paris, then his family moved to Poland. He was half Jewish you know. Watched his parents dragged off to the camps."

"Yes?"

"I studied Polanski. Knife in the Water, Repulsion. You know these?"

Stan shook his head.

Her hand came up and gave a weak wave. "It's not important. But, I studied everything he did. It's why I came here, to United States, Hollywood.

"You sit in a theater. You see a movie. I used to watch in Gdansk. A little theater. I'd watch over and over and I studied the films. I watched the credits. They showed so many people who worked on these films. I thought, 'how could so many people work on one film?'

"I came here to work in film, be on film, to be a success." She dropped her eyes and gave a short, harsh laugh.

"I did not expect that so many people would be here. But I was a fool. Thousands of theaters. Millions see these movies. I was a fool to believe that I was the only one who saw these and wanted to work with Polanski and Alfred Hitchcock. You know Hitchcock?"

"Of course. Psycho."

Mallory entered and handed the water to Ilsa who took it without a thank you.

Mallory looked at Stan and mouthed, 'psycho'?"

"You think Psycho," said Ilsa with a smug smile. "You think of the dark ones. Americans always think of the dark ones. Americans' only experience with darkness is sitting in the dark watching it happen to others. Yes, you remember the dark ones."

Ilsa raised her eyes to Stan. "You never lived in the dark."

Stan reached for his notes. "You said James Marston raped your daughter? This is James Marston Junior we're speaking of?"

Ilsa didn't answer but seemed lost in thought.

Stan studied her. Rape of a child. Revenge of a mother years and years later. Sinew.

"When was this rape? When did it happen?"

"I never thought there would be so many. So many people. So many women, girls. So many who would do anything to get what they wanted. So many.

"Miss Pokovich."

"I was naïve. Like a little girl, I was. I had no experience with all that. I had no experience with men like him."

"You mean Marston? You worked for Marston?"

Stan saw her refocus on him.

"Did I work for him?"

Stan nodded. "That was the question."

She smiled. "I spread my legs for him. I got on my knees for him. I got down like a dog for him. I did things…"

Stan looked at the woman. The beauty was years gone. She was an arrow going through time, day by day. Only the core endured. Pretense and innocence skinned away. What remained was ramrod straight and didn't give a shit.

"It was no use. I got the disease and two years of shame." The words were bitter now, not for remembering, but for the stropping, it gave to her anger.

"So, you never worked for him?"

"Professionally? No." She gave a rueful smile. "It was always, 'Next Week, I'll have something that's just right for you, Darling'."

She looked up at Mallory. "That was usually while he was humping me in the ass, you see. He always wanted to give the women he was fucking some hope. The carrot. He dangled the carrot while shoving the stick, eh?"

She made a weak, but universal sign; her middle finger moving between the 'V' of two other fingers.

Stan needed to get things back on track.

"All this was when?"

She sighed. "Why do you want to know this of me? Why is it important when he fucked me? Why do you like to hear that he made me feel like an animal? Like a pig sucking up his slop. Why?"

"Miss Pokovich…"

She brought her skeletal hand down on the table with more force than either Stan or Malory expected. They both flinched. The cellphone fell over.

Ilsa Pokovich turned to Mallory. She pointed up to her. "I'll tell you. I'll tell you how it feels to be fucked in the ass when all you want is to work. When all you can think about is getting the job. When really all you're getting is cleaned out. Know what I mean?"

Mallory let the words flow past her. She kept her face impassive as she righted the cell phone.

Stan continued. "Miss Pokovich. I'm sorry. I see it pains you to speak of this. But when did all this happen?"

Ilsa turned back to Stan. She didn't answer for a moment, then the answer came in a sigh.

"'98. Late '97, then '98."

"How did you meet him, Marston?"

She fiddled with the folds of her hospital gown and rooted inside. A cigarette appeared between her fingers, but she made no move to light it.

"I started seeing a nice fellow from the makeup and effects department. Marston's wasn't a big outfit, but they did a lot of sort of bloody films. Vampires. Women in trouble, you know. Women, always put down…" She seemed to be seeing things as they once were.

"Who was the man you were dating when you worked for Marston?"

"What? Oh. I started dating Frank from special effects, so I was always hanging around. I really wanted a way into the studio, you see. I would've licked up dog's vomit if that had let me be on the studio lot. I figured I had a chance to meet somebody if I was there every day.

"He must've seen me one day." She looked down at her hands on the table. She tried working the knuckles. The thin skin stretched tight and wouldn't allow her fist to close.

"I looked better in those days. I had a face. A body. Doesn't matter. Next, I knew I was asked to do a screen test, by personal request of James Marston.

"I was impressed. Hah! I knew from nothing about nothing. But, I knew it was my only chance. Especially when I heard that Marston himself would be reviewing it."

Mallory spoke up. "And he loved it. Or said he did, right?"

Ilsa gave a rueful smile. "I was supposed to be the new Polish 'Titanic' type girl, a Kat Winslett or Helene Carter. You know these people?"

"Of course," Mallory said, not bothering to correct her.

"He gave me script after script to read. Once in a while, between screwings, he had me do another screen test.

"'Course, it was later when I found out that about ten others were given screen tests on a regular basis. Like life-giving vaccines. Boosters. To keep our hopes up."

Mallory could feel the bitterness in the woman.

"Funny, it was Frank, my nice guy from special effects, the guy I had been dating only to be able to get a screen test. To get a shot, you know. It was nice Frank who told me the secret, of course. There was never any film in the cameras after the first test. For any of us."

Stan looked down and studied the papers before him, though he knew the contents. He looked up at Ilsa.

"That's when you attacked Marston. That correct?"

"What? No."

"It says here you attacked him in 1998. You were arrested and convicted."

Mallory didn't let Ilsa answer. She opened and read from the file.

"Ilsa Pokovich, Los Angeles, convicted in July of '98 of assault with a deadly weapon, was sentenced to 25 years for the attack on James Marston, CEO of Marston Studios."

Both Stan and Mallory waited for an explanation.

Ilsa sat up, her chin thrust out against past rebukes.

"I came in that day. Pretended to water the plants. I could hardly hold the can steady. I was crazy hurt. He had hurt me and my child."

"I know he was surprised to see me. Men are so stupid. He didn't figure out that I wasn't carrying water. He raised his arm up at the last second. That was the only thing that saved him from looking like the freak he was."

She looked at Stan and cackled. "Battery acid. Melts the skin. Burns the hair. Seals the pores."

Neither Mallory nor Stan said anything.

"You see, not only did he rape my girl, my little girl, but he shot film of it. He shot film. And he showed it all around. He couldn't put film in the camera to shoot those of us who were regularly spread-legged or on our knees, those of us taking his cock up our ass. No film for us. But, plenty for her."

Ilsa lowered her head.

"What happened to your daughter?" asked Stan.

Ilsa took a few deep breaths and didn't answer right away. When she did her voice was harsh with remembering and regret.

"What do you think? You think she came running to me, crying, claiming that the great Marston had raped her? You think that? No!"

She looked from Mallory to Stan.

"No," she said softer. "No. She developed a taste for it. She loved having anything in her cunny. Anything. Anyone. More than one. She couldn't get enough. And she was rich, you see? In this Hollywood of yours, sex is the currency. And she had plenty. Get it?"

"At least when we lay down we did it to get something, a screen test, a shot at getting noticed. We were doing it for our reasons, right or wrong. We did what we thought we had to. We wanted to be in film. On film. Hollywood. But, she… she did it 'cause she liked it. And, God help her, she was good at it."

She lowered her head. "Marston used her for years, I found out later. Passed her around. Used her like an appetizer at meetings with investors. Money men fucked her. She made them feel good and so they gave their money to Marston."

"So where is she now," asked Mallory again.

Ilsa turned with difficulty and reached over to her purse. Mallory stood straighter, alert to what might come out of the purse. Alert to what Ilsa Pokovich might do to either of them or to herself. The older woman undid the clasps and pulled out a folded piece of paper.

"Most would say she's where she belongs. I..."

She said no more but, working her fingers, she tenderly unfolded the paper and spread it out on the table before her.

Mallory moved around behind Stan as he turned it to read it.

It was a clipping from the L.A. Times. Stan could tell it had been folded and unfolded many times. Even handling with care, it had worn thin as parchment.

The headline read, 'Woman on Beach Identified'

The pregnant body of a 19-year-old Los Angeles woman has been identified as Elizabeth Portnoy, nee Pokovich, as the one discovered on the beach near the Baymark Country Club last month.

Portnoy was an actress employed by Marston Studios in Los Angeles. Cause of death was listed as drowning due to an apparent suicide. It is believed Portnoy jumped to her death from the San Diego-Coronado Bridge sometime last month. She was six months pregnant at the time of her death.

Ilsa gave them time to read it, then slid it back, picked it up, and carefully refolded it.

"They sent this to me when I was in prison. I heard later since no one came to claim the body, that the Country Club where she was washed up took up a collection among some of its members and they had her cremated."

She put the newspaper clipping back in her purse.

"That was nice of them since many of Marston's investors who belonged to Baymark Country Club had also screwed my daughter."

She held Stan in a steady stare until her eyes rolled back and she collapsed sideways.

Stan reached for her, coming away with his only prize, a large brown wig.

Mallory hesitated, but went to the hallway and called what passed for a nurse.

CHAPTER 45

"Again?" asked a weary Jessie. "Are these the only places you know to go?"

She looked at Michael then back at the one-story structure that was the rear part of Fourth Redeemer Lutheran Church.

"You have a problem with God?" Michael asked, pronouncing 'God' like he heard TV evangelists do.

"Yeah right. We're so here to see God."

"We need shelter from the storm," intoned Michael. TV again.

"Whatever. I need to sit down. I'm tired."

Michael raised his arms.

"Praise be and suffer the little children to come on in and sit a spell."

"And who is the fourth redeemer?" asked Jessie as they passed the front reader board.

"Ah, the fourth redeemer was Jesus's second cousin once removed. Harold. Harold Christ. Ran an ox cart repair shop a few huts down from Jesus's woodworking venue. Jesus never liked him. But what could he do? Family is family."

They bypassed the main front entry that, if it followed Lutheran form, probably led into a foyer then into the sanctuary. Instead, Michael opted to try one of the back doors. It was afternoon now and Michael hoped the place would be like the desert, and all the Israelites would have fled.

Wrong.

The lone car was an older grey Nissan. Church secretary, Michael guessed, working on the coming Sunday's bulletin or sending out reminders to contribute to the building fund or the clothing drive.

Best not to disturb her.

There were two concrete walkways from the back parking lot to the building. The Nissan had grabbed the Handicap spot in front of one. Michael steered Jessie up the other one.

"This way my little lamb."

"Who made you Mr. Cheerful all of a sudden?"

"I am filled with the holy spirit of a narrow escape."

Michael glanced up to the eaves of the building as they made their way to the far door. Motion lights, but it didn't appear there were any CCTV cameras. Those Lutherans. What a trusting bunch of good deed doers.

He put his hand on the door handle and paused. He winked at Jessie. Then he pulled. It opened with a loud latch click.

"And the gates of heaven shall be opened unto you."

Jessie took off the flowered backpack as she entered the coolness of the back hallway. Michael followed and eased the door closed.

The first door they came to was the choir rehearsal room.

"Must be the Sunday school wing."

"Why?"

Michael pointed up to the signs on the other side of the hallway that stuck out above the doors.

One said 'Creepers'. Another 'Leapers'. The last was 'Pre-School'.

Michael had been in many churches. It wasn't the first time he'd seen such cuteness.

"Now what?" asked Jess.

"In here" Michael opened the door to 'Sleepers'. "It's right across the hall from the kitchen, if we want a snack or something."

"Yeah. Sure. We'll just help ourselves."

"As usual."

Michael checked the hallway before he softly closed the door.

"Good." Jessie made beeline for the stuffed bean bags and plopped down.

Michael hefted the backpack he had grabbed and wondered why the hell he'd taken it. Maybe so Jessie would have something to wear. He wasn't even sure there was anything of value in it. And he had no idea where they were going, what they would need.

It was all so perfectly wrong.

It had been a panic and a struggle to get themselves and the backpack out of the small bedroom window. Trailer windows were meant for cross ventilation, not for slinging one leg at a time over the transom, sliding your ass out then falling to the ground. Though it had worked.

He and Jessie had worked their way behind two other trailers before emerging onto the main road in Sunshine Vista. It was obvious from the milling crowds and the hoopla that something big was happening at Aunt Jane's trailer, it just would not be happening with them.

The cops were about to leave, so Michael turned Jessie around and headed them back toward the trailer.

"What are you doing?" Jessie had shrieked in a panic, wanting to turn around.

Michael grabbed her hand and explained that if the cops were looking for two kids now they wouldn't be looking for two kids going toward the trailer to see what all the excitement was. They'd be looking for runaway escapees, going in the other direction.

They only had to take a few steps when the cops passed without giving them any kind of once over. They immediately reversed direction. When they got to the pillars at the entrance to Sunshine Vista, Michael pulled Jessie behind one of the pillars.

"Now what?" she'd asked.

"Wait."

It was a few minutes later when Michael pointed to the car that stopped at the trailer park entrance ready to leave Sunshine Vista and launch back into traffic. Inside were the Grand Duchesses of CPS enforcement, Mrs. French and Mrs. Warner. They did not look pleased.

It was a ten-minute walk to the Quick Mart. Michael had planned to call a cab, but in truth had nowhere to tell the cabbie to go. Besides, their trail would be easy to follow – two kids in a cab from the nearby Quick Mart to where? Sacramento's version of the Waldorf Astoria?

Hoofing it to The Fourth Redeemer it was.

"M, what are we doing here? What now? When can we go back?"

Michael checked out the window and cased the parking lot.

"Sleep my little lamb. Go to sleep."

"I'm not tired."

Michael turned to her. "Get some rest. We've got some travels ahead of us."

Jessie brightened. "Like Arizona?"

Michael smiled.

"Okay!"

"Now go to sleep."

"You serious?"

Michael nodded. "Like a heart attack."

It was his father's favorite phrase, almost. If Michael ever dared question his father on something, his father would grab the front of Michael's shirt, bring him spitting close. 'Hey, boy, I'm serious. Like a fuckin' heart attack'.

"Not funny M."

"Yeah, I know. Now, close your eyes."

Pitic switched off the lights and coasted into the gravel parking lot of the Fourth Redeemer Church.

He steered the car to the far end of the deserted lot, skirting the bushes that lined the lot and provided cover from the road. He stopped under some linden branches and rolled down the windows.

And listened and waited.

The rain was Sacramento steady. A steady misting with big drops falling after collecting on the branches above the car, making pinging sounds.

God, he hated the Cooper kids.

He picked up the phone and dialed.

When it was answered, he whispered.

"I've got 'em…No…no, they were walking on the highway. It was too busy. Had to wait until they're alone…What...? I know, I know…"

Pitic picked up the newspaper. He folded the page back and brought the picture closer to his face. He cradled the phone as he studied the picture of the little girl and the cop and the bear.

"It's a church…A church…Place is all dark, but I saw 'em through a window."

He carefully shredded the paper into strips.

Damn that little Cooper girl. This was all her fault he tried to tell himself.

He listened dutifully, finally shut off the phone. 'Don't fuck it up,' he repeated silently to himself.

He felt for the knife on his belt.

Sure sir.

Alive.

Unless they struggle.

It was dark when Michael woke. The Nissan driving church lady must've left. Evidently, she had not bothered to check out the Sunday school rooms, as Michael knew she wouldn't. No reason to.

But now they were locked in for the night. Probably any attempt to leave would send alarms to an untold number of alarm companies and security patrols, if not the cops.

Couldn't have anyone walking out with the silver dogwood-petaled candleholders or a boatload of Lutheran hymnals. Jesus, God, what would happen on Sunday. A mute and dark service.

Fourth Redeemer was dreaming a quiet dream.

And Jessie was still napping.

Michael went to the church kitchen. He pulled open the heavy doors of something called a Turbo Air refrigerator. It was massive and deep and pretty damn empty.

"What's today?" he asked himself.

He mentally calculated today's date with the date on the round Tupperware tub. It had 'Men's Bible Study' scrawled in red marker on top with a date.

As the date was tomorrow's date, Michael assumed the tuna salad was destined for tomorrow's meeting and hence perfectly fine for enjoying tonight.

He rummaged in the cupboards until he found crackers, but no bread. He'd have to make do with Poisson-sur-Saltines.

Searching the rest of the fridge, all he saw were sugared sodas. Plenty of those. Guess Lutherans didn't give a shit about rotten teeth or contributing to pre-diabetes.

He opted for a club soda. The only one left.

"What are you eating?"

"Ah. She wakes. Tuna. On crackers."

Jessie rubbed her eyes and worked her tongue and not in a good way. "What else is there?"

"Crackers. With a side of tuna salad."

"Ha-ha." She moved to the refrigerator and peered inside.

"Well, there's some milk- "

The splinter of broken glass in the nursery down the hall stopped everything.

"M!" The milk carton crashed to the floor exploding in a spray of white.

"I'll be back."

"No!"

Michael ran into the nursery and froze. Someone was on his belly struggling through the window, fighting to hang on to the drapes for purchase.

Michael moved to the side of the window. Just as the little man raised his head, Michael went to deliver a mighty kick. But stopped.

"You!?"

Pitic turned his head toward Michael, let out a growl, and grabbed for Michael, snagging his shirt. From somewhere a knife flashed.

Delivering what he'd planned in the first place, Michael let fly with a solid boot to the chin driving Pitic's head up into the sash. The upper part of the window cracked, shards broke away from the frame, and guillotined into the side of Pitic's head. The knife fell to the floor at the same time an ear-splitting alarm erupted.

Michael took one second to snatch the knife and caromed his way back to the kitchen. He thought to throw the knife in the trash, instead shoved it in the backpack. With Jess in one hand and the backpack in the other, they crashed through the side door.

Outside the klaxon alarm echoed off the trees, alerting everyone for miles that the good Lutherans of the Fourth Redeemer were being robbed this night.

"This way" Michael half dragged, half carried Jessie across the parking lot in the spitting rain.

.

CHAPTER 46

"Detective Steiner, I didn't expect to hear from you this soon. Are you asking me out on another date?"

Samantha Barnes' voice was slightly mocking and the whole not answering with a Hello but with his name thing, threw him.

"What? No. How… did you know it was me?"

"You're the detective, you tell me."

"You recognized the number."

"Well, I wouldn't have, but I have your card and the other night I entered your name with your number in my phone with all your… pertinent information."

He wanted to ask what pertinent information she had of his, but moved on, especially since Mallory was tapping her pencil and giving him a 'what-the-hell' look.

"Listen, we need you to take a look at someone and see how much she might resemble the woman you saw that night out on Jones road."

"You mean like a lineup type thing?"

"No, not exactly. A lineup is not possible in this situation."

"But, you have a picture then?"

"No picture. We'd like you to view this person, in person." It sounded stupid when he said it and even worse when she repeated it.

"A person in person. I'm not quite getting you."

"This…person is in a recovery center so we would need you to come and view her there."

"So, she's under guard and you want me to take a look at her. Do I need a special password to get past the guard?"

He wasn't sure whether she was kidding or slightly clueless. Second thought told him she wasn't clueless.

"We will be there with you. Some of our OID team." He glanced at Mallory who rolled her eyes and mouthed, 'OID team?'

"When? When would you like to do this viewing?"

"As soon as you can make it. We'll pick you up."

"Where is this?"

Jake checked the address and gave it to her.

"I'm actually not far from there. I can walk and meet you. That seems more convenient, don't you think?"

"So, you're available now?"

"Are you sure you're not asking me out? I'm free."

Jake hoped Mallory wasn't overhearing any of Samantha's comments. He didn't need office derision.

"I…"

"Never mind, I can see I'll have to be the one calling you for second dates. Anyway, let's meet in half an hour. You and I and your team and we'll all do this together. There's probably a lobby. See you there."

And she hung up.

Mallory shook her head. "You are so suave. You'd think you were asking her out on a date or something, you know."

"She'll meet us there."

"I heard."

Samantha Barnes hit speed dial number one. After he answered, she told him.

"It's all set. This should do it."

She didn't wait for an acknowledgment but gathered her purse and coat and before she left, she went to the side of the bed and kissed her mother on the forehead.

"You ready to do this?"

"Bring 'em on," answered Ilsa Pokovich.

Then she left room 227, outside of which there was no guard, and took the elevator down to the lobby to wait for Jake Steiner and his 'whole team'.

CHAPTER 47

Mallory took one side of the bed, Dr. Parker paced alongside the other. He stood with a disapproving expression on his face and had spent the last few minutes registering his Hippocratic displeasure, both at this intrusion, as well as Mallory and Stan's previous interrogation of his patient.

After Mallory explained for the third time that they wouldn't be bothering anyone, least of all the patient who only had to be still and do nothing, did Dr. Parker relent. Now, he stood like a watchful hawk alert for any sign of distress.

While waiting for Jake to arrive with Samantha Barnes, Mallory realized that it didn't matter what the Pokovich broad had claimed about where she had or hadn't been, how sick she was or wasn't. If Samantha Barnes does verify this crone was the one she saw standing in the rain next to the BMW on Jones Rd. on the night of May 13th, it would close a circle and weld a link in the continuing chain of bad news for the old lady.

Fingerprints in the car and now a witness who might place her certainly in the car. Clang go the bars, closing this old woman up for the rest of her life, which, Mallory realized may only be months.

Even though the pallor on the woman was just north of death, her eyes shone with an alertness that belied Dr. Parker's dire predictions. If she had cancer, it wasn't in her brain. Her body might fail and soon to be eaten up, but the old lady remained cat-like vigilant. Nothing seemed to escape her attention.

Even Mallory's observations.

"The hell you lookin' at?" snarled Ilsa, her eyes boring into Mallory.

Dr. Parker put a calming hand on her arm which she shook off.

"Tell this bitch to stop bothering me." Ilsa raised up on her elbows. "I have cancer!" she hissed, snake-like.

Mallory didn't respond, even when the woman whispered, "You're just a wracked-up, scarred-up whore. Couldn't get a man if you paid for one."

Mallory resisted the desire to trace her scar, instead gripped the bed rail a little tighter and forced a smile.

When she didn't answer, the woman spat. "Silence is truth, dearie. Wait 'til you're an *old* scarred whore. Not even the stinking, toothless homeless bum'll take pity on your sorry ass."

Dr. Parker finally felt compelled to speak.

"I think that's enough now."

Ilsa Pokovich shot him a look but said nothing else.

Just then, Jake guided Samantha Barnes into the room. None too soon thought Mallory.

Jake made sure all the fluorescents were on as well as the overhead room light. He'd had to inform Ilsa Pokovich this was to be an official interrogation, even though she needn't do anything. He'd received a growled 'fuck off' for his courtesy.

As soon as Jake and Samantha entered, Ilsa lifted herself up off the pillow.

"The shit is this?"

Jake and Samantha stood at the foot of the bed. Samantha stared.

Ilsa looked to Dr. Parker. "Who is she?"

"Just be quiet now," came his calm answer.

"Like hell, I will. I wanna know who the hell she is and what she's doing here."

When nobody replied and nobody moved, Ilsa banged her hands on the bedrails. "Too many staring people in this room. Get out, all of you! Now!"

Samantha turned to Jake. Mallory and Dr. Parker watched as Samantha Barnes nodded.

Jake took her arm and guided her out.

"The rest of you, get the shit out!"

Ilsa continued banging until Dr. Parker took her arms.

"What?" asked Ilsa. Innocent, as if she hadn't been bloody hysterical seconds before.

Mallory left and joined Jake and Samantha in the hallway.

"You sure? asked Jake again.

"Yes," sighed Samantha. "I told you that was the woman who stuck her face into my window. It was the voice that threw me."

"I thought you never heard her speak," challenged Mallory.

Samantha did a slow turn. "I didn't. Hear her speak, I mean. I meant it was her voice that kind of threw me off now. I didn't expect it. An old lady to talk like that." Then, pointing to Mallory's face, she said, "That's one nasty scar. Maybe you should have it looked at."

She directed her attention back to Jake. "But that's the woman. I'm sure."

"And you never heard her speak before?" Mallory again.

Samantha ignored Mallory, leaned into Jake. "I'm sure. And I'm leaving."

She started down the hall. "This was loads of fun detective and... *team*. You know where to find me. If you uh...need anything."

Mallory watched Jake watch her walk away. Finding her voice, she said, "This seals it for Pokovich, doesn't it?"

Jake rubbed his temples. "What? Yeah, gets us Pokovich..."

Mallory pinched Jake's arm. "Okaayy. Now what?"

"Ow! Yeah, Pokovich. But you know she wasn't alone," he said, turning his attention to Mallory. "Hell, even if she was twice as strong weeks ago, there is no way this time she would be able to sneak up on Marston, get a noose around his neck, and saw like a mother. Not like sneaking up with goddamn battery acid in a watering can."

"Is it so unusual that a felon cooped up in California Women's for umpteen years wouldn't make a friend or two?" Mallory asked. "Wouldn't she have developed contacts? Couldn't she have put the feelers out for a few heavy hitters to join her in her little revenge?"

"Of course," agreed Jake. "I'm sure that's close to what went down, but it doesn't answer the question of why not just shoot the bastard."

Mallory shook her head. "You're a man."

"Thanks."

"You only know a woman scorned from your side. From stories you've heard, or in your case, maybe personal experience."

Jake smiled. "Me? Never."

"You ought to see it from in here. Scorned is not pretty. It's red and ugly and festers, and it magnifies and mutates and exaggerates and it gets drenched in acid and it starts to eat and it settles deep. Deep where it can't be removed. And if the hurt is bad enough, really bad, it becomes part of you, it becomes the whole you, maybe. And it is you. And only retribution, bloody goddamn revenge will help."

Jake looked at her, searching her face for farce, for serious, or for a personal incident that would've manifested itself in deep hurt.

"Shit, Mallory. Are all women like you?"

Mallory, burned, remembering Samantha Barnes' comment about her scar. "Of course."

As they left the Recovery Center, Jake opened the door for her. And made sure to let her go first.

"So where you headed?" asked Mallory as Jake returned from retrieving his dog from the security office.

Jake, preoccupied, searched the street, both ways.

Mallory petted the dog. "Okay, I think I'm headed home, maybe back to work, possibly rob a bank," she offered, checking Jake's reaction. "What about you?"

"Okay, have a good night. See you tomorrow." He pulled out his phone and headed off on his own.

"Sure, Mal, let's go celebrate," grumbled Mallory. "Maybe head over to Beatty's Bar and clink drinks, Have fun. Relax. You know, the two of us."

The dog looked back at Mallory but stuck with Jake as he walked away.

Twenty minutes later Mallory entered OID. She didn't bother turning on any office lights but went straight to the back sink, flipped on the work light, and stood, debating whether to fill the coffee pot or not.

"You have coffee now, you'll be up all night," she said to her image in the cracked mirror over the sink.

"Yeah, so what?"

She picked up the empty carafe, rinsed it, filled it, poured the water in then pulled out a bag of some of Jake's special coffee he'd already carefully ground.

She read the label. "*Colombia San Sebastián Reserva from the hillsides surrounding the town of La Plata.* Damn. I hope this shit's expensive."

She filled the basket and got it started.

While watching the coffee drip, she unexpectedly felt something against her leg.

"Whoa!"

Jake dog stared up at her.

"What are you doing here you crazy mutt?"

She smiled as she started back toward the glass office, meaning to call out something incredibly rude to Jake, but stopped halfway, frozen in place in the shadows.

The evening moonlight speared into the glass office and lit Jake and Samantha like lovers on a movie set.

They stood together, their foreheads touching.

A delicate few seconds later Jake began making progress with the buttons of her blouse. His hands lingered in one place then moved lower, then lower still. When it came off, Mallory could see headway had already been made on everything else.

With his arms now on her shoulders, their eyes never leaving each other, Jake slowly backed her to the glass wall, toward Mallory.

Mallory slipped further into the shadows and held onto the dog.

Jake put his palms on the glass on either side of Samantha. Her back was arched and her ass was nicely flattened against the glass.

Mallory had no view of Jake but that was unnecessary as his hands started their slide down the glass as he lowered himself to his knees. His hands came around and cupped Samantha's ass. Her body tensed and came away from the glass while her head rested back.

Mallory never thought of looking away. Never. Never thought of interrupting. Never thought about bursting in and making a stupid comment about getting a room. This was wicked, salacious beauty and she could not look away. Her eyes were locked on the scene before her.

Samantha reached down and lifted Jake's head and brought him up standing. She raised one leg, just enough. The rhythmic thrusts started slowly and tentatively, then continued in earnest.

Their familiarity with each other let Mallory know this was not a first screwing. This was a continuation of an on-going screwing. There's was continual lust, interrupted only by periods of normal life and change of location.

Jake was good. Twice she saw Samantha shake and knock against the glass. The last time must've been both together as Jake ended by resting his head on her shoulder. They stood that way for a few minutes, sealing it with a kiss.

Mallory plopped down on the floor and studied her hands. She was genuinely surprised when tears welled and started to fall. She sniffed and wiped her nose like a little kid with the back of her hand.

She didn't watch them get dressed but they must have. She didn't watch them leave, but they must have because the dog was gone. She didn't notice when they turned the lights off, but they must have because she found herself in total blackness with no sound in the office except old building sounds.

She was alone.

And that was the thought that kicked her. Alone.

Not that she didn't want Jake. She admitted it now. It was so clear. She knew what she wanted. She wanted his hardness in her. She wanted to be held. She wanted to arch her back, meet his thrusts, lie awake talking for hours.

What ripped at her wasn't that Samantha Barnes' bare ass cheeks, and not hers, had been plastered up against the glass walls, widening out with each thrust from Jake.

Not that she was jealous of Samantha Barnes. She was. But it wasn't that.

It wasn't that at all.

This whole night, this whole experience had really been about one thing.

She was forgotten. No, more overlooked, disregarded, ignored.

"Oh, what a pity party, Mallory. Man up, will you. And why is it 'man-up'? Why am I saying 'man-up' when restoring my dignity has nothing to do with a man?"

"Good goddamn question Dimante," she answered.

"Then again, maybe it does."

"Shut up!"

What a fool.

She approached the quiet office, her reflection defining herself as she approached. She studied her face, gently illuminated by the moonlight that lit the atrium.

Hope.

She was truly pathetic. She realized that.

She touched her scar with her index finger and traced its length. She knew she'd once been cute. She knew that. Sure, men's eyes still go right to her boobs. Then they jump right to the scar.

She'd tried to imagine what they think when they see her now. In the old days, it was easy. They were evaluating her for sex. It was understandable and easy to deal with and not unwelcome.

But now she was a contagion. That was it. That's how they reacted. As if they, too, could catch a scar. As if her scar was an ad for crabs or herpes. They still thought of sex when they looked at her, but now it was bad sex. Bad things would happen to you if you had sex with this girl. Normal girls, girls without a shitload of baggage or sordid history, didn't have scars. Bad girls did.

That's what they thought.

They were wrong.

She unbuttoned her blouse, working slowly, pulling her blouse free when she got to the last button. She spread it apart and ran her fingers over her breasts until her nipples tightened. She pushed up against the glass and raised her hands and placed her palms where Jake's palms had been.

She rested her head against the glass.

Looking out, the world was still the same to her, except how she was treated. She was on another planet and she'd have to adjust. Learn the language and customs.

But what were they?

She thought Jake understood. Cop to cop. She thought he saw her good parts and ignored the rest because he knew how the scar happened. She thought he could see past the scar. Thought he could see only her.

She didn't realize how much she counted on that.

Still, he'd chosen normal.

And really, why go with damaged goods when you can get new?

She sat slumped on the floor of the archive office. She traced the scar again and again.

Sometimes, though, you just had to admit to yourself that as pathetic and hopeless and idiotic are your hopes and dreams, they are real and they are yours and you will do anything to put yourself in front of them. To be run over by them. To meet them head-on. And accept them when they happen. Assuming they happen.

We hope more than we say. We dream and don't act on our dreams because it's easier to keep them safely locked away like dreams. Dreams are perfect. There is nothing about life that is.

And sometimes when your dreams involve someone else and it requires their participation, when you mess around with someone else's life, when you spy on what they're doing and doing without you, then the odds of making the tough transition from lonely to the best that can ever be are like Vegas odds.

Life 1, Dream 0.

"Enough, you moron."

Just after midnight, knowing they were long gone, when she was sure that the semen on the glass had dried and the panties were picked up and the cock put away, and the place was deserted, only then did she climb to her feet, gather her keys and coat and leave.

With sadness, she realized that without the scar, back the way she used to be, back before Olive Park, she was never forgotten. And she would never have been forgotten. And, if she really thought about it, had things worked out, had the stars aligned, or whatever the hell they do, it could have, should have, been her ass being thrust up against the glass.

Olive Park had left its mark on her as it had on so many others. It was unfair. Everyone else had moved on. Had relished the bittersweet ending to Olive Park and then they'd gone on to other things. Life, career, family, friends.

Some scars were there; you just couldn't see them. Some scars were there and that was all you could see.

She pulled open the outer door and turned and looked back at the wonderful glass office and gave a little rueful smile. Tomorrow, she'd stand back and let Stan wonder what the hell happened because she'd be damned if she would clean the fucking glass.

CHAPTER 48

"I don't know where she is," Susan Spruance stated. "Really, I don't. Maybe her phone's busted. Anyway, this stuff is for you guys. A week ago, she asked me to try and find some background on Marston and this Pokovich broad."

She dumped two files and three DVDs on the conference table.

"And there you go." She stood back and waited for some response from Jake. "And where's Detective Wyld?"

Jake moved from the whiteboard detailing the Marston case.

Susan saw pictures of Marston, Marston's car, Ilsa Pokovich, Peter Berlin, dollar signs, Last Will, and a jumble of other notes scrawled in Jake's scribble, all over the whiteboard.

Some solid, mostly dotted, lines connected the boxes and pictures.

Next to the board was a hand-drawn timeline chart. There was an embarrassing gap between 'Discovery of BMW' and 'Marston Murdered'.

She looked up into the skylights and the four levels above the glass office. She couldn't help herself. It was the first time she'd been in the glass office of OID. Most of the SacPD archive units had been completed on the second and third floors. Billowing out as far as the railing of the fourth floor, Susan could see dirty construction plastic tacked onto the unfinished framing, where construction had ceased. No plans to go further until need warranted.

"No clue?" answered Jake.

"What?"

"Mallory. No clue?"

"She gets to take a day off now and then, doesn't she?"

Jake nodded, admitting he'd heard the term 'day off' before. "Sure, as long as she doesn't make a habit out of it."

"You boys must be peaches to work with."

Jake smiled. "We try. And Detective Wyld is out, 'on assignment' as he likes to say when he doesn't want to say. So, what's up with the DVDs?"

Susan chuckled. "Marston movies. These things are so bad, they put two or three on a disc because they can't sell a disc with only one movie on it. Nobody would buy it."

"According to Stan, somebody's still buying 'em."

"Overseas, probably. Anyway, here are six or seven of them. Hard ones to find. Mal thought you'd like to see these."

"Can't wait," Jake sighed. "It will be riveting. What else?" Jake pawed through the folders.

"Well, it's funny. I had to go to a whole lot of sources to come up with anything on Pokovich, but Marston, holy shit, took me forever to wade through the life and times of this guy. Separating out the truth from the legend."

"Anything that you think'll help us connect him to someone who wants his head gone?"

Susan flipped through the pages, musing as she went.

"Well, he's gay, but you guys knew that right?"

"No, we did not," said Jake, uneasy. "How gay?"

"What do you mean 'how gay'? Seems to me to be gay gay. I don't know. I'm ill-equipped to answer that on a scale of 1-10."

"It's just that we understood that the guy was mainline women user. Especially from his days in Hollywood."

Susan flipped back and forth. "Not seeing that in truth, only in legend. Have you gotten toxicology back on him yet?"

"Danni says another week. Why"?

Susan shrugged. "My guess is it'll show anti-HIV drugs in his system. He had AIDS…uh…but I guess you didn't know that either, right?"

"How come Mallory didn't find this out or know it to begin with? She knew so much about the guy."

Susan held her hand up. "Hey, she assigned Marston to me. She would normally be getting this stuff to you two, not me. I'm merely the lackey here. And, she wouldn't have known about his sexual preferences, probably. He kept it pretty well hidden. And the other guy found with him. My guess, he is…was, his current live-in."

"Except he wasn't," countered Jake. "A private detective. Former SacPD. Don't think he'd ever known where Marston lived until last week."

"Well, what's he doing in Marston's car then?" Susan asked.

Jake pointed to the dotted line on the whiteboard connecting Marston with Peter Berlin. "Yeah, well. We're working on it."

"Huh. So, according to one source, Marston had a nickname in the gay community back in L.A." Susan flipped a page. "Man-Eater."

Jake remembered released felon Ilsa Pokovich and her insistence that Marston was the biggest abuser of aspiring female actresses in L.A.

"I have a bad feeling about this," said Jake. "And what about Madam Pokovich?"

Susan switched files. "I had to go, well you wouldn't believe the sources I used. I even tapped two of those Find-Your-Relatives sites to trace part of her family."

Jake studied the list of facts under Pokovich's name on the whiteboard.

"So, she was born in Gdansk, Poland, right?"

"Almost. Hungary."

"Mother was a hooker?"

"Probably not. Her father held some Russian government post, which was how she was able to get out. If her mother was in the couch-bouncing business that would've been awkward."

"Out of Russia or out of Hungary?"

"Yes. No. Her father was in the Russian bureaucracy assigned to Hungary about the time Hungary decided to flex its muscles and revolt. Father was stuck in Hungary. Died there, too."

"So, how did she get out?" asked Jake.

"This part is funny. I can only go by sketchy immigration reports. But, it seems their father lied a bit and got them out by finding a sponsor here in the U.S. to take them."

"Them?"

"Oh. Yeah. Sorry, Ilsa is the youngest of three. They all made it out. Ilsa and her two brothers. Yeah. Her father lied and said they were child circus performers and he found a guy in Florida to employ them, even as kids. A special work visa."

"Florida?" Jake felt the blood drain. "A circus in Florida? What was the guy's name?"

Jake held his breath as Susan flipped to one of the first pages.

"Rendell. Roger Rendell. Ran some two-bit circus…what?" Susan studied Jake as jumped up and walked to the whiteboard.

"What?"

Jake took a deep breath and let it out. "Was one of the brothers named Rudy?"

"I…" She traced the name with her finger. "Rudolph Pokovich Yes. Rudy."

"Bloody hell. I don't believe it," muttered Jake.

"What?" Susan flipped pages. "What is it? What did I miss?"

"I don't get this," continued Jake. "The hell is going on?"

"Jake, what're you talking about?"

He came back to the conference table and addressed Susan. "You have proof that Ilsa Pokovich is Ruby…Rudy Pokovich's sister?"

Susan, cautious now. "Right here, Jake. I'm sure. Rudy Pokovich is Ilsa's brother. Pokovich, Pokovich. I have it right here."

Jake shook his head and sat on the conference table next to Susan. "That means Ruby Everheart, who we thought, who we were sure was really Roger Rendell, is, in fact, Rudy Pokovich."

Susan looked puzzled. "Wait. Who's Ruby…?" Then she remembered. "Oh! Oh shit, shit, shit."

Jake reached for his copy of Pokovich's file. "You said there were three siblings."

Susan was still digesting the Ruby information. "So, what does that mean?"

"I'm very much hoping you'll tell me," said Jake as he made his way to Stan's desk, pulled out a half-empty Speyburn bottle, grabbed two paper cups, and poured a generous shot in each. He lifted each with care and placed one before Susan and one before himself on the conference table.

"And, did Ilsa have a daughter?" continued Jake.

"Yes," answered Susan. "Born in '82."

"I'm guessing, though, she didn't commit suicide by jumping off the Coronado bridge."

"There's absolutely no record of her after her birth at Cedars-Sinai. Nothing."

Susan stared at the scotch, then back at Jake.

"What are we drinking to?"

"Whack-A-Moles mysteries. And their eventual demise."

She started to ask then changed her mind. She watched Jake tip and drink in one gulp. Not being a hard liquor person, she sipped the biting, peaty liquid.

"Wow," she managed, as it burned its way down. "Whoo. Yow."

Jake held his cup in anticipation of her finishing.

"You want me to go? Just down it?" She held up her cup.

"Yep."

"Here goes." She tipped the rest and coughed it down.

As soon as she finished, Jake crumpled his paper cup, swiveled, and fired at the wastebasket. Missing.

Susan made it.

Jake ran his fingers through his hair, picked up the Pokovich file, and flipped to the last page. "You're sure that this Rendell brought three kids into the country?"

"That's what I show, yeah."

"Positive that Roger Rendell is not Ruby Everheart aka Rudolph Pokovich?"

"Positive. Why?"

Jake stood up. "You see, according to what Ollestad who researched this, we were under the impression that Everheart's real name was Rendell and he ran a circus that was based in Florida and traversed the country, ending up in Sacramento. In Olive Park.

"I…" began Susan.

Jake interrupted. "So what happened to this Roger Rendell?"

Susan shook her head. "Not a clue. Mallory asked me to follow Pokovich. Besides, if this Rendell really did bring the Pokovich clan into the country, he'd be, what, seventy probably."

"You said three siblings," repeated Jake.

"What? Yes," said Susan, pointing to the file. "Youngest is Ilsa, then Rudolph, then there is an older brother. No records on him, yet."

Jake added Rudy and a ?? to the board. He included them in a newly drawn circle with Ilsa.

"I didn't see employment for Ilsa listed. What years did she work for Marston?"

Susan laughed. "You're kidding, right?"

When Jake didn't respond, Susan affected a serious tone.

"Jake, I thought you knew. Ilsa Pokovich was married to James Marston for twelve years. She was his wife."

CHAPTER 49

Stan turned off Highway 50 into the little pullout. Since the last time he'd been here, two, three months ago, the boulders blocking the path into the woods had been shoved out of the way. Now, in the late afternoon sun, it was easy to see the path was clear and well-trodden. Unlike the trailer park, the location of the bodies discovered in Olive Park was not well publicized. Otherwise, there would be a continuous swam of gawkers sniffing the air, pawing the ground, wondering where all the bodies were buried, where Ruby Everheart was found. Where it all came to an end under the moonlight in a clearing in Olive Park.

He closed his door. There were no other cars around. He pushed aside a branch and found his way to the clearing.

The wind was sweeping the branches of the trees around the clearing, but the same as the last time he'd been here, there was a sullen stillness about the place.

The mound in the center was still there. The mound of dirt on which Everheart's body had sprawled, stuck through the chest, steaming in the night air.

Now, in daylight, the whole place seemed tired, lifeless.

It was not a happy place.

"Enjoying the view?" came the voice from behind him.

Stan started and was miffed that he did so.

"What the hell Ginger. Why here?"

Phil Ginger shrugged.

"Sorry, chum. Bad memories, eh? Well, c'mon. Let's take a walk."

Stan started to follow Ginger, but Ginger only moved as far as the mound in the center of the clearing.

"I understand this is where Everheart was. Right here. Stuck with what did you call it? A broom handle?"

"Shovel."

"Yeah. Shovel. Right here."

Stan couldn't take his eyes off the mound. All he could see was a steaming corpse in the moonlight.

"Why," he asked quietly. "Why are we here?"

Ginger continued as if he hadn't heard. "Thanks for the tip on the head. Made me look like I was on top of things again. So, why are we here?"

Stan nodded.

"Because I owe you, brother. I owe you. Though, we shouldn't even have to be here, if you'd done your job, you know."

Stan studied the red-haired reporter.

"What are you talking about?"

Ginger kicked the side of the mound.

"You're thinking your case was all wrapped up, right? Perp is dead. Dead kids recovered. Parents notified. All Olive Park loose ends wrapped up, eh?"

"Case is closed," said Stan. "Closed."

Ginger shrugged. "Maybe."

"Meaning?"

"Let me ask you a question. They carted Everheart's body outta here. Took it to the morgue, right?"

"Yeah. So?"

"Then what?"

"Autopsy, of course."

"Right. End of story. Dead perp. Cut open. Didn't find anything. Just a man. Cause they couldn't look into the warped part of the brain and see what was really wrong. Just a body cut up."

"What are you getting at?"

"You think your case is closed? Then tell me where the body went after Forensics had finished with it and the Coroner had done the autopsy?"

Stan opened his mouth. And closed it.

"Yeah, pal. I didn't think so."

Stan recovered. "I assume it was given to the next of kin, except there was no next of kin we could find."

"So?"

"So, it would've been cremated or buried in a state plot." Stan looked abashed. "But, I don't know."

"I do," said Ginger.

He looked at Stan. "Someone did claim the body."

Stan felt the hairs rise on his neck.

"Shit, Who?"

Ginger smiled.

"Let's take a walk."

He headed deeper into the woods before Stan could object.

Ginger beckoned and forged ahead. They moved past the disturbed earth where the additional nine graves were. Stan studied the spot where Mallory's brother had been found. It was all so innocent now. Simply freshly turned earth with victims that had now been set free and put to proper rest.

Ginger didn't stop.

"Hey. C'mon," Stan protested. "Where we going?"

But Ginger didn't answer, only kept tromping through the woods, elbowing aside Aspen saplings and stepping through the salal and brushwood.

They came upon a semblance of a trail. It led straight ahead, right to the back of the Sunshine Vista trailer park. Right to the entrance to JOYLAND.

Ginger pointed to two rectangular bare spots. The spots where the two Everheart trailers used to be. Instead, now empty lots with bare, embarrassed dirt and pale shoots of weeds that had had the misfortune to attempt to grow without sunlight.

Stan looked down and saw what was left of the metal pole that had held the neon sign. The sign advertising 'Fortunes by Ruby'. Someone with a sizeable cutting torch had sheared it off at ground level, most of the gleaming cut was already rusting. Severed electrical wires flowed up from a conduit and flopped uselessly next to where the pole had been.

Ginger turned to Stan.

"You know what happened to those two trailers?"

Stan nodded. "Yeah. I do," he said, finally sure of something.

"We, rather Forensics, had a whole crew out here for days, sifting through both trailers. They printed every inch of space. They cataloged every item. They took for evidence the stuff that appeared to be relevant. They returned to the two Cooper kids their stuff. The rest they left. They did the same in both trailers, at least what they could in the torched one."

Ginger sniffed.

"What's your point?" continued Stan, still unsure why they were here.

"Well, Mister Detective. Where are the trailers now?"

Stan was about to say he didn't know or care but something about this whole trip made him hesitate. He knew Ginger wasn't a fool. Just shrewd and relentless.

Stan took his best guess.

"I'd assume as soon as we were done with them, the owners of the trailer park probably insisted they be destroyed. Hauled away. It wouldn't be good for business."

Ginger laughed. "Definitely not good for business. But, do you know who took 'em. Who hauled 'em away?"

"Does it matter?"

Instead of answering, Ginger approached the fenced-off gates of the abandoned amusement park. The shuttered arched opening with the unlit sign above, JOYLAND, at once welcomed and barred entry. Ginger went to the chain link and shook it. Waves of answering wobbles continued in both directions.

"You know," mused Ginger, peering past the fencing. "At one time, this whole place was under one ownership. The carnival, the trailer park, the woods of Olive Park."

Stan joined him. "I know. Guy named Rendell, alias Ruby Everheart. Used to use this as winter quarters for this freak show 'til he ran out of dough. Sold the land for the trailer park. Kept this and the woods. Started the psychic business, changed his name to Ruby Everheart, a woman. A woman who tastes ran to kids. I know all this. We all know this."

Ginger turned to Stan. "But you don't."

"What do you mean?"

Ginger raised his head and stared at the sky, then back to Stan. "You ever hear the name Pokovich?"

Stan recoiled. "Pokovich? Did you say Pokovich?"

"Yeah," smiled Ginger, but he displayed a hint of disappointment. "So, you know it? You know all about it, then?"

"Know what?"

"I thought you said you'd heard the name?" asked Ginger, his brow furrowing. He never wanted to give more of his diggings away than he had to.

Stan shrugged, playing the game. "Name's come up."

"In what context?"

Stan shook his head. "You go. You dragged me here."

"You know when I came across this…Pokovich, I asked around. Dug for something, dug deep, because nobody seemed to care and I needed a story. You guys were all focused on this Ruby Everheart whose alias was Rendell. And now Everheart was a smoking mass of dead and the dead kids were found and everybody simply wanted to put the whole thing behind them.

"So, I'm thinking what can I do? What part of the story doesn't anybody seem to care about? All the young hotshots have the big, hot story; that was you and your guys and a shovel up the perp's asshole. So, I came out here. I thought I'd have a look around the trailer. Find out about the life of this Everheart. Wanted to get here right after your forensic crew finished and before the curious picked the place clean. I thought, what the hell, I'll have a look-see.

"Of course, I do my best exploring at night. So 'bout eleven one night a few weeks ago, I pull in and damn if two bigass semis ain't pulling outta here, one with the remains of the burnt trailer and the other with the complete other trailer. Shit, I said to myself. Ginger, you're too goddamn late. There goes your story.

"What the hell. Better follow my story, I thought. I turn the old Saab around and don't go but a few feet and flashing lights cut me off."

"Our guys?"

Ginger shook his head. "Nope. Private asshole. I tell him to get the hell outta my way when I see he's not for real. Not a real cop. But guess what. Fucker pulls a gun. Whoa!"

"What!?"

"Yeah. Thing is. He didn't ask for I.D. or anything. I told him who I was, what I was doing. That this was a public street and that I needed to leave. Funny thing though. It came clear he was just stopping me from following those semis. Kept looking to make sure they were well gone before he lets me go."

Ginger touched his nose. "This never fails. Now, I knew I had my story.

"You find where they went?"

Ginger scuffed the ground. "Hell no. But rent-a-cops with guns are only a minor setback for this guy. And you know everybody leaves a trail, somehow, somewhere, there's a pile of shit that some dog forgot to cover up."

"And?"

Ginger knelt down and picked up what his shoe had uncovered, a scorched red tennis shoe. He turned it over and the swagger left him.

He continued in a quiet voice.

"Like everybody, I thought Rendell was the man or woman who owned this. Rendell is the name on the tax records. With a Post Office in Florida. Figures. Tax records still carry the old Florida address. Why not? If you're going around pretending to be a woman doing shit to kids you'd damn well better have an alias and a different address."

"We know," Stan said. "That's how we put Rendell and Everheart together as the same person."

Ginger shrugged. "But you see, all of this isn't owned by whom you think. Rendell, Everheart, or whatever his name is, was. In fact, the same person who owns JOYLAND and the woods, also really owns the trailer park. See, it was never sold, only the name was changed."

Stan didn't like playing catch up. Hated it.

Ginger smiled. "God, I love it when I do the work for the mighty Sacramento PD. Makes me feel like I still know my way around a pile of bullshit."

"So…"

"You still don't see it yet. The one person behind this, the one person who owns all this shit, the one person who paid for the trailers to be removed, who paid for the neon sign to be taken away, and most importantly, the one person who claimed the remains of your precious Ruby Everheart…"

Stan finished the sentence for him. "That one person is Ilsa Pokovich?"

Ginger went to agree but his mouth hung open.

"*Ilsa Pokovich*?" Ginger's voice rose. "Who the hell is *Ilsa* Pokovich?"

"But…"

"Stan, it isn't Ilsa Pokovich. It is a Pokovich all right. But it ain't any Ilsa. Stan, the name you're searching for is Nicholai Pokovich."

"Who?"

"Yeah, pal. That's what I thought."

CHAPTER 50

Stan didn't know why he hadn't done this before. It was something Mallory said a few days ago. It had nagged at him ever since.

He'd left a gloating Phil Ginger an hour ago at the Blue Moon and now approached the curve on Jones road at a slow speed. It was late, near midnight. The traffic was light and no one was coming up behind him at the moment.

The Tule fog was thinning but a veil still clung to the road.

He pulled as far off the road as he could at the exact spot Marston's car was found and put on his flashers. They pulsed a weak crimson giving the car an alien glow.

He thought this would help, coming out here. Mallory was right. There was something about this spot. There was a reason Marston's car was dropped here. It wasn't random. He didn't know why, but he… felt it. Like meeting someone out of context. They are known to you, you're just not sure how.

Of one thing Stan was sure. He had been here before. Not merely passing by. Not out for a drive with Bea. And not on official business.

Because he remembered this section of road. And he remembered the fog. And he remembered he was looking for an address.

He glimpsed the tail end of a memory, but couldn't seem to catch up.

Stan got out and closed the door and listened. The fog muffled, taking away the sharp noises and filtering them into a somber grey. Except for distant traffic, there were no other identifying sounds.

Across the road he knew, after studying the map on his phone, were a few gentlemen farms, tidy five-acre plots with sizeable homes set far back from the road. Surrounded by white rail fences and plenty of well-tended, sweet-smelling grass with a paucity of clucking chickens or well-manured rows of soybeans.

He took out his flashlight, flicked it on and off, then left it on while he studied this side of Jones road. Beyond the road's shoulder was a thick stand of eucalyptus guarded by a low menace of Brickell bush and salvia.

Through the trees, he could make out the yard lights of a row of houses.

Stan checked the road for oncoming traffic both ways, figured his car with flashers was safe, and started for the development. He pushed his way through the low brush, enjoying the heady fragrance of the mature salvia.

The stand of eucalyptus, ripe with its own woody aroma, gave way to neatened backyards. No swing sets or sandboxes here, merely quiet gardens and the occasional gazebo with cushioned metal framed patio sets.

Some yards were fenced, some were hedged. He moved along the backs of the yards until he came to an empty lot, an open area where he could find his way to the street without having to skirt past someone's kitchen window.

At the sidewalk, he brushed off the burrs that clung to the bottom of his pants, straightened, and turned off his flashlight.

Stan took in the curve of the street. Houses lined both sides, equally set back with identical, manicured lawns.

He saw the clumps of double security mailboxes painted the distinctive blue, and the classic street lamps, black fluted poles with white acorn globes, which lined the street, alternating sides as they made their way around the street's arc. This was a section of one of the thousands of housing developments California was famous for - winding streets, 3500 square foot boxes hard up against their neighbor, all with muted, forgettable facades. Depending on the neighborhood, these California-blah houses either collected families with passels of kids, or retirees looking for some quiet.

His eyes scanned the houses up and down the street until they stopped on one near the top of the cul-de-sac.

The hairs on his neck prickled. His heart thudded. He had to get out of here because he now remembered when he'd been here He remembered who he'd been here to see. And he remembered why.

And he realized something was very, very wrong.

CHAPTER 51

From behind the dumpster, Michael watched to see if the little brown man would recover and begin searching for them. He didn't think so. It had been a pretty good field goal boot.

Instead, almost as suddenly as it had started, the alarm stopped.

Night sounds rolled in with the rain.

The car the little man had come in was still in the shadows, half hidden under some tree branches. Nobody was running toward it or shambling for that matter.

Nearby, the few house lights that had come on with the alarm now winked off.

"MMM! What is it? Is ssssomeone here?"

Michael looked at his sister. She was shivering and hugging herself. This had not been the plan. To hide out behind the garbage in the fucking rain. Jesus. What had he been thinking?

'C'mere." He motioned for Jess to come to his side. When she did, he rubbed her arms.

"Whooss hhere?" she asked again. "Who was it?"

"Get close to me. We can try and keep each other warm, okay?"

Jessie tried to look around the dumpster. Michael pulled her back.

"Stay back will you."

Rain ran down his back. He was nearly soaked and they had only been outside for a few minutes. He could feel the water in his shoes.

"Whaat are we dooooing?"

"Hiding. Just hang on."

Michael pulled her tighter. His hand shook as he pulled out the business card and punched in the number on his cell.

"Whoo you caaallling?" Her teeth chattered when she tried to speak now.

Michael disconnected when there was no answer. He tried the second number.

He peeked around the dumpster while he listened and hoped someone would pick up. The car was still there. All dark. He thought he saw the end of a cigarette but with the chill and the rain, he wasn't sure.

"Whhenn you neeeed help you call 911."

Then he was sure there was a lit cigarette. Then he was certain when the car door opened.

"Move back." Michael pushed his sister away and rose up enough to push up the top of the dumpster. He reached inside. He felt paper and something soft. More important whatever it was, was dry.

"C'mon. Step on my leg, boost up, and get inside."

"Whaat?"

Michael stared at his sister. "We could be here for a while. It's dry in there."

Jessie whimpered. "It's garrrbage, M."

"C'mon. Yeah, I know, but it's dry. C'mon. Up."

"You're seeerrrious?"

Michael managed a smile. "Like a heart attack."

He held his sister's arms while she stepped on his thigh and stood up. She peered over the top into the deep gloom of the parking lot.

"I dddon't see anything."

"In! Get in will you!"

Michael raised the top a little further, Jessie reached her arms inside.

"It smells, M"

"Go! In!" Michael hoisted her legs up and she went headfirst into the dumpster.

There was the sound of thrashing around.

"Hush up!"

Michael swung his right leg up and caught the rim with his foot while holding up the top with his left arm. He squirmed under the top and fell all the way in. The top clanged down.

Pitic made it to his car. He threw the cigarette away. The dirty rag he'd found in the church was soaked with blood from his scalp.

Then he heard what sounded like a door. Maybe they were still in there after all, in the dark.

He re-tied the rag around his head supporting his jaw. He didn't feel the pain when he pulled it cinch tight.

Instead, he was savoring the thought of twisting the chunk of blade around Michael Cooper's gut.

If only he hadn't lost his knife.

Michael called the third number.

CHAPTER 52

It was after midnight when she punched in the door code and slipped into OID. She stood perfectly still in the doorway and scanned the whole office until she was confident no one else was in the office, screwing or whatever. She wanted to work without having to answer where she'd been all day. What she'd been doing.

She certainly didn't need to see a repeat of the Adam and Eve show.

Mallory pulled her sweater tighter. The building stayed warm 24/7 but at night there was an unfriendly, empty chill to the place. Echoes carry no heat.

She glanced up. Not even a moon for company. Sky had clouded over and spits of rain dotted the glass four stories above her.

Rain.

On her laptop, she reduced the map program she'd been studying a few days ago and pulled up the weather almanac for the night of May 13th, the night Marston and dear Peter Berlin were abandoned.

Rain. Half inch.

It was raining. Great. What was the timeline for that night? And there was still something eating at her about the location of the car. While she had been staring at the wallpaper in her room, it was the location of the car that had been warping her brain.

What was it?

"Let's start at the beginning." Her words echoed into the darkness four stories above her head.

She sat head in her hands, not thinking. Fuming.

"Fuck it!"

She jumped up, made her way to the side of Jake's desk. She studied the arranged items, then chose the hapless victim, sure it would be something personal, something he will be pissed about, something that will disrupt his life. She picked up the green-shirted, yellow rubber duck mascot.

"So, who cares if you went to the University of Oregon, asshole." She smiled. "Yeah. Asshole."

She took one of the pencils from his holder and shoved it up the duck's ass. She broke off the rest so there was about an inch sticking out. When she replaced it in its place of honor, it sat catawampus, kinda like it had a stick up its ass.

Satisfied, she resumed her seat at her desk.

"Okay. That's done."

She tapped her pencil while she studied the blank notebook in front of her.

All right. Start over. From the beginning.

She shivered and glanced over at the brand new bank of four monitors. For some reason, the alarm guys had mounted them next to Stan's desk. When he was in the office he usually threw a jacket over them not wanting to watch himself. He complained that any movement kept catching his eye and ruining what concentration he could muster.

All four were flat screens, color, arranged in two and two, side by side. Evidently, there was a switch by which you could dedicate all the screens to one view. But, none of them had bothered to learn that. Eyes had glazed over during the instructions on how to operate the entire security system.

All any of them knew or cared about was the passcode for the security door.

Mallory scanned all four screens. One camera was mounted outside the front door and was supposed to clearly show the face of anyone begging entry. Supposedly, one could switch it to show the parking lot, which was silly because no one had yet mounted any lights so all you'd be able to see would be blackness, occasionally illuminated by a passing car.

The second screen showed the view from the camera mounted up on the third-floor balcony, aimed down at the office. It was near useless for security as it showed the office as a small square of light.

The third screen had bothered Stan the most. It was mounted atop their glass wall and could capture images of Stan and Mallory while they worked. Or didn't. Worse, there was a quarter second lag which drove Stan crazy, watching himself with a delay. No one really knew if there were budget dollars earmarked to fund recording equipment. Like any retail store, the idea being their exploits would be instantly reviewable for some period of time. Jake had called bullshit on that grand scheme. The Styrofoam cup he had secured over the fourth camera still held and blocked anyone from seeing what he and his violated Oregon duck were doing.

It was never stated explicitly, still, they believed the security line was piped to SacPD downtown, or soon would be. But no one had yet called them when Jake did his vanishing act, so they assumed, once again, SacPD had left a project underfunded and unfinished.

Mallory saw herself on the third screen staring at what appeared to be Stan's desk. She raised her hand and waved a lonely hand at herself.

"Hey, girl."

As if alerted on some cerebral plane her cell rang.

She checked the incoming number on her screen. It wasn't one she recognized. After midnight and the phone rings, it is never good. No one waits until you're asleep, or should be, to call and ask how your day was or to remind you of your dentist appointment the next day.

Her finger hovered over the phone. Very few had her number, a few bygone boyfriends, remnants of her family, exactly five friends, Stan and Jake. That was it.

It wasn't an 800 number which was good.

What the hell. Bad news never waits. You can try and ignore it, but it always is what it is.

"Yes?"

There was silence, then breathing.

Great, a breather.

"Look…" she started.

"Detective Dimante?"

The voice sounded young and faraway.

"Who is this and how did you get the number?"

On his end, Michael Cooper checked the name associated with the number again. It was scrawled in blurry pencil on the back of Detective Stan Wyld's business card.

Wyld hadn't answered when he'd tried a few minutes ago. This was the last number he had.

He tried again.

"Is this Detective Dimante?"

Mallory silently accepted the promotion to detective though she did not understand who would give her the new title.

"This is Mallory Dimante," she answered, leaving off 'detective'. "Who is this?"

"This is Michael Cooper. Um. Maybe you remember me. You know. From the trailer park…"

"Michael! Michael Cooper! Yes. How are you?" Mallory said, letting the excitement come through. "We were, Detective Steiner and I were just talking about you the other day, wondering how you and your sister are getting along. How are you? I didn't know you had this number."

"I have this number because you gave it to me. That night. Olive Park. The woods. You wrote it down and you told me to call if I ever needed anything and I know you probably say that to a lot of people, trying to be nice, and you don't expect them to call you but I need something. Help, actually. And kinda quickly."

"I'm happy to help you in any way I can. I can hardly hear you. How's your sister? Jessie, isn't it?"

Michael interrupted.

"Really a bad time for a chat, detective, we're in…"

"Michael?"

Mallory heard the ambient change on the phone with clothing rustle and low beseeching in the background. More rustling.

When he came back on, his voice was hushed to a hoarse whisper and the phone was right up against his mouth. Mallory could hear him breathing.

"Detective, I hope you can hear me. Listen, not sure…"

He was interrupted by someone in the background.

"Who's there with you?"

Michael ignored her question or didn't hear it.

"No time. We need you to pick us up or call all the cops you know. Fourth Redeemer Church, out on Highway 50."

"Michael, where's your aunt?"

More rustling, then a conversation in the background.

"Shit, get down! Down!"

"Michael?"

"Detective?"

"I'm here. What is it? What's going on?"

And then Michael Cooper came on for the last time.

"I think he sees us."

CHAPTER 53

She punched the lighted button beside his name repeatedly at the same time she called him on the phone. For a fleeting moment, she wondered who would answer, and then she didn't give a shit. Then she did.

"C'mon."

Mallory held the phone to her ear, listening to the fourth ring while she alternated the phone ringing with the buzzer going.

She hoped his phone was ringing simultaneously with the buzzer. That should be enough.

When he answered he seemed more confused than mad. He'd obviously seen her name on his phone.

"You drunk, Dimante? And stop with the buzzer. It's bothering Jake."

"Is it bothering anybody else?" She struggled to keep the 3 A.M. sarcasm out of her voice but failed.

"What…?" But Jake understood. There was a bit of pause. "What do you want?"

Mallory took her finger off the button.

"Open up."

His voice dropped to a whisper. "Why?"

"Because I said so."

"Is this really important?"

"10 on my Richter scale. Unlock it."

She could hear him begin to ask why again, but didn't.

"Give me a minute." He hung up.

Mallory shivered in the chill. The rain had stopped, but the black wet cold lingered. She checked her car. The windows were closed; the car was running. Inside she knew the heater was flowing full blast, not that it did much. She only hoped Michael and Jessie were getting warm. She'd given them the emergency blanket she'd had in the trunk. Wrapped them both up and turned on the heater. She'd left her coat with Jessie who covered herself up to her eyes.

Mallory hoped she was doing right. She didn't know about child protection laws and custodial rights, but even so, it wasn't kidnapping and she figured she had at least a few hours before they had to make the kids' presence known to whomever.

She was still unclear about the details even though she'd made Michael repeat it twice.

Even after she heard it, she insisted on driving them back to their trailer. Against Michael's wishes, she'd pulled into a quiet Sunshine Vista trailer park. At least she tried to.

She wasn't prepared for the scope of the invasion. Four large white TV production trucks were crowded in front of and in one case, mired partly on the front lawn of Jane Cooper's trailer. Numerous support vehicles lined the street. Inside, she could see people sleeping.

Jane Cooper's trailer was dark.

The only other thing Mallory noticed were the spotlights on tripod stands that formed a semicircle around three chairs positioned in front of the trailer, facing the street.

She had to weave in and out of the parked vehicles and drove to the end of the trailer park, the forgotten end where the two Everheart trailers had been, and turned around. She backtracked her way out.

Just before she pulled out of the trailer park, she turned and checked the backseat.

Michael Cooper was awake and staring at her.

"I'm not lying."

"Not about that," Mallory acknowledged.

"You can take us to a hotel. I have some money."

Mallory didn't want to ask where he'd been able to secure enough to rent a room. But she had about a thousand questions and the only reason she didn't grill him further was that he

eemed to be telling the truth about the Hollywood circus, that
nd the fact that both he and his sister looked about ready to conk
ut.

Mallory said nothing but headed for downtown Sacramento.

"Where are we going?"

"Someplace safe where nobody knows where you are."

"Where?" But the voice was slurred, overcome with warm
elief, and didn't continue.

She smiled in the rearview mirror.

Their two heads were nested together. And they were not
tanding in the rain behind the dumpster they just climbed out of
n the back parking lot of the Fourth Redeemer Church where
he'd found them.

She'd pulled in and as she'd expected in the middle of the
ight, there was no redeeming happening. Just the lone mercury
apor light illuminating the misting rain as a shimmery blue wavy
vash.

No activity. One empty car parked out of the way under the
rees.

She'd circled the parking lot, then steered to the small lot
ehind the church.

Nobody.

"If this is some kind of sick kid joke…" she muttered.

Mallory opened the door and stood.

"Michael!" she shouted. "Michael Cooper!"

Out of the wet shadows from behind a big blue dumpster came
wo figures on the run. When they got closer, Michael held out
is arm to stop his sister. They approached a few steps at a time.
Michael scanned the parking lot.

"Detective Dimante?"

"Yes, now get in."

She opened the back door and Michael clambered in. Jessie ran
traight for Mallory and wrapped both arms around Mallory's
egs. Mallory hugged her back. "Let's go, okay?" Jessie let go
nd let Mallory help her into the back seat.

"Can you turn the heat up," chattered Michael.

It was then she could see how cold and soaked they were.
Mallory had retrieved her emergency blankets from the trunk and
ad bundled them up as best she could. She got in the driver's

seat and put the heater on full. She shifted in her seat and looked at the boy. She would not drive anywhere until Michael explained.

Instead, he leaned forward, intent on scanning the quiet parking lot.

"You need to leave. Now."

"Not until I understand what's going on."

"Do you have a gun?"

"What?"

For the first time, Jessie's small voice was heard.

"Please do as he says, detective. The man might be coming back."

"What man?"

Michael put his hand on Mallory's shoulder.

"Go. Now. Please."

"Fine. But this better be good."

CHAPTER 54

The door opened and a sleepy Jake stood there in his boxers, hair askew and sleep creases on the right side of his face.

The dog moved past him and licked Mallory's hand.

"He doesn't have his kerchief on."

"He wasn't expecting company. None of us were. What do you want?"

"Why don't you put a bathrobe on when you answer the door?"

Jake looked uncertain. "I don't own one. Never have. Never understood the need."

"But, it's raining."

"How silly of me. And to think I was planning on frolicking in the wet at whatever the hell time it is in the morning. What is it, Mallory? Are you really drunk?"

Mallory looked him up and down. "Jesus. C'mon. Follow me."

"Mallory."

"Trust me. Just come on." She turned back. "You won't be sorry."

"Trust you? Hah!" Jake patted the dog. "That trust ship has sailed, hasn't it boy? I'm already sorry."

Mallory went to her car and opened the back doors. "Jake!" she hissed.

"C'mon, then." Jake urged the dog who hung back, having second thoughts about getting his paws wet, but that was superseded by animal curiosity.

Jake danced his way to the car on the wet walkway. When he dipped down and looked into the backseat, he turned to Mallory.

"Are they dead?"

"Help me carry 'em in."

"In where?"

"Your spare room. I assume all the action is elsewhere."

Jake straightened. "How do you know I have a spare room?"

Mallory ignored him and attempted to rouse Michael.

"C'mon, wake up Michael."

Then to Jake, "Keep the blanket around her, would you?"

Jake hesitated a few seconds, then knelt on the seat and scooped up Jessie and the backpack, careful to pull the blanket snug.

"You know, if you wanted kids so badly, you could find a sperm donor, or adopt." He stopped. "You didn't steal them did you?"

"Funny."

Mallory shut off the engine and kicked both doors closed.

She led a dazed Michael up the steps and into the building's entry. Jake followed with what appeared to be a bundle of bedding.

"Upstairs," urged Mallory, guiding Michael. "Fifth floor. Unfortunately, this cheap building has no elevator."

"Cheap!" Jake whispered. "I'll have you know I pay a great deal to live here and be quiet, don't piss off the owner."

Mallory, from the landing above, "Shut up Jake. You own the damn building and the two lots next door. You've had it ever since your parents willed it to you."

Jake said nothing more until they entered his apartment. Mallory immediately turned right and headed down the hallway.

"Where are you going?"

Mallory opened the door to the guest room and turned on the light. "In here," she said to Michael.

She was surprised at what she saw. She'd expected a barebones, unmade bed, small bedside table maybe, single lamp, a few unpacked boxes – your basic bachelor spare room.

But what was presented was warm, homey, and inviting. Plush white carpet, polished oak queen-sized sleigh bed, even a corner-sized matching roll-top desk. The complementary bedside tables were graced with shiny brass lamps with soft pleated shades casting a gentle light. The loveseat sized tufted couch and small ottoman had the same matching fabric as the bedspread. On the opposite wall, there was a small gas fireplace under a painted mantle.

What astonished Mallory, even more, were the special touches – four throw pillows geometrically arranged on the bed, a bed skirt between the mattress and box spring, two sets of towels stacked on the foot of the bed, bath towels on the bottom, hand towels, then washcloths on top, all in a blue and white pattern that somehow seemed to tie into the paintings of sun-washed white and blue houses, backed by an azure sea, of Greece she guessed.

And the whole room had an airy just out of the dryer floral freshness. Not overpowering, only suggestive.

"Jake, this is…"

Jake swept past her, pulled the covers back, and set Jessie down. She stirred but nestled into the blanket further and her breathing evened.

Mallory rummaged through the backpack searching for some pajamas for either of them but ended up pulling out a random assortment of shorts and tops and socks and a stuffed bear. She thought about making the bear Jessie's bed partner, but the girl appeared so sacked out, she replaced the bear and all the clothes back in the backpack.

She turned to Michael, now slumped in the bedroom doorway. "Okay, Michael. Shoes off. Jake will…Detective Steiner will find some dry clothes for you, maybe even some pajamas, if he owns any."

Without a word, Jake went to the guest closet and from the top shelf took down a pair of chocolate brown pajamas. Mallory couldn't help notice they were tied with a matching brown ribbon.

He handed them to Michael.

"Bathroom's in there," Jake said indicating the door next to the closet.

Mallory watched Michael kick off his shoes and make his way to the bathroom door.

"Get some sleep, Michael. We'll talk later."

Michael back. "Where are we?"

"Detective Steiner's. No one knows you're here."

"Okay." He buried his face in the pajamas and smelled. "I need some sleep, I think."

He went into the bathroom and before he shut the door he turned back to Mallory.

"Thank you," he said. It looked like he wanted to say more. Maybe how sorry he was for all the trouble. Maybe sorry for how he balled things up by trying to be a hero. Maybe sorry that everything he'd tried to do to keep him and Jessie safe was sodden failures.

Instead, he shut the door.

As Mallory turned down the lights she heard soft crying coming from the bathroom before the shower turned on and drowned it out.

Jake came out of his bedroom. Still barefoot, he had pulled on jeans and a plaid work shirt.

Mallory was examining kitchen cupboards, high and low.

"Are those two who I think they are?" he asked.

"You know they are. What do you have to drink?"

"You should know. You seemed to have knowledge of just about everything else in here. And besides, before you say anything, I had someone come in to do the guest room and this room and, you know, get the whole place up to par. But, you probably already knew that."

"Don't need to apologize. I wouldn't think less of your masculinity, you know if you had done it. It looks nice, Jake," Mallory said, trying to be sincere. "He, she, they did a good job. And listen, don't tell me you didn't have me checked out before you met me. We all like to know who we're working with. Where they live. What they own. Their history. Who they are, really."

"Beer in the fridge. Hard stuff over the fridge."

"You want anything?"

"Answers."

Mallory sighed. "Me too."

She pulled down a bottle of Tanqueray, rummaged in the fridge for something to mix it with, gave up, broke open some ice, and poured a healthy slug.

Jake had settled onto one of the arms of the 'L' shaped leather couch. Mallory came back into the living room and took the other arm.

She took a sip. Her whole face scrunched while she swallowed. "Whoo." She put her feet up on the table.

"Those are the Cooper kids, right?"

Mallory blew on her drink as if that would impart some mellowness to it.

"Yeah. Michael and Jessie."

"So, what's going on? Why are they here?"

"They need someplace safe."

"Who from?"

"I don't know. The only thing I do know is what he said when he called me and then in the car. It was a little crazy. One thing for sure, they were scared, Jake."

"He called you?"

"Yeah. When he couldn't get a hold of Stan. Or you. Or anybody else he trusted."

Mallory began a disjointed retelling of everything Michael had told her.

Jake was quiet for a few minutes. The dog, with his head on Jake's lap, was twitching in dreams. Jake smoothed his fur.

"Where's their aunt?"

"Right after what happened with Everheart, the aunt went a little crazy it seems. She was committed. Michael said all she could do was wring her hands and say she was sorry about putting them with that sick bitch. Over and over."

"Everheart was a he."

"Of course, but you didn't talk to her…him. I did and it was creepy."

"Who ended up with the kids if the aunt is nutso?"

Mallory smiled for the first time. "That's when good old Michael decided he could fend for himself. They were trying to hook up with some relative in the Southwest, it seems. They needed money to get there. Plus, trying to dodge CPS. Then there was something about a TV show he was needing to avoid. An arrangement the aunt had made with some production company. I drove past their place thinking I could merely take them home.

"He was telling the truth. Whole conglomeration of vehicles scattered all over the trailer park, most in front of the aunt's trailer. Seems he's been a very busy boy."

"So who was after them?"

Mallory shook her head, remembering Jessie running to her and hugging her.

"We'll know in the morning. I've gotta go."

Jake stood. "I don't think so Dimante. It's after four. Give me your keys, I'll go lock your car. You can camp out right here on the couch."

Mallory closed her eyes. "I'll think about it."

When Jake got back he took the glass of perilously tipping gin from her hands, found two blankets, and covered her with them.

He turned out the lights and for a few minutes, watched her sleep.

She was lightly snoring.

Jake dog jumped onto the couch and curled up next to her.

"Traitor."

The dog swallowed twice and settled on his paws.

Jake whispered. "Yeah. You're right. Good dog."

When he opened his bedroom door the only thing he said was, "You have to go."

Outside, Pitic scuttled back into the shadows after noting whose name was on the nameplate. He smiled. It was all under control now.

CHAPTER 55

Officer Mark Pennington had to call for reinforcements. While he waited for additional cavalry, he addressed the problems in the order he deemed most critical.

First, was the problem with the missing children. To deal with the three people from CPS he had to push aside, literally, the producer and various assistants for some L.A. TV production company, threatening them with arrest if they again came within ten feet of him.

He also had to forestall Arthur Dewees, the uptight property manager of Sunshine Vista who, from what Officer Pennington could conclude, had a laundry list of issues. Mr. Dewees was insistent on getting resolved, 'right here and now', the traffic bedlam caused by the TV trucks, the fact that one of the trucks had singlehandedly destroyed one of the pillars at the entrance to Sunshine Vista, and the overwhelming chaos caused by 'those damn kids.'

Pennington turned to the CPS group.

"Officer, I'm Julia French- "

Officer Pennington had had enough. "Not now!"

The wiry woman shut up.

"There's a lot to deal with and I am taking you first. So, if you want my attention, you will listen to what I say and do what I say, got it?"

The group nodded in unison.

"I.D.s please, then."

The three dug out the Children Protective Services identifications. Officer Pennington took a picture of each I.D. badge, while also noting their names in a small notebook.

"All right. In as few as words as possible, tell me what's going on with missing children and CPS. Just one of you."

The man was about to speak, as his mouth was open, but with a sigh, he turned and deferred to the small wiry woman next to him.

"Officer, I'm Julia French. For the last few months, I've been dealing with the two Cooper children involved with the unpleasantness here. You know, Olive Park."

She raised her chin to the far end of the trailer park.

Officer Pennington looked up when she said 'unpleasantness' but let her continue.

"This is where they were living with their aunt who had taken them in, temporarily. There was a growing concern for their welfare as it was becoming apparent that their aunt, Miss Cooper, was increasingly unable to care for the children due to her escalating instability. Mental instability as we found out," she added as if there was a question.

"Arrangements were made to place the children out of state with a relative who was suitable and willing to care for them- "

"Are one of you Mrs. French?"

Everyone turned to Jake who, with his I.D. out, had come up behind Officer Pennington.

Pennington saw Jake's SacPD badge and smiled. "Relief," he said. "They're all yours." He snapped his notebook closed and moved off to extinguish other fires.

"Thanks," replied Jake, not sure he was.

"I'm Janice French. Who are you?"

"Jake Steiner, Detective with OID." Jake held out his hand. Mrs. French went to shake when she realized Jake was instead holding three business cards. Embarrassed, she took one. As did the other two.

"You were dealing with Michael and Jessie Cooper and their aunt, Miss Cooper?" said Jake, focusing on Mrs. French.

"We weren't 'dealing' with them, we were overseeing their care, as I was explaining- "

"I understand. Well, there's been a change of plans."

"A change? I don't- "

"Michael and Jessie Cooper are in protective custody with our department."

The three exchanged worried glances. Jake stole a glance to his car parked half a block away with Michael and Jessie inside.

"Exactly which department is that?" interrupted the man.

"Who are you?" demanded Jake.

"CPS area supervisor, Sy Grant."

"Well, Mr. Grant I'm with the Keeping-Children-Safe department."

"I don't think so. That's our jurisdiction."

"Not in this case."

The standoff went awkward for a few seconds. Sy Grant held up Jake's business card.

"Detective, you'll have to do better than that. I have no idea who you are. In fact, I'm going to need a confirming call from your supervisor. We are responsible for two children and while we get some very bad press for not keeping tabs on our charges and letting some slip through the cracks, I can assure you we take our duties seriously. We were about to issue an Amber Alert."

He looked to the two women who nodded in agreement.

"Commendable," said Jake with a dose of sincerity. "Now, I'll have my people call your people and we'll be all on the same bus. Please excuse me."

Jake moved off toward the street, satisfied that at least part of the tale Michael Cooper had spun at breakfast this morning rang true. He texted Mallory, letting her know somebody should send a memo to CPS regarding the Cooper kids, otherwise CPS was on their backs.

He rejoined Officer Pennington now dealing with a gaggle of Hollywood sunglasses.

Contracts were being thrust in Pennington's face and arms were flying up and down, beseeching and pointing to all the equipment setup, all the vehicles, all the personnel.

Jake thrust his arm into the middle of the group like he was the team coach calling for hands-in before the big game.

"Folks, Miss Cooper is not available and won't be for some time and Michael and Jessie Cooper are in protective custody with Sacramento Police."

Of all the things that could be said to stop a torrent of protests, that was number one. No one spoke as Officer Pennington gave another goodbye smile and stepped away.

Jake was about to follow him when the man with the largest sunglasses spoke for the TV organism.

"Great! We can use it! Police custody. On-going threat. It's all good. We'll work it in."

Nods all around.

He stepped up to Jake. "Are you a cop?"

Jake dug for another card. "Detective Steiner."

A murmur of approval waved over the group. Sunglasses man gave Jake an up and down appraisal. He stepped closer.

"Detective, how would you like to be on TV?"

Without waiting for an answer, the man turned. "Where's Smith with the camera?"

A flurry of activity began. "He doesn't need any makeup, just hit the shine a bit, turn one of those floods around, we can use the general background, where's the sun, do we want him in the chair?"

Jake backed away as an earnest young thing with ragged blond hair approached him with a large powder puff.

"Stop!"

Sunglasses turned, surprised. "Detective, detective." He again invaded Jake's space. "Listen, it won't take but a few minutes for you to catch us up on these exciting turn of events…on camera of course, and…" He raised his eyebrows and nodded. "The money is very, very good," he whispered. Nodded again to make sure Jake really understood.

Jake clapped him hard enough on the shoulder the man's sunglasses went askew.

"Great. I'll have my people call yours. In the meantime, you and your whole crew need to vacate this area. Now."

Sunglasses, unperturbed. "But, when can we see the kids?"

"Can't."

"No, I don't mean right now, I mean like in a day, like tomorrow how 'bout?" He wasn't asking Jake; he was asking the group.

Assents of 'Sounds good' and 'Works for me' spilled forth.

Jake gripped the man by his shoulders and brought his face so close he could see his own reflection in the man's darkened lenses.

"It will not happen. Pack up. Go home."

Jake smiled and added, "Sounds really good and works for me."

He headed for his car and the two Cooper kids. What caught his attention was Officer Pennington squatting before the front door of the Cooper trailer, examining the door lock.

"What's up?"

Pennington stood. "Just noticed lock's busted."

Jake tried to peer in a window but inside was all dark.

He used his elbow to push on the door. It swung all the way open.

"Ho-ly shit," exclaimed Pennington. "Place's been trashed."

Jake took in the damage.

Pillows ripped, chair cushions slit, tables overturned, gaping holes in the sheetrock, carpet turned over and mounded against the far wall, refrigerator contents displayed in a trampled array, every single book torn from the bookshelves.

"I wonder."

Pennington looked at Jake. "What?"

"If they found what they were looking for."

CHAPTER 56

The jingle of Jake's collar let Stan know Mallory and the dog were back from their walk.

For the last ten minutes, he'd been trying to reconcile what he discovered out on Jones Rd with what he just confirmed. He wanted to wait for Jake, to run it by him and see if he could make sense of it, but Mallory would have to do.

"Dimante!"

"What," she yelled.

"Where's Jake? He's supposed to be here with those kids."

"Jake'll be here. He's got 'em. On the phone, he said he was taking a quick detour to the kids' trailer to see about the aunt."

"Well, come here then. I need you to see this."

"In a minute. Need to get myself and the dog cleaned up. When I said I'd watch the dog I didn't realize how much he loves river mud and how he needs to share it. I'm going to take him back to the janitor's tub."

"You said there was no record of a call to either dispatch or 911, right?"

"Jake checked on that. He said there was nothing. Then I went over and talked to both 911 and dispatch. Thought I was crazy. There was nothing Stan."

"Okay. Listen I need you to find what you can on another Pokovich."

But Mallory had already disappeared toward the back bathroom.

Stan ran through the SacPD employee roster again, this time combining it with the map program. The roster was cybersecurity locked. There had been too many instances of citizens using the roster and the cops' home addresses to harass the officer who had stopped them for a DUI or had arrested them for domestic violence or even had given them a parking ticket. There were more than enough public outliers who fancied themselves as payback machines, modern-day Rambos willing to give a cop, or his family, some of his own back.

Two years ago, the public's right to know where the cop lived had been curtailed. Now the only way to access the database was with a security password which only department heads possessed.

Stan watched as the area around the sharp curve on Jones Rd filled in with blue numbered dots, each corresponding to a member of SacPD.

There was only one. It was on the street in the development with the black fluted lamp posts and the nice houses, a short walk from where the BMW was found.

Only one.

He felt Mallory's presence behind him.

"Okay," he began. "So there was no call to dispatch- "

He froze when he saw the image in the security monitor to his left. The view was from the overhead camera and showed the entire area within the glass walls. Visible were the other two desks, the conference table, and himself seated at his desk looking at the monitor to his left.

It wasn't Mallory who stood behind him.

Stan turned in his chair slowly as a gun emerged from the pouch of the hooded sweatshirt and the barrel leveled at him.

Revolver noted Stan. Colt. The limited number of options available to him was sickeningly small.

He glanced to the far side of his desk where his Glock lay, ready to be cleaned.

The hood followed his glance, then shook its head.

He did a quick inventory of the person before him. Smallish, dark jeans, dark blue sweatshirt, hooded, no logo, cheap white tennis shoes.

He'd heard nothing since Mallory left to clean the dog. It was as if whoever this was materialized like a ghost.

Jake was supposed to be walking in with the two Cooper kids any minute. And Jesus Mallory, how long does it take to clean a dog?

Random, spurious thoughts rattled through his head as he stared at the gun.

Then, with professional dread, he noted the latex gloves.

"What do you want? Money?" He kept his voice as level as he could. But he felt his Adam's apple working to keep some saliva. He could feel his pulse pounding in his head.

He'd been shot at three times. But that was in the heat of pursuit or in a domestic abuse case gone wrong. Each time, he'd been prepared, had cover, and hadn't been hit.

He'd never been surprised. He'd never been this vulnerable.

Stan forced himself to breathe. Easy.

Whoever this was had made it in without him hearing. Past the security door. The whisper-quiet security door.

"Well?" He sounded more confident this time.

The hood shadowed the face, but now Stan could see there was a mask, a knitted ski mask pulled up over the mouth, leaving solely the eyes which glinted like two glistening, dead dots.

Mallory let the water run in the tub until it was warm. She glanced at Jake who sat next to her, his leash still on, the end of which was under her foot. The dog tried to ignore what she was doing, subtly pulling on his leash.

"I'm sorry mutt, but I told you not to crawl around in the river." She held her hand under the stream to test the temperature. "You didn't listen, did you? And now look at you."

Jake took no notice. His focus was elsewhere.

"Don't be looking back there. Stan's not gonna help you. Nobody loves a dirty dog."

Jake was standing now, straining. Not so much to get away from the incipient bath but more to get back to Stan.

"Whoa, there. Quit struggling will ya. This won't take- "

Jake jerked free and took off.

"C'mere, you coward."

Stan swallowed. His mind searched for an out but all he could think about was Bea and how mad she will be when he was dead and how silly this was to be shot at his own desk and how he still didn't understand how someone had snuck up behind him.

He played for time. For seconds. "I don't understand."

"Yes you do," came the muffled demand. The hooded head flicked side to side, searching.

"But- "

"Give it now!"

"Look, I'm here alone," Stan tried protesting.

Just then, Jake came padding around the corner dragging his leash and stopped.

Stan tensed, waiting for the attention to swing to the dog, waiting for his chance, but the gun never moved.

Jake just stood there panting, looking for a sign. Deciding, was this good or bad?

"C'mere Jake. C'mon boy," called Stan. Anything to distract. Anything to buy time.

But, Jake didn't move or acknowledge Stan. Instead, he cocked his head to the side. Good or bad?

Then Stan knew.

Then the Gun knew he knew.

Stan tried to keep eye contact. "It's not here."

The gun paused. The hand holding it extended the barrel toward Stan.

"I will shoot," it rasped. "Now give it, unless you want to walk on stumps."

The gun barrel lowered toward Stan's left knee.

A low growl. Jake tensed. His eyes slitted.

Stan knew this moment. Knew it. How many times had he promised Beatrice he'd be careful? And he had. Wore his bulletproof in the field whenever he thought there was a chance of a situation going bad. Watched his driving, balanced the urgency of his job for someone's else's life with his own and that of his family. He'd done his best, but often the wave is bigger than you are and you will be ground under no matter what you do. Sometimes you look up and you know the wave will crash and pin you to the bottom, with you choking for breath.

"Shooting me won't get what you want," he managed.

But, he knew this moment. It happens with a desperate inevitability in intractable slow-motion.

Knew this moment.
He took a breath.
"I know."
Jake lunged.
And the gun fired.

For a second Mallory didn't know what it was. The crushing reverberation exploded through the four-story atrium, its booming rebound knocked her into the wall by the bathroom. She covered her ears against the noise and dropped down out of instinct.

Her mind raced with possibilities. But then she knew. It wasn't like the range, the sharp crack her Glock made. Still, she was sure.

She rose up to call out to Stan. Wanted to demand what the hell he was doing.

Then she sprinted. She stopped short when she saw it through the glass.

A dark figure with a gun. She almost laughed. She could see a wisp of smoke coming out of the barrel, like a cartoon.

And she could see Stan. He was standing, his hands clenched at his side. He wasn't shot. Jesus, he wasn't shot. But he wasn't looking at the gun or the person who held the gun. He was looking to his left, down at the floor.

And then she remembered the dog.

Oh, Christ. Jake.

Without taking her eyes off the scene which seemed frozen in time, she keyed the emergency icon on her phone.

As soon as she heard the 911 operator answer she whispered carefully and slowly, "Mallory Dimante, Sacramento PD I.D. number 55723, officer down, another held hostage. We are in the OID building, 5th, and Commercial Blvd. Unknown is dressed in dark black jeans and hooded sweatshirt. He's has a gun on detective Wyld. Door code for our security door is…"

She stopped. She knew the code yesterday. What was it?

And then it didn't matter because she remembered her coat and what was in it.

And then nothing mattered because she saw the gun raise up and point at Stan.

With a concussive boom, the glass walls detonated in a shattering rain.

The hammer blow from the bullet ripping into his shoulder rocked Stan sideways. He tried to grab for the desk but nothing seemed to work. In agonizing slow motion, his good arm flailing for support, he now fell backwards, his head cracking off the desk edge. Helpless, on his back, he stared, not believing or understanding.

Except, the last thing he heard was one more shot.

When it came, it hit the hooded figure full in the back and exited out the center of the chest, taking with it a healthy chunk of the sternum. As if deflated, the figure sank to its knees, then fell sideways in a final, gruesome acknowledgment of one already dead.

Mallory held her shooter's pose until she started crying. The Glock shook in her hands and she realized she was gulping in breaths between sobs.

"Jesus."

She tried to think. Tried to force her brain to work. Make it decide what she should do next.

Jake was shot.

Stan was down.

The person pointing the gun was down.

Or were they?

"Shit!"

She lowered her weapon but kept it tight in a two-handed grip as she advanced in a halting shuffle.

She wiped her face with the back of one hand then replaced it on the gun.

Three panes of glass from the office walls were gone. She stepped on small square chunks of glass as she advanced. She tried kicking them out of her way, but they were inches deep.

She couldn't see anyone over the conference table.

"Stan?" She called out but her voice sounded high and thin.

"Stan! You all right?"

Nothing. Only the distant echo of gunshots bouncing around the upper stories of the building and in her head and the acrid gunpowder smell were proof that some bad shit had happened.

But she couldn't really hear anything. Her ears were shocked into deafness. She scraped her shoes along in the glass.

Nothing.

She used a hand to run over one ear, massaging it back to usefulness.

She worked her way around toward the entrance to the glass office.

She knew she needed to call for help. For paramedics. For Cops. Call the shittin' cops again. Call an ambulance for chrissakes.

But, still, she inched her way through the door.

"Oh, God."

To her right was Jake, thrown up against a glass wall. Heaving breaths, slowing now, making desperate ripples in the blood that pooled from under his fur.

Stan was on his back, his arm thrown over his face. His shoulder was bleeding and the blood was mixing with Speyburn dripping from his desk, pooling in a rich crimson. He was breathing and the breaths were regular.

She moved a few steps further around the conference table. The gun held out at the ready.

But there was no need.

The hooded figure was face up. The front of the black sweatshirt was blacker still in a growing circumference surrounding a small exit hole, right about where the heart used to be.

There was nothing more going on there.

Mallory moved next to Stan. She put the gun on the floor next to her. Carefully, she removed his arm from his face. He didn't look like he needed CPR, which was good, because now she couldn't remember much of what she was supposed to do, even though she had taken the renewal course last month.

Then she noticed the blood dripping from the gash on the side of his head.

"Shit, Stan."

She removed her cell from her pocket. What? It was all bloody. She looked at her hands. Dripping with blood. She looked around her. Blood from Jake had made its way over to her. She didn't realize a dog had so much blood. Her hand marks were on the floor in his blood.

On the phone, 911 still showed on the screen.

Through the ringing in her ears, she could just make out the subdued wail of approaching sirens. Dully, she remembered summoning the ambulance and backup and help.

She looked down at Stan. She stroked his arm.

She stripped off her sweater and put it under his head. Then realized she shouldn't have moved him.

"I'm sorry, Stan. But, help is coming, okay?"

She kept stroking his arm until she heard the banging on the brand new security door, which she noted in her fuzziness, did a gold-standard job of keeping out the people she needed in while letting in scum with guns and very bad intentions.

In the few seconds before the world descended, Mallory pushed herself up onto her knees and crawled her way over to the other figure on the floor. Being careful to avoid touching anything but the ski mask that covered the face, she carefully peeled it up and pushed it back into the hood.

And recognition struck.

She was still staring at the face when rough arms pulled her away.

CHAPTER 57

Pitic watched from his car the crowd of workers from the nearby warehouses who gathered to watch the horde of cops and technicians come and go from the OID office. He had plenty of time to change the bandages on the side of his head twice because it was hours later when the coroner finally arrived.

Then it took one minute to confirm the worst. A black body bag.

And no one arrested.

Which meant Pitic knew who was in the body bag.

With a trembling hand, he dialed.

"Yes?"

Pitic took a deep breath.

"Something went wrong."

PART FOUR

CHAPTER 58

Jake found Danni Harness sitting on one of the stone stanchions that would eventually ring the new parking lot, but now was one of many scattered around the front path to OID. She sat on one and rested her back on another taller one. She was smoking and trying to blow rings when Jake came out.

"Jesus, you guys don't give up do you?" she said. Her sarcasm was tinged with obvious fatigue.

"How long have you been here Danni?"

"I don't know. Cop is down Jake. No time to rest."

Jake could see her swagger was propped up by little or no energy. Her legs dangled. Her shoes rested on the ground, toe over toe.

"Danni..."

"Yeah, well, the crew's pretty much wrapped up. I just...I just wanted to make sure we didn't miss anything for Stan's sake."

"Fine. Then, before you fall asleep, before I fall down, just tell me how she got in, okay? How did she get in without anyone seeing her, hearing her? How did she get the drop of one of our best cops?"

He asked but in his heart, he thought he knew. He at once did and didn't want an answer. Really didn't want it.

Danni flicked her ash toward the front door and the newly-installed code box.

"Easy. She entered the code. Or somebody let her in."

"Nobody let her in."

"Then she entered the door code and waltzed in and shot Stan and then your little Melanie, Mallory, plugged her good. But she entered the door code, Jake. She didn't break in and if she wasn't let in, then she knew the code and helped herself."

Jake swallowed. "You're sure? How sure are you?"

"If I weren't resting my dogs and if I thought it would make you understand, I'd get up and show you how I know. But I'm not, getting up that is. I will tell you. Go take a look at the code box."

Jake went to the obscure metal box. From a good distance away it could be mistaken for another historical brass plaque. Only this one was small, about six inches by three, and there was no lettering on it. Could have been the cover to a letter slot. Up close it appeared to be a standard garage door keypad with the brass weather cover plate held up and out of the way by a rubber band.

"Don't touch it, now," sighed Danni.

"Wasn't going to," answered Jake as he examined the box. The faceplate with the lighted buttons was covered in fingerprint dust, as were all the buttons on the keypad.

"You know the code obviously."

"6-9-6-9, Enter."

"Which you'll need to change soon as I'm done."

Jake had not a clue how to reprogram the door code and would leave that to somebody else.

"So, knowing the code numbers, what do you see?"

"That you've made a mess of the code box with your print powder."

Danni ignored him.

"Look at the numbers 6 and 9. What do you see?"

It was obvious. "Prints. Smudges."

"Which you would expect. Now, what about 1-2-3-4-5-7-8?"

"Shit."

"Yeah. Shit. You see nothing on those numbers. That means whoever accessed your keypad and entered that door, knew the code. They didn't try and screw around with other numbers. They knew it. Punched it up. Opened the door."

Danni took a long drag and stubbed out her cigarette on the side of the stanchion.

"That's how she got in. Now, you better start coming up with an explanation of how she got the code 'cause I'm sure somebody's gonna be all over your ass about it soon."

She slid forward, slipped on her shoes, and stood up and stretched.

"Helluva security system," she said. "You'd a been better off with a guard dog." She looked quickly at Jake.

"Shit, I'm sorry Jake. About the dog. Really. I'm just tired. That wasn't a good thing to say. I'm really sorry."

Jake pretended to study the keypad some more.

"Yeah. Well..." He cleared his throat. "It didn't help either that they replaced the old metal door with a nice silent open-silent close one, where you can't hear anyone come in."

He placed his hand on the door.

"Even a dog can't hear it."

Danni touched him on the arm. "Maybe. Maybe not. There is another explanation of how she got in."

Jake turned. "What's that? Osmosis? Ectoplasmic reconstitution?"

"I'm serious, Jake."

"Well tell me then how she got in."

Danni studied Jake.

"Maybe she was already in."

CHAPTER 59

"Excuse me, detective."

Jake stepped aside at the entrance to the glass office as the cleaners began mopping up the more extensive blood pool in the middle of the office.

Lightheaded, he steadied himself against the glass wall and tried to make sense of what the hell had happened.

Hours ago, he'd seen Forensics wade through the sea of exploded tempered glass, mixed with papers and mouse pads and Scotch tape and staplers and calendars and blood and whiskey. When they had finished photographing, measuring, and removing what evidence they felt was necessary, Danni had two of her crew carry out the body of Ilsa Pokovich.

Now, the mop-up had begun.

He didn't believe bad things roll in on a wave of threes. He didn't want to believe it, yet the evidence was all around him.

Mallory had been attacked and scarred and nearly burned to death in the investigation of the Olive Park murders. And now Stan, working this benign missing person case, shot.

And then there was his Jake.

He tried not to think about Jake. The bloodstain where the dog had been hit was still there. He traced the size of the stain, where it had traveled.

Jake knelt down, touched a fingertip to the nearly dried blood. "For what?"

He straightened, moved to his desk, and touched his finger to Jake's picture, leaving a crimson promise.

He slumped into his seat and herded some of the glass chunks off his desktop.

Maybe in a few weeks or months a shiny shard, a piece of this night, would ...just appear on his desk as if it had been falling in slow motion all this time.

Maybe, in one of its silvered facets would be the answer to what had happened. What Mallory had done.

Mallory!

What if she hadn't been here? What if she hadn't recognized the situation for what it was? What if she hadn't acted?

"What?" Jake sat up.

"Christ Steiner. I said this is a goddamn bloody mess you guys have gotten us into."

Detective Rodriguez advanced on Jake, kicking at the glass, scattering jagged sparklers further into obscure corners.

Captain Ash Carruthers stood with his back against one of the glass panels still in place. His hand was cupped in front of his mouth. He appeared as white as a sheet as he surveyed the damage.

Jake, idly checked his watch. It was now after eight. He'd been awake since yesterday morning. How long ago was it he'd left Bea sitting bedside, holding Stan's hand. How long ago had he listened to the doc tell him it wasn't the shot through the shoulder that was Stan's problem, it was the bang on his head.

Hours and hours ago.

Rodriguez raged on. "Look, Steiner, you sure that psycho assistant of yours didn't shoot Wyld. He still hasn't regained consciousness-"

"He has and she didn't shoot him," stated Jake, lifting his head.

"All right. Okay. So where did she get a Glock for chrissakes and why did she bring it here? And how did this other person, this Plokovitch woman- "

"Pokovich."

"Whatever she was, who you say was sick with cancer and a felon! How the hell did a felon get access through your brand new security system...?

"Not my system."

"...and then was able to shoot one of our best detectives?"

Jake stopped listening and closed his eyes. He replayed his brief conversation with Mallory last night after she was released.

Rodriguez and Carruthers had acquiesced and agreed to wait and take her full, formal statement later.

Hyper with adrenaline but unsteady on her feet, paramedics had made the decision to take her to the hospital with Stan. The second ambulance, the extra one, had taken the dog at Mallory's determined insistence.

When Jake finally saw her in the ER hallway, Mallory had reminded him of a refugee, sunken cheeks, hollow eyes. Only her voice had remained strong with a scared resolve.

She appeared not to recognize him for a moment, but when she did, tears welled up and she flung her arms around his neck.

He could tell she was holding back sobs that she needed to let go.

She pulled away.

"Sorry," she mumbled. "Oh, Jake." She stood, head down, arms drooping by her side.

He took her chin and raised it.

"It's okay. It is." He tried to engender confidence he didn't believe was truly warranted. But, she'd saved Stan, whether she shot him or not.

She shook her head. He wasn't understanding.

"It's a mess. All of it."

He knew what she meant. How did they miss what was now so obvious? How did he miss what was so obvious? How had it gotten out of control?

"I'm sorry," he said. "I'm just…"

"Jake."

"Listen, go home now," he said, recovering. "You're fine. Stan'll be fine."

At the mention of Stan's name, more tears spilled down her cheeks.

"I didn't shoot him, Jake. I didn't."

Jake started to say something, changed his mind.

She took a few steps, then turned back to him. "Jake? Can you come by?"

Jake saw her face and the mask of false bravado that hid a childlike vulnerability.

He studied her, gauging her need and his strength.

He nodded.

"Yeah. Okay. I'll be there."
She mouthed a 'Thank You' and left.

"Hello, Steiner. You listening Steiner?"

It took all of Jake's effort to get himself standing. At the sight of Rodriguez's face, he knew he'd had enough.

Ever since Carruthers had dumped this piece of shit into their lap, nothing had been right.

Stan had said it days ago.

The machine was off. Somebody had tossed a cog into the works. The case was tilted. Skewed. They'd known it. But, then they hadn't known anything.

"I'm going home," Jake said with a finality that left no room for argument.

Still, Rodriguez piped up, "Hell no. You're staying…"

"Rodriguez!" barked the Captain, pushing himself off the wall. "Leave it for chrissakes. Just leave it. Let the man go."

Carruthers turned to Jake. "You and Rodriguez work this tomorrow. Take whatever, whoever, you need. Okay?"

Jake looked into Carruthers' eyes, but all he could see was evasiveness.

Jake picked up his leather jacket and Jake's leash and went to call for his dog.

Then he remembered.

CHAPTER 60

Jake made it to the Corvette, opened the door, got in but didn't start it.

He sat and brushed his hand through Jake's empty vehicle restraint harness.

A lot of things seemed silly right now. Unimportant. And empty.

He really needed a few minutes. He'd promised Mallory, but, he needed a few minutes.

Jake dug his fingernails into the leather harness until his fingers turned white and the tightness in his chest passed. He opened his mouth and shallowed his breath.

What the hell.

What shocked him awake was he didn't remember pulling out of the lot. It wasn't until he found himself halfway down Jefferson Boulevard that he realized he was even driving.

He made it to Mallory's in fifteen minutes. He'd been there once before but all these newer condo places looked the same. He crisscrossed the parking lot twice until he was sure he knew where he was.

Or, he was simply delaying, killing time.

After he knocked he felt the presence behind the door, looking through the peephole.

"Hello? I'm here."

Two locks clicked and the door opened.

Jake took a few tentative steps inside. All of the shades were pulled and he didn't see her right away, just a gauzy silhouette by the sliding glass door that led to the patio.

"Hey," he said softly.

She didn't turn around, instead gave a half-hearted wave.

"Thanks for coming over. I just needed someone, you know, to talk about it."

"No, it's fine." He stood uncomfortably.

She turned.

"I just...wanted somebody on my side."

He understood. "Yeah. I know. Anyway, we are. All three of us."

"What?"

"Me, Stan, and Jake."

Mallory looked away. "Oh God, Jake. Poor Jake. That was it," she rushed on. "When I heard her shoot Jake. I heard it and I called dispatch or 911, maybe both, I don't know. Then I saw her raise her gun and I knew I had my gun and she was aiming at Stan and I don't know, I fired. I tried to remember everything you're supposed to remember when you shoot at somebody, but...I just shot at her."

Jake said nothing. He tried to picture the scene, but couldn't.

She looked up, blinked. "Jake?"

"It's okay. Really. You saved Stan's life. Focus on that. Don't let anything about the shit that's going to come down make you forget that. It's not that you shot somebody. It's that you saved somebody. Your partner."

Mallory began to cry again, but feeling embarrassed, started for the kitchen.

She wiped her eyes with the back of her hand.

"I'm going to make some soup."

"Soup?"

She didn't address him but dragged out a pan and a can of soup.

"I need to start over, you know. My mother gave me soup when I was sick. She always said the reason you gave someone soup was that it was a basic food and you needed to start with basic and build from there. You needed to let your body heal and you do that by starting back at the beginning."

"Soup," Jake said.

"Yeah, soup. I'm making mushroom. My favorite."

"Mallory..."

When she didn't turn right away, he repeated it.

"Mallory. You did the best anybody could do."

She stopped turning the can opener.

"Did I?"

"Yes."

He moved to her, turned her around, and wrapped her in his arms. She rested her head on his shoulder and leaned against him. They stayed that way, savoring the closeness, listening to the stillness.

He wanted to tell her nothing was her fault, that he was the one to blame. More than anyone knew.

"You know," he said quietly. "You're going to be embarrassed by all this hugging tomorrow."

"Probably." She hiccupped into his shoulder. "I hope so." She held on.

But Jake released her and held her away from him so he could look at her.

"I know. I'm not a kid anymore, Jake."

"No. You're not."

They stared into each other's eyes. The silence was awkward and both knew this was a point of no return.

Jake broke it. He looked away. "I need to rest and then go back and see to Bea. And Stan."

Mallory sighed, understanding. "You do, I know. I should go too, sit with Bea but I can't. I just…"

Jake looked at his hands. "They said with that bump he got, they'll keep him a few days. When he comes around, short term memory might take a while to recharge."

Mallory nodded. It made little sense, but there was no way she wanted to see Stan and Beatrice right now. When she'd cradled his head and seen where he'd hit it and seen the blood and the dog's blood, she'd thought everyone was dead. She thought she was the only one left.

"I have to eat soup." She turned and finished opening the can.

"Before I go, tell me again what happened. Before you go through it all with Rodriguez and Carruthers, tell me. All of it. The good and the bad this time."

Mallory stopped fiddling with the saucepan.

"Tell me. Partner to partner."

"Partner to partner," she whispered. "You mean the unvarnished truth. No cover my ass stuff. That type of partner to partner?"

"Something like that, yeah."

She avoided looking at him, looking into his eyes, avoided asking him about coming to terms with his own unvarnished truth. Instead, she dumped the soup contents into the saucepan. Merely watching the soup heat up gave her some energy.

Jake found a stool at the kitchen counter. "First, tell me where you got the gun."

"Oh. The gun." She shrugged. "It was my Dad's. Left it to me, along with the small life insurance policy that covered his funeral almost to the penny. He was an accountant after all."

Jake would pursue it further but he was too tired and it didn't matter except Carruthers and whoever else would investigate this as an officer-related shooting and would lean hard on her.

"Okay, lay it out. Where were you?"

"In the back. I had Jake with me. We'd come in from a walk. When we came in, Stan asked me to come look at something he'd found. I had to go to the bathroom first and I wanted to scrub Jake down 'cause he'd been in the mud and all. So we went to the back. I started the water and he took off running. I thought he didn't want to be washed, but I think he heard someone...her." She took a deep breath, remembering the dog on the office floor. She stirred the soup and wiped her eyes again. It was nearly a minute before she continued.

She looked over the counter at Jake. "And that's when I heard it. The shot. It was huge and echoed. I thought. I don't know what I thought. Something had hit the building, I don't know. Then I thought Stan was screwing around with his gun. So loud, God. But it wasn't anything hitting the building. And it wasn't Stan. It was when she shot Jake."

"I was about to yell to Stan when I saw her. She had her back to me. Stan was standing, I think. His body was facing her, but he was looking down at the floor. At Jake, I think."

"Then what?"

Mallory looked down at the stove, concentrating.

"I...I could see Stan and I knew he wasn't shot. And he didn't have a gun in his hand. But she did. I didn't know about Jake then. I believed somebody had shot a weapon, but I saw two people standing and neither was hurt."

"Then you drew your gun? Where was it?"

"In my coat. But, no. Not yet. I had my cell in my pocket I think and I called 911 first. Yeah, I did. But, I couldn't remember the door code. It didn't matter because I saw that bitch with her gun on Stan. I couldn't hear them but I could tell by body language that something was going to happen."

"You couldn't hear them?"

"No."

"So you couldn't hear if she was threatening Stan or what?"

"No."

"But you shot her anyway."

Mallory slammed down the spoon into the soup some of which slopped out onto the stove.

"Goddammit, Jake! She was going to shoot him."

"You're sure?"

"Fuck you! You had to be there. I knew she was going to. We don't need to have this discussion now do we?"

Jake held up his hands. "I'm asking the questions you're going to be asked tomorrow." He shrugged. "Or today. This is nothing compared to Rodriguez."

Camaraderie had vanished. "Is this how it is now, partner to partner?"

Jake shrugged but didn't let up.

"So, you called 911. You say you saw she was about to shoot. Then you pulled your weapon?"

"This is sounding like a goddamn interrogation Jake." Then she added with all the sarcasm she could muster, "Partner."

Jake's mouth went to a tight line. "Stan and I have been together for more than 15 years. He's been shot. So, yeah, I guess this is an interrogation. Because I'd like to find out what exactly happened to him. Because I wasn't there and you were. And you fired two shots. And one shot is still unaccounted for."

Mallory felt her body tightening up. Both her fists balled. Her voice was stretched and raw.

"I did not shoot Stan, Jake. I didn't. I know it."

"Like you knew she was going to shoot? That kind of know it?"

"Listen, asshole. I was shooting through glass. Half inch glass. At an angle. I didn't know what that would do. I didn't want the shot to go haywire, so when I fired I first aimed for the corner of the glass to bust it out, okay? I didn't aim for Stan or whatshername. I aimed for the glass to break it. I didn't shoot Stan. I broke the glass on my first shot."

Jake's face gave away nothing. "Why didn't you say that to begin with?"

"You didn't give me a chance. If you'd just listen instead of accusing me. Just listen, okay?"

"Okay. You busted the glass."

Mallory shrugged. "Second shot hit home." She held up two fingers. "Shot one, glass. Shot two, perp. Got it?"

When he didn't answer she reached out and switched off the stove.

"Sounds convincing," he said at last.

"It's the truth."

"And it sounds convincing. You'll do fine with Rodriguez. And that was smart thinking about the glass. I've seen rounds bounce off a car windshield and when they do punch through, they can go…haywire."

He stood. "Two more things before I go. First, tell me exactly what Stan said."

"You mean when I came in?"

"Yeah. Exactly."

Mallory carefully ladled soup into a bowl while she played everything back.

"It wasn't much. Just, 'Hey, come here. You gotta see this.' Or, 'You won't believe this.' Something like that."

"You don't know what it was?"

"No clue."

"Okay. Last. How did she get in?"

Mallory turned away.

"Jake…" The image of Jake with Samantha Barnes in the moonlight pressed up against the glass would never go away. Shit, it was all jumbled. Samantha Barnes, the one witness they had who Jake had invited into OID. Samantha Barnes, the one witness who identified the woman at Marston's car as Pokovich.

Now that Pokovich woman had skulked into OID and shot Stan and precious Jake.

She wondered if she would be asked about Jake and Samantha Barnes.

And she wondered how much she would tell. Or, if it mattered at all.

They were both quiet.

Finally, "I don't know how she got in," Mallory replied. "The door was shut when I came back in. I made sure."

Jake rubbed his eyes and stood. "Okay. I'll go now."

"But what are we going to do Jake? About the case?"

"I don't want to think about it or talk about it right now. Let me help Stan and Bea. Today, later today, or tomorrow, Rodriguez, you, and I will tackle it. Try to figure out how this got so screwed up. How we... how I missed so much. Tomorrow."

"I'm not supposed to come back to work until this is all sorted out. Carruthers' orders."

"Yeah, well, forget Carruthers. We're short-handed and what with the time to try and bring Rodriguez up to speed with all we know, we'd be further behind. So, yeah, I know you're not supposed to be around but forget that. You come in when you're ready. Maybe on the quiet."

Jake paused. "We need you. I need you."

Mallory let that comment hang in the air.

"Soups done," she whispered.

"How do you know?" Jake searched the ceiling and gave a rueful smile. "The smoke detector hasn't gone off."

She grabbed a ladle and dribbled some into a coffee travel cup. She covered it and walked it to him.

"Here. Sip this on the way home."

"Mushroom soup?" He looked at it as if it was the last thing he wanted to put in his mouth.

"It's my recipe. You'll like it."

"You opened a can."

"Yeah. So?"

Jake sniffed the top.

"Tomorrow. 9 A.M."

And then he was gone.

CHAPTER 61

"What are you doing?" Jessie entered the kitchen and sidled up to her brother, her eyes half-glazed with sleep.

"It's weird."

"What?"

"I've called everybody. Nobody answers. So, I'm fixing some breakfast. I'm hungry."

"Nobody answers? And where's the dog?"

"Like aliens have taken them."

Jessie shuffled to the window, pulled the curtains aside, and scanned the street.

"Normal people are still here. I see cars and there's a garbage truck."

"I'm making eggs and toast."

"M, maybe their batteries died in their cell phones."

Jessie plopped down on the sofa and played with the remote. "Whatever. We can go home now, can't we?"

Michael stirred the eggs and put the toast down.

"Can't we?" Jessie continued. "I want to go back with Aunt Jane."

"Jess, she's crazy. Why would you want to go back?"

"I just do. I don't want to keep going from place to place. It's like we're lost kinda. So can we? Go home?"

"Maybe. Hey help me find some jelly or peanut butter or something, will ya."

"You're the cook. You're responsible."

"Tired of being responsible," muttered Michael with his head fully engulfed in Jake's meagerly supplied refrigerator. There was mustard and ketchup, some beer, a few lamb chops, Michael knew because they were labeled, an old cucumber and brown lettuce in the produce bin, and a few apples.

He did find butter for the toast.

Just then the TV came on.

"What're you doing?"

"It looked like a cool TV. I want to see what's on."

What was on was a replay of hockey. Sacramento Kings, from their glory days, claimed the announcer.

"I hate hockey," said Jessie. "You can never see the pucky thing."

"When have you ever watched hockey?"

"I just don't like it."

Jessie played the remote like a concert pianist. Starting at the low channels, she paused only long enough to get the gist, not even allowing the audio to catch up.

When she stopped surfing, she stopped for a reason.

"Michael. Michael, look at this."

"I'm serving eggs and toast. It's dished, come and get it."

"Isn't that our detective? From last night? Isn't that him?"

Michael set the two plates down on the coffee table and studied the screen. It was a frozen shot of Jake talking to a black-haired woman in front of a stone building.

The announcer droned on, but all Jessie and Michael could focus on was the banner across the bottom of the screen.

'1 dead in Sacramento Police Shooting'.

And the picture of Detective Jake Steiner.

"Michael? Isn't that him? And now someone's dead?"

"Shh. Turn it up."

"Don't bother," came the authoritative voice from behind them.

Michael and Jessie jumped. It was as if they were seeing a ghost.

"We thought you were dead," whispered Jessie. "The TV said."

Jake Steiner ran a hand through his hair.

"Well, I'm not. As you can see."

He moved to the kitchen and saw Michael's handiwork.

"I'm sorry I...we forgot about you guys. You got something to eat?"

Neither Jess nor Michael moved but watched Jake navigate his way around the kitchen. He opened the refrigerator, grabbed an Anchor Steam, twisted the cap, and took a long swallow.

When he finished half, he looked at them.

"Breakfast. Okay. I've had mine. And it looks like you've made your own, so eat up."

Neither child made a move to eat the food.

"What happened?" asked Michael. "It said there was a shooting. It said one died."

Jake fished two forks out of the drawer and set them next to the plates. He settled on the other wing of the couch.

"You eat. I'm fine but Dimante would kill me for sure if you weren't fed."

"Is this because of us?" Michael indicated the TV which droned on, endlessly repeating what little information there was. "Because of us being here?"

Jake looked away and didn't deny it. "There was a shooting. Someone broke into our police offices and threatened one of the detectives. Mallory…Miss Dimante shot the intruder."

"Dead?"

"Very."

"So, it was a bad person who died, not a policeman? Who was he?"

Both Michael and Jessie awaited the answer.

"Wasn't. Wasn't a 'he'. It was a woman. A very bad one. She's dead now."

Jake didn't want to talk about it anymore. Didn't want to have to explain about Stan, about the trouble Mallory was in, about the wreckage of the OID offices, about how he was accountable.

He stood and finished his beer.

"I'm sorry you guys, but I have to get some sleep. Can you amuse yourselves? Watch TV, movies, something like that while I get some rest."

"Sure," said Michael. "No problem."

When Jake was almost at his bedroom door he heard Jessie's small voice.

"Where's the dog? Where's Jake, the dog?"

Jake stopped, held himself against the jamb, but didn't turn.

"Don't open the front door for anyone, hear me."

And then he closed the bedroom door.

PART FIVE

CHAPTER 62

"No offense, but you've looked better," chided Susan Spruance as she slipped into her seat across from Mallory.

"It's the lighting in here." Mallory gave a doleful smile as she licked the shade of the small table lamp then pulled it over and held it under her chin. "See. Everything's the same."

The waiter arrived, reached over, and replaced the lamp back into its proper position.

He smiled as if this was a regular occurrence at Rhinos.

"You want to eat?" asked Susan.

"Just water."

Susan sat back. "Whoa. Water?" Turning to the waiter, "Two gin martinis and a water."

"Sue, I don't know…"

"It's medicinal."

The waiter hovered.

Susan nodded to him. "She's good. Two martinis and a water."

"Thanks," offered Mallory. "I'm decisioned out."

"How was your tete-a-tete with Internal Affairs?"

"Done with for now. I think they don't know how to handle a non-cop."

"No waterboarding? Hot coals? Harsh lights?"

"Nah. After ballistics determined the bullet that hit Stan was not from me, pressure was off. I had the feeling they were confused or maybe impressed with what I did. Anyway, they were almost smiling at the end. I think those were smiles."

"Hard to tell with Internal Affairs."

"Mostly, they grilled me on who she was and if I knew why she attacked Stan."

"This is the woman that the witness said she saw at Marston's car, right?"

"The same."

"So, she broke into OID and was going to shoot Stan. Well, how the hell did she get in?"

Mallory let the question hang.

"Well?" pushed Susan.

Mallory bit back the answer. Last night she had decided to keep what she knew about Jake and Samantha Barnes to herself because it probably meant nothing. There was no connection to Pokovich. Now, sitting with her best friend, she wasn't sure. She wasn't sure about a great deal lately.

Mallory shook her head. "No idea."

Susan studied Mallory, trying to weigh the truthfulness of the answer. "Huh. Okay. Well, how is the old Mr. Wyld?"

"Mending," replied Mallory, brightening, happy for the change of subject. "I took him some scotch, even though he's not supposed to have any. We toasted. He only took a sip and gave me back the bottle. Said I'd be needing it more in the days to come."

Susan settled back and watched as the waiter placed the two martinis in front of her and a water before Mallory.

"Very funny Jeeves. Begone."

The waiter smiled and retreated. Sue redistributed the drinks.

"Bottom's up," she quipped. "Always my favorite position."

She raised her glass and waited for Mallory to do the same. They clinked and sipped.

"Okay, so what's this I hear about Carruthers horning in on your investigation?"

"Hah! Bastard got us started on this. He should take it over. Besides with Stan recovering, it would only be Jake and me."

"That would be okay, you know," Susan smiled, raising eyebrows.

"Yeah, right."

"But what the hell? This is the Captain we're talking about. Why would he personally get into this? Why not have shithead Samuels or Rodriguez come to the rescue?"

"I don't know. Rodriguez was first on then off the case. Carruthers pulled him off. Says he, Captain Ash Carruthers, can handle it with us."

"Big woop."

"And, he started off by having a big fight with CPS 'cause he wants to interview the Cooper kids. God knows why. Far as we know they have nothing to do with all this."

"Where are they?"

"CPS gorillas swooped in and took the kids to a temporary foster home. Won't tell anybody where. Even Carruthers. I think they could've stayed at Jake's, but he's got enough right now."

Susan nodded. "Yeah. He does."

Both of them sipped in silence, lost in questions.

"And now what about that private investigator you said had evidence that there was some connection between, you know, Olive Park and Marston?"

"God. Poor Peter Berlin. Really nice guy," sighed Mallory. "Yeah, well Jake found something, and…shit, I'd forgotten about that. We'd forgotten with everything else happening."

"What was it?"

"Seems, Berlin was casing the Marston mansion. Why? We don't know. Jake found some notes in Berlin's office." Mallory gently teased her ice cubes. "And he tried to contact me before he disappeared."

"Berlin? Why you?"

Mallory shrugged. "Yeah, why me? He didn't know what I was working on. The only connection we had was through my brother."

Both women fell silent. Mallory raised her drink, held it up to the lamp, and studied the designs the gin made.

"What are you looking for?"

"Solutions. You know, I'm studying the solution for a solution."

"Good luck. I'll tell you the solution you need. You need to know why that bitch pulled a gun on Stan. 'Course the dead don't talk, not the way you shoot 'em anyway. Still…"

Mallory's eyes widened.

"What?" asked Susan, alerted.

Mallory deliberately set her drink down.

"Mal? What?"

Mallory went visibly pale. She swallowed. She reached out her hand to Susan.

"Oh my God."

"What?"

"We do know."

"Know what?"

"Why she did it. Oh…fuck. We gotta go."

Mallory gathered her coat.

"Mallory?"

Mallory grabbed Susan's arms.

"We have it! The security system! It's all on the security system!"

CHAPTER 63

"Close the door please," came a voice from the gloom.

Susan pushed Mallory further into the room and pulled the heavy door closed. The latch snapped with what sounded and felt like a permanent clunk.

The lights from the monitors cast a glow over a control panel and two operators who sat at the controls. To Mallory, it looked like a TV master control room.

"This is new," she whispered to Susan.

"You don't have to whisper. We made it past security. It's okay to speak."

"We would've made it past security anyway. It's after eight, the night guys are on and no one's issued any bulletins about me not being allowed in the building."

"At least not yet."

Mallory moved behind the older technician and studied the bank of twenty monitors. Their split-screen pictures, mostly in color, kept changing every ten seconds.

Mallory grabbed Susan's arm. "Where did all this come from?" hissed Mallory. "This wasn't here when I was around."

Susan spread out her arms. "This is Ollestad's dream-"

"Ollestad's debacle," smirked the younger tech, a college-age woman with thick glasses and obvious attitude. Her picture I.D. on her lanyard said, Alicia Simms. "But, you didn't hear me say anything."

Susan ignored her. "Evidently Ollestad had this in the works with the upper echelons for a while, even with Homeland

Security. It is the… how did she put it? 'The security terminus for all of Sacramento PD'. They've got feeds from all over the place and not just for the department mind you. Besides areas in the department, they monitor every floor, every inch of HQ, practically, plus a number of high profile buildings, some street corners, and some other places that if I told you about, they'd kill me."

"No shit. We have to see what they have on us."

Susan leaned over the older operator. "We want to see the playback of the feed from the OID.

Both operators turned as one and stared at Susan, then Mallory. "Say what?"

"The OID," repeated Mallory. "On-Going Investigation Division."

"Like we're supposed to know what that is?"

"You don't have any security feed from the OID?"

"No, ma'am."

Mallory had an idea. "How about the archive storage."

"Not even from the archives," intoned the older tech. "Is it important?"

"Yeah, we do. Have a feed that is," corrected the young woman.

The older man looked at her. "We do?"

"Connected a few days ago."

"We have to see the playback from there?" asked Mallory, trying not to fidget.

"Yeah," added Susan. "I think we can all see the big monitor in the middle. You can show it there."

The woman adjusted her glasses. "Not sure they connected it up to any of the digital recorders. They just ran the line."

Mallory gave her an encouraging smile. "But you can check can't you? It is important."

The woman pulled out a folder that had been stuck between two of the monitors, opened it, and scanned the first page.

"You have it right?" Mallory kneaded and twisted the leather on the back of the woman's seat.

"Just a moment."

"I doubt it," contributed the older tech. "I've never heard of it."

"And so that makes it official?" chided Susan. "Cause a man said it?"

Mallory nudged Susan hard in the ribs.

Alicia turned halfway in her chair. "Got it. At least where it's supposed to be. It says it's hooked up to one of the two-day units," she volunteered. "It is not one of the newer digital ones that can record a month on one disc. This old unit still uses tape and is limited to 48 hours."

"Why is that?" asked Mallory. "Why only 48 hours?"

Alicia turned all the way around before answering.

"I guess it was felt that the security system for the archives can use the older tape system because, at least the explanation I heard, was that nothing ever happens over there."

She took off her glasses. "You work over there? At the archive place?"

Mallory leaned on the back of Alicia Simms' chair, harder than she meant to. "Is there or isn't there something recorded from there," demanded Mallory.

Alicia shrugged. "We'll see. You never know if those guys hooked everything up. We may only have two days of static. Idiots. Some stuff works, the rest, maybe." She held up the folder again and punched some numbers into her keyboard.

The young woman leaned back in her chair, satisfied. "All righty. If it's there, we'll know it now." She keyed a lighted button on her console. The center screen switched from a picture of a vacant parking garage to a paused picture showing a shimmering frozen split screen of four quadrants of the OID offices.

"That it?"

It was disconcerting then maddening to Mallory when she realized Jake was right. It was Big Brother watching. Viewing her empty desk from above she felt exposed. Like someone had hidden a camera in her department store changing room or a Peeping Tom had telephoted into her bedroom. It was out-of-body creepy.

"Audio?" asked Susan.

"Your guess is as good as mine. Should be. Here we go." Alicia started the tape. "Old technology. You never know what you're gonna get."

A hollow sound expanse from the speakers filled the room. Alicia thumbed up the volume and reached out with her pencil and pointed to the top left. Its square was blank.

"Okay. Looks like there are supposed to be four cameras but there's either no feed from the fourth camera or there's no camera there."

The pencil moved to the top right square which showed no discernible picture, but it was evident the camera was on, if not functioning.

"I don't know. If I didn't know any better, I'd say they left something in front of the lens. That's what it looks like."

Mallory groaned to herself. Thanks, Jake.

"And this one," said Alicia, pointing to the bottom left screen. "This one is pointing upwards, looks like. I see a railing and a door."

She turned to Mallory. "They don't seem to be aimed very well."

Mallory shrugged, but her eyes were glued to the last screen.

"What about the last one?" asked Mallory studying the monitor. "There's something there."

"Yeah," offered Alicia. "Two people looks like."

"From about as far away as you can get." Alicia touched the lower right square and it filled the screen. It was the camera from the third story looking down onto the glass office and their three desks and the conference table in the middle.

"Oh, shit," whispered Mallory. "Oh, shit, there's Stan. And the dog. And her."

"Want I should run it?"

"Just a minute," Mallory said. She leaned over.

"Can you make it bigger?"

"You mean zoom? Zoom in?"

"Right."

"Yeah. I can definitely make it bigger." She smiled.

"Okay, but first run it this way without zoom in. We'll get the whole view."

"Hold on. Here we go."

The picture jerked frame by frame, a new frame every few seconds. The sound was continuous but as if coming from the back of an empty auditorium.

"What's wrong with the picture?" asked Mallory with more force than she intended. "What is it?"

"Like I said," soothed Alicia. "You guys got the real dog of the units. This is one of those, like, hand-crank units that scan a frame every three seconds instead of continuous like a video. So, when you play it back you get the herky-jerky playback."

"What about audio?" Mallory asked.

"It's continuous, but not great." Alicia pushed the volume up all the way. Only the cavernous echoing of indistinct voices came through along with a pumping rush of an empty room.

Mallory looked to Susan. "Can you make anything out?"

Susan shook her head.

"Jeez. And, it's low res black and white too," said Susan. "Cheap bastards."

On the video, Ilsa Pokovich was already confronting Stan who was seated in his chair with his back to the desk. Except for the muzzle of the gun, just visible, it could be imagined that they were having a civil conversation, until both their heads turned as the dog padded into the glass office.

Then, everyone froze.

Without taking her eyes from the screen, Mallory gripped Susan's arm. "Oh shit," she whispered. "No!"

The next frame saw Stan lean over toward the dog. Stan's arm moved back and forth on his thigh, calling to the dog.

But, the dog's stare never left Ilsa Pokovich and the gun. And he never moved.

Mallory's grip on Susan's arm tightened.

Stan suddenly straightened up. He started to rise.

The muzzle of the gun swung quickly over toward the dog.

Stan's arm went up.

The next frame caught the dog skewed in mid-air, flying back from the bullet's impact toward the glass wall.

"Oh God!" screamed Mallory.

"Jesus!" Alicia and Susan both jerked as if shot themselves.

Mallory turned away and held onto Susan with both hands.

"Jesus fucking Christ, they shot a dog," whispered Alicia. She had both hands over her mouth.

In the next frame, the gun was already back on Stan, who sat back down in the chair, his gaze going from the dog, now hard up against the glass wall, then back to Ilsa.

The gun rose, narrowing the target.

Stan gripped the arms of his chair.

And then the world exploded.

The frame was filled with silver glass slivers coming from somewhere lower right of the camera's view. A faint muzzle blast could be seen from Ilsa Pokovich's gun.

The next frame almost obliterated the scene with small portions of Ilsa Pokovich exploding outward toward Stan.

And that's where the screen went blank.

No one said a word until Alicia Simms whispered, "Well, I guess they were wrong."

"About what?" asked Mallory, quietly.

"About nothing ever happening over there."

Susan cleared her throat. She spoke quietly. "Ms. Simms, please play it back and see what you can do about the audio."

"I'm going to try the audio from one of the closer cameras, see if I can patch that around while we watch the high camera's video. Here we go."

Playback started again with the picture cropped so the view was much closer.

Nothing changed. The same bullets fired. Jake was still thrown up against the glass wall by the bullet's impact, the glass wall behind Ilsa Pokovich still exploded, Stan still went down hitting his head on the corner of his desk, and Ilsa Pokovich's still crumpled in the same place.

Only this time everyone heard the audio and for the first time, it became clear why Ilsa Pokovich had risked her life to break into a police facility and confront a SacPD detective.

Only five words mattered.

"Give me the fucking bear," demanded Ilsa Pokovich.

"What?" asked Susan. She turned to Mallory for an explanation.

But Mallory was already gone.

CHAPTER 64

Helen Pinsky had made this mistake before. She would not let it happen again.

In the mirror, she practiced her stern but professional countenance and what she would say to Jake Steiner.

'When we had this discussion detective before you even adopted that dog, I asked you whether he would be in any danger and you assured me he wouldn't. You said and I quote, 'He'll be bored because you don't chase criminals and you hadn't shot your gun in years.'

"That's what you said. And now you're back here. Well, I'm sorry. The answer is no. And, I feel I'm going to have to alert the other vets in the area and tell them what happened. I feel strongly they will feel as I do and give you the same answer."

She attempted a knowing, understanding, smile. "I'm sorry to have to say all this, but I feel I must, if…"

Shawna interrupted her as she pushed through the double doors to the animal bonding area of the Willowood Animal Hospital and Shelter.

"He's here. Detective, um, Steiner. He's out front." Her eyes glittered and she started twisting her hair.

"Tell him I'll be right there," said Helen, adjusting her smock and pulling the sash tighter.

"You don't want him to come back here?" Shawna looked as if she didn't understand. "I mean, he's here to…"

Helen cut her off. "I know why he's here. And that's not going to happen. Over my dead body."

Shawna started to say something, but instead retreated and eased the double doors closed as if there was a bomb in the backroom and she didn't want to set it off.

"'Course I know why he's here," muttered Helen.

She checked herself in the mirror again and took a few deep breaths. Fortified, she pushed through the doors and headed to the reception area. With luck, nobody but the detective would be there; she didn't want to cause a scene.

But the reception area was empty. Shawna wasn't even behind the desk. Helen marched to the front door and scanned the parking lot. A bright red Corvette sat by the walkway. She could see an empty harness from the dog restraint system suspended above the passenger seat.

"Shit."

Helen turned on her heel and steamed back to the infirmary, shoving open the doors, stopping when she saw them.

Shawna was smiling and crying. "He's so happy!" she choked through her tears.

Jake's tail was going. He was licking Jake's face and hands overjoyed the person he belonged to had come back for him.

His eyes held the gratitude of the innocent believer.

Jake Steiner was full down on the floor, his back up against the wall, his legs stretched out before him. Both his hands were cradling the dog's head, acknowledging the dog's joy and trying to slow the licking.

"Hey, Jake, fella. Come on. We have work to do, you and me. We can't have this."

Jake dog would have none of it. He kept licking any place he could and started a whine. Even with his whole right foreleg bandaged he managed to hobble his way in front of Jake for a better licking angle.

Helen grabbed Shawna's arm and backed them both out of the room.

Jake Steiner reached up and wrapped his arms around the dog's neck.

He buried his face in Jake's fur and did not let go.

CHAPTER 65

Stan sipped the homemade tomato soup Beatrice had set on the TV tray next to his chair.

"Jesus, woman."

He dropped the spoon back into the bowl.

"I wanted soup, not lava."

Beatrice watched her husband from the kitchen doorway. Her heart did a little leap, but she had promised herself years ago when she married a cop to treat every day as if it was the last.

It wasn't a religious thing. It was a love thing.

She pushed away from the doorway and moved to stand in front of him. She shook her head slowly. "My big, strong cop can't handle a little hot liquid. Thought you were tough."

"I burned my tongue on your so-called soup, you know. Nobody's that tough."

Beatrice avoided looking at her husband's limp right arm and the sling and the bandages around his head.

Stan was silent for a second, then volunteered, "And my heel hurts like hell, too. I don't know what happened there, but, shit, it feels like someone took a goddamn samurai sword and sliced the back of my foot. Not to mention my head's like a pounding bowling ball."

Beatrice fingered her apron. "I'm supposed to ask you what you do remember. The doctors said it should come back if I bug you enough."

"They said that? Or that's your idea of wifely torture?"

She picked up the spoon, scooped some soup, blew on it, and held it to his lips.

Stan slurped at it and settled back. "I don't know. I remember meeting with Phil Ginger and then walking along the highway where that car was found. Then there's a gun and noise and Mallory doing something. Kinda blurry after that."

She picked up the spoon, dipped another spoonful, and blew on it.

"Here, eat, tough guy."

She tipped the spoonful into his mouth.

"And, if you're a good boy and eat all your soup, there's dessert."

Stan brightened. "What?"

"A big slug of scotch and three pain pills."

Stan settled back and closed his eyes.

"Thank you."

Bea stood.

"But first, you have a visitor."

"Jake's here?"

"No," said Danni Harness from the doorway.

Stan shifted higher in his chair and straightened his bathrobe.

"Danni! Hey! What is Forensics doing here? I'm pretty sure I'm not dead so you must be here to comfort me in my convalescence."

Danni moved to his chair. Stan saw she was dressed not like Forensics Danni, but in street clothes. It was such a change Stan tried to remember the last time he'd seen Danni anywhere but the basement of SacPD.

"Oh, Stan, Stan. Convalescence, my ass. Jake said you hurt yourself chasing your girlfriend."

"He would say that."

"Anyway, I think you're milking this," chided Danni, glancing at Bea. "Making your poor wife wait on you hand and foot, all the while you could be up and about, digging up more headless bodies for me to work on."

At first, Stan thought the difference in Danni's demeanor was because she was unused to the etiquette of paying sympathy visits. Coming to soothe and comfort the injured. So not Danni Harness's style.

He thought that right up until he saw the file in her hand.

"Listen, Stan, I know you're not going to be back in action for a few days, but you're still running cold cases, though I have to say that if this past month is how you're planning on running this division, beheading people and shooting witnesses, I'm going to need more help."

Stan raised a weak arm, fingers up.

"I promise, Danni. We're done."

Danni suddenly looked uneasy.

Stan saw her look away. "What?"

She sighed and tried to smile. "Look, maybe I should give this to Rodriguez. Let his RH boys work on it. I can see this isn't the right time for this. Actually, I should probably dump it in Jake's lap."

"I'm fine. Really. What is it?

Danni fidgeted.

"It's not done. You're not done, Stan."

"What do you mean?"

"Marston." She set the file folder down on Stan's TV tray. He reached for the folder but stopped when she put her hand on his.

"Don't bother," said Danni. "I'll tell you."

"Okay."

"Remember we found only two prints in Marston's car and one was Pokovich's."

"Yeah," he drawled. "Don't believe the doctors. I remember most things, only not the night this all happened. But I recall the two sets of prints."

Danni laughed in spite of herself. "Sorry. This isn't funny." She shook her head trying to erase the smile.

"The second print. We got it. The ID. And it was only luck that we found it at all. You know our computer search for fingerprints defaults, I mean, is programmed to search all known databases, but in reality, we usually truncate the search because we only have so much time, you know, so we typically only hit the DOJ and AFIS and the three state files of known perps. If we're talking felony-level here, we feel reasonably confident we can eliminate the civilians with their prints on file because they work at a military base, or elementary school teachers who had to have their prints taken when they went to work for the school.

"We usually skip those searches, especially in a case like this."

"Danni, I know all this."

"Yeah. Okay. Well, it seems Cissy, one of our interns, started the search yesterday afternoon because paperwork showed we hadn't searched all the sources. So, she started the query running, but her daughter was sick, anyway, she had to leave and so she left the search running. Ran into the night. Ended up searching every place, every database we have access to, even the obscure ones. This morning, there was one hit."

"Danni!" Stan leaned forward. "You know who it is?"

"Yes. But, you're not going to like it."

"Why?"

"Because you're not going to believe it."

"Try me."

"Her name is Anna Chase."

"Okay. Anna Chase."

"She lives in Plainfield, New Jersey."

"New Jersey?"

"Yeah…but."

"What Danni?"

"Stan, Anna Chase, your other killer is in the fifth grade at Parkway Middle School. Anna Chase is 11 years old."

CHAPTER 66

While no one was watching, in the deathly quiet of a fog-laden night, at the very far end of Crimson Park away from the Marston mansion, between the restlessness of the neighboring woods and the shadowed trailer of what was once Ruby Everheart's, there is a sharp electric crackle and the insistent flicker of long-forgotten neon.

High above the fields, welcoming all, the lights have come on.

Evil has been reborn.

Fortunes by Ruby is once again open for business.

Acknowledgments

I am simply the gatherer of wit and wisdom, notions and potions. My sack, its contents once emptied out on the table, re-arranged, massaged, put in order, only then become a book.

Those who contributed to the collection are hereby acknowledged.

First, I thank all those who enjoyed OLIVE PARK (and told me so). Those are the readers for whom the Park trilogy was birthed. The overwhelming response to the story of OLIVE PARK and especially the characters was the tidal momentum I rode in writing CRIMSON PARK.

Second were the individuals who assisted in ways they could not imagine and to this day probably have no knowledge of their contributions: author and journalist Dawn Ius, author and agent Michael Neff, agent Katherine Sands, Indie publishing expert and author Debbie Young, attorney Mike Larson, consultant Derek Pacifico, and author James Patterson. Special note of merit to Sgt. Robert McCloskey, part of the Cold Case Unit of the Sacramento Police Department, for his insights into the workings of that unit.

Thirdly, Beta readers, whose varying points of view, strict adherence to a rational story timeline, and insistence on the correct use of the English language, are essential to any writer. Mine was invaluable. I bow down to their patience and feedback. Elizabeth Booth, Sarah Adams, Michael Brown, David Booth, Trace Adams, Jo Booth, and Kayleen Nichols.

A book's cover must convey part of the story. For that, I thank Jessica Bell who not only re-designed the covers of OLIVE PARK and the cover of the forthcoming third book in the Park trilogy but with the assistance of Sarah Adams, captured the curiously sinister feeling of CRIMSON PARK.

Finally, a writer tends to collect an assortment of friends who usually have something to say and add to the development of the story, or if not that, just general cheerleading. They are always appreciated – Julie and George Gorveat and Teras Karlinsey and Pete Cummings.

Most of all, at the literal heart of this writer's support, is my wife, Elizabeth.

Words are not enough, only feelings.

Thanks, babe.

ABOUT THE AUTHOR

Following his careers in radio and TV broadcasting, motion picture and video production, C. J. brought detectives Stan Wyld, Jake Steiner, and Mallory Dimante to life in the fiction novel, OLIVE PARK, the first in the series involving Sacramento's fictional OID – Ongoing Investigation Division, the cold case division. Winner of the Bronze medal in Popular Fiction at the 2012 E-Lit awards, named one of the Top 5 Mysteries for 2012 by the Reader's Favorite Awards, OLIVE PARK went on to be awarded the Best Mystery of 2012 at the Global E-Book awards

CRIMSON PARK, the second book in the Park trilogy, is part riveting police thriller, part spellbinding mystery and continues the story of Michael and Jessie Cooper and the detectives of the On-Going Investigation Division of the Sacramento Police Departmen

C. J. has studied fiction and creative writing with Judith Guest (ORDINARY PEOPLE), Rebecca Hill (A KILLING TIME IN ST CLOUD), Christopher Short (THE BLACK CAT), Gary Braver (TUNNEL VISION, SKIN DEEP), Elizabeth Engstrom (LIZZIE BORDEN) and screenwriting with David S. Freeman ("Beyond Structure").

An author of numerous short stories, including Pushcart-nominated "Relentless", he is currently working on the third novel in the Park trilogy as well as the screenplay for OLIVE PARK.

C.J. lives with his wife on an island near Seattle, Washington.

Facebook and Twitter @cjboothbooks
Email cjboothbooks@hotmail.com

An excerpt from
ANGEL PARK
Book 3 in the
Park Trilogy

"Stan!"

Mallory sat bolt upright, her heart pounding. She frantically searched her dark room terrified that someone had shouted at her.

She pulled the blanket close. Her bed shook with her hard breathing. She felt her heart.

Then she understood she had been the one yelling.

"Jesus, get a grip, girl."

And she remembered the nightmare and then she remembered why she yelled. Why she had to yell, had to get Stan's attention.

She threw herself sideways, flopping over the edge of the bed trying to secure the vomit from erupting because she remembered the bottle of Tanqueray she'd tried to conquer and she really, really didn't want to have to clean that up.

She braced herself with her hands against the floor and let the cold sweat drip off while she talked herself into not throwing up.

After five minutes, assured she was safe to be mobile, she slithered off the bed and went to the bathroom, and ran the shower.

Mallory stood inhaling the steam for minutes before she got in.

She let the spray buffet her head while she leaned against the tiles.

It was so clear now. They'd been so close to the damn trees they couldn't see the forest or the path through it. She straightened up suddenly. Maybe she was the only one that knew this. She'd given them the information too, but neither Stan nor Jake had put it together.

Of course, neither had she, until now.

She rubbed her nose, stopped the shower, and cleared her eyes. In the bedroom, she found her cell.

She couldn't call Stan.

She dialed Jake's number.

Somebody answered and fumbled with the phone on the other end.

"Jake?"

"There was a pause, then, "He's busy," came a female reply.

Mallory stabbed her phone to end the call. The voice was vaguely familiar.

She sat on the bed hoping now he wouldn't see it was her who had called and call back.

Stan's out. Most certainly Jake is out. Asshole. "He's busy," she mimicked.

Please tell me you're not sleeping with a witness.

She couldn't call Rodriguez or any of the Robbery-Homicide crew because there was the small matter of her being officer-involved-shooting material, sort of, and she was not to do anything officially departmentally or OID-related until they officially sorted out what had happened. Who had shot whom?

Anyway, even though there was ballistic evidence to the contrary, Mallory still felt most of them were certain she was somehow responsible for Stan being shot. Tough, let 'em think that.

Wrapped in a towel, she dialed the only person that was left.

"Hey…it's me…yeah, I know what time it is. Listen…just listen, I need you to pick me up…Soon. Now is better…am I drunk? Why do people keep asking me that? No, well, I was, but I'm not, so come get me…it's important…because I want a witness. I'd rather not say…just come…no, it won't be long…do I promise? Yeah, I think so…so when? I'll be out front. Oh, and bring a crowbar."

Mallory ended the call. And thought about what she said.

"Because I want a witness? Bullshit. Because I'm scared and I don't want to do this alone."

She ran to the bathroom and finally ridded herself of her gin martinis.

"You okay?" asked Susan Spruance when Mallory slid into the passenger seat of the Lexus.

"Ducky."

"I meant, you know, after what happened?"

"Well, I've stopped shaking and throwing up."

"Speaking of, you do smell a little like the night before."

"I gargled. Twice. Hey, nice car."

"My ex's. Mine's in the shop. He still thinks we're going to have sex. Roll down your window a bit. I'm hypersensitive to smells like that when I first wake up."

Mallory did as asked and stuck her head out the window. She let the early morning air whip past her face.

"Hey, so okay I'm just driving here. I have no idea where I'm supposed to be going!" shouted Susan. Mallory brought her head back in.

Susan flicked on her brights. "And why did I have to bring a crowbar?"

"You bring the gun too?"

Susan looked over with delight.

"Always packin'. What's wrong with yours?"

Mallory shrugged. "They pinched mine. Evidence. So, um, head straight. I'll tell you when to turn."

She pulled a scrap of paper out from her jeans opened her phone and found the address on her phone's map.

"Head across the river. West Sacramento."

Susan looked at her sideways. "At this hour?"

"Get off at Jefferson."

Susan shifted her shoulders and bore down on the wheel.

"Now I know why I brought the gun.

"Orleta, just off Jefferson after the canal."

Susan looked at her.

"Sure about this?"

"Right here. Go right."

Susan turned onto Orleta. The sparkling white car stood out against the abandoned storefronts and rusted sheet metal that secured many of the vacant buildings.

"I can't see any of the addresses," said Mallory, squinting into the darkness.

"That's because they shot out all the streetlights."

Mallory's phone finally came to life.

'In 200 feet, your destination will be on the right.'

"Slow down. I can't see."

"I'm just going to pull, over. Lock the doors."

Mallory looked at her. "Lock the doors? There's nobody around."

"They always say that just before the zombies smash through the window."

"If they're coming through the window, locking the doors won't help."

"You'll see." Susan guided the quiet car to the curb. Mallory opened the door and got out.

"What are you doing?" hissed Susan. She reached up and turned off the dome light.

Mallory stuck her head back in. "We're here. C'mon. And, where's the crowbar?"

"Backseat."

"Where's the gun?"

"In my hand. What are we doing?"

Mallory reached into the back seat and pulled out the crowbar.

"Putting two pieces of a puzzle together. Right after breaking and entering. It'll be fun."

Susan got out and stood next to the car, guarding it. She checked both ends of the street.

"What's wrong with daylight? You allergic to being safe?"

Mallory wedged the crowbar behind the weathered, graffitied plywood that sealed the entrance to a storefront office.

"Mallory?"

Mallory paused and looked the length of the street, both ways, as if seeing it for the first time.

"We're fine. Nobody's around."

Susan sniffed. "You can't see 'em, but they're around."

Mallory put her weight against the crowbar and worked it back and forth. The rusted nails screamed with every move of the wood.

"C'mon Mal, you'll wake everybody."

"Give me a hand then," puffed Mallory. "Grab and pull."

Susan added her hands to the edge of the plywood and together they worked the board back and forth until they could raise their grip along the side of the door's covering, enlarging the gap.

"Brace the crowbar against the doorframe. We can squeeze in."

"Is this a felony or just a gross misdemeanor?" questioned Susan. "I mean, I remember going over this during training, but it's a bit different when you're actually committing the crime."

"Neither. This is investigation." Mallory turned and smiled. "This is fieldwork. C'mon. You can slip under."

"What size do you think I am?"

Susan checked the car and the street and the dark before she inhaled, turned sideways, worked her ass a bit and followed Mallory into the tenuous opening.

"Don't touch the bar," admonished Mallory. "It slips and the wood springs back into place, and we're stuck."

"I'm not touching anything."

The door glass behind the plywood had long ago been victim to a rock or a heel. They crunched on dusty shards and splinters of wood as they stepped through the door frame. Susan caught a glance of the faded gold lettering atop the door as she stepped through.

'Acme Distributing'

"You kidding me? Acme Distributing?" whispered Susan. "Are we in a cartoon? Some safe going to come crashing down?"

Mallory was already steps ahead and had switched on her flashlight.

They were in a reception area. That much was evident. Reception chairs, albeit ripped to shreds, were along one wall. A high desk, which someone had graciously put a foot through, stood guarding a dark hallway.

Evidently, whoever had decided to trash the place, had decided not to urinate or shit anywhere, which was surprising. But there was a raw mustiness to the place that made her nose twitch.

"What is this place?"

Mallory turned.

"This used to be owned by Marston or one of his companies. Used to be a distribution point for many of his old films. Closed it a few years ago."

"So, I'm afraid to ask, why are we here?"

"A hunch."

"And you called me?"

"Who else?"

"Thanks so much. Look, hasn't this been cleaned out? I mean, if it's closed, didn't they take all the films?"

Mallory stopped before a padded double door. She raised her flashlight to the sign.

'Screening Room'

"We're not looking for films."

Mallory was about to open the door when she stopped. She pulled her sleeve up over her hand and with the cloth against the door, pushed it open.

Complete darkness loomed. No light from anywhere except the meager beam from Mallory's light.

They moved forward and the door swung closed behind them. The feel of the room was large and open. The raw mustiness smell was stronger, riper.

"Mal?"

"What?"

"I hear something moving."

Continued in
ANGEL PARK
Book 3 of The Park Trilogy

Author's website
www.cjboothauthor.com

Author's Amazon Page
CJBoothAuthor

Made in the USA
Las Vegas, NV
17 November 2022

59688298R00213